Falling Through the Roof

Falling Through the Root

Thubten Samphel

Rupa & Co

Published 2008 by
Rupa . Co
7/16, Ansari Road, Daryaganj,
New Delhi 110 002

Sales Centres:
Allahabad Bangalooru Chandigarh Chennai
Hyderabad Jaipur Kathmandu
Kolkata Mumbai

Typeset in AdobeGaramond 11 pts. by
Mindways Design
1410 Chiranjiv Tower,
43 Nehru Place
New Delhi 110 019

Printed in India by
Nutech Photolithographers
B-240, Okhla Industrial Area, Phase-I,
New Delhi 110 020, India

*'For Rabten, Yugyal, Dekyong and Namgyal
with much love'*

Contents

☯

Acknowledgements

☯

The mantra must be recited. This is a work of fiction. The characters that people this novel are works of the author's imagination. Any resemblance to persons living or dead is coincidental. Most of the places are real enough, though not all. Some of the events described here are now part of Tibetan refugee history. The rest is fiction, including the spurious theories regarding the origins of the Tibetan script.

I remain deeply grateful to Pico Iyer for his encouragement throughout the years, starting from the time when I showed him the hesitant beginnings of the story. His gentle coaxing and taking time away from his own creative life to read my drafts have kept me going.

I also remain deeply grateful to Tenzing Sonam for his constant encouragement and the time he set aside from his busy schedule to read my drafts and make extensive comments. They have enormously improved the final outcome.

My gratitude goes to Zosawmpuii Bhatia for her patient reading of the manuscript and her detailed comments.

I owe this book to Rajiv Mehrotra. He brought the manuscript of this book to the attention of Rupa & Co. I am grateful to Smita Khanna Bajaj of Rupa & Co for her thorough editing of the manuscript. To both Rajiv Mehrotra and Smita Khanna Bajaj, salaam and namaste.

I would like to thank C.B. Josayma for allowing me to use parts of her excellent English translation of Dekar's annual Losar recitations called *Dekar – Song of the Pure Old Man*, which appears in vol. I, No. 2, 1987 of *Choyang, The Voice of Tibetan Religion and Culture*.

I would like to thank Tashi Tsering, the director of Amnye Machen Institute, for his groundbreaking article on 'Nyag-rong Mgon-po rnam-rgyal: A 19th Century Khams-pa Warrior' that appeared in *Soundings in Tibetan Civilization*, edited by Barbara Nimri Aziz and Matthew Kapstein, published by Manohar, Delhi, 1985. His article has been the inspiration for the One-Eyed Golok, who plays a significant role in this book.

The poem composed by Gendun Chophel comes from the Library of Tibetan Works and Archives' *The Guide to India: A Tibetan Account by Amdo Gendun Chophel*, a biography of the famous Tibetan scholar by Toni Huber.

I thank the Department of Information and International Relations for permission to use passages from the late Tendar's excellent English translation of *The Mongols and Tibet: A Historical Assessment of Relations Between the Mongol Empire and Tibet*, published by the Department of Information and International Relations, the Central Tibetan Administration, Dharamsala, 1996.

I owe a great deal to the *Tibetan Review* and the lengthy quotes on the formation of the Tibetan Communist Party. Since its birth, the *Review* has become an important chronicler of the fortunes and misfortunes of the Tibetan people. The *Review* will serve as an essential and invaluable source for future scholars researching on this critical period of Tibetan history.

I am grateful to *Studies in the Grammatical Tradition in Tibet* by Roy Andrew Miller, University of Washington, Seattle, published by Amsterdam/John Benjamins B.V., copyright 1976-John Benjamins B.V., for the connection between Shyambhadra and Thomi Sambhota.

I benefited a great deal from *Kashmir and Central Asia* by P.N.K. Bamzai, published by Light and Life Publishers, New Delhi, 1980. The chapter on 'Evangelization of Tibet' has helped me develop the theory that Thonmi Sambhota might have had an ethnic Indian origin.

1

The Delhi Days

Prologue
Majnu Ka Tilla

☯

Majnu Ka Tilla was a ghetto of desperation, a jungle representing the elemental struggle for survival. To eke out a living had a harrowing meaning for its inhabitants. They awoke everyday in the heat and dust of despair, wondering whether they would get through another day. This question, quite like their prayers and their courage to hope, would be met by the day's blistering gaze. No, there was no way out. There was no way they could get out of the trap, out of this poverty, out of this mess which was a product of history's injustice. More than most Tibetan refugees, Majnu Ka Tilla Tibetans were the real victims of imperial ambitions asserted and realised. Of great armies moving in, scattering small people.

For a long time, no one wanted to do anything about these people. They were beyond help and hope. Their camp was a dark, illegitimate secret, an orphan that no willing parent would step forward to claim. Not even their own community. It stood there like an uncertain home, an embarrassment, more so because of its dubious reputation.

The haphazard Tibetan camp in Majnu Ka Tilla was sandwiched between the mosquito-breeding banks of the placid Yamuna River and Bela Road, a national highway growling and choking with thick traffic. It was a sprawling place dotted with wooden huts and their dust-covered tarpaulin roofs. It was festooned, in a half-hearted attempt to assert its indeterminate personality, with dejected prayer flags, made heavy and listless by thick coats of dust. Its narrow, dirty alleyways led you to an inevitable chang shop or a gushing water pump or to a stinking open toilet that served as a crowded bazaar for scavenging dogs and pigs. Other Tibetan refugees elsewhere in India, who considered themselves more fortunate, punned into existence a place with a distinct Tibetan accent called Ma-jon pai Tro-lha: the dregs of failure. Such refugee wit provoked derisive refugee laughter. In the food chain and on the shaky ladder of social prestige of the dispossessed, Majnu Ka Tilla by a wide consensus was dismissed and relegated to the very bottom.

Like all unplanned settlements, it has no birthday. No one knows exactly when the place sprang into existence. Some say it was in the late 1960s. Others say it was in the early 1970s when the Delhi police herded the Tibetan refugees, who had been illegally camping out in the compound of the Ladakh Dharamsala or Ladakh Buddh Vihara, near Delhi's Inter-State Bus Terminus, which provided free accommodation for Ladakhi pilgrims. The police ferried the refugees in vans up north, a ten minute drive, and dumped them opposite the Punjabi Basti, along the bank of the sullen Yamuna. The depressing hutment that grew on the riverbank became one of the many shantytowns that disfigured the metropolis of Delhi. These refugees led a fringe existence, foraging for metropolitan leftovers. The evicted Tibetans took to moonshining. Chang, Tibet's barley wine, brewed the Tibetan camp into an unlawful but tolerated existence. The place thrived, fuelled by the resourcefulness of the desperate and the traffic of people and refugee commerce servicing the pockets of an émigré community scattered across the subcontinent.

The tables have been turned. Now Majnu Ka Tilla finds itself at the very top of the Tibetan refugee heap. It is humming with entrepreneurial industry and sparkles with a nervous Chinatown energy, an enclave of ethnic exclusivity, feeding on a precarious prosperity. Majnu Ka Tilla is the money town of the Tibetan exiles, attracting the energy, ambition and dreams of the young, transforming the place into a brave imitation of Kathmandu's Thamel. A commercial capital, a meeting-point, the hub of refugee enterprise. The MTV generation of Tibetan exiles has given the place a halo of cultural orientation. This generation refers to Majnu Ka Tilla simply as MT, the initials ennobling the place and making it sound exotic, glamorous and familiar.

The growth of Majnu Ka Tilla and its gentrification is the story of the Tibetan community in exile.

Changistan

☯

Tashi and I had safely put away the last of our marathon history exams at the Delhi University and quite on the spot, decided to go on a drinking binge to Majnu Ka Tilla. Majnu Ka Tilla had a reputation for cheap chang, a welcomed substitute at a time when Delhi was going through a stiff bout of prohibition. As if in gratitude, the local Indians joyfully salaamed the place as Changistan.

'Let's celebrate,' said Tashi, as we ambled away from the steaming exam hall into the blistering sun. Tashi and I were friends. He was the intelligent one and I the studious one. He liked me because I was a compulsive note-taker and I shared all my notes with him. Whatever the professors, their eyes fixed on the whirring ceiling fans as if ticking off one century after the other of their exalted labour, dished out, I had it all down in my notebooks: dates, names, historical trivia, great moments, insignificant incidents which precipitated momentous events. During the exams, we dished it all back.

'Kipotang! Mi-tse thun thun re,' Tashi said with excited anticipation, his dark glasses gleaming in the evening sun. This was a new and favoured mantra of Delhi University's Tibetan students of our days. It means, 'Have fun! Life is short,' which, in our case, invariably meant attending a drinking orgy in Changistan.

'Kipotang!' I responded, feeling great about having managed to graduate from the heat of Delhi and Indian history, all five thousand years of it, with not a single insignificant year missing, all accounted for and each either contemptuously dismissed in a footnote or remembered in laboured detail in a full-blown chapter.

'Why can't India have a reasonable history?' Tashi said, fuming. He said this in English, perhaps finding his Tibetan too inadequate to convey the weight of his thought. 'Two hundred years, that's manageable. But why five thousand years? And why do we need to remember it all?'

I didn't have an answer and suggested that perhaps a great civilisation needed a long history. Nevertheless, I accepted Tashi's argument that each nation could do with only two hundred years of history. Being, like Tashi, an orphan of two languages, I responded in English, 'Look at America, it's doing very well with only two hundred or three hundred years, much better than India. Maybe Indian historians should put away the rest for good. Makes life much easier for us and for India. A long memory complicates things.'

'Dhondup Kunga, I think you make sense,' Tashi said with a grave professorial nod.

When we reached Majnu Ka Tilla, we dropped in as usual at Ama Penpa's wooden shack, which greeted us with its pungent smell of sour chang. Ama Penpa didn't serve the best of chang, but with her pretty daughter doing the serving, who could complain? 'She's a goddess,' Tashi said whenever he talked about her.

Tashi had many rivals for the heart of Metok. Some were students but many were businessmen with lots of cash to throw away. But Tashi, with his easy-going manner was both Ama Penpa and Metok's favourite. Naturally, he adopted the I'm-a-part-of-your-family attitude.

But that evening the place was deserted. Usually it was filled with young, rowdy Tibetans, drinking chang and eyeing the daughter, with Ama Penpa, all of one storey tall, making sure nothing outrageous came out of either the drinking or the eyeing. Ama Penpa had plans of sending her daughter off to be married to an elderly Tibetan in Switzerland. This was perhaps why Tashi sometimes referred to her as 'export quality'.

Ama Penpa and Metok were in the inner room which served as their bedroom. The two of them sat at the feet of a long-haired lama who had their undivided attention.

I had never been in this room before. Perhaps Tashi had ventured in. The room which was surprisingly clean and smelled of freshly lit incense, was dominated by what looked to me like a very expensive large wooden altar, with elaborate carvings of peacocks and deer. Two beds, covered with hand-woven woollen carpets with the Great Wall of China motif, were placed on either side of the altar. The altar held the usual religious knick-knacks: Buddha statues, statues of various deities whom I couldn't identify, and photos of the Dalai Lama and other lesser lamas. A single butter lamp, placed at the centre of the seven copper bowls of water offering, flickered before all this piety.

'Ama-la, Metok! We finished our exams!' Tashi screamed in Tibetan, arms outstretched, as if Metok would come running into them. 'I'm an M.A.!'

Ama Penpa immediately shooed us away. 'No, not today. We're closed,' she said. 'Anyway, look at you. All you've done is finish a simple school test, but the way you go on about it seems as though you've fetched us Tibet's independence,' she barked. 'Go away, we're closed.'

'Let them stay,' commanded the long-haired lama who had a sharp, east Tibetan style sculpted face dominated by a protuberant nose. He was probably in his sixties and sported a longish, sparse beard, greying at the edges and a thin Thirteenth-Dalai-Lama moustache and dark glasses. His long hair was tucked away in an enormous bun held together by a red sash. The main attraction of this unusual personality was the bundle of cloth sitting on top of his head like a defiant crown. His demeanour exuded the confidence, dignity and brutality of some Central Asian despot. Even in the searing heat of Delhi, the lama wore white robes and a white shawl with maroon trimmings. He looked like a ngaba, someone endowed with magical tantric powers, or so older Tibetans believed of people like him.

'Your best chang, as usual, Metok,' said Tashi, ignoring Ama Penpa, ignoring the lama, always cheerful in Metok's presence.

'No, not on the bed. Here, sit here,' growled Ama Penpa, stern-faced, pointing to the floor.

We sat on the hot, sweltering mud floor, below the high table, below the wooden bed, on which the long-haired lama sat, leaning against the wall.

'What's wrong with you today?' demanded Tashi. 'We have finished something important in our lives. Maybe not as important as Tibetan independence, but still important to us. We are educated. Educated, you see. Not simply literate, but educated. We know the hows and whys of things. Now treat us like educated people,' and he promptly sat on the bed.

'Because you, luckless, good fortune-dried up young man, you are in the presence of a high lama!' Ama Penpa shot back, taking Tashi by the neck and dumping him on the floor. 'You can't share the same table as him,' Ama Penpa barked in an angry whisper. 'Do you know who he is? He is Drubchen Rinpoche, the abbot of Drubchen monastery, the master of the biographies of all the reincarnations of Drubtop Rinpoche. You should consider yourselves fortunate that Drubchen Rinpoche has permitted you in his presence. And we don't serve chang today. Now, prostrate and receive Drubchen Rinpoche's blessings and be on your way.'

'What, no chang!' Tashi screamed, still ignoring the lama and his elevated title. 'Oh no, we won't prostrate or receive any blessing. We came to drink chang, and chang we will drink. Look, look at him!' Tashi growled, pointing at the lama, 'He's drinking and he's a lama! A drinking lama!' Tashi said, laughing at the irony. 'We have money,' he added puffing his chest in a mock show of pride and tapping the pocket of his spotless shirt, indicating where his money was. 'We came to share this important moment with you because you are like family to me. Now some chang,' he said, sitting on the bed again.

Tashi took off his dark glasses and placed them on the table, revealing his blind left eye, and ran his hands over his face. For some reason the lama seemed fascinated with Tashi's blind eye. Probably he hadn't seen anyone with a blind eye before, I thought.

'Bu,' Ama Penpa said, using the Tibetan word for boy in a condescending way, 'you're in the presence of a great lama and yet you are crying about chang. Get down from the bed and sit on the floor.'

'What!' Tashi screamed, standing up. 'Milarepa is long dead and still people know his name. I'm alive and you have already forgotten my name? It's Tashi. Add a la, now that I'm a graduate. Tashi-la.'

'Give them chang and let this one sit on the bed,' the lama said, laughing.

'See? He's a modern lama,' said Tashi, slipping off his shoes, and tucking up his feet on the edge of the lama's bed. 'Modern means he's broad-minded,' Tashi explained, extending his hand to the lama.

Surprisingly, the lama gave Tashi a firm handshake. 'Educated people don't squabble about little things like chang or where to sit,' Tashi said with an unsmiling face. 'So what's your story? What's this Drubchen Rinpoche thing?' he asked, turning to the lama, at his irreverent best. He pulled out a Wills packet, lit a cigarette and blew the smoke into the lama's face. I also pulled out a cigarette from his pack, but lit mine hesitantly, not knowing how this obvious show of disrespect would be received by the lama.

'You really want to know?' the lama asked, expansively stroking his beard.

'Really. Why would I ask if I wasn't interested?' Tashi said, digging his elbows into his knees, his hands cupping his chin and his body bent forward, indicating that he was all ears. The cigarette dangled jauntily from a corner of his curled mouth.

'It concerns the first Tibetan scholars sent to India by Songtsen Gampo,' the lama explained.

'Whatever you like, I don't care. Make up a story. Tell us how, instead of slinking away from the Chinese like a scared fox, you fought them single-handedly. Tell us about your many victories,' Tashi said. 'You know, a lot of older Tibetans say that they did all this and more. And I wonder how we still managed to lose!' Tashi said, puffing on his cigarette.

'Tashi!' screamed Ama Penpa, towering above him with flaming eyes and quivering nostrils. 'How dare you speak to our Rinpoche in that tone! If you don't want to receive his blessings, stop insulting him. If you continue like this, I will throw you and your blasphemy out of here.'

'That's all right, Penpa,' the lama said. 'Young people these days are like this. At least they are honest. Well, to answer your question, I did run away like a frightened fox. And I didn't fight the Chinese

I'm a good Buddhist, at least I hope I am,' the lama admitted. 'As I said, I will tell you about the first Tibetan scholars, especially about the first Drubtop Rinpoche,' he added and clasping his hands and closing his eyes in prayer and reverence.

'The history of Tibet is encapsulated in the life of Drubtop Rinpoche,' the lama explained.

As was my habit, I took out my Elephant notebook and Bic ballpoint pen from my Free-Tibet cotton shoulder bag and started to jot down what the lama said, translating the lama's guttural Tibetan into my strained English.

Tibet Memories

☯

'What was all that blabber about last night? All the way from Majnu Ka Tilla to the mattress, you were shouting "I'm Drubtop Rinpoche, I'm Drubtop Rinpoche".' I rolled over and there was Tashi, as fresh as the early morning sun peeping over snow-capped mountains, up in the verdant Himalayas. He was as chirpy and breezy as if Metok were there beside him. He had washed, brushed his teeth and was now deliberately wiping himself with a small colourful Chinese towel in front of the cracked mirror on the wall.

'What time is it?' I asked.

'Time you got off that mattress, Dhondup. I can hardly move without tripping over you or the mattress.'

I got up and headed for the common bathroom located at the end of the long L-shaped corridor. I was still in a stupor from both last night's chang and the lama's story. A potent mix, I thought. I felt better after the bath. 'And you have read all these books?' I asked Tashi, with a contrived cheerfulness as soon as I entered his book-strewn room. The bulk of his books were haphazardly piled one on top of the other in a genuine attempt to erect stepping stones to a higher stage of disorganised learning. Several slim novels were scattered on the floor as if flung away, rejected. A couple of P.G. Wodehouses, gathering dust, peeked guiltily from under his high bed, as if afraid of making their presence too prominent and revealing their owner's taste for bourgeois flippancy. Several books on how to start a revolution were stacked and arranged nicely on the low bamboo shelf that lay on the hot cement floor. There were also books on Marxism, communism, Che Guavara and Mao. A copy of *Das Kapital*, occupied centre-stage, flanked by lesser communist wisdom, on this bamboo altar dedicated to the gods of Marxism and the religion of the poor and oppressed. The only ancient heresy to share space on this modern man's revolutionary altar was a copy of Sun Tzu's *Art of War*.

'Yes,' Tashi said, slipping into his Bata shoes and tying the laces. 'Yes, I've read them all. Books are a better form of education. Better than those dry, boring lectures.'

'Some books are also dry and boring,' I said. I pretended to struggle to pick up his copy of *Das Kapital*. 'For example, this,' I said, holding the volume above my head.

'You can always shut a book,' Tashi said. 'But you can never shut up people who think they have fancy theories.'

'Talking about people, why have we never heard about Drubtop and Drubchen Rinpoches before? Seemed these are two important lineages. The lama made them sound very old,' I said.

'Who knows, who cares? Perhaps the lama has a habit of telling tall Tibetan tales,' Tashi said. 'Perhaps that's his way of giving himself some degree of self-importance. Why dwell on it? Let's go and eat.'

I suggested that we eat at my college where the food was better. We took the short cut through the compound of the Delhi School of Economics. 'The brains of India,' Tashi remarked dryly as we walked past the School.

Dripping in sweat, we entered the college dining hall, a huge room, easily half the size of a football field. Ceiling fans whirred. Forks and knives clankered on crockery, a low beat and loud clatter, a symphony produced by a crowd of earnest young hands working in dissonance. On rows upon rows of long polished teak tables, glasses and pitchers glinted, as if in a sparkling clean readiness to quench the thirst of anyone who walked into the orbit of this large orchestra of a banquet. In the non-veg part of the dining hall we spotted Samdup, Phuntsok and Rigzin and walked to their part of the hall. Samdup, in his usual dapper cream safari suit, was jabbering away to Phuntsok, mustachioed and stout, clad in spotless white cotton kurta and pyjamas. We sat across the table from them.

'So when do you leave, Dhondup?' Phuntsok asked, hitching up the glasses perched on the beak of his nose.

'A week or so,' I replied. 'How did Shakespeare go?'

'Okay. I'll pass, I suppose,' Phuntsok said, nodding his head with excessive cheerfulness now that the last of the gruelling exams were over and done with, joyfully epitaphed and epilogued.

Phuntsok said he was off to see *The Blue Lagoon* with Rigzin. 'Brooke Shields, man, Brooke Shields. You should see it, man.' Phuntsok said this in English, another of those whose enthusiasm opened up by new horizons could not be expressed in the language of losers, as if this would corrupt both the thought and the enthusiasm.

'That's right,' Rigzin added, standing and slapping Phuntsok's shoulder. 'Really hot stuff, man.' Rigzin hitching his Levi pants higher over his premature paunch grabbed Phuntsok's shoulders, swung him around and pushed from behind, as if launching him towards another level of excitement. Rigzin, with lumbering steps, followed Phuntsok out of the dining hall.

When the three of us had finished our breakfast, I said I wanted to go back to my room.

'Sleep it off, man,' Tashi said. 'We'll be back later to fetch you for another round of the lama's stories.'

'That's right, we'll be back to fetch you,' Samdup said, flicking off dust from his safari suit. The two of them sauntered out of the dining hall.

Lately, I had noticed that Tashi and Samdup were coming closer. They were close buddies all right, but the time they spent huddled together, whispering, and the suddenness with which they stopped talking whenever I or any other Tibetan bumped into them seemed to make them more than just friends. They were like comrades-in-arms, plotting something big, something mysterious. I wondered what secret linked the two of them. What were the two of them up to? I wondered.

I could not get a single word out of the two of them. I had an enigmatic article Tashi had written for the *Tibetan Review*, published out of New Delhi, for a clue. The article raised a few heckles that veered dangerously close to becoming a full-blown storm. However, this particular storm proved to be mild and no visible damage was done.

Some insinuated that the article was Tashi's attempt to reject his Buddhist beliefs. Others were openly sceptical of the claims made in the article, of Tashi's ability to remember so much and in such excruciating detail. Still others condemned the article as the new generation's sacrilege. 'Who does he think he is, writing about the Sixth Panchen Lama, as if the Panchen Lama was just another lama next door? And what proof does he have in stating that the Sixth Panchen Lama's sister was married to that Bogle guy?'

Part autobiography, part slice of history of Tsang, part his meditation on the Tibetan exile scene, the article's scattered thoughts mirrored the confused impulses and the contradictory yearnings of a restless soul in search of a ship to a new port. I didn't think he really cared what ship or which port, as long as there was a ship and a port to sail to. Like all wanderers, Tashi's real passion was travelling, not the destination. The article was entitled 'Memory'.

To be made an orphan of your past, having no clue about it, is worse than fate relieving you of your parents. We, our generation of Tibetans, are the true children of Tibet's Age of Orphans. We have no memory, having been robbed of it by either deliberate forgetfulness or by Chinese bullets or treacherous Himalayan passes and left lying in deep green crevices and buried in snow, ice and human indifference. Not knowing what went before you, not knowing where you come from is worse than not knowing where you are going. On the other hand, in this respect I consider myself lucky. I remember and I remember it all. The world I remember is not necessarily the world I claim as my own. But it is the world I was born in. If any man could base his wealth on his memory, I am exceedingly rich. I have lots of memories, memories to share and memories which are an education in themselves, painful and expensive. Memory is what we want to forget but are forced to remember. Memory is the interplay between sleep wakefulness. I myself was in this state when I was sprawled on the bed, half asleep, one eye closed, permanently, one eye watching the restless ceiling fan. I was rummaging through the confused depths of my aching head for something to lay claim on, for anything to cling to. I was digging into my head for the smell of old Tibet, for patches of mildewing memories, for scraps of old Tibet. I managed to scratch only the transition period, the transition from the old to the ugly. The violent transition burst upon us, as the gate of old Tibet through which the ugliness pounced upon our lives was blasted open. That's what happens if you keep your gate locked too long. One day someone is bound to gatecrash, tear it down.

Well, if you ask me, it was the biggest blast in my life. I still remember the exact shapes of the scattered cumulus clouds that drifted across the azure canvas above the plateau as the force of the blast hurled me on the ground, my face turned heavenward, my stunned mind contemplating the silent clouds framed by the courtyard, till they too were overpowered by the dust and smoke from the smouldering blast. Till then I thought the gate of the Moti Linka mansion where my mother served the household of Sey Kusho, an important aristocrat of Shigatse, was as solid, as permanent, as the brooding Samdrup Tse Dzong which overlooked Tibet's second biggest town. This was the gate that we approached with deference. The gate symbolised authority and tradition. Behind the gate was everything we respected.

Regardless of what stood behind it, the gate itself was a piece of Tibetan craftsmanship. It was framed on the top and sides by a two-inch thick slanting, carved wooden awning. The gate was solid wood, held together at intervals by cast iron strips. The brass door handles grew out of the mouths of two lions. The handles were decked with multi-coloured tassels that sagged with age and dripped with tradition.

Through the gate marched the history of Shigatse and much of Tsang and beyond. Moti Linka was the place where the Fifth Dalai Lama and the twenty-eight year old Gushri Khan, the brash and bearded Qoshot Mongol chieftain, conferred with the Great Fifth and made his ascent to Samdrup Tse Dzong in 1642 to assume authority of all Tibet, from the borders of Ladakh in the west to Dartsedo in the east. Lingering Shigatse rumours whispered that Moti Linka was one of the pleasure parks of the Sixth Dalai Lama during his long absences from the Potala. Many of his love poems were inspired by its comely maidens. Moti Linka gave a Panchen Lama to Tibet and claimed the life of a Manchu amban.

Moti Linka was the first stop of the Sixth Panchen Lama's cavalcade when he returned to Shigatse with George Bogle. The Panchen Lama, the one who authored the Guide to Shambhala, had temporarily abandoned

Shigatse because of an outbreak of smallpox. Moti Linka was where the secret marriage between George Bogle and the Sixth Panchen Lama's supposed sister took place. Two daughters were born whose descendants still live their lives in the Scottish highlands. The Sixth Panchen Lama, or the Third Panchen Lama to some and the Teshoo Lama to the British, had earlier intervened on behalf of Bhutan in the hostilities between it and Cooch Behar, which sought the arms of the East India Company to push back the aggressive Bhutanese. The Panchen Lama's intervention provided Warren Hastings, the Governor General of all East India Company's territory in India, the ideal opportunity to dispatch in 1774 George Bogle, an 'English gentleman to Tibet... to explore an unknown region for the purpose of discovering, in the first instance, what was the nature of its production; as it would afterwards be, when that knowledge was obtained, to inquire what means it might be most effectively converted to advantage.' The Company was interested in Tibet because it wanted to expand its trade beyond India and the Teshoo Lama, as George Bogle discovered, was interested in the Company for the sake of larger peace.

The Teshoo Lama told Bogle, 'In the event of war between Russia and China, I may perhaps be able, through means of the Company, to do something toward bringing peace. And that,' the Teshoo Lama concluded, 'is the business of us Lamas.'

Those words and the world shaped by them were blasted away when the People's Liberation Army stormed Moti Linka in March 1959.

My mother sent my brother to inform the officials of Moti Linka, or whoever was left, that the Chinese soldiers were at the gate. Then my mother picked me up in her arms to flee. To do this we had to cross the courtyard and that was the time when the gate was blasted away, and the impact of the blast threw us on the ground and we watched like frightened rabbits as teenaged soldiers of the People's Liberation Army, as frightened as we were, but with rifles in hand, crept into courtyard.

My mother and I were the only ones wounded. Grenade shrapnel caught us in the legs. We were allowed to spend the night in our own house. The next day, I was taken piggyback and my mother in the palanquin used by Cham Kusho, Sey Kusho's wife, to the People's Hospital behind the walls of Moti Linka.

That was how we were liberated—from our history.

I remember how several months later, my mother recounted the episode to one of our neighbours. According to her, as the PLA soldiers approached, the two of us were flung on the ground awaiting our inevitable fate. Then I had put forward my two little dirty hands, thumbs up—the desperate gesture of a man begging for dear life—and said, 'Ku-chi, Ku-chi, don't kill us. If you kill my mother, kill me too.'

My mother said the PLA soldiers were either lousy soldiers or good men or simply understood Tibetan, because we were spared.

Besides liberating us, they also led us out of the mansion because they said they needed the place for setting up the Shigatse branch of the Preparatory Committee for the Tibet Autonomous Region. We were sent packing to Takdrukha, a farming area on the outskirts of Shigatse, sprawled along the banks of the growling Tsangpo River.

A year or so later, I was sent to the new school and was promptly recruited into the ranks of the Young Pioneers, a notch below the Communist Youth League, from where the Chinese Communist Party recruited its members. I didn't make any extra effort to get the honour. From my dust-covered face rinsed and, perhaps redeemed by one astonished eye, our Chinese language teacher must have instantly concluded that here was a real proletariat waiting to be recognised and reclaimed for the revolution. A Young Pioneer red scarf was given to each of us, which we wore on our necks as proud emblems of our baptism in the fire of Chinese communist revolution. It also served as protection against the pitiless wind.

But there was no hint of a revolution in our Tibetan language classroom. It was all good old feudal Tibet with the Tibetan teacher in his chuba, glowering over our heads glued to our jang-shing, with all of us wondering when the tyranny would come to an end. Questions were frowned upon as an act of crass impudence or outright stupidity. The quality of our Tibetan calligraphy marked us as either good or bad students. A student whose writing on the wooden board reminded the teacher of a yak gone mad was placed last in the row. A student whose calligraphy reminded the teacher of a dignified aristocrat making stately progress among the ranks of his subservient retinue was placed first in the row.

After the examination and as a fitting way to announce the results, our teacher lined us up in a single file and gave the first student a stinging whack on his cheek with a split bamboo reed because his handwriting, though brilliant, was not good enough. The first student gave two smacks to his immediate neighbour and down the ranks the smacks were added on till I, whose calligraphy reminded the teacher of a blind louse who had lost its way on some important and itching head, was smacked twenty-two times.

But then I forgot the pain and was more concerned about whether the balls of tsampa I would stuff in my mouth at meal times would pop out from my split left cheek, only to be grabbed by my elder brother who could then stuff them into his mouth.

I returned home to find our mother waiting anxiously. Unfortunately for me, her cries of despair at seeing my savaged, bloated, swollen cheek did not prevent her from depriving me of my evening meal for coming scandalously last in my class. 'You are a disgrace to our family! How many times do I have to tell you that your grandfather was the best shoemaker in Shigatse? Why can't you have the best handwriting in your class?' That was also the question uppermost in my mind, but I couldn't come up with a reasonable explanation because I was made to sit cross-legged, with the jang-shing on my laps, to practise my calligraphy, trying to upgrade it to anything else except a yak gone berserk or a blind louse meandering on some important feudal head.

One day our teacher decided that we all deserved a picnic, which started as a promise and ended as a lesson. Off we went, clanging our pots and soot-laden pans, to a cemetery. We didn't know why our teacher decided that a traditional Tibetan cemetery was an ideal picnic spot. Perhaps he wanted in his tyrannical fashion to remind us that this was where old Tibet lay dead, cut to pieces and offered to hungry, waiting vultures. Or perhaps he wanted us to know that this spot would be the graveyard of communism in some future, happier times. We, his serf students, wearing our bright red revolutionary Young Pioneer scarves, didn't really know which.

One sunny, windless day the Takdrukha neighbourhood committee decided to get rid of our Tibetan teacher. The whole school was called to witness this grim exposure of a feudal element lurking amidst bright and young revolutionaries. One reason cited for the struggle session was our teacher's habit of instituting feudal habits like whacking his students with split bamboo reeds on their cheeks. A dunce cap was placed on his head and the incensed strugglers assaulted him with the full savagery of the revolutionary vocabulary. This display of class struggle over, the neighbourhood committee packed him off to a prison in Shigatse.

Our witnessing a struggle session or wearing the Young Pioneer scarves around our necks wasn't our real baptism in the fire of communist revolution. Starvation was. It swept through our part of Tibet like a terrible curse and lingered on like a hungry ghost. Soon the people of Takdrukha were busy borrowing tsampa from those better stocked. Even this surplus ran out. That was when we took to the PLA soldiers, who were always well fed. One day the cook of the PLA platoon who we had been regularly pestering with our bright revolutionary scarves, urchin faces, running noses and trembling hands, handed us a large chunk of raw meat. We divided the meat and ran home with our day's booty. But my mother was suspicious. Could be horse meat, she said after the meal. This piece of suspicion stayed with us like some secret shame. But hunger was a stronger force than shame or guilt.

As long as the horse meat stock lasted, we stayed away from the PLA soldiers. As soon as the stock ran out, we were back to pleading with the soldiers who ate their midday meal out in the open, in pairs, chopsticks furiously active before their busy mouths.

While we were thus bravely battling hunger and starvation, one day my eldest brother, the ex-monk, showed up at Takdrukha, just as suddenly as he had eloped. He brought, to our disbelief, was a lot of cash and a big bag of tsampa. More than the cash, the sight of that bag of tsampa triggered in us sentiments similar to those that must have overcame exhausted pilgrims when after months of travel they first sighted Mount Kailash: reverence, elation, fulfilment, relief, joy…

That was one practical reason why my mother at once forgave and perhaps forgot my eldest brother's scandalous exit from our lives and welcomed and embraced him like a dream come true. The other reason was that my mother might have been a good housewife but she was a lousy farmer. Giving her a plot of land, like the others who had been displaced by the Chinese communist authorities might have been a magnanimous gesture, but distributing land to people who hadn't a clue about farming went beyond being communist and revolutionary. It turned out to be a disaster. My mother had to hire extra farming hands for plowing, sowing, reaping, and threshing and all her income was spent in paying their salaries. And we the deserving proletariats of the revolution, except what we could digest of communist verbiage, were left mighty hungry. For that reason my mother thought or at least hoped that my eldest brother would be the one who could replace those extra hands.

But this was the exact reason why my brother wanted all of us to move with him to Rachu, just across the Nepalese border, where he worked in a road-construction unit. He said conditions were a lot better in Rachu. Conditions being better naturally meant that there was food. To our disbelief, he said a leg of mutton could be had for a bag of tsampa. 'One whole leg of mutton for a small bag of tsampa,' he emphasised, stretching his arms apart to indicate the size of a mutton leg in south Tibet. The effort he made in trying to stretch his arms as far apart as possible made it seem as if the sheep in south Tibet were the size of yaks and he talked about mutton legs as if he were having them for breakfast, lunch and dinner and was quite bored of consuming them. But my mother and my two other siblings were not permitted to move to south Tibet. In the end it was I who accompanied my brother, remorsefully, after extracting a promise from him that he would not beat me when I wet my bed. But the most compelling reason for my agreeing to go with my brother was that piece of mutton leg he described in such detail. The mystery of that leg of mutton baffles me to this day.

But the pain of being so abruptly snatched away from my mother was mitigated by the marvel of one whole day's truck ride down the meandering valleys of south Tibet. At dusk the truck disgorged us in Dingri, a quiet village with pretensions of being a town, spread all over a low dusty, lone hill. We walked to Rachu nestled across the Dingri River, in the arms of a towering hill, where my brother's wife welcomed us with a wan smile.

Rachu was famous for two things. One of them was a breathtaking view of Mount Everest, or Goddess Mother of the Earth to the local Tibetans. In Rachu my vocabulary became enormously enriched when I learned the word for mist, which perpetually garlanded that piece of rock and snow piercing the turquoise sky. On this side of Everest it was Tenzin Sherpa who first stood atop that famous rock. A ditty composed by the sherpas living on the other side of the Himalayas and brought to our side by the shrill wind and the occasional trader celebrating the exploits of their famous son. Why did he bother, why go through all this effort? Was there food on top of the summit or what? That was our attitude then as I suppose is the attitude of every starving people who think any effort directed at not acquiring food is an effort that is rendered criminally stupid.

Some Tibetans whispered knowingly that there was a golden frog on the summit of Mount Everest and those who heard its croaking would be endowed with fame and fortune, beyond anyone's wildest dreams. That, I supposed, explained Tenzin Sherpa's scatterbrained action.

Anyway, I always wondered what lay beyond those mountains. More mutton legs?

The other reason Rachu was famous was the bravery of its people and that of Razam Gyapon. Razam Gyapon had been a captain in the Gadang regiment of the Tibetan army headquartered in Shigatse and a hundred of his men were defiantly deployed in Dingri to guard the border. The PLA had pacified the whole of Tibet, except Dingri, which resisted it with a ferocity that still lingered in the hesitant whispers and hushed conversations of a stubborn but subdued people. After taking on the PLA soldiers single-handedly with sniper-shots from the terrace of his house, Razam Gyapon, his energy spent, his ammunition exhausted and his soldiers and family obliterated, yielded to his enemies. Their efforts to execute him became a legendary failure until a PLA soldier who was acquainted with the superstitious ways of the Tibetans divested the man of all the amulets and talismans he wore on his neck and waist. In his stark nakedness, his life rendered meaningless by the sudden, brutal deprivation of all the physical accoutrement of his culture, Razam Gyapon died instantly, survived by no one in particular, except a growing legend and a reincarnation, orphans of a brave past.

Since then his house, below the tiny village of Rachu, which stood all alone on the northern bank of the Dingri River, was blemished by a frantic, flapping Chinese flag planted on its roof, a daily reminder of China's conquest of Rachu and its victory over Razam Gyapon.

But my brother's glib talk of mutton legs being had for bags of tsampa proved outrageously illusionary. Rachu was mutton-less and as far as other foodstuff was concerned, in the same appalling, tsampa-less situation as Shigatse. My encoring eyes were met by my brother's who pointed to Mount Everest, the habitat of a golden frog who croaked incessantly of the promise of more mutton legs further down in the lush, sub-tropical valley. So one early morning the three of us enveloped in the easy camaraderie of sherpa traders trekked toward Mount Everest in the hope that we would hear the croaks of the amphibian resident of the highest peak in the world. That night we slept on the crest of a mountain, dwarfed by the dark, brooding goddess mother of the earth. That was also the night when I didn't wet my bed. And try as hard as we could, we heard no croaking by any frog, golden or otherwise.

In Solo Khumbu, we left the poverty of the bare Tibetan plateau behind us. In Nepal we first encountered India in the form of two crisp ten rupee notes, an indulgence from a fellow refugee.

The twenty rupees and our own coolie work for some Amdo businessmen took us across to India. After a ten-day hike through the breadth of the lush Nepalese terai, burdened by back-breaking loads and bothered by the insufferable heat, we showed up at Bodh Gaya, an enforced pilgrimage, all in search of a piece of mutton leg.

Bodh Gaya, the setting where the Buddha attained enlightenment, was also the spot where an exile confronted the place of his exile. And where, for some strange reason, the homeless felt at home. This was the spot where the world's first exile discovered his true home. And we his followers wanted to do the same. We wanted a home where we felt at home. We felt our two situations were similar. Both he and we had run away from home.

But he ran away from home to renounce the world.

We, what did we do?

We ran away to pronounce the world.

In which case, should our prayers be the same? We came in search of more of the material world because in Tibet, we were liberated from our dreams, and, what was critical for us, from the very stuff that kept body and soul together. For these practical reasons we wanted to reclaim our world, our material world.

As an afterthought, was the place where we, with ruddy cheeks and bewildered eyes, discovered our true identity. We found we were called refugees.

Our ethnic identity, Tibetan, preceded and was made to qualify our new one, of being refugees, stateless, tossed about. It was a lengthy education in the various expressions of dispossession, in the vocabulary of not belonging, in the language of loss. We graduated. From refugees we became exiles, with a brand new world to ourselves, the world of the Diaspora. That was a comfort. We filled the vacuum world of our longings with things that we longed to have. Mostly, we ended up filling this world with bits and pieces of remembered furniture from our shattered home. Sometimes, this required great ingenuity because the repairing work demanded the skills of seasoned exiles. But we were not seasoned exiles. We were babes in woods. And the woods were the latter half of the twentieth century and not the medieval woods we left behind in a rush to be out of Tibet. Didn't the first refugees when confronted with the modern world in India say in bafflement of the hermit that everything was strange except the selfsame earth and sky? We had a world of catching up to do. This catching up took its toll: confusion, anger, despair. Whether we really caught up or all this business of catching up is a good thing is beside the point. The point is that we survived. That itself was a small victory. We were yet to recover what we had lost but our surviving gave us the hope that those would be recovered. Our survival was more amazing because in all of our history we have been fiercely home-keeping people. We refused to let the world in. Well to test a silly theory, we were thrown out to find out for ourselves what was going on behind our mountains and how we dealt with what we saw.

Seasoned exiles or not, experience became our true dharma, our best refuge. At least we could say that we had been abroad, that we had seen the world and flicked off the dust of cosmopolitanism from our well-travelled shoulders.

Yes, I remember it all, this and more. And I know that remembering is deliverance. Or, if my dear readers prefer, memory is a trick which others don't play on you but which you play on yourself. With this I rest my autobiographical case of memory colonising my mind and taking over and looting and in so looting colouring my precious perspective. Yes, I believe memory changes you, memory after memory, breath after fresh breath, depending on how far into the past you remember and how much life you breathe into what you remember, life after new life.

Different Dreams, Different Tibets

☯

As promised, Tashi and Samdup barged into my room late that afternoon. 'Time I went to see Metok. You and Samdup should also hear some more Drubtop Rinpoche yakshit,' Tashi said, giving a dig in my ribs.

When we entered her place, Ama Penpa did not shoo us away as she had yesterday, but simply asked, 'You're still alive?' with a look of mock surprise. The lama was seated on the bed.

When we were seated, I said, 'Rinpoche, Tashi said I shouted that I was Drubtop Rinpoche last night. Is this a good sign?'

'In your dream?' the lama inquired, taking a gulp from his glass of chang.

'No, no, when I was dragging him to my college last night,' Tashi butted in. 'All the way he kept saying he was Drubtop Rinpoche.'

'I interpret only dreams,' Rinpoche said firmly.

'Rinpoche, tell us more Drubtop stories,' Tashi said.

This pleased the lama and he asked, 'Where was I last night?'

'When the Drubtop Rinpoche returned to Tibet, after inventing the Tibetan script,' I said.

'It's not just any script,' the lama said testily. 'It's the Word! The Word! The one that makes us speak, the one that makes us remember and store what we remember for those in the future to learn again and again and remember and pass on to others through the endless cycle of birth and death and rebirth. It's the Word, the one that opens to us the wisdom of the Sakyamuni who frees us from the cycle of karma. The Word which leads us to freedom and saves us from going round and round in small, meaningless circles drawn by our ego—forever going, forever reaching nowhere.'

'The Word and the Sound that brought the universe into existence...' Tashi said, dreamily. He gave a shrug in my direction to indicate that was not too difficult. He closed his eyes and said, 'The Word that creates and teaches us the emptiness of its own creation...'

'And first uttered in the Land of Snow by our Lord and Master, the maker and keeper of the Word,' the lama intoned. He had brought his hands together in prayer, casting a penetrating look at Tashi.

I waited for the lama to continue his recitation, not wanting to terminate the magic of the moment, but he fell silent, now and then looking sideways at Tashi. In an attempt to revive the spirit of the moment, I said, 'Yes, after the Drubtop Rinpoche coined the Word.' The lama remained silent. 'The Word that makes us remember and not forget,' I said, trying to fall in sync with the lama's mood in an attempt to make him remember his own story of the night before.

'I'll skip the rest and tell you the story of the last Drubtop Rinpoche,' he spoke up, breaking out of his languid mood. 'The last one was the nineteenth Drubtop Rinpoche. The Drubtop lineage is the longest lineage in Tibet.'

The way Tashi tried to suppress a yawn I knew that he regretted asking the lama to tell more Drubtop Rinpoche stories. This time Tashi did not try to interrupt the lama by making any clever remarks. I took out my notebook and Bic.

The lama's story was focused on only one theme. How the Chinese communists by struggling the last Drubtop Rinpoche had killed him. By the time he came to the end of his tale, he was barely audible. He was sobbing. 'And I didn't lift a finger to save my teacher,' he moaned with uncharacteristic gentleness.

What could Tashi and I do, except gulp down more chang? We came to be touched by the magic and exuberance of our isolated past and here we were confronted with the reality of our wretched present. When the lama had wiped away the last of his tears with the fold of his robe, I turned to see how Tashi was doing. He was slouched on the lama's bed, his head resting on the wooden wall plastered with glossy posters of Hindi movie stars, a hobby of Metok's and a topic of inexhaustible interest to her. Tashi was snoring.

Samdup shook him and told him we should go and leave the lama alone. On the way out, we met a pock-faced Gyaltsen, the president of the Delhi TYC. He said the next day, a Sunday, was the last meeting of the youth body. As usual the meeting would take place at the school at three in the afternoon.

When Samdup and I entered our college, we bumped into Rigzin and Phuntsok.

'Brooke Shields, man, Brooke Shields,' Phuntsok said, by way of a greeting.

'So how's rangzen-shangzen?' Rigzin asked.

'Same as before. It's still a struggle-shruggle,' I said.

'Have you started writing the brochure on Ladakh?' Rigzin asked. 'It's going to be a big tourist season in Ladakh this summer and that brochure will be very useful.'

'Give me a few days,' I said. 'I have something else to do at the moment. Once that is done, I will start on the brochure. I will have it ready for you before you leave for Ladakh.'

The next morning I walked to Phuntsok's block, but the early bird had flown away with the familiar formidable padlock guarding the door. I dropped by Samdup's block. He was there and we walked to the college cafe and ordered scrambled eggs, buttered toast and coffee. Samdup was silent for a while and then abruptly leaning forward and lowering his voice to a hushed, conspiratorial whisper asked, 'You know the latest news?' His eyes were trained on mine, burning with un-blinking misgiving.

'Tibetan independence is around the corner?' I said breezily, trying to shake off Samdup's uncomfortable stare and refusing to be ensnared in his conspiratorial plans.

'Maybe,' Samdup said, hesitating.

'Independence, not around the corner? So what's the big news?'

'We … we've formed a communist party!' he whispered.

'A communist party!' I blurted. 'Enough jokes for the morning.'

'No joke, man. This is serious. We have formed a communist party.'

'When did you establish this party and who's the "we"?' I asked, ordering for more coffee.

An unbecoming gravity marred Samdup's chubby features. 'Just between the two of us,' he said, looking around to see if anyone was within earshot and then continuing, 'Tashi and I have already had an audience with the Dalai Lama. He has approved of and blessed the party.'

'You form a communist party and the first thing you do is to get it spiritually endorsed?' I asked.

'Why not? We'll unite with all the positive social forces,' Samdup said pedantically.

'Aren't you going to make a public announcement of this historic event?' I asked sardonically. 'The Tibetan refugees should know of this. They should know that they'll be free once again, and pretty soon at that. But why are you telling me all this?'

'You don't have to be sarcastic,' Samdup said, a flash of anger clouding his face. 'We are doing what we think is the right thing to do. We knew that we would be alienating a lot of people. So be it. It's all for rangzen and a decent socialist Tibet. For your information, communism might be the only thing which connects us with the people in Tibet. For the last twenty years or so they have known only communism. The next issue of the *Tibetan Review* will have everything you wish to know about us. And we thought you may be interested in joining it,' Samdup said, with what I thought was a sigh of relief.

'Join the communist party? Whatever for?'

'Tashi thought you might be interested... in joining.'

'Fat chance! What do we need a communist party for? We don't need a revolution. The Tibetan exiles are equally poor, we are all refugees, remember? What urgent social compulsions could kindle a communist revolution?'

'We thought you might be interested, that's all.'

'A communist party is a serious thing. You can't be so cavalier in your invitation. Are you serious about it?'

'How can we make it look more serious? Invite you to a dark cell and make you swear allegiance and take an oath of secrecy?' Samdup fumed. He pushed the wicker chair back and his hands gripped the armrest for several seconds. With a grunt he stood up and walked away, leaving me to pay for his half-eaten breakfast. The communists! I muttered. The first thing they need to learn is to pay for their own breakfast. Won't even pay their bills and want to start a revolution. Who would foot the bills for the revolution? The people? No way!

I sat in the cafe for sometime, letting everything sink in.

A Tibetan Communist Party in exile? Then the realisation hit me like a bucketfull of freezing water thrown at me. Tashi and Samdup had been plotting the formation of a communist party for a long time. Perhaps for three years now. That was how long Samdup and I had been collabourating in a common interest. For three years we had taken turns editing *March*, the magazine of the Delhi branch of the Tibetan Youth Congress. Two of us wanted to change its name. *March* seemed so prosaic, uninspiring. We wanted to change the name to *Young Tibet*. That name had a whiff of revolution, a faint smell of blood, a willingness to do away with the odour of the rotten past and promises of new beginnings. But the others rejected the new name. They explained that the magazine was called *March* because it recalled the heroic efforts of the Tibetan people in the uprising that occurred on 10 March 1959. 'It's our homage to men and women who died to get rid of Chinese rule. *March* also indicates the willingness of the exiled Tibetans to continue the struggle for an independent Tibet,' they said.

Samdup and I, after some intense haggling, lost our steam and didn't protest any more. Whatever the symbolism of *March*, we enjoyed bringing out the mimeographed magazine, once every two months, posting it to the embassies in New Delhi, to TYC branches all over India and Nepal. We had the articles typed on stencil sheets and made about two hundred mimeographed copies. The magazine was polemical and strident and full of anger. However, when it was Samdup's turn to edit and put the articles together, he would erase every derogatory reference to communism. His explanation was that we shouldn't make our struggle ideological. 'We are against the Chinese occupation of our country. But by always lumping communism with China, we would lose support of the socialist world and half the world is socialist. We need all the support we can muster. We will be confusing the socialist bloc and playing into China's hands. As it is they are portraying our struggle as a bunch of feudal lords crying over their lost privileges.'

There was logic in his argument, but since no Chinese government in history had occupied Tibet with the brutality displayed by the communists, to me it seemed only right that the Chinese be qualified as communists. In my naivety I sought Tashi's advice. His response was simple, 'I think Samdup is right. Remember, His Holiness the Dalai Lama said our struggle is not against communism or any ideology, but against the Chinese government occupying our country.'

I left it at that, but when it was my turn to edit the magazine, if communism or communists were made to qualify or more accurately demonise the Chinese, I let these words hang on much to the quivering editorial outrage of Samdup. I countered Samdup's tendency to indulge in editorial butchering by using his own logic. 'We need to make a distinction. The regime ruling Taiwan is also unfortunately Chinese. Why piss them off. After all, one day we may need their support. We need to make it clear to them that our struggle is directed not at all Chinese but against the Chinese communists who are brutalising our country and culture.'

During the last such altercation, Samdup, instead of stamping his feet, sulking and staging a walkout, was all charm, sweet reasonableness and, despite the scorching heat, volunteered to deliver the articles to the Modi Correspondence Institute. I was delighted, not because of Samdup's willingness to help, but by his sudden change in attitude. A week later I negotiated my way through the dense traffic of cars, rickshaws and cows in Kamla Nagar and sauntered to Modi Correspondence Institute to collect copies of *March*. Modi, a paan-chewing man dressed in a spotless dhoti, told me that all the articles had been stenciled but that his Gestating machine had broken down. He was waiting for the repairman. He told me to come the next day.

I told Samdup that he and others should gather at Tashi's room the next evening to collate, staple, stamp and mail the copies of *March*. 'Four hundred rupees,' Modi said when I went to collect the copies the following day. Modi spat out the paan and his potbelly twitched, rumbled and convulsed in a fit of exhaustion generated by this enormous physical effort.

'Why? It was only three hundred the last time.'

'Inflation, inflation. Price of paper going up. So are the labour charges.' Modi pointed his index finger to the high ceiling of his crowded office where he indicated everything would eventually land. Prices of all items shooting up through the roof of his office.

'Receipt?'

'Here, I write it down.' Modi opened his desk draw and produced his company's letterhead that had a logo of a sari-clad woman, cheerfully typing the evident good news of the establishment of Modi Correspondent Institute. 'Fifty rupees for typing, hundred for forty-eight stencil sheets, two hundred for about ten thousand A4 paper sheets and fifty for the use of the Gestetner machine.'

Fifty rupees for typing wasn't fair especially since Modi made some of his students taking the typing course type the articles for free even as he collected a handsome fee from them. Anyway, my predecessors had paid up and I wasn't in a mood to haggle. I handed over the money, slipped the receipt into my shirt pocket and hailed a rickshaw, which deposited me and the latest issue of *March* to the lawns of Tashi's college. A crowd had gathered in Tashi's room. While others got busy collating the magazine, I made a complete set and browsed through the loose sheets. I discovered that Samdup had struck off all references to communism. Samdup had sat up all night to delete what he considered offending references. For all I knew, he might have even bribed the typist to perform this service.

'Samdup, you rotten saboteur!' I screamed, throwing the offending sheets at Samdup. 'You have edited the editor! Why did you delete all references to Chinese communism? I explained my reasons for leaving this reference intact. I'm going to stop this issue being mailed. This is an illegal issue,' I screamed and heard some scattered muffled laughter from the group. 'Yes, this is an illegal issue,' I repeated. 'And I declare it so!'

Samdup stood there with a smirk on his face, as unruffled as his safari suit. 'I did this for Tibet and the Tibetan people,' he replied grandly. There was no evidence of guilt either in the irritatingly measured tone of his voice or in his attitude.

In fact he seemed proud and happy with what he had done. He struck a martyr's pose—an innocent victim of mad, jealous people throwing wild accusations. 'Why use communism in a derogatory manner. We will lose support from the communist world,' he explained with maddening reasonableness.

'Lose support?' I shouted. 'Have we got it already? The only thing you have lost is my trust.'

I stormed out of Tashi's room. My walking out was a strategic mistake because in my absence the others had collated the loose sheets, stapled them, stuck a one-rupee postage stamp on each copy and launched forth the sabotaged magazine on to an unsuspecting world.

As a way of apology, Samdup came to my room that evening with a forbidden bottle of whiskey. He was a person who thought that every problem could be solved by bribery. At least with me it always worked.

But Samdup and Tashi's love affair with communism wasn't just confined to sabotaging *March*. I was told that a year or so back when the TYC held a major conference in Dharamsala to discuss a suitable ideology for the Tibetan movement, the two of them passionately championed communism. 'We must counter fire with fire,' Samdup supposedly thundered before an appalled audience. Later the pair was dubbed 'the communist duo'.

That was it. I had all the clues, but concluded nothing. Not interpreting, not assessing their curious actions was worse than conniving in their conspiracies. I drained the last dregs of coffee, paid the bill and walked out of the cafe, dejected, feeling betrayed and used. On the way I met Phuntsok.

'Some nimbu pani?' he offered.

'Why not? Do you know what Samdup just told me? He and Tashi have formed a communist party!'

Phuntsok raised the loose front of his kurta before his bored face to fan himself. 'What's the big news? It's an open secret. They asked me to join. Months back.'

I was surprised that the party's politburo had asked Phuntsok to join their gang.

'No, what's the point?' Phuntsok said, still fanning himself. 'A communist party needs a revolution to justify itself, to sustain itself. Do you think the Tibetan society is on the verge of a revolution, corruption and a repressive system oppressing it? No! The Tibetan refugees had never had it so good. They're free and, if not prospering, at least making ends meet.'

'Surely, Tashi and Samdup know this. Why do they persist? They're doomed to fail.'

'I don't know. I was told that His Holiness supports the idea. Perhaps it's an attempt to reach out to the Tibetan communists in Tibet. To say that if a solution could be found, Tibet would not revert to the old feudal system. That the Tibetan communists in Tibet could run Tibet.'

'That I understand but the way Tashi and Samdup explained it seems that two of them really believe that there is a need for a major revolution.'

'Well, they are in for a major disappointment. A revolution has already taken place. Dharamsala is now manned by common people like you and me. So what do they want to change?' Phuntsok said. He stopped fanning himself.

I had many questions, but Samdup ignored me when we gathered for the last TYC meeting. When I approached Tashi on the subject, he kept his mouth shut. A scowl surfaced on his face when I teasingly said, 'How are you today, Mr Chairman?'

The meeting was a wrap-up. Gyaltsen, the president, stood up and cleared his throat. Whenever Gyaltsen stood up to speak, most of us would just be waiting for him to finish even before he had begun. Gyaltsen reviewed the TYC's activities during the past year rating all of them highly.

Before the meeting broke up, Tashi and Samdup to everyone's surprise surrendered their TYC identity cards. 'We quit the organisation,' Tashi said brusquely and refused to answer the questions fired at him.

Gyaltsen accepted the two ID cards, wordlessly. Later he said he felt betrayed. He felt Tashi and Samdup had betrayed the ideals and spirit of the TYC. According to him, 'TYC defines our generation. It serves as a platform for the expression of our hopes and dreams. By disowning the TYC, Tashi and Samdup, have disowned our refugee identity, and all the hopes and dreams which go with it.'

Chastened and subdued, in groups, we left for our favourite chang houses. I persuaded Phuntsok to accompany me to Ama Penpa's chang shack in the hope that I would hear more lama stories.

Tashi was there, sullen. Samdup stared at the dirty ceiling when he spotted Phuntsok and me walking in. The lama was in, seated on the bed and he was in an expansive mood. Perhaps sitting on the bed the whole day was boring even for a lama and he needed someone to converse someone like me who was the perfect listener, curious, respectful and noting down every word he uttered.

By now I had five Elephant notebooks, filled with my scribbling of the lama's fascinating stories. And the notebooks kept piling up.

'Soon the whole history of Tibet will be contained in these pages,' I said with a smug, satisfied smile, pointing to the notebooks which filled my cotton shoulder bag. I was speaking to Phuntsok.

'The history of Tibet?' Tashi laughed. 'Call it the fable of rinpoches, gods and ghosts, all reincarnating with exasperating frequency.'

'What are you going to do with them?' Samdup asked.

'Publish them,' I said, surprised that such an obvious thing did not strike him. 'After getting permission from the lama.'

Tashi and Samdup burst out laughing.

I had a ready response to their laughter. 'Tibetans of his generation are dying,' I said, pointing to the lama, 'and if their experiences are not recorded, how will the coming generation of Tibetans know about our experience and the experience of the Tibetans of the lama's generation? And about communist atrocities in Tibet?' To get back at them for rubbishing my lama notes, I mentioned to the lama in passing that Tashi and Samdup had formed a Tibetan communist party. There was a shriek from Ama Penpa who dropped a glass in her anxiety. It shattered into fragments. Metok looked at Tashi with alarm and helped her mother pick up the broken pieces. But the lama's reaction was unexpected. He just smiled and did not say a word. He sat there, smiling and nodded in a knowing way. Strange, I thought.

Tashi and Samdup responded with a piercing look with the word 'traitor' was clearly formed on their quivering lips.

Since the lama did not seem too disappointed with the news, the two communists turned to him to explain their reasons for forming the Tibetan Communist Party. Were they trying to recruit the lama into their party? As they explained their intent eyes were focused on a gleaming future for Tibet, preferably shaped by them. To them the Tibetans could only have an indestructible identity in a socialist Tibet.

Tashi and Samdup bluntly told the lama that they had depopulated their mental world of its traditional tenants. The lamas, oracles, spiritual teachers and rinpoches had been sent packing to some other minds. In fact, in their eyes any Tibetan above the age of thirty was a suspect, who, according to the communist duo, was responsible for losing Tibet to China. Their revolution in essence was young Tibet versus the old. Their heroes were Tsarong Datsang Dadul, Lungshar, Gendun Choephel, the Pandatsang brothers, and Baba Phuntsog Wangyal and others who in the first half of the twentieth century tried to shake Tibet off from the slumber of isolation and monasticism and warned the Tibetans of the gathering clouds of war, revolution and the inevitable invasion. 'But their efforts were the classic case of too little, too late,' they said, quoting from history books.

They explained that they considered themselves the inheritors of this unfinished revolution, the keepers of the flame, the authentic reincarnations of modern Tibet's failed heroes.

The lama simply nodded his bulky head in understanding, an amused smile playing on his face. But he did not express his support or approval of their foolhardy initiative.

The Old China Hand and the Avenging Golok

☯

Next day, before going to the farewell party at the Bureau, I paid a visit to Tsering Migmar in New Delhi. Samdup and I while editing *March* had benefited a great deal from Tsering Migmar's insight into Chinese policies in Tibet. Tsering also contributed articles, which we translated into English and published in *March*. I walked to Mall Road and took a bus to Tsering's place. Dechen, Tsering's wife, answered my knock. Without waiting for her to ask me in, I walked past her and shouted my tashi delek, more to greet Tsering. 'Tashi delek,' Dechen responded, from behind me, after a long pause.

I detected some hesitation. Was I not wanted? Had I dropped in at the wrong time? Wasn't Tsering Migmar at home?

But I couldn't expect answers from Dechen. She was a woman of few words. She believed that time spent in idle chatter was time wasted away from the business of earning a living and keeping the family fed. That was why during winter, Dechen, like so many other Tibetans, supplemented her husband's income by going to Ludhiana to buy sweaters and travelling to Nagpur to sell them. Off-sweater-selling season, she weaved pangthens. For Dechen, like all refugees, bread-and-butter security meant putting in twelve hours of solid work every day. Even now the dull thud and high twang of her loom meant that Dechen was back to her perpetual anxiety of not being able to feed her family. For Dechen wealth and security lay not in the result of hard work but in hard work itself. Hard work was her therapy for anxiety.

For Tsering Migmar words were his life. He did nothing else but talk and read and write. He literally lived by words. Tsering worked as a newsreader at the Tibetan unit of the All India Radio, a job that carried some social prestige in the Tibetan Diaspora because of the princely salary. It was not a demanding job and gave Tsering Migmar time to indulge in his primary passion: writing.

I strode to Tsering Migmar's study room and my greeting was replaced by a groan of astonishment when Tashi and Samdup stepped in from behind the door.

'What are you doing, hiding from me? I see. You three are the communist party! You're holding the politburo meeting?'

'Nothing of the sort. Just came to say goodbye,' Tashi said, taking off his glasses and running his hand over his face.

'But why hide behind the door?'

'Just wanted to surprise you. That's all,' Samdup said.

'You surprised me all right. So have the three of you decided to announce your party? And why were you so evasive when I asked you if you wanted to come with me to see Tsering-la?' I demanded of Samdup.

'Tsering-la here is not a member. Just as I said, we came to say goodbye. Sorry, the two of us need to run. Tashi delek, Tsering-la. We'll keep in touch,' Samdup said and the two of them rushed out.

'Sure you will,' I said. 'The three of you will be in touch day and night. Are they trying to recruit you?' I asked an amused Tsering.

'They want support, they want support,' Tsering said, dismissively, gathering together the loose sheets he had been writing on and stowing them away in the drawer of his high writing table. 'They want advice. That's all,' Tsering said, eyeing me, sideways.

'And your response?'

'I'm with Deng Xiaoping. It doesn't matter whether a cat is black or white as long as it catches mice,' Tsering Migmar said. 'Our mice is Tibetan independence. Or, as we Tibetans say, as long as it bring happiness to the Tibetan people, it doesn't matter even if a nun becomes the king of Tibet.'

'But they are not nuns. They are communists. And they want to follow an ideology that has made us suffer. But I don't have to point this out to you. You've been through the whole thing. And did they ask you to join them?'

'Why go on with who's in the communist party? These are details. What matters is that there is a Tibetan communist party,' Tsering said. The Chinese were master strategists. We needed to think like them, to anticipate their policies. 'Would Buddhist compassion and non-violence be an adequate counter-strategy to China's plans for Tibet?' he asked. 'We need to play fire with fire.' His bright eyes burned with rage. 'We are in this for the long haul. What happens if His Holiness passes away before we get back Tibet? Do we just say we give up? No! That's why Tibetan communists will be of benefit. They will learn to think like the Chinese, strategically, minimising weaknesses, amplifying strengths and probing and prodding for weak links.'

It was his fervour that compelled Samdup and me to see Tsering again and again. We felt that understanding communist China was a key to understanding Chinese policies in Tibet. Tsering Migmar was a new refugee and had been educated at the Central Instititute of Nationalities in Beijing and his knowledge of China and Chinese politics was profound. We started publishing a great deal of articles on China in *March*.

That day Tsering said he had to be at the All India Radio office to put together the evening programme for the Tibetan service. 'I need to leave now.'

While we walked to the bus stop, Tsering narrated an incident in Beijing that I instinctively knew linked Tsering with our lama in Majnu Ka Tilla and his nineteenth Drubtop Rinpoche. 'We had the Drubtop Rinpoche in the Beijing Nationalities Institute. He was from Golok, my region, and the highest lama in Golok. What did he become famous for?' Tsering asked. 'For killing,' Tsering shouted. 'For killing, like his grandfather. But the Drubtop Rinpoche killed not people but flies. He was declared a national champion! A Tibetan, a Buddhist monk, the highest rinpoche of my region! What shame! What laughter among the Tibetan students when the real reason for his fly-killing success came to be secretly known! But he himself came to a well-deserved end when the people of Kyitsel struggled him to death!'

Tsering said this with a trace of viciousness I had not detected in him before. He did not notice my shock at the way he vindictively dismissed the nineteenth Drubtop Rinpoche's tragic end.

We stopped at a pavement paan stall. I wanted to buy a cigarette. Tsering too decided he needed a smoke. We lit our cigarettes from the smouldering jute noose hanging from the branch of a tree next to the paan stall.

'The fly-killing campaign was meant to clean Beijing. It was a nation-wide campaign. You know how Drubtop Rinpoche managed to kill the number of flies?' Tsering's giggling face made it seem that he couldn't get over the irony of the incident, even after more than a quarter century.

'I think I know,' I replied. 'He turned a part of the Institute's library into his own personal toilet. And the flies came swarming in. Drubtop Rinpoche swatted them and presented his loot in ink-bottles to his proud teacher, everyday.'

'Who told you this?'

'You should meet Drubchen Rinpoche in Majnu Ka Tilla. He was in Beijing and was the teacher of the nineteenth Drubtop Rinpoche. You know Ama Penpa who runs the chang shop in Majnu Ka Tilla? The lama is staying with her.'

Call it premonition. As soon as I opened my mouth to release this piece of information I regretted it. I was staggered by the change that came over Tsering Migmar. And I feared for the lama.

'That grandson of the one-eyed butcher is still around!' Tsering fumed. 'Where is the grandson of that mass murderer? His grandfather massacred half my family, two generations ago!'

'Are you sure it's the lama's grandfather who did it?'

'Are you sure it's the Chinese communists who are making Tibetans in Tibet suffer?' Tsering asked, pinning me with his angry eyes. 'The case is well known. And it's in our memory, in our blood.'

'Tsering-la, calm down. That is what I call ancient history,' I said hastily. Despite my cavalier attitude, my shock turned into outright fear. I had opened old wounds. Because of my fear, fear for the lama, I became clumsy. Instead of ointment I was rubbing salt on old wounds. My fear grew not only from what Tsering said, but from the transformation that came over him. From a mild-tempered person with a ready smile, Tsering turned into an avenging Golok fired by the brooding blind grassland anger. His face became blue with seething rage and his eyes turned bloodshot.

'Ancient history! The One-Eyed Golok butchered half of my grandfather's family. And you call that ancient history! To me it's alive and still hurts. It hurts deeply. But I should be taking revenge instead of babbling on like this.' Tsering, his clenched fists tightening around an imagined broadsword, was ready to leap into the heat of ancient feuds.

'But the lama should not be held responsible for the misdeeds of his grandfather. Why harm him?'

'Because revenge is in our blood. Because it's our nomadic tradition. That's why.' Tsering's purple fists still clung to his imaginary broadsword.

'Anyway, the lama is gone from Majnu Ka Tilla. No one knows where. And what about Buddhist compassion and non-violence and forgiveness?'

'We were nomads before we became Buddhists. We are still nomads after we became Buddhists. It's in our blood and in the culture of the grasslands.'

'Well, if that's your attitude, you had plenty of time to take revenge during your time at the Nationalities Institute. Why didn't you? Anyway, Tsering-la, here's your bus to Parliament Street. Get in. You'll be late.'

Tsering dismissed the bus. 'For the simple reason that the two had left the Institute before I arrived,' Tsering said, turning his cold eyes towards me. He stared at the departing bus.

I was becoming increasingly frustrated with these memories of ancient feuds and the possibility that they might spill onto the streets of Delhi. I confronted Tsering, my eyes staring into his, looking, searching and trying to discover whether I was talking to an avenging, provincial

Golok or an educated Tibetan with an all-Tibet vision. 'Tsering-la, I respect you, for your tolerance, for your broad-mindedness and for your love of Tibet and Tibetans. Now you have turned yourself into a petty Golok brigand, ready to loot and avenge. What's the point? We have a bigger score to settle. Try to forget about old petty quarrels.'

'What's the point?' Tsering repeated. He squinted his eyes, trying to remember something. The lama's face? Or that of the nineteenth Drubtop Rinpoche? 'What purpose will it serve?' Tsering asked, still staring at his departing bus, perhaps regretting not having hopped onto it. His face assumed its usual warm glow and his eyes regained their softness. 'Yes, what's the point? We have a bigger feud to settle. That's right, the biggest of them all. But still the way that One-Eyed Golok killed his victims. It's unspeakable!' Tsering said, still as moved by horror I supposed as when he had first heard of it from his devastated parents. 'He fed his victims, men, women and children. Even children!' Tsering shouted. 'Fed them with milk, forced them to drink milk, till their stomachs were bloated and about to explode. Then the One-Eyed Golok had his men hurl the victims down the fortress rampart.' Tsering had raised his arms and suddenly brought them down to release his mind's victims onto the steaming asphalt street. 'As the victims hit the ground and their stomachs burst, shooting up fountains of milk in the air, One-Eyed Golok there he would be, legs apart, arms astride, on the edge of the fortress's rooftop, rolling with laughter.'

I stood there on the crowded street, beside Tsering, waiting for my bus. The merciless memories Tsering evoked came hurtling towards me like a DTC bus, driven by a mad monk whose furious, almost violent, meditation on compassion had been disrupted by the accidental viewing of *Sholay*, a three-hour film on dacoits, revenge and unending gun battles.

Tsering stopped talking, perhaps imagining the way his grandfather and others in his family met their gruesome fate. His eyes scanned the other side of the street, trying to spot another Parliament Street bus. 'But the Tibetan government put an end to more horrors,' Tsering said. 'At least it did something right. Just one thing,' he said, raising his index finger in a mock show of counting. 'Just one thing right. The

One-Eyed Golok was subdued and killed. He became a spirit, tamed by the Sakya lamas and chained in their monastery.'

Tsering's bus came rumbling from a distance. But he was in no hurry to catch it. 'And don't worry. I don't want to know where that lama of yours is. And you don't have to warn the lama,' Tsering said, anticipating my fear and intention. 'I don't want to waste my energy and time on that lousy grandson of that mad butcher.' He then strode across the street wading through traffic, holding up his hand to stop tolerant cars, and, like any old resident of Delhi, dodging the impatient vehicles. Just before he boarded his bus, Tsering shouted across the bustling street, 'But that lama of yours, he's another yak. Another yak! He recognised his own half-brother as the nineteenth Drubtop Rinpoche! His own half-brother! Can you believe the audacity? Just like the One-Eyed Golok. He made his own half-brother the exalted Drubtop Rinpoche!'

The lama and the nineteenth Drubtop Rinpoche are brothers, I mulled, watching Tsering's bus speed away. I would need to re-confirm this with the lama. Would it seem rude, I wondered.

I was relieved by Tsering's change in attitude. I supposed it would come as a relief to the lama too when he came to learn about this. Still, I wanted to warn him. One never knew with these Goloks. The very word 'Golok' in the dialect of U used to be a synonym for mischief. He played Golok meant he wreaked havoc. The literary meaning of Golok is still a word for 'rebel'. Yes, the lama must be warned. My anxiety was heightened by horrible 'escape' stories of tribesmen from eastern Tibet, who, just as they were fleeing for their lives from Chinese communist atrocities, were also busily settling tribal feuds...in blood. There was the famous bloody affair of a small group of clansmen who just as they reached the safety of the Assamese border were massacred by a superior rival tribe. Men, women and children were slaughtered and the little that the butchered clan was able to carry with it looted clean.

Was the lama's past coming to haunt him? Were the characters of his stories, distant and remote when I first heard them, actually popping up in the streets of Delhi in flesh and blood to play Golok on him?

Tsering Migmar might forgive and forget. But how many descendants of the victims of the One-Eyed Golok in exile were not so forgiving and secretly plotting revenge, unknown to the lama?

Fearful, I took the Mudrika to Lajpat Nagar.

Farewell to All That

☯

A yellow two-storey building housed the Bureau of the Dalai Lama. For most of the Tibetan students in Delhi, the Bureau was the source from where the funding for their college education came. Or the agent through which their scholarships were channelised.

The official farewell ceremony was over by the time I had arrived. The students were down in the basement where Boney M was already blaring from two old soundboxes placed at either end of the L-shaped room. Samdup was hopping up and down on the floor, now and then, assisting Dolma, his girlfriend, with setting up the table, which would be used as the counter for the sale of beer, cold drinks and food. Crates of beer were stacked against the wall, and there were two large buckets of water with ice and beer bottles floating in them.

I went through the door in the back wall of the Bureau which had a couple of chai shops and entered the first one for tea and a smoke.

The first chai shop showcased the stand-off between Tashi and Gyaltsen. They were locked in the Tibetan refugees' latest feud. The two pillars of the Delhi University Tibetan Students' body were at each other's throat on some issue relating to the formation of the communist party and its relevance, now an open secret. Tashi was at the receiving end and he was receiving it with growing impatience. Gyaltsen, and two new faces, Gyaltsen's gang of two, perhaps, were grilling and hectoring. Gyaltsen had just told Tashi that the Tibetan communist party was like a drop of crimson blood, which defiled the purity of the milk of the Tibetan struggle.

Then employing another comparison, Gyaltsen barked, 'You build a house and only then do you decide what colour you want to paint it—red, white or something else. And anyway,' Gyaltsen demanded, switching from Tibetan to English and back, 'from where are you going to get your support? From the Tibetans in Tibet? No, they have suffered enough from communism. From the Tibetans in exile? No, we ran away from Tibet to escape communist persecution. And for your information, comrade, with the exception of a few people like you or Samdup, the rest are all devout Buddhists. Tibetans will never abandon Buddhism to follow communism. By starting this bloody thing, you are trying to make us less than what we really are. You are trying to take away our cultural pride. Our culture is the only thing we have.'

He paused to wrap the sandal wood prayer beads around his wrist. Like an excited monk debating with his hands and legs, he thrust his left hand forward and brought his right hand on it and stomped his right leg forward in a thunderous triumphant dismissal and bellowed, 'Tsa! And for all that the Tibetan government did on your behalf, your school education, your college education, you now want to lead a revolution against the Tibetan government,' Gyaltsen shouted. 'You,' Gyaltsen pointed his finger at Tashi in total incomprehension, 'you have wasted Tibetan government tin-mos. In fact, you are a wasted tin-mo!' Gyaltsen shot an accusatory finger at Tashi.

'Wasted tin-mo?' Tashi bleated. He sounded alarmed at his new identity. 'The Tibetan community will be a better judge of my wasted tin-mo status,' he shot back, defensively as if he was already a public figure. 'We are not leading a revolution against the Tibetan government. Ours is not a struggle for power. We want social justice. Just that.'

Tashi paused and took a sip of tea from the stained glass. 'And as far as I know,' Tashi said, going off on a tangent, 'Tibetan Buddhism at the present stage deals more with superstition than the real teachings of the Buddha. Spiritual con men writhe and stagger and utter absolute nonsense to fool ordinary Tibetans and this passes off as Buddhism. This is not Buddhism. It's superstition! It needs to be cleaned up. As the Tibetan saying goes, if people get desperate, they consult gods. When gods get desperate, they tell lies. We need an ideology which will strengthen us, which will make us tread on the path to freedom, not some mumbo-jumbo. There should be transparency.'

'Transparency?' Gyaltsen barked in English. 'That's democracy and not a one-party communist dictatorship.' Gyaltsen spat out those words. 'Let me tell you another Tibetan saying comrade, if you take refuge in the arse, you get a load of shit.'

Gyaltsen's gang broke into smiles, appreciation to indicate the appropriateness of their idol's use of the old Tibetan proverb.

'Load of shit? Well, what about the TYC? If you want a load of shit, you're sitting on it. You're an establishment organisation. Yes, we want independence but we also want social change. And we can do this by saying what's on our mind, instead of treating the TYC as another stepping stone to a prized posting in the bureaucracy.'

'And how are you going to go about bringing social change?' Gyaltsen countered. 'Social change has already taken place. It's ordinary people like us who are manning the bureaucracy in Dharamsala.' Gyaltsen pulled himself to his full six feet. 'It's tsampa power,' he repeated, his clenched fist cutting through the hot air.

'Tsampa power?' Tashi looked up at Gyaltsen.

'Tsampa, the ordinary food of the common Tibetans. Yes, tsampa power,' Gyaltsen said, looking at his gang of two, pleased with the new phrase. 'It means the common Tibetans have taken over. Your revolution is obsolete. Your revolution is a little too late. A revolution had already taken place. The ordinary Tibetans don't want you. And regardless of the sentiments of Tibetans, I suppose you will now start shouting your new slogan, China's chairman is our chairman? No?' With that Gyaltsen strode off triumphantly back to the Bureau's basement. His face was flushed with seething anger. But his accomplices stayed behind. One of them raised his hand as if asking for permission to speak and without waiting chirped excitedly, 'I know that one. Yes, I know that one. China's chairman is Tibetan chow-mein. China's Mao is Tibetan mo-mo. Whatever the Chinese do, we do double best and we cook it well. Please visit Zhong-go Xizang Restaurant for your next best meal in New Delhi.'

Tashi rejected the invitation and flapped his hand, as if to say, stop this nonsense. He took off his glasses, went over his face with both hands, wiped the dust and dampness from his lenses and slipped them back on. 'Tsampa power? What does he think he's talking about, tsampa power? Words, words, and some more catchy words. That's all he's good at. Well, it's a failed tsampa power.' He stared at Gyaltsen's retreating figure, which disappeared through the door in the wall. Abruptly turning around, Tashi confronted the two and demanded, 'And what do you think?'

'Gyaltsen said what we feel,' one of them spoke up. 'The revolution has already taken place. We've told as much to your comrade, comrade Samdup.'

'Chai,' shouted Tashi in response. Tashi was, I thought, about to give the official explanation for the reasons behind the sudden birth of Tibet's first communist party.

'We started thinking about it when His Holiness told Tibetan students in Chandigarh that he was not against communism, a year back. Our key reason is our frustration with the TYC. It's an establishment organisation. It's a rah-rah-type. It will make noises but there is no will to introduce social change. The upper-class dominates the TYC. Those who toe the official line will get prize postings.'

'This is not true,' interrupted one of the two again. 'Maybe one or two cases, but these are exceptions.'

Tashi shrugged off the interruption and continued with his chain of thought. 'Those less obliging are always tucked away in some remote place like Tezu or Ladakh to rot. Our main message is that it's okay to be Tib and red. But more than independence we want social change. The officials tend to keep certain information from His Holiness. This is wrong. We got started for another reason: to inform His Holiness about everything.'

'But you can make an appointment with him and tell him what you feel. The Dalai Lama meets everyone,' it was the same fellow who spoke up again.

'Yes, we know that. But there has to be a system in place.'

'You mean that you want to be an official consultancy firm?' he said, realising how tenuous Tashi's arguments were becoming. 'You told us minutes back you wanted social change. Now you want to be a part of the official package.'

'Yes, informing His Holiness about what needs to be changed.'

'So, how many of you are there exactly, besides the broad masses?' this time it was the other one.

'Three, four core members. But there are others.'

'Perhaps you would like to tell us about the others?'

'And jeopardise their jobs?'

'You mean some of them are working in the Dharamsala establishment? You have undercovers in the government?' the first one aked in astonishment.

Realising that the duo was picking his brains, ferreting out information, maybe for Gyaltsen, Tashi said, 'This leads nowhere.' He stood up and walked away, without waiting for the tea he had just ordered.

The gang of two waited for a while. Then, the one who seemed the brighter of the two confided, pointing at Tashi, 'He doesn't know who puts butter in his butter-tea.' The two stood up and followed Tashi, at a distance, like a discarded double shadow. I fell in step a little later.

The basement was cool. The exhaust fans were doing their work. Gyaltsen was manning the entrance fee counter. The gang of two kept guard behind him.

When I had a moment alone with Tashi, I whispered that he should warn the lama to be careful. I mentioned the gruesome fate of Tsering's grandfather at the hands of the One-Eyed Golok.

'Tsering-la, taking revenge?' Tashi said in an incredulous whisper. 'After so many years? You are imagining things,' Tashi said. He stepped forward to smell my mouth, confirming whether it was me or the beer which was doing the talking. But I wasn't done yet. I described the way in which the One-Eyed Golok killed his victims. Tashi listened, his own one eye opening wide in apprehension. 'That will do. I'll warn the lama,' he said.

At this point, Editor, staggered in with a mischievous grin working on the corners of his mouth. Everyone welcomed him with a loud

'Yeah!' Editor 'yeah-ed' back and the party was declared open and got started in real earnest.

Samdup had already opened a beer bottle and offered it to Editor. Tashi left his friends and came over. Both he and Samdup had one question for Editor. 'So when's the next issue coming out?'

Before answering, Editor took a gulp from the bottle and made a face. 'It came hot from the press today. Sorry, I don't have a copy with me right now,' he said. 'It has an item on your party.' Editor looked around and deciding that secrets were quite redundant at this point added, 'The issue also carries an item on your communist party. On the formation of the Tibetan communist party,' Editor said loudly, repeating himself, not believing why anyone would ever do a ridiculous thing like forming a communist party.

'I'll come tomorrow to get a copy?' Tashi suggested with a grim face.

'Sure.'

I whispered into Samdup's ear to keep an eye on Tashi and Gyaltsen. Their heated argument might just spill on to the dance floor.

But I needn't have worried. The two kept their peace. The crowds were gathering even as Boney M continued his pounding. The hesitant dancing by a few slowly gathered collective rhythm and enthusiasm. Those who were not dancing had formed into small knots from where occasional laughter burst forth, as if the whole damn thing was one big joke. Experiences were narrated and turned into shared witticisms. The young men and women seemed comfortable in this party setting. It seemed as if they had known only this world, the world of pop and rock 'n' roll, as though the old Tibet had been left far behind. So was Tashi's world of social change and revolution. Tashi's and Samdup's broad masses had other ideas of how they could spend their time and money.

When the party was over, most of us just crashed right there on the basement floor. Some went up on the terrace, where it was much cooler. Later, cursing high Shangri-La, they came scrambling down, chased by mosquitoes. They cursed because they were bitten, bitten because they cursed those spiteful ones demoted by karma to flitting lowly beings, banished from Shangri-La. And the flitting lowly beings took revenge on us, those newly banished by non-karmic forces. Or was karma behind the second mass banishment too? And the spiteful ones spoke Tibetan, a curse inflicted on them by karma as a reminder of their earlier existence as human beings on the roof of the world. Never, ever take your life on the roof of the world for granted. Otherwise, you get pushed down to the bottom of the mountains. Or down the bottom of the stairs.

The next day I accompanied Tashi to the office of the *Tibetan Review* located in Jangpura, walking distance from the Bureau. Tashi was silent all the way, except for some slight grunts of impatience. Perhaps the silent war had begun. I took security in my thoughts and thought about the paper.

Since my first year in college, I spent most weekends at the office of the *Tibetan Review*. It was an office, during office hours, and a residence off-office hours for both Editor and Nyima who was the accountant, administrator and Editor's drinking buddy all rolled into one. My first encounter with Editor took place during my first year in college. In the blazing heat of post-prohibition Delhi, Rajesh Khanna, a Tibetan who resembled and went by the name of an Indian movie star, and I sauntered into the office of the *Tibetan Review* to raid Editor's fridge. Like the man himself, the fridge was alarmingly bare and devoid of goodies. Except for—the very picture of temptation itself—a bottle of Golden Eagle beer, with life-giving droplets oozing down its side. No discussion was required. The two of us emptied the bottle in several thirsty gulps. Afraid of the inevitable editorial rage, we decided to de-camp with the loot safely tucked into our stomach. That was when Editor walked in and headed straight for the fridge. He put his round, chubby face in the fridge only to discover the beer gone. Thinking that his large round glasses were playing tricks on him again, he raised them and tried finding the bottle with his naked eyes. No luck, no beer.

'All right,' he swung around and snapped, 'The next round is on you two.' With that he sent us off to the nearest liquor shop. I excused myself, pleading student poverty as a reason for shirking the honour. Rajesh Khanna volunteered and bought half a crate.

There was something about Editor which managed to turn even a crisis into a party. And somehow, those around him always responded in the same generous, party spirit.

Editor made a refugee rag into the favourite magazine of the literate exiles, turning it into an influential institution of the Tibetan world. The *Tibetan Review* gave birth to a whole new generation of Tibetans who were born in Tibet, educated in exile and who used the forum provided by the publication to discuss ways to redeem its sudden loss of inheritance. A generation inspired, fired and energised by the power of a new vocabulary. This generation spoke the language of the world.

I turned to Tashi. He was still not talking. Perhaps he, like me, was in intimate telepathic communications with his thoughts, far away, all excited and brewing in the socialist camp. Or the sullen war had definitely begun. I went back to my thoughts, about the *Tibetan Review*, the new vocabulary, the written word and all that. Then I thought of the Word. I shoved my hand in my cotton shoulder bag and pulled out my Elephant notebook. I was not going to take notes of my conversation with my thoughts. I was consulting my notebook because more words were there, including the Word, claimed by the lama, to have been invented by the first Drubtop Rinpoche. I held up my hand to indicate to Tashi to halt.

Tashi looked irritated. 'You want tea or something?' he demanded.

I shook my head. I flipped through the pages and found the passage where the lama narrated what Gar Tongtsen told the first batch of students Tibet ever sent abroad.

'You are being sent to India to master the art of reading and writing, whatever that means, and the ideas and philosophy of the country. Tibet is a powerful military state. But military force is fickle. It is like an un-faithful mistress.' And Gar Tongtsen cupped his hand on his mouth and whispered aloud, 'And all mistresses are unfaithful.' All hundred and eight students shook with suppressed laughter. Gar Tongtsen continued in his stentorian voice, 'Military might, it is here today and gone tomorrow. Far more than military might, ideas will hold our empire together. Ideas in written words, whatever that means.

They will make our people one. Arrows rust, bows don't bend and swords lose their sharp edges, but ideas, no matter how dead, tend to retain their enchantment. Well, go and get those ideas and bring them to Tibet in writing, whatever that means.'

My nose was buried in my notebook. Tashi tugged at my shoulder. 'The bloody exams are over.'

I shook him off, trying not to let him disturb my conversation with my thoughts.

Yes, the *Review* was our new idea. It was our generation's Word. China had its People's Liberation Army, but we the young Tibetan exiles had our *Tibetan Review*. We had words. They had arms. We had ideas. They had even more arms. Well, anyway, they did not have the Word, the beginning of every brave enterprise. Didn't a storyteller say 'by the power of the written word...before all to see?' My thoughts said the Chinese didn't see because they were blind. They were blind because they did not have the written Word. Ideograms did not count. Alphabets made people logical and reasonable. Ideograms. Original, yes, but logical? No way, man!

With my thoughts whispering this consoling and conspiratorial idea in my heated mind (one of many places in Delhi that has no air-conditioning), Tashi and I reached the office of the *Tibetan Review*. No air-conditioning here too. Housed in a barsati, situated on the top floor of a flimsy two-storey structure, the *Review* office bore the brunt of Delhi's scorching heat. Editor was shirtless, pounding on his massive Remington with two fingers. He too was busily conjuring up the Word. Nyima, the accountant, more practical, brewed tea.

Editor handed Tashi the latest issue of the *Review*, saying, 'Here's on your party.' More words. I immediately snatched another copy lying on the messy desk.

And there it was, the April 1979 issue of the *Tibetan Review*. 'On May Day this year, the workers of the world will receive greetings from an unexpected quarter—the Communist Party of the Tibetans in exile. Discussions on the desirability of such a party have been going on for several years now in the columns of this paper as well as other forums. Such discussions still continue unaware of the fact that the party was actually formed nearly a year ago.

'Membership of the party increased by fifty per cent when, a few months later, Namgyal also joined it. Namgyal is in fact the most suited of the three to be a member of such a party, thanks to his background. Brought up as a Communist from his young days, Namgyal was a trusted security guard in Chinese-ruled Tibet until his escape to India in 1974.

'The main aim of the party is to "prepare the Tibetan exiles" for independence. They believe the Tibetans should be able to unite, without any internal disagreements on minor issues, if they want to make post-independence Tibet a happy place to live in.

'Tashi and Samdup maintain that until now, no one else except the three members have been aware of the existence of the party. They have not informed even the Tibetan Government-in-exile about it. They have not approached any other party, organisation or government with any plans or ideas.

'Another reason why they have felt the news should be released now is that a few people suspect the existence of the party and have even identified one or two of its members. However, some people frequently seen in their company are also suspected of being members. So the real members decided that in the interest of the non-members, it was better to reveal their identity.'

After carefully reading the whole news item Tashi left, clutching a copy of the latest issue. He said he had work in some part of New Delhi.

Hint of Inheritance

☯

Since ideology had started to estrange relations between Tashi and me, I found myself gravitating towards Phuntsok. The next day when I returned to college I managed to persuade Phuntsok to go with me to Majnu Ka Tilla. Ama Penpa was in the chang-room, serving chang to a couple of Indians. She was in a furious mood, barking in Hindi at an amused rickshaw-wallah that a rupee note he had handed her was too torn and wrinkled to buy even a drop of chang. Metok, it seemed, had gone off to the bazaar to buy vegetables and meat or to see the latest Amitabh Bachchan film. I didn't ask.

'Go right in. Rinpoche is inside,' she said when she saw us enter.

'Tashi delek, Rinpoche,' I greeted the lama, parting the dirty door curtain. The lama sat crossed-legged on the bed, his back leaning on the wall. He wore a welcome smile.

Phuntsok greeted the lama and immediately said he wanted to see some of his friends and that he would be back later on and promptly walked out.

'You liked the story of Drubtop Rinpoche killing flies in Beijing?' the lama asked me as soon as Phuntsok had left.

'Yes,' I said. 'Is it because he killed so many Chinese flies that Drubtop Rinpoche came to such a bad end?'

'Don't know,' the lama admitted. 'Maybe because it's in his blood. The nineteenth Drubtop Rinpoche came from the line of the One-Eyed Golok.'

'Yes, I came to hear about him, about the One-Eyed Golok,' I said, picking up the Bic. 'But Rinpoche you should be careful. There are still descendants of the victims of the One-Eyed Golok. The other day I met Tsering Migmar. He's from Madoi, from your region of Tibet. He said the One-Eyed Golok slaughtered half his grandfather's family.'

A hint of aggravation scurried across the lama's impassive face. Ama Penpa entered the room and setting a glass on the table, poured out some chang. I immediately drained it and held the glass up for a refill. The lama sipped his chang and turned to Ama Penpa, 'Penpa, you know anyone in New Delhi called Tsering Migmar. Dhondup here says he's from Golok.'

'Yes, he came recently from Tibet,' Ama Penpa said. 'Why do you ask?' she asked.

'His family name? His family name?' the lama demanded, impatiently.

'I think it is Thangshawa,' Ama Penpa said.

'Thangshawa!' the lama repeated, nearly jumping out of his skin, toppling his chang glass. 'Thangshawa, the only clan which refused to make a blood pact with our family.' The lama's voice trembled. His eyes rolled back into his skull and went blank. Ama Penpa, seeing the lama's change of tone stood transfixed, holding the plastic chang jug in her quaking hands. 'Is that bad?' she asked.

'Bad? It's our nightmare. Their clan was notorious. They were known for their ferocity. They held nothing sacred. Except revenge. They did not forget or forgive. They were merciless. They burned, looted and killed and left nothing to chance. I still wonder how the One-Eyed Golok managed to subdue that tribe. The One-Eyed Golok's victory over the fearsome warrior-bandits of the Thangshawa tribe made him a celebrity throughout Amdo and beyond.'

The lama murmured a prayer and fell silent. The silence turned meditative, dwelling on how actions, performed long past, could still trigger unpredictable catastrophes for individuals far removed from that scene by time and space.

'And these people fought like the hordes of Hor. They pinned rival warriors with their spears on walls like so many dead frogs,' the lama mused.

Ama Penpa need not have asked the reason why. She instinctively knew. She expressed our fear. 'Will he take revenge ... on us?' Fear hung powerfully in the air like the pungent smell of sour chang.

'I don't know about that Tsering Migmar, but in the past, others of the Tangshawa clan tried to avenge themselves at every opportunity,' the lama said, sipping chang. 'Most of the time we fended off their attacks. But they looted a caravan to Lhasa. Those brigands made their way from Golok to loot on the Chamdo-Lhasa trail. And such a distance,' the lama mused. 'They even tried to sneak the caravan leader whose life they had spared into our household as a spy.' The lama withdrew into his usual silence. Ama Penpa was standing, the chang jug in her hand, her other hand covering her gaping mouth and her anxious eyes fixed on the silent figure of the lama. I sat there, my Bic in my hand, my eyes staring at the notebook and then at the lama who had inexplicably retreated into a pregnant silence.

'I'm going to Manali in a couple of days,' the lama said, suddenly coming out of his reverie, regaining his composure and terminating his meditation on the consequences of human actions.

'But the One-Eyed Golok. I want to hear more about him.'

'Later,' the lama said.

'Tsering Migmar also said that you and the nineteenth Drubtop Rinpoche are half-brothers.'

'That is true,' the lama said, giving me a piercing look, trying to figure out what I was up to. The lama went back to his plans for the trip to Manali. He said he had a monastery of sorts there, but wasn't a big monastery. The only monk looking after the place was the lama himself. He got by on donations offered by devout Tibetans on whom the lama would bestow the blessings of all the nineteen reincarnations of Drubtop Rinpoche.

The main attraction of his wooden hut, which he called a monastery, was the thangkas, which hung on the walls of his hut. The thangkas were portrait paintings of all the Drubtop Rinpoches. Some thangkas dated back to the tenth century. Come to think of it, the lama was sitting on a virtual gold mine. Whenever he travelled he pulled down his nineteen thangkas and locked them in a steel box. Wherever he went, the steel box accompanied.

The lama pointed to a steel box resting on a wooden shelf above his head and said, 'That's where all the nineteen large brown leather suitcases, all bulging at the seams.' When the lama spotted my eyes focused on the suitcases, he said, 'These are the biographies of the eighteen Drubtop Rinpoches.' He left it at that and I didn't press on.

The lama was Ama Penpa's half-brother. They were born in Chamdo in Kham but considered Kyitsel in Amdo as their real home.

'The same Kyitsel as Drubtop Rinpoche's Kyitsel?' I asked.

'The very same,' the lama said.

The lama said his and Ama Penpa's father had kept three wives, all sisters. The lama was born to the third wife, Ama Penpa and the nineteenth Drubtop Rinpoche to the second. Tsering Migmar had forewarned me about this. But still coming from the horse's mouth, so to speak, this was news to me. Both the abbot of Drubchen monastery and its highest incarnate lama came from the same family. 'Now I will tell you the story of the One-Eyed Golok, since you brought up the subject. It's not about the lineage of the Drubtop Rinpoches,' the lama explained. 'It's about my family, about my grandfather, the famous One-Eyed Golok, who catapulted our ancestral household into brief but unprecedented eminence and endowed our blood with the violence and strength of the cold, silent, brooding grasslands of Golok.'

The lama said that from Golok in the late nineteenth century emerged Tsensong Dorjee, one of the greatest Tibetan warriors, who united all of Amdo under his rule before being crushed by the Tibetan government. With tact and diplomacy Tsengsong Dorjee, or the One-Eyed Golok as he is better known, might have had the whole of Amdo, even Kham, under his rule. The One-Eyed Golok was brave and a great general, but he was sometimes tactless and his henchmen were too intimidated to offer better counsel. He had plans of hoisting someone from his own family as the next Drubtop Rinpoche of Kyitsel, thus combining his growing military might with the enormous spiritual prestige of Kyitsel's highest incarnate lama, but he was no match for Lhasa's superior diplomacy and deceit.

'Consider this my autobiography,' the lama said, as he sipped chang and braced himself to re-visit and re-examine his life and soul and the history of his violent forefathers.

'This is my gift to you and to that generation of Tibetans who missed the opportunity of having lived in old Tibet,' the lama said. 'You missed the bus,' the lama said, uncharacteristically.

I was stung by this remark, missing the bus, implying that we were less Tibetan than he and his generation. Missing the bus, indeed.

'Yes, we missed the bus. But remember we came on the same express yak service from occupied Tibet, running away from the Chinese army,' I shot back. 'I was born in Tibet and my generation's hopes for Tibet are same as yours. Does this make us less Tibetan than you and your generation?'

'You may have been born in Tibet, but you haven't lived in Tibet. There's a difference. There's a little less of Tibet in you than in us. Our memory is greater, our burden heavier. In a way you have been liberated from Tibet. Whereas, we are enslaved to the country by our memory.'

'Wait a minute,' I demanded, gulping chang and nearly choking in my hurry. 'One minute you're implying that having lived in Tibet is a great privilege and the next minute you're implying that it is a burden. Which is which?'

'It is both a privilege and a burden. Depends on how you use it.'

'And to which category do you belong? Tibet as a burden category or Tibet as a privilege category?' I pressed on aggressively, an aggression stimulated by chang.

'I belong to both. Old Tibet, the Tibet of my childhood, was a wonderful place until the Chinese communists turned it into hell.'

'And what are you doing about it? Just telling stories, drinking chang?'

'I am giving you memory, memory to base your hopes for Tibet on. What is more important than that? Without memory, there's no hope,' the lama said grandly, slicing the air sideways with his large brown hand, indicating the end of the discussion, the end of a debate on the topic of who missed what bus and who came on which yak express service.

But I had a question for the lama. 'Why do you keep telling us these Drubtop Rinpoche stories?'

The lama looked pleased.

'For two reasons,' the lama said. 'First is to inform young people like you about Tibet. To let you know where you came from, what you have lost. The second reason is personal.' According to the tradition of Drubchen Monastery, each abbot of the monastery has to write a detailed biography of the Drubtop Rinpoche he served, the lama explained. 'But I haven't done that yet.'

'Why?' I asked. 'Aren't you neglecting your spiritual duties?'

'I can only start writing the biography of the late nineteenth Drubtop when I have fulfilled my more important spiritual responsibility of finding his authentic reincarnation,' the lama said, with a sigh.

So, in a way, before writing the biography of the nineteenth Drubtop Rinpoche, the lama was practising his narrative skills on me. Bouncing ideas, seeing what was gripping and what was boring. By urging him to tell stories, I wasn't inconveniencing him. I was doing him an inestimable favour.

'What happens if you die before you either find the next reincarnation or manage to write the biography of the earlier reincarnation?'

The lama stroked his moustache, bedewed with specks of chang. He took a long swig from the glass, wrapped his prayer beads around his wrist, stood on the bed and opened the large steel box placed on the shelf along the wall just above the bed where he had been camping these last few days. He took out a large packet, wrapped in blue brocade, the colour of royalty.

With excited and trembling hands, the lama un-wrapped the packet. The packet revealed what the lama called the 'inheritance of Drubchen Monastery'. The inheritance consisted of a red upturned hat, two copper seals and a piece of light brown Tibetan parchment paper with Tibetan characters written on it. The parchment scroll was stamped with a seal and in red ink.

The lama climbed down from the bed. Holding the packet high above his head like a recovered crown, he walked forward, a prayer, silent but still said with the same unwavering faith, played on his lips.

The lama placed the items of possession, of recognition, on the space he made on the crowded altar. He bowed and murmured,

> May you never depart,
> May you never forsake us,
> But forever be our guide,
> Be our lamp,
> To that goal,
> To that joy
> called Enlightenment.

'I said these words when I recognised the nineteenth Drubtop Rinpoche way back when I was just twenty-four years old,' the lama said, turning around to face me. 'I hope to repeat this prayer when I recognise the twentieth reincarnation.'

The lama, towering over me, stood bare-foot for long. He turned his back on me, his head bowed, pondering over something. Whatever he was mulling, he must have made up his mind because he swung around and looked deep into my eyes and told me in an excited whisper, 'I have found my rinpoche, my refuge, my master!'

'Where, who? A little boy here in Majnu Ka Tilla?' I blurted.

The lama put his finger to his lips. 'You will know in due time, the world will know in due time,' he whispered. 'The fact I have displayed the inheritance of the Drubchen Monastery to you means that my search has come to an end. It means I have found him!'

I was a little confused. Why was the lama telling me all this? Maybe he thought I was the next Drubtop reincarnation. 'Is it me!' I whispered, pointing to myself, half-believing, half-teasing the lama.

'No,' the lama shrugged, scowling, shocked at the blasphemy.

'Why can't I be the next Drubtop Rinpoche?' I persisted, pained by his forthright rejection. For a fleeting moment I became fascinated by the idea of myself as an important incarnate lama dressed in rustling maroon robes, accompanied by breath-sucking attendants.

'At least, consider me a candidate,' I pleaded.

'Not even a candidate. You don't have the requirements.'

'What requirements?'

'The necessary requirements.'

'Like a big, wealthy family?'

'No, not that. Just necessary requirements.'

'What necessary requirements?' I pressed on. 'What do you look for when you're in search of a reincarnation? What guides you?' I demanded.

'Prophesies, omens, physical features and dreams. Mainly dreams. I'm an interpreter of dreams,' the lama said. I thought he was boasting this time, but the lama was simply stating a fact. 'And you don't appear in my dreams,' the lama said. 'We are what we are because of our dreams,' the lama explained.

'Holy stuff, but you consider anyone who walks in your dream as the reincarnation you're in search for?'

'Yes, but in auspicious circumstances, like sitting on a throne, blowing a conch shell which indicates that his teachings will spread far and wide, in all four directions. The rays of the morning sun striking on his figure while he sits cross-legged. And these must occur frequently in circumstances of ascending auspiciousness.'

'How can I enter your dreams?' I asked.

'It's not up to you. Since I do the dreaming, it's I who project my hopes into my dreams. And the physical features of the person, those are also very important.'

'And I don't have any of these?'

'No,' the lama said, his voice breaking into a soft whisper.

Seeing it was useless, I gave up my newfound spiritual ambition. 'Whoever it is, when are you going to identify him? Or is it her?' I whispered. 'Is it a woman lama, this time?'

'You will know in due time. In due time. But I have more stories for you.'

I re-opened my notebook and picked up my Bic.

The lama re-visited the ancient wind-swept landscape where the fortunes of his family were made, lost and made again, and in the end, like all other Tibetans, lost – irretrievably. There was a feisty edge to his voice this time, a sublimated vibrance on the verge of exploding into the brilliance of words, a wordy rainbow to halo his prayers. In this mood, sometimes the lama's narrative, regardless of the tragedy of some of the events he described, scattered into an east Tibetan brigand's guttural tones, choked with the incoherent anticipation that the fattest loot was yet to come, an easy picking, just beyond the next grassy knoll.

At the end the lama said, 'My stories should end here with the discovery and enthronement of the new Drubtop Rinpoche,' the lama said, unwinding his prayer beads from his wrist and bringing his hands together in reverence. 'It is auspicious. It is a good omen. We mustn't spoil it by telling more stories.'

'But you haven't announced your discovery.'

'I will, I will…soon. When the circumstances are right, when they are auspicious.'

I slammed shut the notebook and stashed it away in my shoulder bag. 'I promise that I will have all this typed and give you a copy,' I said, as a way of thanking the lama for his time, for his stories. These stories were a legacy of sorts, his legacy. 'Perhaps you could get someone to translate it back into Tibetan so that you could check it for accuracy,' I suggested. The lama thumped his hand down as if to say it was a waste of time or too tedious.

I became obsessed with the lama's stories. As long as the lama was in Delhi I visited him everyday to take notes of his narrative. I used the substantial library of the office of the *Tibetan Review* for reference to fill in details of the lama's stories. Wherever the lama's narrative was not clear or if I thought I had missed an important point, I went back to him to crosscheck. When I was done, I wrote a short introductory background. I opened the steel box, which contained the notebooks filled with the lama's stories. There were seven of them, all numbered. I put the latest one on the pile and stacked them on Nyima's desk and asked him to type the whole lot. Nyima looked at the pile and resorted to bureaucratic technicality. 'I need Editor's permission. His permission to use my office time to type this mountain of yours,' Nyima said, dismissing the request.

'Please, I need these typed. I want to give these to the lama.'

Nyima resisted. I persisted. In the end I resorted to outright bribery. I dangled a bottle of whiskey before him. This made him change his mind pretty quick. 'Make carbon copies,' I said. 'Two carbon copies. And there will be another bottle after you have finished the whole lot.' Nyima's fingers flew over the Remington.

The manuscript eventually came to a hundred and eight typed pages, double-spaced. I went to Majnu Ka Tilla and said to the lama, 'Rinpoche, I came to present these to you, your stories. These are all typed. Perhaps Tashi will translate these stories back into Tibetan for you.'

'What use will they be to me?'

'To write, to write the biography of the nineteenth Drubtop Rinpoche? Won't these be of help?'

'No need, I have them all here,' the lama said, tapping his head, 'Give these to Tashi. He may find the stories interesting. He needs to know more about his country's history and its culture.'

I walked out of the chang shack, found Tashi and handed him a copy the lama's stories. 'Here, the lama wants you to have these,' I said. 'These are my notes of the lama's stories. I suppose this is the lama's gift to you. It is certainly mine. He wants you to know more about Tibet and its culture.'

2

The Lama's Stories

Lost Pieces of a Jigsaw Puzzle

☯

The lama seemed to hold the key to the mystery of why a bunch of Tibetans, children of the wide open spaces of a nomadic culture, had camped, dislocated and confused, in the messy congestion and chaos of Delhi's disorienting urban sprawl, far away from the bracing mountain air of Tibet. The lama seemed to know every rock and stone of the terrain of our geographic karma and the reasons why we were blown away beyond our old grazing patch. I saw in this stranger—this mysterious figure from our past—our chief herdsman, who would point the way to our past trivia. He was our memory made reliable by a dose of exuberant faith, the memory that reflected and predicted our future.

But to the lama his story was Tibetan history itself. He told it without entertaining any of Tashi's snide, caustic comments, which he brushed off by stretching his hand, palm open, before Tashi's babbling mouth.

I never knew why the stories the lama told me fascinated me, drew me in and clung to me. Perhaps in his stories I felt that the old Tibet, which moulded the world in which the lama lived, would not die and would perhaps come alive in its telling. Or perhaps I thought the certainties and assured beliefs of the lama's Tibet would rub on me and I could get on with my life, without any of the nagging doubts and questions which followed my refugee existence like a pair of nervous shadows scared of being reduced to irrelevance by the gathering darkness of collective forgetfulness. In the back of my mind, I thought that I would be able to discover a piece of myself, my reflection, in the stories the lama told me. Or a jigsaw puzzle that, when all the lost pieces were found and put together, would reveal the entire picture. Then, I thought, I would find myself. And the puzzle would become an answer.

I also took my role as the biographer of the lama and his family saga seriously. I did some research into the history of his part of Tibet, managing to put dates to events and names to personalities.

Thinking about it, we made a mutually sympathetic pair, the lama and I, two searchers, the lama in search of his master and I in search of myself. The lama said he had found his master, his teacher. Would I find myself? We made a pair in another sense. The lama had a story to tell and I was eager to listen. We were joined together by the bonds between a storyteller and listener.

The lama sensed my uncertainty, the struggle and the turmoil I was going through. When he saw me taking out my notebook and ballpoint, he took the cue and braced himself by taking a long sip from his chang glass and began his tale.

The lama had two techniques of telling his stories, depending on his mood. One was by packing a lot of details into his narrative. When he did that, he acted out his stories. With labourious effort he stood on his bed and took up the roles of the characters of his stories, their mannerism, the modulations in their varied voices, the whispered conspiracies they hatched. He would dramatise the One-Eyed Golok astride his horse, with his broadsword in hand. Or make a face so gruesome as to make you believe that the corpse of the One-Eyed Golok was staring at you in Ama Penpa's scorching room. Or with a few swift movements of his hands, the lama would create a scene of a nomadic encampment set in the backdrop of rolling grasslands flanked by towering snow-capped mountains.

Or, sometimes the lama, like the Nechung Oracle, would tell the broad outline of a story. It was left to my imagination to fill in the details. Even then the lama managed to create uncluttered, but distinct contours of an episode.

The lama said that he was born in 1925 in Chamdo. In fact, he was born Namgyal Dadul, the one who was taken by his uncle Dawa to be enroled at the Drubchen Monastery in Kyitsel. Helped by his uncle, our lama rose through the monastic ranks to become the abbot of the monastery, the oldest in Tibet. He talked about the last New Year and the last childhood days he spent with his family in Chamdo. Those were his happiest memories, he said. He enroled at the Drubchen Monastery which immediately hijacked his childhood. The Monastery took over his life, overwhelming him with a strict and relentless regimen of prayers, study and meditation.

These stories are culled togther from my copious notes. They included the events and circumstances of the lama's own life and that of his precious Drubtop Rinpoche and the role they played in our lives.

I created scenes to provide easy passage from one episode to the other. Ultimately this is the lama's story. He said this was his gift to us. He hoped that it would provide us with an idea of the enormity of what we had lost. He said we did not just lose a country. We lost a world.

The First Literate Tibetan and His Mastery of the Word

☯

In the language of India, what the lama intoned with his hands folded in fervent prayer, is 'Om namo, tantrayana, gate, gate!' In the language of Tibet, it is simply rendered as 'Ema!' There it is, the wisdom of a whole culture reduced to a mantra. In English the mantra is translated as 'The Word became flesh and ventured to the great beyond and the story thereafter'. I hope this is an accurate translation. Poor translation between cultures is always the source of mutual incomprehension and eventual contempt. Anyway, this salutation served as grace, especially before a big spiritual feast. It used to be murmured with our earnest faces turned southward to Arya Bhumi, from where the aroma of sandalwood groves of south Malaya riding on the monsoon clouds drifted in through the cracks of the Himalayan mountains to perfume our dry and less endowed tableland. It was also murmured to show off our bilingual skills, to offer respects to our spiritual homeland, to trace the root of the Tibetan verb and the origins of the excitement of the Tibetan soul. Some directions are respected by the Tibetans, regardless of where the morning sun rises. We turn south with our eyes closed and our hearts open in prayer. To the east our eyes are always wide open in alertness and our knowing hearts closed to premonitions of disasters to come. Being nomads directions are important to us. Because they show the way, we have given even colour to the two pivotal directions. The south is the Great White Expanse. The east is the Great Black Expanse. But later, much later, we were taught to say 'the East is Red'.

We chanted, 'the East is Red', and under our breath, more to remind ourselves than anything else, muttered, 'stained with blood'.

Without going any further into the laboured preliminary prayers and elaborate chants of the lama, but not excluding one or two derisive interruptions from Tashi, the gist of the story of the Tibetans confronting the written Word for the first time, according to the lama's exuberant, almost visionary, history, went something like this…Tibetans will tell you that it was the first Drubtop Rinpoche who mastered Sanskrit, ultimately making Tibet bilingual. He was the one who invented the script which made Tibet literate.

But in 1949 the Chinese came. They said it was the wrong script.

'Ah-tzee,' Tashi butted in, moaning in utter disapproval of the lama's ignorance of Tibetan history. 'The man's name is Thomi Sambhota. He's the one who invented the Tibetan script. Don't you read Tibetan history? It's all there. Anyway, is this history or what? But I think the Chinese are right. It is the wrong script!' Tashi said with disgust.

But the lama would have none of Tashi's attempt to make him stick to what he considered irrelevant facts.

The story of the Tibetan script, the lama continued, began in the seventh century with king Songtsen Gampo. He was a liberal and flung the doors of Tibet wide open.

His open-door policy was triggered by an incident at the borders of Nepal. Songtsen Gampo had unified the numerous Tibetan-speaking tribes under his rule. He went on to subjugate diverse foreign tribes, and these, his new subjects, soon acquired the manners and mores of any cultured Tibetan. They learned to respectfully stick out their tongues for royal inspection.

But in Nepal he came across this shrivelled-up Brahmin who kept his tongue in his luckless mouth.

Songtsen Gampo knew that though a king his philosophy was simple. He knew that the universe originated from a cosmic egg, that spirits, good and evil, dwelled in the high mountain passes, the lakes and rivers and these should not be desecrated. Like any man of his day, Songtsen Gampo held impeccable Bonist beliefs and wanted to know from the Brahmin what was wrong with his beliefs.

However, at that time all Tibetans were monolingual and in the absence of an interpreter the opportunity was lost. But the unfazed gaze of the Brahmin said it all. For the Brahmin, like all Brahmins, was educated and was staring at an illiterate tribal chieftain demanding respect.

For the Tibetan king, the display of cultural arrogance by this single Brahmin took the fun out of his conquest of Nepal. But Songtsen Gampo did not become the king of Tibet by letting disappointments get in his way. And when he understood the implications of writing, he was happy. The introduction of such an invention to Tibet would mean that messengers did not have to ride from one end of Tibet to the other, only to discover that they had forgotten what the message was all about. It could be written down at one end and read at the other. There would be no deliberate or inadvertent inaccuracies, no deletions, and no additions. A script would become a useful defence acquisition for the military machine the Tibetan king was operating throughout high Asia, if only it could be mastered. And he was determined to master it if not by himself, then by the brightest and best of the youth of Tibet. At his command they were sought and found.

One of those who gave up his inheritance to go to India was Drubtop, whose career, life after life, reincarnation after reincarnation, spanned the centuries of Tibet's history and of this story.

The nomadic encampment of Kyitsel was situated not far from the south shore of Tibet's largest lake, Koko Nor, or as the Tibetans call it, the Blue Lake, at the other end of the Tibetan plateau. Cooped in a slight valley, in a vast grassland surrounded by low snow-capped mountains, the encampment decked itself for the farewell. It was a proud moment for Kyitsel. Drubtop, a youth of their own flesh and blood, would soon master that invention called writing which would preserve the collective memory of their village and their race. And to Kyitsel, Drubtop would bring back the religion, philosophy, culture, literature and folklore of India to enliven the dull and desultory conversations around the firesides in the winter evenings of wind-swept and snow-sprinkled Kyitsel.

But Ama Bhuti's feelings like that of any mother's were mixed at best. With repeated warnings of the climate, of jungles infested with tigers and snakes and the need to keep to a simple tsampa diet, she bade Drubtop a tearful farewell. The whole encampment watched as Drubtop's receding figure—Lhasa-bound—became a mere dot in the azure blue of the horizon.

In Lhasa, Drubtop and his two companions were guided to the place where the rest of the brightest and best were staying. The next day, Tibet's famed minister, Gar Tongtsen, tall, clothed in a robe of dazzling brocade, gave a run-down of the mission. Here is a reproduction of what Gar Tongtsen told the youths.

'You are being sent to India to master the art of reading and writing, whatever that means, and the ideas and philosophy of the country. Tibet is a powerful military state. But military force is fickle. It is like an unfaithful mistress.' And Gar Tongtsen cupped his hand on his mouth and whispered aloud, 'And all mistresses are unfaithful.' The hundred and eight muffled their laughter. Gar Tongtsen continued in his stentorian voice, 'It is here today and gone tomorrow. Far more than military might, ideas will hold our empire together. It will make our people one. Arrows get rusted, bows no longer bent and swords lose their sharp edges, but ideas, no matter how dead, tend to retain their power. Well, go and get those ideas and bring them to Tibet in writing, whatever that means.'

The next day the hundred and eight trooped to the palace of Songtsen Gampo. The palace was a majestic tent. The floor was carpeted, grass to grass, and in the middle of the tent on the highest pile of rugs sat Songtsen Gampo. When the king saw that all the brightest and best had been seated, he cleared his throat. He knew that the dispatch of this lot to India would prove a momentous decision and the occasion called for some drama, some speech making. He spoke in simple, plain Tibetan, not yet cluttered by the verbosity of Sanskrit.

We have created an empire but we are still looked down upon as barbarians. Our dzongs—the symbol of Tibetan authority—cover the whole area we call the Land of Snow, but honestly, we need a bit of polishing. And come to think of it, despite our conquests, we are still an illiterate lot. We need to turn our conquest into quest and you need to learn to read and write. Go to India. Learn the ABC of the world down below. Go and master their Sanskrit, their philosophy, and their culture. Yes, go and come back and make us civilised. I want to wipe the sneer from that Brahmin's face.

The journey to Nepal took two months. Some of the brightest and best unable to cope with the heat and humidity and the prospect of living for years in a yak-less land, returned to Tibet, to their yaks, to their tsampa, to their butter-tea. The rest endured the jungles infested with snakes, tigers, the great fever and the general terrors on the road and reached Nepal. From Nepal the others headed for Nalanda, the famous monastery in north India. Drubtop struck west and braved new jungles infested with new snakes and tigers and reached Kashmir.

In the valley of Pallahari, Drubtop came across this pretty girl. The Tibetan translation of her name is given as Dolma. Drubtop didn't speak her tongue and Dolma was ignorant of Tibetan. But this hardly mattered. As the months passed, Drubtop became competent and even fluent in her language. The early Tibetan translators were that sort of people.

From Dolma, Drubtop learned that Birupa was the best of all teachers. Hearing his name mentioned, Drubtop felt an immense joy and happiness well up within him. He immediately made three prostrations northwards in the direction of Birupa. Even today it is said that the trees of Pallahari are bent northwards as a witness to that historic bow of Tibet to the wisdom and culture of India. Sceptics say it is because of the south wind sweeping over the hills and trees.

When the monsoon rains were over, Drubtop told Dolma, 'I must be going now.'

'Why so soon?' she asked with concern.

In reply Drubtop broke into a spontaneous song,

> I am a man with a mission
> In search of an invention
> Which can make us read
> Our dark and dismal future

In your glorious scripture.
We want to think
What you think.
We want to dream
Your dream.

Dolma too had something poetic of her own,

To Drubtop, the Bhotiya
From beyond the Himalaya
Where Shiva and Parvati
Hold eternal consort
This is an advice of sort.
Ages in making is our civilisation,
Taken in a gulp, you may suffer indigestion.
Making the right choice is a person wise
For momos turn up in samosa's disguise
Making you eat our own Holy Cow!

Drubtop thanked her for her dietary warning and her hospitality and took to the road. He walked for two whole days. On the morning of the third day, he came across a stream bubbling along the foot of a low hill. He crossed the stream and found a narrow footpath winding up the hill.

Some magic made him follow the path, which led him to the top of the hill and to the mouth of a cave lit by the morning sunlight. In the cave was seated Birupa, the best of all teachers. Drubtop had found his lama.

Bearded, naked, and sitting cross-legged in the position of the Buddha, Birupa broke out, 'I was expecting you.'

Drubtop was surprised but didn't show it. Since coming to India, he had had his share of culture shock. But now, the snake-charmers, the rope-climbers, the jungles infested with snakes and tigers, the monsoon rains and the rest of the terrors and wonders of India held no surprises for him. Drubtop had adjusted. This gave him a certain confidence.

'Good, I came looking for you,' Drubtop said carelessly, after putting down his load.

'Did you bring any gold?' Birupa asked.

'I thought the teachings of the Buddha are for free,' Drubtop said.

'You think so? Your astonishment will not last long. Haven't you heard: When the iron-bird flies and horses run on wheels and when the Tibetan people are scattered like ants across the face of the earth, then the Dharma will fetch a good price in the land of the white men. Well, it seems I'm speaking out of turn. It's supposed to be Padmasambhava's line. Anyway, doesn't matter. Yes, yes,' Birupa continued with unnecessary excitement, 'Your later reincarnations will discover that in their time the price of Dharma has shot up. We might as well fix the exchange rate now.'

No use arguing, Drubtop thought. He might think the Tibetans had ran out of gold. From the ample folds of his robe, Drubtop pulled out a bag of gold and laid it at Birupa's feet.

It was then that Birupa did a strange thing. He untangled his legs, stood up and positioning his hands above the gold bag, muttered,

> Mind and matter
> Clatter and patter.
> Gold is sand
> And sand is gold.
> It's written in our scriptures old.

And lo! And behold! in a flash the gleaming pieces of Tibetan gold were turned into dull Indian sand.

'Why did you do such a silly thing?' Drubtop demanded with some exasperation, losing his poise.

'To prove the obvious: all that glitters is not gold. It's our first lesson in Buddhist metaphysics. It belongs to the mind—the only school. By the way,' Birupa said, stroking his bread, 'that will cost you another bag.'

'Thanks!' Drubtop replied. 'This time I'll pay in sand, which at your leisure, you could turn into gold.'

Birupa jumped down from his rocky seat and flung himself in prostration before an astonished Drubtop.

'That's it, that's it. You have gone beyond our conventional wisdom. Each item is precious according to the value we give it. You have been the first who has dared to give sand the same value as gold, and why not? And why not? Birupa asked after he had straightened himself. 'True wisdom lies in not being stifled by existing values,' he said.

That's how Drubtop met his lama who became his guide, philosopher and friend. The archives of the Drubchen Monastery record that Drubtop spent seventeen years in India with Birupa. He mastered Sanskrit and all the branches of Buddhist learning: ethics, logic, psychology, metaphysics, epistemology and others. Most important of all, besides inventing the Tibetan script, Drubtop mastered Cho-pa.

Birupa himself initiated Drubtop into the mysteries of the Cho-pa, which required each practitioner to meditate alone at the dead of night in the village cemetrey and visualise and summon the fierce dancing gods, demigods and ghosts who people the world of tantric Buddhism. The point of the practice was to realise that all the dancing figures were nothing but the mental projections of each practitioner. To realise this was to realise the Buddha's teachings of the basic impermanence of life given solidity only because of the illusions of the unliberated mind. To forget this during the period of visualisation and give the dancing forms the substance they lacked, was to allow oneself to be overwhelmed by the terror of appearances produced by one's own psychological disorder.

The day Drubtop departed for Tibet, Birupa filled a bag with sand and transformed it into glittering gold coins. 'Here take these. These are my parting gift. May the sand, and perhaps the waters, of the Indus and Sutlej make the deserts of Tibet bloom,' Birupa said, laughing. 'The point,' Birupa said, stroking his greying beard, 'is not whether one set of beliefs is right or wrong. The point is what you believe in, because your beliefs, whether right or wrong, change your world.'

Those words stuck in Drubtop's mind as he retraced his way down the hill, leaving the Indian master stroking his beard and contemplating the same old world in the old sun lit cave on top of the old hill.

Drubtop returned to Tibet and presented his invention to Songtsen Gampo. The Tibetan king commanded Drubtop to teach the script to a new group of a 108 of the brightest and best of Tibet. Later, the script was introduced throughout Tibet. Chaired by Drubtop, a committee translated all the scriptures of India into the Tibetan language.

At last Songtsen Gampo was able to wipe the sneer from the shrivelled-up Brahmin's contemptuous face. The Brahmin was aghast. He found himself looking at a mirror image of himself. 'You have become like me,' the Brahmin said feebly. 'And speak my language.' Songtsen Gampo through the linguistic enthusiasm of the first Drubtop Rinpoche had finally succeeded in giving the Tibetan people the power of the written Word. They're still pondering over its implications, still squabbling over who coined which word first.

The Death of the Nineteenth Drubtop and Beijing Flies

☯

On a bright summer morning in 1959, the lama said, the people of Kyitsel were confronted with a shocking sight. On the middle of a hurriedly constructed stage was the nineteenth Drubtop Rinpoche surrounded by several PLA soldiers, rifles in hand. The crowd, shamefaced and helpless, burst into a long groan. Four Tibetans climbed up the stage. They were the accusers, Drubtop Rinpoche the accused. He was going to be subjected to one of the inventions of the Chinese communists: struggle or class struggle in the form of a stage drama. The four Tibetans trotted up to Drubtop Rinpoche and recited a litany of crimes he had supposedly committed. One man carried away by his own violent eloquence struck a blow on Drubtop Rinpoche's nose. The lama staggered and fell.

Immediately one of the soldiers caught hold of the accuser. 'This is a peaceful struggle. You must not hit,' the soldier said. 'We must be reasonable with this man. We must try to educate him and let him see for himself the wrong he has done.'

Convinced of this, the later accusers contented themselves with simply spitting on the lama's holy face.

Shock and confusion covered the faces of the men and women gathered there. They knew something was coming to an end. There were groans and a murmur of prayers. But no one lifted a finger.

The last accuser was a light-complexioned, oval-faced woman in her mid-thirties. She slapped her chest and demanded, 'Do you know me?'

Drubtop Rinpoche didn't answer.

'Perhaps not. You were so high and mighty that you wouldn't recognise one of your own slaves. Do you know who fetched water every day from the river to the monastery? It is I! Me! And other women like me. But today I am free!' A fraud perpetrated on our village for a thousand years has been exposed. And he is the fraud!' the woman screamed, pointing her finger at Drubtop Rinpoche who was bent low with his two hands resting on his knees to ease the strain of standing.

'And for a thousand years,' the Market said, 'we, the labourers, have worked, toiled and sweated to maintain this fraud. Look at him! Even now he doesn't feel ashamed of the suffering which his gang of yellow robbers and red bandits inflicted on the people. Our Chinese comrades have saved us from our suffering. They have liberated us,' she said. Raising her clenched fist and bringing it down, she shouted, 'Down with him and up with us who have been down for so long!'

'Down with him and up with us who have been down so long,' the other three accusers replied.

The Chinese soldiers, strutting to and fro, made a show of restraining the woman from assaulting Drubtop Rinpoche every now and then. The people of Kyitsel watched this with horrified helplessness. But who could argue with loaded guns?

After this performance, the first soldier spoke to Drubtop Rinpoche. 'Today the people of Kyitsel have pointed out your misdeeds to you. You must confess all your past crimes. This is the time. Confess and the Chinese Communist Party will treat you leniently. Be stubborn and you will be treated harshly. Confess and correct your thinking. Confess now!'

The victim was standing alone. Alone and forlorn. He had been standing there on the stage the whole morning in the full glare of the hot sun. There were obsequious attendants to carry a parasol over his head now. The heat and the assaults exhausted Drubtop Rinpoche. He felt he was back in the midnight loneliness of the village cemetrey. Uncalled for, unsummoned, the masters of the cemetrey, the lords of dead, the ghosts, the gods, the spirits and demigods, their mouths overflowing with human entrails, arose and surrounded him from all sides. To the supernatural beings, the nineteenth Drubtop Rinpoche offered his ultimate sacrifice.

Dancing the dance of the Lords of the Cemetrey and singing the prayer of the practitioners of Cho-pa, Drubtop Rinpoche chanted his last hymn, 'For ages in the course of countless rebirths, I have borrowed from lives that have provided me with food and clothing. Now I pay my debts, offering my body, my flesh to the hungry, my blood to the thirsty, my skin to clothe those who are naked, my bones as fuel to those who suffer from winter's chill, my happiness to the unhappy ones, my breath to bring the dying to life.

'Lamas, spiritual teachers, heroes and sky-fliers, come, join me in this dance. And you, all those hungry, thirsty, greedy and jealous. Eat and eat!'

After a few swirls, astounding in the controlled dignity of his steps and in the vibrance of his movements, the nineteenth Drubtop Rinpoche, the highest lama of Kyitsel, dropped on the stage–dead.

'Murder! Murder!' the Tibetans shrieked.

'Suicide! Suicide!' the Chinese replied.

Then it happened. The nineteenth Drubtop Rinpoche's body and his robes, which lay in a crumpled heap on the stage, transformed into a wraith. It rose and drifted into the sky. It circled the sky and changed into words. 'Go to India. I await you there.' With these words, the wraith vanished, sucked up in the blueness of the sky.

Before his passing away to the heavenly fields, the nineteenth Drubtop Rinpoche had a different kind of encounter with Chinese communism. He was at the Central Institute for Nationalities in Beijing from 1953 to 1955. Situated on the outskirts of northwest Beijing and within the city's academic district, the Institute, covering two acres, was near the Beijing Zoological Gardens and the Nationalities Dance and Music School.

Before the founding of new China, the Institute had been a graveyard for the nearby village. But the new construction boom had gobbled up the graveyard and other ghosts of China's past. A Soviet-style auditorium dominated the campus, and around this were spread the dormitories for students and members of the faculty, classrooms and seven dining halls. Newly planted pine and willow fenced the campus.

There were about 26,00 students from forty-seven different nationalities. But the majority of the Institute's student body consisted of Tibetans, Mongols, Uighurs, Kazakhs, Koreans, Manchus and Hui Muslims. During Drubtop's time, there were about one thousand Tibetans. When they returned to Tibet, the Chinese authorities hoped, these Tibetans would become the standard-bearers of the new faith.

The Institute consisted of a primary and middle school and a university. Drubtop Rinpoche attended the middle school.

Drubtop Rinpoche's presence in Beijing coincided with the time when the country went on a fly-killing binge.

The campaign was introduced to the Nationalities Institute by Principal Wang Yao himself, who on that historic day strode into the auditorium, puffing on his cigarette, with a fly swatter tucked under his arm. He stood behind the bare table on which he slapped his Mao cap.

'To kill flies is to make China beautiful, socialist and clean,' thundered Dr Wang. He handed each student a fly-swatter and an empty ink bottle. Having suitably armed his students, Dr Wang urged, 'Kill flies.' Make China clean.'

But that hot summer day, Drubtop was bored. He didn't want to kill flies because he was a good Buddhist. The flies, which were normally everywhere, buzzing in his ears, sitting on his nose, were scarce as a yak meandering on Tiananmen Square. In a city as clean as Beijing, no fly could survive for long and with the whole of the city's eight million inhabitants on a fly-hunt, what chance did the flies have?

Disheartened, Drubtop crouched on the steps of the Institute's library, cupping his chin in his hands, the ink bottle and the swatter lying listlessly beside him. All of a sudden he had this urgent need to go to the toilet. The toilets were located at the other end of the Institute and Drubtop knew he couldn't hold it that far. He ran around to the back of the Library, found a quiet corner protected by two willow trees, squatted and relieved himself.

Soon the surviving, starving flies of Beijing swarmed in, buzzing in utter astonishment around this rare piece of steaming Tibetan turd.

And from the capital the good news must have spread to the rest of China like communism, since the place became black with hordes of flies from other famine-ravished provinces.

Drubtop couldn't believe his good fortune. To hell with his Buddhist beliefs, he thought. He had a reputation to recover. He ran around to the front of the library, recovered the ink-bottle and the fly-swatter, and in one mad frenzy, pinned down flies on trees, and on the Library ground and wall. At the end of the day, Drubtop Rinpoche's bottle was brimming with flies.

Dr Wang was pleased. He looked at Drubtop Rinpoche's brimming ink-bottle and compared it with the empty bottles of the rest of the students. 'Keep it up,' he said.

And Drubtop kept it up. As long as China's fly-killing infatuation lasted, Drubtop's ink bottle was always full of bloated bluebottles and lesser flies. Soon students crowded around him to learn his secrets. Drubtop kept mum.

Later when he returned to the sanity-inducing mountains of Tibet and his native Kyitsel, Drubtop recovered from his Beijing madness. He was sure that karma, the Buddhist law of you reap what you sow, would exact its inevitable retribution.

The Ancestors of the One-Eyed Golok

☯

The lama said that the nineteenth Drubtop Rinpoche was fond of saying that he came from a race of kings. The other Golok tribes, the victims of the ravages of the One-Eyed brigand, countered, 'No! You come from a race of bandits.' This brought a twinkle in his good eye. He would content himself by simply saying, 'Aren't we all?' He would say this more in resignation than in confession of guilt or admission of shame. This time he had more comments to add. He wanted to say that to a greater or lesser degree we all belonged to that particular race. Some had their misdeeds glossed over by minstrels and bards who were desperate for an audience that would willingly replenish the storyteller's tsampa bags and provide bowls of steaming butter-tea. The minstrels and bards too wanted to make a killing from telling the stories of successful scavengers. Robbers we were since the wheel of time first started its grinding spin. Robbers we would remain till the day the clock of time stopped ticking. Only some came up with a more convincing excuse for their daylight robbery. Depriving others of their inheritance still remained the world's greatest story when embellished and given a stirring tune by an inspired minstrel. Tribes we were and tribes we would remain, no matter how much varnish was added to cover our predatory instincts. All laws, the Rinpoche wanted to add were self-serving tribal laws laid down to demarcate and preserve hunting grounds. But this particular tribal discussion group lost interest and the words that sprung to the

Rinpoche's lips to articulate his un-Buddhist thoughts were swallowed back again, un-said, trapped in tribal incoherence.

When they were not debating the finer points of their thieving genealogies, fighting among themselves or looting one another's cattle or wives, the Goloks raided the lowlands of China. When they saw the clouds of dust raised by those dreaded horsemen from the Tibetan highlands, the Chinese peasants would cry out, 'Flee! Flee! The barbarians are coming! Take your daughters, but leave your wealth.'

When the dust settled and the Golok war cries were only an echo amid the smoke and dust of their despoiled village, the mortified peasants would return to the scene of despoilment and nomadic crime. They would look at one another and at the distant cloud-shrouded mountains of Tibet and shake their fists, 'We'll kyi-hee-hee them back one day. Their bloody female yaks must have stopped giving milk again.'

These curses were blurted out in the din of the fading echo of the Goloks' victory song when they, in a single, disciplined column, pranced back to the highlands after every successful and substantial raid.

The biggest of these contemporary bandits was Tengsong Dorje. He was famously known as the One-Eyed Golok, who at the end of the nineteenth century brought the tribes of 'the eight districts of ten thousand each' of Golok under his brutal rule. But the One-Eyed Golok's ancestors were despoiled by the biggest bandit in all human history, the Lord and Master who commanded the Devil's own horsemen, those who thundered out of the steppes of Mongolia and onto the pages of world history.

The stalking scene around AD 1200 in that part of the world was quite simple and it was the perfect hunting season. China at that time consisted of three states: the Chin empire up in the north, the Sung empire down in the south and the Tangut empire in the northwest. The Mongols surveyed the scene from afar, almost salivating at this easy loot.

The Tanguts on the other hand were still a mystery piece on this imperial chessboard, a Tibetan people who had become sinocised and who roamed and lorded over the present-day Gansu-Ningxia corridor. Songtsen Gampo, the one who initiated the Tibetan people into the world of the written Word, tried to introduce the Word and the meaning of the Word to the Tanguts. The Tanguts refused to be subjected to such an education in subservience. They played truant, fled Tibet and took up residence in China. They preferred the Chinese characters. The ancient Chinese chronicles called them Xi Xia. The Tibetans called them Mi-ngak.

The Tanguts had long since curbed their nomadic instincts and had taken to agriculture. They straddled the region that separated the barbarians from the urban civilisation of China. That was why they were included within the confines of the crumbling Great Wall meant to keep out the marauding nomads.

Genghis Khan's ultimate targets were the Chin and Sung empires. The Tanguts were in the way. He led his soldiers mounted on their steeds from the great Mongol homeland to neutralise the Tanguts, but it wasn't as easy as the great Mongol chieftain had anticipated. It took him more than fifteen years to exterminate the Tanguts, from his first tentative forays in 1205 to his ultimate victory in 1227. One reason was the unexpected stiff resistance put up by the Tanguts. Till they confronted the Tanguts, the Mongols under Genghis Khan's leadership were fighting other nomads who did not have any fortified defence. But the Tanguts dwelled in cities, protected by walls and guarded by watchtowers and ramparts that let loose a steady hail of arrows on the attacking Mongol horsemen. The Mongols were about to return to their great Mongol homeland when a crafty ancestor of the One-Eyed Golok produced a book before the great Mongol Khan that resulted in the crumbling of mighty empires from the east to the west. The plotting Tangut minister stole over to the Mongol encampment in the cover of night and handed over the book to Genghis Khan. 'Here,' the plotting Tangut minister said, jabbing his finger at the book, 'is how you demolish the Mi-ngyak fortifications. And I want to replace that rascal as the next king of Mi-ngyak.'

The Mongol court roared in laughter. 'A book! A book in exchange for a kingdom!' the mighty khan retorted, a cruel derision lacing his booming voice. 'We don't read books.' Another burst of contemptuous laughter rent the night air. 'And we don't know how to! And there is no reason that we should!' The burst of laughter that greeted this comment from the Great Khan nearly ripped apart the roof of the royal yurt.

'Yes, a book in exchange for a kingdom,' the minister insisted, defiance, anger and contempt competing for prominence on his gaunt face. 'The book is in Chinese and the kingdom should be Tibetan. The book will bring the whole world at your feet. A mere kingdom would be piece of camel shit for you.'

Genghis Khan snapped his fingers in amusement. In response, a tall figure, wrapped in a scholarly cloak, appeared beside the Great Khan. 'Read the book,' the khan commanded. The tall figure read and translated page after page of Sun Tsu's *The Art of War*.

Now there is a story about how China's most prized military secrets and other useful inventions were leaked out to the unsuspecting barbarian world. Centuries before, but not before the Great Wall or the great book burning by the anti-scholar emperor Qin Shihuang whose ruthless savagery welded China into one country, an emperor in his imperial wisdom, had instituted a bureau to prevent Chinese inventions from falling into barbarian hands. The establishment of the Imperial Bureau of Chinese Copyrights and Inventions was prompted by the stark warnings issued by an anxious minister. The Tibetans who were frequently knocking at the gates of Tang China were demanding copies of Chinese wisdom books.

The newly-instituted Imperial Bureau of Chinese Copyright and Inventions was charged with the task of keeping an inventory of the number of books published; who possessed what books and the identity and exact addresses of the proud possessors of all Chinese wisdom books. The Bureau was also charged with the task to prevent Chinese inventions like the compass, paper, paper money, printing, gunpowder, gun, cannon, rocket, silk, vaccination for smallpox, wheat grains, city sewage system, playing cards and a host of other inventions from crossing over to non-Chinese territories. Every year before the autumn harvest, the minister of the Bureau had to present the details of the inventory in public before the majesty of the descendant of the Yellow Emperor, none other than the Son of Heaven himself. If one item of invention or if one single copy of Chinese wisdom books was unaccounted for, the minister of the Bureau and all his minions were condemned to death by a thousand cuts. Immediately an imperial army was dispatched to recover either the lost book or the stolen item. In this way China was successfully able to keep the rest of the world in the dark about what the Chinese were really up to. But then there was a serious breach in this imperial decree. The culprit was none other than Wengcheng Kongsho herself, the Green Tara, the Mother of all the Buddhas, the very source of compassion, who in her human form was the most celebrated of the Tang princesses, the gifted exponent of the Chinese harp, whose beauty had kings and princes of half the barbarian world scrambling to Xian for her hand in marriage. She was a picture of the classic Chinese beauty, with small eyes, a small mouth and chubby cheeks and her hair coiffured in the latest Japanese fashion. She was given away in marriage to the barbarian king who made the biggest nuisance of himself, Songtsen Gampo, the fast rising king of Tibet. Just before Wengcheng Kongsho mounted her sedan chair on her long journey to Tibet, the imperial concubines body-searched her. The concubines discovered no Chinese wisdom books or inventions on her, but they were mistaken. Tucked in her vagina was a wheat grain. Earlier the princess had toyed with the idea of presenting a silk worm as a gift to her barbarian husband but she quickly dismissed the idea, knowing a barbarian, even if he was to become her husband, had no use for fineries like silk. And she didn't know for sure whether mulberry bushes grew in Tibet. She was afraid he might even laugh at her. So practical as ever, she struck on the wheat grain idea. Food and the source of food and the means of cultivating it, she thought, was an appropriate wedding gift. Wengcheng Kongsho might have got away with this but for the unfortunate fact that half way to Lhasa the Tang princess became a walking wheat field in full harvest. The imperial entourage was aghast. A Tang princess, the celebrated Wengcheng Kongsho herself, caught in the act of delivering China's prized inventions to barbarians! The entourage was made to halt at Kyigodo, deep in barbarian territory, while a messenger, accompanied by the best soldiers, was sent to Xian to inform the Tang emperor of Wengcheng Kongsho's deception and to relay back the severity of imperial punishment. But when informed of Wengcheng Kongsho's breach of imperial policy, the Tang emperor, the doting father of his favourite daughter, simply smiled indulgently. 'She is smart,' the emperor said. 'She's not helping her barbarian husband. She's helping her imperial father. Well-fed barbarians will always be well-behaved barbarians. They will abandon their nomadic life and become peaceful farmers and less of a nuisance for the empire. Look it up. It's on page forty-eight of Sun Tzu's book. Read it. Yes, there it is. Yes, that's right. She's smarter than many of my generals.' Later the emperor decreed the Imperial Bureau of Chinese Copyright and Inventions to make a distinction. Non-military inventions and books were to be permitted to cross into non-Chinese territories. The Bureau was charged on the pain of death by a thousand cuts to be ever more vigilant about inventions and books that had a military bearing which if they fell into the wrong hands could be used to undermine the empire.

The plotting Tangut minister came in possession of a copy of *The Art of War* because of the disarray that followed imperial decline rather than any brilliant initiative on his part. China's fragmentation into the rival Chin and Sung dynasties meant that the two rivals were willing to make China's wisdom books and other high-tech knowledge available to barbarians who in turn were willing to help undermine the other imperial rival. The Tangut minister was a useful ally for the Sung when it re-captured the imperial capital from the Chin. His reward for this service was the usual booties, including a copy of Sun Tzu's book. Reading it, re-reading it, he knew that within these pages were the means to acquire a kingdom and his chance came when Genghis Khan and his hordes came thundering down from the great Mongol homeland.

Now the secret was out. Having successfully hidden this classic from prying barbarian eyes for more than sixteen hundred years, China's wisdom was thus leaked out. The nocturnal lesson in the art of war over, the next day, Genghis Khan renewed his attack on the Tangut capital of Lanzhou, fed by the Yellow River. After a fierce assault the advance Mongol horsemen feigned a retreat. This made the Tangut horsemen and soldiers rush out of their fortifications in hot pursuit. When the Tangut cavalry and foot soldiers had crossed the Turquoise

Bridge, the retreating Mongol horsemen swung around and faced the astonished Tangut soldiers. Tangut retreat was cut off by Mongol archers and warriors who crept from the bed of the Yellow River and under the Turquoise Bridge. The Tangut soldiers were disarmed and Genghis Khan made them lead the Mongol troops. The Tangut capital opened wide its gates to welcome what it thought were its victorious heroes. Before anyone realised the mistake, the real massacre took place and the city was torched to its skeletal fortifications. Contemporary Chinese chronicles say that for weeks the stench and smoke of the annihilation of the proud Tangut people lingered in the air. At the end of the day, Genghis Khan ordered the execution of the Tangut minister who had plotted its downfall. 'The first rule of war,' Genghis Khan said, 'according to the book is never spare a traitor, even if he betrays your own worst enemy to you.'

Genghis Khan repeated this ruse whenever he wanted to flush out the enemy from effective strongholds. Always beside him in his campaigns was the tall figure, wrapped in a scholarly cloak translating Chinese wisdom into the keen ear of the Mongol chieftain. Tribes, kingdoms and empires were crushed one after the other like grass under thundering hooves. Whispering into the other keen ear of the conquering Mongol was a Tangut Buddhist priest. Like a commoner who accompanied a Roman proconsul to his victorious welcome in Rome, the Buddhist priest whispered, 'They won't last, victories and the fruits of victories. They won't last. Turn to Dharma, the only true path and the only road to lasting peace.' Genghis Khan hired this murmuring Buddhist priest who was from the same family as the plotting Tangut minister. A shamanist priest, belonging to the home-grown religion of Tibet and Mongolia, whispered the secret teachings of the white Bon to the mighty khan. Later, the three priests collaborated on a book to celebrate the exploits of Genghis Khan. The tall figure, wrapped in his cloak, worked on the strategies of battles, the feigned retreats, the sudden, bold attacks and the inevitable ambushes. The Buddhist priest made Genghis Khan into the foremost defender of the Buddhist faith. The Bonpo priest, in a state of shamanist trance, recited the stirring battle songs that had come to inspire succeeding generations of grassland brigands. The epic is called the *Gesar Khan* or *Gesar of Ling*, the world's longest. It is still growing as some minstrel is visited yet again by the grassland spirits to impart, teach and sing anew the deeds and conquests of the merciless warrior.

The acquisition of Sun Tzu's book forged the Mongol empire. Tearing up the pages of the book became a vital cause for its fall. While he was alive, Genghis Khan had the Chinese classic bound in wooden covers and chained to a lectern that was placed behind his throne. The book was guarded day and night. Two mounted horsemen stood on either side of it as a mark of respect to the book which was responsible for most of the conquests of the Great Khan. Before he died, Genghis Khan divided his empire among his four sons. But he instructed that the book must remain in the Mongol capital for the exclusive use of the son who guarded the great Mongol homeland. But as soon as the Great Khan left this world to journey to Shambala to help protect that western paradise from malignant forces, the four sons tore the book into four equal parts. However, before they departed to their respective parts of the empire, the third son, Ogedei, and the one appointed by the Great Khan as his worthy successor, had the foresight to suggest that four Mongol scholars memorise the text of the book. The task was given to the four sons of the man who, wrapped in his cloak, had for all these years translated the book for Genghis Khan and helped him become victorious. They were to pass their knowledge to their sons and their sons to their sons so that the wisdom of ancient Chinese warfare never died. Thus was born in Mongolia the warrior priests, those who advised the Mongol khans on military stratagem. But the line of warrior priests came to an end because at one point of time no male issues were born to the warrior priests and the Mongol khans were too busy fighting to thunder across the length and breadth of the empire to consult the missing parts of the great book. The loss of the book's knowledge spelt the empire's doom.

According to another version, a Tibetan master, endowed with tantric powers, determined to lead the Mongol khans onto the Buddhist path, was incensed by the warrior priests for advising the Mongol chieftains on their slaughter across two continents. He put a curse upon them: the loss of memory. Chapter and verse of the Chinese classic on warfare, the warrior priests clean forgot. Since the four priests forgot, they had nothing to pass on to their sons. And the great Mongol khans with no guidance from their warrior priests slowly lost control of their empire. Some believed that the incensed Tibetan tantric master condemned the four priests and their sons to reincarnate in Tibet. There on the Tibetan plateau recovering their lost memory these reincarnated story-tellers aroused by the spirits of the grassland, and as a form of apology to the Mongol khans for failing in their tasks in their earlier warrior-priest incarnations would spontaneously break into singing new and fresh exploits of the Gesar of Ling.

As for the other family members of the Tangut minister and the rest of the surviving Tangut people, chafing and sulking under Mongol tyranny, they fled Tangutistan en masse and took refuge in Tibet, to be subjected to an education in subservience, to learn the meaning of the Word. Many settled in eastern and northeastern Tibet. Some trekked the breadth of Tibet, crossed the Himalayas and found a safe haven in present-day Sikkim. Others walked further afield and settled in Nepal, in full view of the Goddess Mother of the World. Their descendants are called the Sherpas. It literally means those who came from the east. The family of the Tangut minister did not venture that far. They settled along the southern shores of Lake Koko Nor, in Kyitsel, and reverted to a nomadic way of life.

The lama said that the family chronicles of the Tangut minister and his descendants indicated that a strong streak of cruelty as well as piety ran in the family. The family was torn between impulses of war and the attraction of the Word. As if making amends for the Tangut minister's assistance to Genghis Khan, one of his sons acted as the interpreter when a delegation of Tibetan Buddhist priests, led by the Sakya Pandita, arrived in the Tangut region to plead Tibet's case before Godan Khan, a Mongol prince, whose forces had briefly plundered monasteries in central Tibet. In return for an annual tribute and the lama's teachings, Godan Khan agreed to spare Tibet any further Mongol devastation. Scholars called this a piece of Tiblomacy.

Alternatively, the family of the One-Eyed Golok produced some of Tibet's finest scholars and its fearsome robber-chieftains. It seemed that the family wanted to make up for the years of war, bloodshed and pogrom by offering its sons to the Buddhist clergy as a form of penance for ancestral wickedness.

The most influential of the Tiblomats was Khewang. Though only in his late twenties, Khewang had a pronounced stoop from years of poring over Buddhist scriptural wisdom. He was a gentle soul, devoted to his spiritual practice and committed to the spread of the Buddha Dharma. But he inherited enough guile from his ancestor to be petulant with the petulant and haughty with the haughty. He had a knack for unravelling knotty problems, of finding common ground where others saw only a yawning chasm, of spotting simple solutions for complex situations that defeated astute minds. He learned this side trade from Queen Chabu, Kublai Khan's wife. The two were instrumental in preventing the second Mongol assault on Tibet. Khewang was recalled from the Drubchen Monastery to act as an interpreter for Drogon Chogyal Phagpa, a nephew of Sakya Pandita, at the court of Kublai Khan. Phagpa, just nineteen years old, in turn had been ordered by Kublai Khan to make it to the Great Khan's splendid pleasure dome at Shangdu, popularly known as Xanadu, post-haste, to provide spiritual ministry to him and members of his court. At the time Khewang was in deep meditation and had left strict instructions with his fellow monks that whatever the contingency, nothing should be made to disturb his retreat. The night before the messengers of Phagpa came thundering into the courtyard of his monastery's cell, Khewang had a dream. The world was in turmoil, churned by a band of horsemen who were wreaking havoc on villages, towns and monasteries. Now they were threatening Shambala itself. Khewang found himself on a mountain top, facing the rising sun, sitting cross-legged, meditating. A sky-flier from Shambala alighted on his mountain perch and urged Khewang to stop the horsemen from invading Shambala.

'Can't do that. I'm busy.'

'Busy doing what?' the sky-flier asked.

'Meditating.'

'What is the purpose of meditation?'

'To help attain enlightenment.'

'What is the purpose of enlightenment?'

'To help free sentient beings from suffering and show them the path to freedom.'

'There you are. Your saving Shambala would help you attain the goals of your arduous meditation,' the sky-flier said. 'The leader of the horsemen is a good man at heart. Help teach him the wisdom of the Buddha. Help give him the Word of the Enlightened One. Make him free. He will listen. He will receive the Word and act on it. Save Shambala, save the world. In this way, you will truly help sentient beings to free themselves from suffering.' Khewang nodded and bowed before the logic of the sky-flier who invited him to hop on to a strip of nimbus cloud that drifted away to the east. The cloud floated above a pasture filled with horses and yurts. The place was dense and thick with packed animals and the rush of men in battle gear. The cloud made a swift descend and parked itself above the heads of men and beasts. Sitting in the lotus position on his throne of woolly clouds, Khewang taught the stages of the path to true conquest. The expectant and awed nomadic warriors felt doubly blessed by the wise words of the lama and the divine presence of the sky-flier. They discarded their arms and swung themselves on their horses to pursue true profession: herding yaks and sheep.

The next morning to the astonishment of his fellow monks Khewang cut short his retreat, saying he was expecting visitors. So when the galloping messengers pounded on his wooden door, Khewang, without the messengers having to say anything, knew what their message was. He had received divine intimation. Khewang and Phagpa's messengers sped across the grasslands of Kyitsel to Lanzhou, where Drogon Chogyal Phagpa was waiting. Khewang found the young Phagpa haughty and irascible and refused to prostrate before him, making it clear that he was not Phagpa's student, but his interpreter. If Phagpa did not find him good enough he could start looking elsewhere. But the vision he had of saving Shambala was so uplifting and real that he decided that Phagpa's haughtiness was a necessary quality if the Great Khan was to be shown the true path to peace. However, Khewang had a better opinion of Phagpa when the encounter between the Great Khan and the Sakya lama took place. Phagpa's insistence on the strict observance of the nuances of the guru-chela relationship proved perilous for Mongol protocol. The Great Khan expected the lama from Tibet to perform the ritual kow-tow. Phagpa had other ideas.

'Why is he not kow-towing?' the Great Khan demanded, sitting on his throne in his audience hall. Queen Chabu sat beside him. Below them on the throne's right were a shamanist priest and the medium for the court oracle. On the left, standing with due deference were the ministers and commanders, staring with stern contempt at the young Tibetan lama and his retinue. Amongst them was a strange white man, wrapped in yak skin, with a pair of owlish, astonished eyes about to take wings.

Khewang translated. 'Tell him,' Phagpa demanded in response, his pride rising to the height of the mountains of Tibet, 'why is he not prostrating before me?'

Khewang, ever the fastidious Tiblomat, hesitated, not daring to translate this piece of indignity. Phagpa flew into a rage. 'You said your job is to interpret. Now interpret. Word for word.' Khewang translated. The Great Khan thought he had misheard or the translation was wrong and demanded that the interpretation should be done in Mongolian and not Chinese. Khewang spoke Mongolian to the Great Khan who shot up from his throne and asked incredulously, 'What, I, the master of the universe, humble myself by prostrating before him! Is this what this mad lama is suggesting?'

Phagpa turned to Khewang and said, 'Suggesting? I'm demanding it. And tell him he must stop calling himself the master of the universe. He is nót.'

Khewang looked plaintively at Phagpa, waiting for greater tact and a softening of tone, but the stubborn son of Sakya ignored Khewang's look and was hitching the folds of his robe higher on his shoulder and wrapping his prayer beads around his wrist to prepare himself to engage in a verbal duel with this nomad sitting on the throne.

Khewang translated. The Mongol court groaned in anger. Swords were drawn from their sheaths. Above the murmur and groaning, the sharp voice of Kublai Khan rang out, 'Explain.'

'I'll explain when I must,' Phagpa said. 'I'll express an opinion when I'm in the mood to. Explanation means teaching and the traditional protocol requesting a teacher to teach has not been observed. Anyway, didn't you invite me to Mongolia to give you lessons in spirituality? Or to simply explain things?'

'That's right, to give teachings,' the Great Khan conceded.

'In which case,' Phagpa said, slowly, deliberately, 'I'm your teacher and you are my student. Now make three prostrations before your teacher,' Phagpa demanded, his finger pointing to his feet.

'I refuse,' the Great Khan said.

'In which case, I refuse to teach.' Phagpa turned on his heel and walked away. His entourage followed. Khewang hesitated and then joined the Tibetan crowd, leaving behind the Mongolian court staring at one another in baffled shock.

'You made a mistake,' Khewang shouted when he caught up with Phagpa. 'A big mistake! Now the Khan will unleashed his hordes on Tibet again. Even if you didn't want to prostrate, why did you have to demand that the Khan prostrate before you? We are finished,' Khewang paused for emphasis and said with sharp indignation, 'Tibet is finished.'

Phagpa turned around and wrapped his rosary around his wrist and looked into Khewang's frightened eyes. 'Interpreter, your job is to interpret. I'll make the decisions here. Kublai Khan invited me. Not you. Don't worry your head over what the Khan will do or not do. We are his guests. No harm will come to us. I'm ready to go back to Tibet anytime. But let's wait a day or two for the nomad sitting on the throne to come back to his senses.'

Rather than wait and do nothing, the Tiblomat sought an audience with Queen Chabu to open negotiations. He was made to wait. While he cooled his heels in his quarters and tried to take his mind away from the excitement generated in the court, turning his mind to meditation, he heard quick footsteps and the swish of robes. Someone pounded on his door. Before he opened the door, the shamanist priest, the oracle, and the white man swaddled in yak skin and their retinue entered. Without the formality of an introduction, the shamanist priest said, 'Your lama did the right thing. But the Great Khan is angry. Tell your lama to flee. There is no place for him or you in the court. Dangers lurk everywhere if he waits even for a day.'

Khewang stared at them, wordlessly, suspiciously.

The white man spoke, in Chinese. 'We are your friends. Your lama must leave now. The Khan will want to avenge the great indignity. He will spare no one, including you.'

Khewang was puzzled by the white man and turning to the shamanist priest, he asked in Mongolian, 'And who is this strange white man who speaks Chinese?'

The shamanist priest said, 'He's a businessman, from a faraway country.'

Before Khewang could make more inquiries about the mysterious white man, the door of his quarter was flung open and in walked the emissary of Queen Chabu. The shamanist priest, the oracle and the white man and their retinue made way for her. The emissary beckoned Khewang to follow her and Khewang did, silently. This was the appointment he had been waiting for. The shamanist priest and the oracle started following the royal emissary, but she turned around abruptly and with a face which bore the severity of the steppes and commanded them to stop following her. Khewang was led to the Queen's private chapel. His anxiety about the outcome of the meeting melted away when he saw that a small, finely sculpted statue of the Buddha as the most revered item on the altar. Queen Chabu asked, 'I wonder what the priests have been telling you?'

'They urged us to leave immediately.'

'Why?'

'They said the Great Khan is furious. He feels insulted and we are in imminent danger.'

'Insulted he is. He's never been treated like this before, in front of his entire court. But no, you are not in danger. The priests don't want any more rivals fighting for the Great Khan's soul. You're more in danger from them, from their sweet words of advice.'

This came as a big relief to Khewang. Here was a real chance to save Tibet, he thought. Now he must get into the business of Tiblomacy in earnest. 'The lama is right, you know,' Khewang said, standing in front of the Queen. 'Prostration is required by tradition. By prostrating the student is showing respect not for the person but for the teachings of the Buddha that he will be transmitting. We must come up with a solution. I know the lama was haughty and he used words that should not have been spoken. Besides, he was tactless and outspoken.' But then Khewang wondered why the Queen would belittle her own court priests in private when they were publicly given such an exalted position. Was this a trap, for him and Drogon Chogyal Phagpa?

'Yes, you are right, but my husband is also right. He is the sovereign of this part of the Mongol realm. You can't expect him to prostrate before your lama and expect the Khan to keep this realm intact. Yes, we must come up with a solution.'

'If the solution is to persuade the lama, the teacher, to kow-tow before the Khan, his student, forget it. The lama is stubborn. You can't expect the lama to debase himself to worldly power and expect him to keep his spiritual integrity. And I think I understand the lama's feelings on this.'

Queen Chabu ordered her chief maid to bring with her a statue of the Buddha and a blue Mongol khata. When they had done her bidding, Queen Chabu smiled and stood up and told her maids to follow her. 'Let's go,' she told Khewang. 'I think I have found the perfect solution.'

'Where to?'

'To your lama's place. To talk to him. To offer suggestions.'

The crowd of the shaman priest, the oracle, the white man and their retainers were whispering excitedly in the courtyard. When they saw the Queen skip down the steps they made way for her and bowed. The Queen nodded and smiled, radiating imperial benevolence. The white man kneeled on one knee and kissed the proffered hand. 'It's not only we Mongols who have strange manners,' the Queen said to no one in particular, giggling impishly. The shaman crowd followed the Queen and her maids at a respectful distance. At Phagpa's quarters, Queen Chabu told her maids to wait in the antechamber. 'Keep them company,' she said, pointing to the shaman crowd. She asked Khewang to accompany her into the lama's presence. Phagpa was saying his prayers when the Queen made her entrance. He made an effort to stand when Queen Chabu made three quick, practiced prostrations. 'Rinpoche,' the Queen began, 'I am sorry that things got off on wrong foot. My husband is a proud man but he is also the lord of this part of Genghis Khan's realm and his prostrating in public before you would have adverse implications affecting his ability to rule.'

'Your majesty,' Phagpa said, interrupting the Queen, 'I am also a sovereign. Of a worthier realm. I acknowledge no authority except the law laid down by the Enlightened One. I know the reasons for human suffering and I also know the path that leads to the end of suffering. Don't you think one of my students not prostrating before me would also have serious adverse effects on my ability to teach the wisdom of the Enlightened One?'

'In that case,' the Queen said, 'give my husband the teachings of the Enlightened One in private. He'll prostrate to you in private. When you give the teachings, you will be honoured with a higher seat.'

'I'll give the teachings in private on the condition that your husband obeys my every instruction.'

'Rinpoche, that will be very difficult to follow.'

'In that case, no teachings, not even in private.'

It was at this point that Queen Chabu, to the lasting admiration of Khewang, put forward a set of arguments that later formed the cornerstone of Tiblomacy that has operated in high Asia since then. She in effect told Phagpa that he should not quibble over protocol and insist on the Great Khan's absolute obedience. Phagpa had within his powers the opportunity to make Mongol rule more benign, in accordance with the teachings of the Buddha. By agreeing to become Kublai Khan's teacher, Phagpa would save Tibet from Mongol devastation and help spread Buddhist teachings over a sprawling realm. This, the Queen said, was the essence of Buddhism, to prevent suffering and to introduce the precious words of wisdom to countless beings. The Queen said this was what the Buddha himself would have recommended. 'Your uncle,' Queen Chabu said, 'the great Sakya Pandita, gave the teachings to Godan Khan. The great Sakya Pandita also earned the eternal gratitude of Godan Khan because he cured the Khan of leukemia. Now is your turn, to perform the noble deed for your country and religion. Don't let this opportunity slip away because I don't want my husband's soul to be lost to that shamanist rascal and his cohorts. They are only for themselves. This is a request. No, this is a prayer, from a disciple to her master.' She made three quick prostrations and presented Phagpa a statue of the Buddha and a flowing blue khata.

'She's right,' Phagpa said after the Queen had left. He sat impassively on the cushion, turning his prayer beads. 'But I must have his unquestioning obedience. Otherwise, what's the point in giving him the teachings, if he doesn't act on them?'

'Seek an audience with the Great Khan,' Khewang suggested. 'Meet him. Talk to him. As the Queen said, you have the power to do great good for Tibet, and for the Buddha Dharma.'

But Phagpa was unyielding. He said it was the Great Khan who sought his teachings. He should be the one seeking an audience. 'I have no reason to come to Mongolia, except that he invited me to give him the teachings,' he said, wrapping his prayer beads around his wrist, preparing for another debate. 'Why should the basis of the Buddhist spiritual tradition be compromised whenever a nomad threatens to wield his sword? No, if I am to become his spiritual teacher, I must have his complete obedience so that the Law of the Enlightened One is practised in the realm that he rules with the sword.'

Khewang, the Tiblomat, had his work cut out for him. He met Queen Chabu and explained to her the reasons for Phagpa's insistence on Kublai Khan's unquestioning obedience on all matters. She in turn said Kublai Khan's obedience to the Sakya lama on all affairs would make it impossible for the Mongol prince to rule his share of Genghis Khan's realm. There would be rebellions, heightened court intrigues, wars from other Mongol princes and the realm with fabled Xanadu as the centre would fall apart. 'We are giving the Sakya lama the protection of the sword to spread the Word of the Enlightened One. Don't let the lama throw away this precious opportunity,' the Queen said.

It was then that Khewang hit upon the idea that contained the elements of enlightened self-interest, practicality and the basis of a compromise that would neither undermine Kublai Khan's ability to rule nor the lama's spiritual prestige among his disciples. 'Will the Great Khan be willing to obey the Sakya lama on all spiritual matters and affairs relating to Tibet? If he is willing to obey the lama on these two matters, I am sure the lama will not interfere in the affairs of the state of the Great Khan.'

Queen Chabu mulled over the idea. There was a gleam of excitement in her eyes and she nodded and said, 'I think this will work. My husband will approve. This is mutually beneficial. I think you have hit upon just the right solution. Does the Sakya lama approve of this?'

'No, I haven't discussed this with him yet, but I'm sure he too will see the benefit in this arrangement.'

'Do so and let me know what the lama thinks. But I feel it is essential for the two of them to meet informally. With no protocol, as privately as possible and without the presence of those shamanist priests.'

Khewang broached the matter before Phagpa who was pleased with the idea of the Great Khan not interfering in the affairs of Tibet. However, he was sceptical about 'spiritual matters'.

'But that term covers almost everything,' Khewang countered. 'It is up to us to put forward convincing arguments to make any issue a spiritual matter.'

Phagpa looked at Khewang. For the first time a smile of approval lit up his face. He said, 'Good. Go, set up the meeting with the Great Khan. I want to see whether he deserves the teachings of the precious one. This interview will also serve as an entrance test.'

The Queen wanted everything to go right. She chose her private shrine room as the most convenient venue for the meeting. It implied the meeting was private which, according to Mongol protocol, would eliminate the presence of the usual imperious and arrogant retinue of the Great Khan. This quirk of Mongol court protocol would also prevent the sly shamanist priest and the erratic court oracle from being in attendance. Just four people, Kublai Khan, Drogon Choegyal Phagpa, Queen Chabu and Khewang, would attend the interview that would determine the fate of Buddhist Tibet and the soul of Kublai Khan. The Queen was anxious that neither man feel slighted, so she ordered seats of the same height for the two and placed them at the same distance from the altar, the object of the Queen's devotion and the source of the room's prestige. She ordered identical tables, cups, saucers and cup covers for them. The two men would arrive at the meeting at exactly the same time, so that neither would have to wait for the other. She also made it clear to Kublai Khan that he must not wear his imperial raiment for the meeting and designed a simple blue robe with a green shawl for him, which avoided giving the impression that her husband was flaunting Mongol military might.

But Kublai Khan, still smarting from what he perceived as the lama's insult the other day, nearly succeeded in wrecking the historic encounter, that Queen Chabu organised with such attention to detail, with his very first question: 'What makes you so proud?' demanded Kublai Khan as soon as the two men were seated. 'I'm proud with the proud and humble with the humble. It's a matter of adjusting to the given human environment,' Phagpa said in a lightning flash. But convinced that the fate of Tibet would be determined by this interview Phagpa took time to explain. 'My pride is confidence, the confidence that comes from being the inheritor of a long history and rich culture. My predecessors,' Phagpa said, citing an example which he thought would make the Great Khan understand the wonder of ancient Tibet, The glorious kings forged an empire that was more extensive than yours. They imported the wealth of the king of Tazik and brought the laws of China and the religion of India to the Land of Snow. The glories of ancient Tibet can match anything in your realm. My predecessors waged wars with Tang China for over a hundred years, captured their capital of Chang'an and installed an emperor on the Tang throne.'

Kublai Khan, who was intent on adding China to his part of the Mongol realm, was disbelieving. 'I think you are just a storyteller. I want documentary evidence, historical proof.'

'Consult the Tang Annals if you want,' Phagpa shrugged.

Queen Chabu dispatched the chief lady-in-waiting to bring the court scholar with the tomes of the Tang Annals. The court scholar who doubled up as the court chronicler consulted the Annals and confirmed every word of the great Phagpa.

'Okay,' Kublai Khan said after a long pause. 'That was then. What about now? What great men do you have in Tibet today?'

'Milarepa.'

'Milarepa?' the Great Khan said. 'Haven't heard of him. What did he do?'

'He's a great conqueror.'

'How come, I, the master of the universe, have not heard of this conqueror? Which kingdom, or land, empire or realm, that remains untouched by the might of Mongolia has this man conquered?'

'Stop calling yourself the master of the universe. You are not even the master of yourself! You haven't even conquered your conceit. No, he didn't conquer any land or realm.'

'So what did he do to be considered a great conqueror?'

'He conquered himself. He is an enlightened being.'

'Conquered himself?' the Great Khan repeated, relaxing and beginning to smile.

'Yes, conquered himself. He's free from attachment.'

'And what is attachment?'

'That is why you have invited me here, to teach you the nature of attachment and how to be released from it so that you become free from suffering. Conquering your negative emotions will make you master of yourself, that is the greatest of all victories. This victory will determine your death and your rebirth, not the kind in which you force horsemen up and down the land to pillage, kill, plunder and bring devastation.'

So according to the Gem Treasure House of the Sakya Genealogy, Phagpa found Kublai Khan a worthy student, curious, persistent and eager to learn. Likewise the Great Khan found the Sakya lama a wise teacher endowed with immense knowledge, who was not afraid to speak his mind or cowed by worldly splendour and might. But before the Sakya lama initiated the Great Khan into the teachings of the Enlightened One, he insisted on chalking out the exact protocol of the master-disciple relationship. According to the Gem Treasure House of the Sakya Genealogy, the following were the principles that governed the relationship: During meditations, teaching and at small gatherings, the great Sakya lama would sit at the head. At large gatherings, consisting of royal families, their bridegrooms, chieftains and the general populace, Kublai would sit at the head to maintain the decorum necessary to rule his subjects. On matters regarding Tibet, the Great Khan would follow the wishes of Phagpa. The Great Khan would not issue orders without consulting the lama. But with regard to other matters Phagpa must not allow himself to be used as a conduit for the Great Khan since the lama's compassionate nature would not make for strong rule. The Sakya lama must not interfere in these matters.'

Having agreed on this face-saving formula, the great lama was willing to teach and the Great Khan was eager to be taught. Phagpa selected the three stages of the Hevajra tantric initiations as suitable for Kublai Khan's temperament. Kublai Khan selected twenty-five nobles amongst his relatives and from the ranks of the civil service as his retinue and whom he considered worthy to receive the initiation. Dressed in blue robes held by blue sashes, their shoulders wrapped in green robes, these twenty-six men received the teachings. In gratitude Kublai Khan offered the thirteen matriarchies of central Tibet to the Sakya lama to rule. Khewang, the devout Buddhist, was against the Sakya lama accepting this offering. 'You can't teach the Word of the Enlightened One and then govern people. You will be compelled to compromise a lot of Buddhist principles to ensure effective governance.'

The Sakya lama said, 'I have gone so far into this and have already compromised my beliefs and principles. Better that a good lama mismanaged a country than a tyrant rule the thirteen trikhors with merciless efficiency. I think this is also the teaching of the Enlightened One.'

After the second initiation, Kublai Khan offered Phagpa a conch shell to signify that the teachings of the Buddha would spread far and wide in all four directions and rule over the three provinces of

Tibet. However, for the third initiation the Sakya lama demanded that he would determine the kind of offering he wanted the Great Khan to make.

'What kind of offering?' Kublai Khan asked, curious and little concerned.

'You have the cruel habit of drowning thousands of helpless Chinese peasants in Miyou Lake every year. What harm have they done to you? They are innocent people just struggling to make a living. I want this practice stopped. No more drowning of the Chinese populace. I will accept this as an appropriate offering. Only this and nothing else.'

'But you agreed not to interfere in the affairs of the state. This is a matter of state. This practice was instituted during the reign of the mighty Khan to reduce and regulate the growth of the Chinese. They multiply so fast that it makes it very difficult for us, the few Mongols, to continue to govern them. And their numbers make it easy for them to revolt.'

'Stop this practice. Otherwise, no further teachings.'

'I can't,' Kublai Khan insisted. 'If I do, I will face a palace revolt. I can't overturn the practice instituted by the mighty Genghis Khan.'

'You promised that you will listen to me in all affairs relating to Tibet and spiritual matters. This is a spiritual matter. It is my commitment to the Buddha to save ordinary, helpless people. I consider this a spiritual matter of the highest order. People rise up in revolt when they are desperate and this inhuman cruelty will give them every reason to be freed from Mongol tyranny. To herd innocent men, women, children and the old and the infirm, like so many cattle, and drive them with bows and arrows, spears, lances, swords, sling shots or whips into lakes and rivers to force them to drown in swift, angry waters, what sense does this savage practice make? No sense. Stop this practice at once and provide them with just and good governance and they will forever be indebted to you. Look at people and a growing population as wealth. See them as profit. Tax them, but tax them lightly and the income you generate could provide you with the resources to expand the means to govern. As I said, ending this brutal practice is the only acceptable offering.'

The Xanadu court gathered in a huddle of bowed heads looking for a solution. It was a new idea, the bowed and excited heads of generals and ministers thought. Seeing people as profit. To see a large and growing population as growing wealth. That was an excellent idea. The huddled heads of the Xanadu court decided they could live with the ban and could profit from the new tax. The huddled heads made an enthusiastic recommendation to a delighted Kublai Khan. The Khan in turn informed the Sakya lama that he would indeed offer to end the drowning of Chinese peasants as the most appropriate gift for his teacher as a gesture of his gratitude for receiving the third and the last of the Hevraja teachings. The Sakya lama was delighted. He taught the third initiation and composed a hymn of praise and long-life for the Great Khan and to his commitment to practising the teachings of the Buddha.

> The colour of the sky is red like blood,
> Under the feet is an ocean of corpses.
> Forsaking of such a practice is
> The fulfilment of the Enlightened One's wish,
> And for the spread of the wholesome Dharma.
> It is a dedication to the long-life of the Great Khan.

In return, in 1253 Kublai Khan appointed Phagpa the imperial preceptor and his personal teacher and later made him the spiritual leader of all Buddhists in his realm. Again in appreciation for Phagpa's inventing a written script for the Mongol court for use in the Mongol bureaucracy, Kublai Khan presented Phagpa a hexagonal crystal seal and a special yap exalting the lama's virtues.

> Below the sky,
> Above the earth,
> The son of the Indian deity,
> Emanation of the Buddha,
> The inventor of the written Word,
> Harbinger of peace,
> Arya Tishi,

The master of the Five Sciences,
Drogon Chogyal Phagpa,
The emanation of the Word,
And the exalted explainer of the meaning of the Word,
That blesses Mongolia.

Kublai Khan also issued two edicts, Bendhey Sheykyima in 1254 and Mutikma in 1264, to carry out the wishes of Phagpa. As translated from The Gem House of the Sakya Genealogy, the Bendhey Sheykyima states, 'Like the sun, the Buddha Sakyamuni's splendour vanquished the darkness of ignorance. Like a lion, the king of the jungle, he vanquished all demons and afflictive emotions. Endowed with the same qualities, Master Phagpa's character, virtues, and his wisdom, ocean-like, won my eternal faith and that of Chabu. For these reasons I became the patron of the Buddha Dharma and its monks. My faith has grown in Lord Sakyapa and Master Phagpa. Believing in the Buddha Dharma, I took initiations in the Water Ox Year. I have received many other teachings as well. I have a special desire to become the patron of the Buddha Dharma and its monks. Therefore, as an offering to Master Phagpa, I issue this wholesome Yasa which orders the protection of Tibet's religion and monks.'

In the Mutikma, Kublai Khan issued the following instructions: 'Enjoying divine protection of the devas and the splendour of great merits, I, the ruler of this vast empire, call on the monks and lay people with this law. For complete prosperity in this life, it is fine to enforce the legal code of Genghis Khan. However, future lives must depend on spirituality. Therefore, many years ago, after examining many religions, I found the Buddha Sakyamuni's path to be the most wholesome. Master Phagpa is the one who has achieved realisation and shown the true path to others. Therefore, I received the teachings and initiations from him and presented him with the title of the imperial preceptor. I call upon the Master to serve the cause of Buddha Dharma, lead the monasteries and take the lead in spreading the wholesome teachings, in learning and practice. Those proficient in the Buddha Dharma must teach the young with firm minds and the young with sound minds must apply themselves to their spiritual studies with new energy. Those who know the Dharma, but are not able to teach, must meditate. This conscientious practice of the Buddha Dharma will help consummate the accumulation of my merits as a patron and a practitioner, as indeed it will be of great service to the Triple Gem of the Buddha, his teachings and the community of monks who continue to study and spread the Word of his wisdom.

'The monks following this path will not be bothered by military generals, ordinary soldiers, powerful persons and the runners of the gold-letter mail. Monks shall not be conscripted into the army or asked to pay taxes or perform corvee.

'I issue this yasa to urge that the monks be allowed to follow the teachings of the Buddha Sakyamuni, to worship heaven and pray for me and for the welfare of my subjects. The runners of the gold-letter mail shall not be allowed to descend on monasteries and the homes of monks. Food and corvee shall not be extracted from the monks. Water and water mills shall not be taken away from the monks. The monks shall not be persecuted in anyway.'

In 1260 Kublai Khan succeeded Mongke Khan, who had died in the previous year, and ascended the great Mongol throne. Kublai Khan incorporated Chin and later Sun China into his empire and moved his capital to Beijing. That was the time when Phagpa insisted that he wanted to return to Tibet. 'I have taught you everything I know,' the great Phagpa told Kublai Khan. 'Now you are on your own. As the Buddha said, be a lamp to yourself.'

The send-off was grand. A thousand mounted Mongol cavalry accompanied Phagpa to Lanzhou and beyond. Kublai Khan and Queen Chabu accompanied the lama part of the way. In the procession, Khewang fell in line with Queen Chabu's sedan chair and asked her the one question he had been dying to ask. 'Who is that white man with the pair of owlish, astonished eyes?'

Queen Chabu parted the tassels of her sedan window and giggled. 'He?' she said. 'He is a businessman who has a strange habit. Kneels on one knee and kisses my hand,' she said. 'And he's funny. He says our yaks are cows with long, shaggy hair.' Queen Chabu was greatly amused by the idea. She allowed herself a long, hearty laugh. 'And he has a weakness for telling tall tales. He says the lama of his country is grander than Lord Phagpa himself. He's Marco Polo. Imports Chinese noodles to his country and calls them macaroni. And spaghetti and pasta.'

Khewang then told Queen Chabu the dream he had the night before the messengers of Phagpa came thundering to the courtyard of his monastic cell to take him away to interpret for the Sakya lama. 'The sky-flier is you,' Khewang said.

'Maybe,' Queen Chabu said. 'We have saved Tibet, brought peace to the empire and the soul of my husband is at peace. Buddha Dharma flourishes in this realm created by Genghis Khan. So that sky-flier in your dream could very well be me.'

The grand procession, kicking up a cloud of dust, wended its way to the faraway mountains of Tibet. But unnoticed by the procession, in the outskirts of Beijing a small group had gathered. With clashing cymbals and loud drums, the group of shamanist priest, the court oracle and their retinue burned incense and juniper twigs as offerings to the gods of the grasslands. These two priests, who had been dethroned from their exalted positions in Kublai Khan's court, invoked the jealous spirits of shamanism to bring doom and disaster on the Sakya lama who had polluted the grand soul of their Khan and poisoned his ears with alien heresy. 'May his soul burn in hell,' the shaman crowd chanted. 'May he face death and destruction. May his land become a land of lost content. May his heresy be scattered by the wind, buried by the snow and destroyed by thunder and lightning. May the monks suffer eternal damnation and the monasteries of Tibet destroyed to their very foundations.'

The lama said the curse was effective. 'Look at us, a people without a country and a country without its lama. We have become a land of lost content.'

Unlike Khewang but like his first recorded ancestor, the plotting Tangut minister, the One-Eyed Golok hankered after a kingdom of his own. The only force that prevented the One-Eyed Golok from carving out an independent kingdom encompassing the whole of Amdo was the band of marauding horsemen of the Tangshawa tribe, who operated throughout a wide area in Kham and Amdo. The Tangshawa tribe counter-attacked, dealing crippling blows to the One-Eyed Golok's forces. The One-Eyed Golok consulted his warrior priest. A marriage alliance was proposed. The One-Eyed Golok offered his daughter to the eldest son of leader of the Tangshawa tribe, who rejected the offer, outright. The One-Eyed Golok persuaded his eldest son, a monk at the nearby Drubchen Monastery and the one who had abundantly inherited the family trait of Tiblomacy, to open discussions with the suspicious Tangshawa tribe. The son willingly complied. The crafting of lasting peace was the real business of the lamas of Tibet, the son told his father. A year-long negotiation followed. The Tiblomat raised cogent arguments on how the proposed marriage would result in peace and he explained the benefits of peace. 'Peace,' the Tiblomat said, 'is killing your yak without having to kill people. Peace is having a leisurely meal without having to look over your shoulder to see whether avenging tribes are after your blood. Peace is the true worship of the gods of Tibet and the highest offering to them.' The Tiblomat then launched into his finest argument. 'Look at this, see this endless pasture. Don't you want it to be rich in tents, herds and men, women and children and black with the traffic of cattle and people? In the midst of this prosperity, your aged mother one day decides to go on a pilgrimage to sacred Gangkar Tise, all alone. She decides to take a bag of gold coins with her. She makes the pilgrimage. She returns after a year. Throughout the journey, no harm is done to her, no robbers steal her gold coins, no brigands molest her. She has walked the length of Tibet all alone and no harm was done to her, not even a scratch. That is the benefit of peace and you have it within your power to bring this about.'

The leader of the Tangshawa tribe accepted the marriage alliance. An oath, solemnised by the drinking of fresh blood of a lamb, took place. The sun, the moon and the stars in heaven were invoked as witnesses to the sacredness of the oath. Hostilities ceased and plans were made for the wedding ceremonies.

On the appointed day, appointed by the astrologers, lamas and soothsayers, the bride's caravan set off. The One-Eyed Golok and a dozen of his most trusted men led the caravan. The look of apprehension on the face of the leader of the Tangshawa tribe was replaced by a welcoming smile when he saw that the bride's caravan was accompanied by only twelve of the One-Eyed Golok's men. He signalled the wedding ceremony to begin by placing a silk scarf on the bride's neck. Songs were sung and dances performed the whole day and late into the night. Chang flowed like the Machu River itself. When the revellers were totally inebriated, the One-Eyed Golok moved his men in swiftly and quietly to disarm the drunken Tangshawa bodyguards. 'Let's continue with the celebration,' he said, his swarthy figure, wrapped in yak skin, convulsing with laughter at this nomadic joke. He stood before the wedding tent, his legs apart, his hands resting on the broadsword tucked under the sash that held his yak skin patsa. 'Feed them, feed them well,' he shouted. 'Offer milk to the women and chang to the men. Yes, feed them well. After all, this is my daughter's wedding.' Then from the highest point of the massive Tangshawa stone fortification, his men hurled the bodies of the Tangshwa men. The first to be tossed was the bridegroom himself, followed by the chieftain of the Tangshawa tribe. When their bodies hit the ground, the bloated stomachs burst open, squirting chang all over the place. The One-Eyed Golok laughed. And even as he laughed, all the Tangshawa bodyguards and all members of the royal family were exterminated. All but one. A son and his family had by a stroke of good karma gone on a pilgrimage to Wutai Shan and thus his piety saved his life and those of his wife and children. He received the news of the slaughter of his parents and his siblings at the Five-Peaked Mountain in China.

In horror, the One-Eyed Golok's daughter renounced her family and the world. She became a nun. She refused to set her eyes on the monster of a father who had turned her wedding into a charnel feast, the one who promised her a husband and then denied her her happiness. 'What reason,' she shouted when she stormed out of the stronghold, 'is there for me to continue to live with this family, which takes such delight in mass slaughter? No reason, except the daily torment of the cruel deprivation of my happiness. And I won't give you this pleasure.' The eldest son, the budding Tiblomat, too retreated for a lifetime to erase the horrific memories of ripped stomachs squirting chang and milk over the heads of the wedding guests. As if providing background music to the mesmerised wedding guests on that fateful night was the low, deep, rumbling laughter of his father echoing and bouncing and swirling in his throbbing skull. He, the Tiblomat, had been used. He had been made an unwitting accomplice. By his own father! Even penance and meditation for several lifetimes would erase the image of milk and chang spraying on horror-stricken heads. And all for what purpose? To increase the grazing patch for the herds of yaks already made fat by chewing on rich, lush grass.

The stream of refugees fleeing the One-Eyed Golok's brutality in Amdo alerted the Tibetan government of the dangerous political situation in that corner of Tibet. Being freed of its preoccupation with the Tibet-Kashmir War and the Tibet-Nepal War, the Tibetan government had now sufficiently recovered to muster the resources and sent a regiment under the command of a cabinet minister, Kalon Phulungpa Tseten Dorje, assisted by General Trimon Chimi Dorje. On its way to the battlefront, the government army recruited substantial forces from Riwoche, Chamdo and Drayab in Kham.

The greater staying power of the government army won the day. Besides, an increasing number of tribes, which had earlier, sworn undying allegiance to the One-Eyed Golok surrendered themselves at the lotus feet of Kalon Phulungpa and General Trimon. The remnants of the fiercely avenging Tangshawa tribe were mighty useful in the government forces' swift advances on the One-Eyed Golok.

The One-Eyed Golok retreated to his fortress of Chagden, the Iron Fortress, which he had built in the intervening years. The fortress nestled on a hillock. It resembled the neighbouring Drubchen monastery. The wood and stone structure looked like it had dropped from the sky in a neat tapering heap.

The government army laid siege to Chagden, securing all supply routes, which forced the One-Eyed Golok to ask for a truce. One day he himself came over to discuss with General Trimon the terms of his surrender. He demanded that the Tibetan government bear all the sins he had accumulated by his mass slaughter of men and horses. He would be willing to surrender only on this condition.

The minister and the general agreed. Together with the One-Eyed Golok they drank the blood of a newly killed lamb as an assurance of the sacredness of the oath. But after the oath, the Tibetan officials ordered the murder of the One-Eyed Golok and his armed escort.

The government army stormed Chagden and massacred all the men. The remnant of the Golok troops were quickly disarmed and sent packing to tend to their sheep and herds of yaks. Chagden, the Iron Fortress, was torched and burned to the ground. The year was 1895.

That night the whole of Kyitsel was lit like the festival of lights itself. The fortress of Chagden became one enormous butter-lamp offering to the gods of Tibet. The fire licked the stones and ravished the wood and burst into a blaze of scorching flames that illuminated the outlines of the distant Drubchen Monastery. Then it was said, the spirits of the grasslands, the spectral presence of the warrior priests and the god of stories, all those who moaned with the winter wind and sang with the spring breeze, who were swaddled in snow and who washed in rain, rose with the flames to sing their hymns. They sang and whispered their secrets to unborn children so that the deeds of men would forever be ingrained in human memory. They rose in the sky with the smoke and leaping flames and they sang and chanted till Chagden, that fortress which housed mighty ambitions and big delusions, was reduced to a big smouldering ember. They sang their chorus. 'They won't last, victories and the fruits of victories. They won't last. Turn to Dharma, the only true path and the only road to lasting peace.' They sang into memory, legend and myth how one man's ambition went up in smoke. And was reduced to dust. Others joined in. The serpents that rippled with the river waters, the nagas who sulked in the deep blue lakes, the stern protective deities of the mountains who sneezed hail and storm and blew wind and blizzard, sky-fliers and the others joined in. They sang: this won't last, military victories and the fruits of victories. They would all be reduced to dust and blown away by the wind. The tricks of Tiblomacy, the sword of Genghis Khan, the pretensions of empire and the arrogance of conquest, won't last. But what would last is this haven we praise, this power-place of the world, this Land of Snow, this measure of the earth and our life on it, this playground of the gods, this piece of eternity carved in mountains that give us our river waters. Yes, this would last, this abode inhabited by men and women whose beliefs give us our existence and blessed by countless lamas whose looms of wisdom have woven the pattern on the fabric of Tibet.

The spiritual band that gathered around the now smouldering bonfire burst into its final hymn of praise, not for a people but for a place that made the people:

> This centre of heaven,
> This core of the earth,
> This heart of the world
> Fenced by snow.

Here the storyteller became the story. He became the lineage-holder, the one who kept the tradition and gave it meaning. He was the end of one story and the beginning of another plot. His was the stream of consciousness that filmed people and places, events, spiritual and worldly. For a moment another photographer wanted to shoot the same scenes or develop the same films. The lama seemed to be taken over by the spirit of the God of stories. Or, it seemed a shaman spirit had entered his Buddhist soul. The lama was seized by fits of hiccups that glazed over his eyes and made his face turn blue. His cheeks swelled up and the creases on his forehead turned into so many knotted lines of rage or pain. The stories that swirled in his brain found no words, only hiccups and a violent jerk that forced the lama to lie prone on the bed.

'Don't worry, he'll recover,' Ama Penpa said when she saw the alarm on my face. After a few anxious moments, the lama recovered, revived by Ama Penpa's gentle sprinkling of water and by the smoke from the smouldering juniper twigs. He sipped some chang. 'Was that a dream?' the lama wanted to know, now sitting upright, cross-legged on the bed in Ama Penpa's chang shop in the sweltering heat of Majnu Ka Tilla. 'Ah,' he said, 'it was just a story.' And he, who lived so comfortably in two worlds, one serving as an explanation for the existence of the other, realised that he was back in the present, his refugee world. 'In the end everything and everyone becomes a story,' the lama added, wiping his mouth with the back of his hand. 'Mighty enterprises and ambitions end up being just another story.'

Earlier I thought that the gods of Tibet had spoken through him, as they often did. I quickly started scribbling on the notebook so as not to make eye contact with the divine presence.

'Ah, yes, I remember. The rest is my family story,' the lama continued, gulping chang and acting as though nothing had happened.

Oh, well, the gods had not spoken through him. The lama remembered. The lama said that after the defeat of the One-Eyed Golok and the Chagden massacre there was a lull, a stunned silence, as if the people of Golok still couldn't believe what had just happened to them. They were either cowed down by the horror of the massacre that took place before their astonished eyes or were stunned by the sheer audacity of what the One-Eyed Golok had tried to accomplish.

Not all the family members of the One-Eyed Golok were killed, the lama said. 'My father survived, saved and protected by his uncle. We too have something to avenge.' This startled Ama Penpa who furtively looked at the lama and offered a glass of chang in an attempt to stop his train of thought, to let his lips be busy with something else than mouthing subversive thoughts against the Gaden Phodrang government.

The lama's father was the five-year-old Sonam Senge, saved by Pon Wangchuck, the half-brother of the One-Eyed Golok. Pon Wangchuk took his family to Kyitsel to seek the protection of the Drubchen Monastery. Protection was readily given because the One-Eyed Golok had been a generous patron and a devout follower of Drubtop Rinpoche. Drubtop Rinpoche instructed the half-brother of the One-Eyed Golok not to instil in Sonam Senge any thought of revenge.

'My father was a quick learner and his uncle a wise teacher,' the lama said, his misty eyes softening perhaps because of the memories that were being evoked. 'When he came of age, he borrowed money from Drubchen Monastery and took to business. He imported brick tea from China and exported wool. Business was brisk and soon my father established himself in Chamdo, the centre of commercial traffic between Tibet and China. He married one of the daughters of the Lingtsang family but even after five years of marriage, no child was born to them. Then my father took the two remaining daughters as his wives numbers two and three. I was the first born child and at the age of five I was sent to Kyitsel and was enroled as a novice at the Drubchen Monastery. I rose through the ranks and after many years I was appointed the abbot of the monastery and the sense of pride and joy I felt then still remains with me. The abbot of the oldest and most revered monastery in Tibet!' the lama said. Wonder and fulfilment made his eyes luminous and his face flushed. The lama's voice became loud and thick with pride. He remained silent. Perhaps he was still unable to believe his elevation to the exalted post, even after so many years.

'I was born to Pon Senge's second wife and the nineteenth Drubtop Rinpoche to the third,' Ama Penpa said, trying to fill in the gap.

'Yes, that's right,' the lama said. 'And I was accused of recognising my own half-brother as the Drubtop Rinpoche, the highest incarnate lama of the Drubchen Monastery. People said that was why he came to such a bad end at the hands of the Chinese communists. But Lhasa confirmed my recognition. But here I am, once again looking for him, the one who gave Tibet the Word and the meaning of the Word, the one who taught us that the greatest victory is victory over oneself. He taught us that non-attachment is the source of true happiness. I have failed miserably in this. You see I am attached, attached to the fortunes of my monastery in Tibet and its real lama.' The lama's eyes were closed and his hands were folded in prayer and reverence. He did not speak another word.

Ama Penpa filled in the gap by recounting her happiest memories of Chamdo. It was of Losar. Her happy memories of that particular year had the whole family sitting on elegant cushions to welcome the Year of the Iron Monkey. Outside in the courtyard they heard the Dekhar singing and doing his rounds of the rich families.

Hail to the Gods, Honourable Sir,
Hail to the Nagas, Honourable Sir
O, this morning I looked to the sky,
There was the fine omen of a good star.
This morning I looked to the earth,
There was the good omen of a warm sun.

'The Dekhar's got it wrong this time,' Pon Senge said to his wives and two children.

'Shhh..., not on the first day,' cautioned the ever-superstitious Tsomo Lhamo who believed that anything nasty said on the first day of the New Year would rebound later.

Then all of them got up and went out into the balcony. From the balcony they saw the dim figure of the Dekhar. It was a different one this year. A younger man. Wearing a mask, the Dekhar stood his staff firmly before him with the whole weight of his body resting on it. He had a tsampa bag slung across his shoulder. Seeing the master and mistresses of the household emerge, the Dekhar stuck out his tongue, made a little bow and sang.

Ha, ha, Honourable Sir,
O, I the old wish-fulfilling Dekhar
Last night had a dream while I slept.
This sleep was more like a snooze
In an eighteen-metre dream.
O, more than eighteen, let's say nineteen.
When I had my first dream,
The good omen of a full bowl of chang appeared.
When I had my second dream,
I dreamt I wore a victory scarf on my neck.
When I had my third dream,
I, Samphel Thondup, the Dekhar
Dreamt my tsampa bag was full.
When I had my fourth dream,
I dreamt that the shade had crossed the rocky mountain.
When I had my fifth dream

I saw the good omen of the shining sun upon the snow.
                    Then I awoke.
              O, perhaps, it wasn't a dream.
        O, could it be that it is actually here before me?

'It's not a dream, Dekhar. It's all true,' Pon Senge said, laughing loudly and gesturing to his servant to give the Dekhar his due. The Dekhar bowed his thanks. 'Why don't you describe everything from the top of your head to the sole of your feet?' Pon Senge asked, playfully, forgetting his sorrow.

'Hail to the gods, again I say, hail to the gods,' the Dekhar shouted, thrusting his staff before him.

              Honourable Sir, you ask me to describe
                    From the top of my head
                    To the sole of my feet.
        O, I the old wish-fulfilling Dekhar, if I must explain
                 My body, head and feet, all three;
          These fleshy feet are the bases, bases like cushions.
                 My knees are the wheel of religion,
                    Where religion is spread.
        My waist is the bell and vajra, offered to the Lamas.
             The upper intestines are the lasso of the gods.
             The lower intestines the lasso of the nagas.
                 My lungs are the snow-white mountains.
                    My liver the rocky mountains.
                 My heart is the Lama's offering cake.
             The rounded areas are where the horse runs.
             The hollow areas where the butter swirls.
                 In front is the place to tie the horse.
             At the back is where the cannon is fired.
        When the barrel booms, the land is filled with smoke!
             When your eyes are rolling, Honourable Sir,
                    You must guard your nose!

Pon Senge laughed. 'Go your way, Dekhar and bless this house,' he said.

'I will, I will. I give according to what I receive,' the Dekhar replied. Pleased with what he had received, the Dekhar bowed and went singing out of the house into the chilly early morning air laden with snow.

> O, this morning I go to the paradise in the north.
> O, this morning I go to the paradise in the east.
> I go when all the black ravens are chattering.
> I go when all the magpies are preening.
> I go like the wild white eagle
> Soaring through the sky.

3

The Protest Demonstration
Generation

Plans for Demonstration

☯

One morning Gyaltsen, the outgoing president of the Delhi branch of the TYC, came rushing into my room, dripping with sweat. He carried a copy of the day's *Times of India* and said, 'The Chinese foreign minister will be in town. We must stage a protest demonstration. Wherever you're going, postpone your trip.'

Well, we couldn't let such an important occasion pass by without our letting the world know what we felt about the conditions in Tibet. The TYC members worked fast. They had the whole Tibetan camp galvanised. The hall of the school in Majnu Ka Tilla, whose setting up Tashi had initiated was converted into a war-room. The atmosphere bristled with action. A chain of command had already been established. Acting as the conquering general plotting another brilliant strategy for a new battle was pock-faced Gyaltsen. He hunched over a big map of Delhi spread on the table. Using a wooden ruler he was pointing at a spot on the map. The burly Gyapon, the camp leader of Majnu Ka Tilla, Nyima of the *Tibetan Review*, Samdup, Dolma, Tashi and a young Tibetan were crowded around the table, listening intently, their eyes following the ruler darting back and forth.

'We'll settle for the Boat Club,' Gyaltsen said. He spotted Phuntsok and me slip in. Gyaltsen scowled, perhaps in disapproval, at our delayed entry and Gyaltsen went back to what he was saying. 'It's the Boat Club then. It's centrally located.' Others around the table nodded. 'But we still need to find out the exact time the Chinese motorcade will drive to Rashthrapati Bhavan. That is vital for the success of our protest rally.'

As the day for the protest rally approached, the classroom was also transformed into an armoury for the weapons and symbols to be used for combat. In one corner a schoolteacher was pounding on the old Remington, making the leaflet for distribution during the rally. Bundles of the Tibet national flag printed on nylon and plastic poles were stacked against the walls. Across the room, on desks, benches and on the floor, foot soldiers were making posters of the new battle cry: 'Free Tibet.' Others were painting slogans on green headbands. They all screamed 'Free Tibet'. A huge framed photograph of the Dalai Lama was set upright on a table pushed against the wall. At the far corner were a dozen or so empty Thumbs-Up bottles.

There was a strong smell in the room. I sniffed. 'Is that petrol I smell?' I asked, puzzled, turning to Phuntsok for enlightenment. Phuntsok twitched his nostrils and sniffed. 'It is petrol, for sure,' he said, a little mystified. 'No smoking!' he said, turning to me, his admonishing index finger wagging in my face.

On Gyaltsen's table were copies of the day's *Indian Express*, the *Times of India*, the *Statesman* and the *Hindustan Times*. The *Times of India* carried two stories, one from Beijing and another from New Delhi. The Beijing story, a PTI dateline, said the Chinese foreign minister was visiting India to revive the Hindi-Chini-bhai-bhai days. The Beijing report said, 'China is in the process of enlisting India's support in the new Chinese version of non-alignment, the struggle of the third world against the rich developed west and the two superpowers.'

The *Times of India*'s New Delhi political correspondent had also listed details of the foreign minister's itinerary while in the Indian capital. But he had a different take on the visit. Quoting an un-named Indian foreign ministry official, the New Delhi reporter said India planned to raise the border issue with the Chinese foreign minister. 'The Ministry for External Affairs will raise the contentious border issue with Mr Huang Hua, the newly-appointed Chinese foreign minister, who will arrive in the Indian capital on 20 April in the first leg of his tour of South Asia. The MEA will press the Chinese side to settle the border issue which led to a war in 1962 and since then has been a bone of contention between the two Asian giants.'

It also carried the nugget of information we were all looking for: the minister for external affairs would receive the Chinese foreign minister at the airport. The guest be would be lodged at Hyderabad House. He would call upon the President at Rasthrapati Bhavan on Raisina Hill on 21 April.

'The foreign minister is staying at Hyderabad House,' I said, waving my copy of the newspaper.

'That's why we are all here,' Gyaltsen said, trying not to sound irritated but hardly succeeding. Seeing that all the members of his war cabinet were present, Gyaltsen told the foot soldiers to leave the classroom. 'We'll call you back in a minute.' The poster-makers and the typist left. Gyaltsen told Phuntsok to bolt the door.

'The success of a demonstration lies in limited information and great timing,' Gyaltsen said, playing with the ruler. 'And a clear message of why we are protesting. It also depends on division of responsibility,' he added. Gyaltsen said the Gyapon would be responsible for transportation and would also see to it that the demonstrators did not turn violent, especially against the police. Pointing his ruler at Samdup and me, he assigned us the task of contacting the media, feeding information to them and drafting a memorandum addressed to the Chinese foreign minister.

Tashi and Phuntsok had to get some 'big' Indian politician to address the rally. 'A big name attracts the media,' Gyaltsen said.

Dolma, Samdup's girlfriend, and Nyima were given the responsibility of raising funds to cover the expenses of the demonstration. Gyaltsen himself would be the point man, the nerve centre of information flowing out and in.

'Any questions?' Gyaltsen asked, tapping the ruler on his open palm.

Samdup's hand shot up. 'A simple question,' he said, combing his immaculate hair, slowly, deliberately.

'Put that thing away,' Gyaltsen shouted. 'Or do you want me to hold a mirror for you? Here we are talking about Tibet, the suffering of the Tibetan people and you are concerned about how you look. And what is it, this simple question?' Gyaltsen asked, impatiently.

'In case you have forgotten, Tashi and I are members of the TCP, the founding members,' Samdup said casually, stuffing his red folding comb into the breast pocket of his brown safari suit.

'And what is the TCP?' Gyaltsen asked.

'I see, you have forgotten,' Samdup said with a look of mock surprise. 'TCP means the Tibetan Communist Party.'

'So?'

'So, we want to organise the demonstration as equal partners, the TCP and TYC. All the press releases and leaflets we distribute should say the demonstration has been organised by the TCP and TYC,' Samdup insisted.

The room erupted in protest. 'Impossible!' Gyaltsen yelled. 'You should be grateful that we are allowing you to participate in our demonstration, in the first place. Mind you, not as communists but as fellow Tibetans,' Gyaltsen said. 'In fact, the TYC doesn't want to be associated with you in any formal way. That's the instruction from Centrex.'

At this Tashi, who had been sitting quietly all this while with his dark glasses on the table, spoke up, 'In that case, Samdup and I will organise our own separate demonstration. The TCP protest demonstration for Tibetan freedom. Let's get out of here.' 'A demonstration by just two people?' Gyaltsen shouted. 'The Chinese foreign minister won't be amused if he discovers that there are only two Tibetan refugee communists.'

'You have the manpower and the resources,' Tashi shouted back, 'but you don't have what we have, conviction. And we don't treat the TCP as a stepping-stone for personal ambition.'

'You have already used the TYC to become the chairman of the Tibetan communist party,' Gyaltsen retorted, 'We should not have accepted your resignation from the TYC. We should have expelled you. You stand expelled.'

'That's a badge of honour. We are happy to remain ex-communicated,' Tashi said, giving one long angry stare before he strode out with Samdup, slamming the door behind him.

'We'll see how many people turn up for their demonstration. And I suppose theirs will be a demonstration to welcome the Chinese foreign minister,' Gyaltsen said. 'They are just using the demonstration to get cheap publicity for their party. They want to ride piggyback on us and get credit for it.'

There was an awkward silence in the room. Then it dawned on Gyaltsen. 'Dolma, you are friends with Samdup. We don't mind if you join them. But you have to make up your mind.'

Everyone stared at Dolma, wondering what her reaction would be. Dolma took her time answering. She pushed her hair back and looked around before she said.'Yes, I'm Samdup-la's friend, but not his comrade in arms. I'm a member of the TYC, and I am proud of being a member. But if you suspect that I will pass any TYC secrets to him, expel me. I won't voluntarily resign from the TYC. It's for you to decide.' Dolma stacked the receipt books one on top of the other and pushed them across the table before Nyima.

We turned to Gyaltsen. 'I didn't mean it that way. We want you to stay,' Gyaltsen said, looking to us for encouragement. We nodded our heads vigorously. 'Anyway, why don't you and Nyima start going around Delhi to raise money? I think you should start with the restaurant people in New Delhi. They tend to donate more in times like this. Here take these.' Gyaltsen pushed the receipt books across to Dolma. Dolma left the room with Nyima, carrying them under her arm.

Gyaltsen turned to the young Tibetan beside him. 'Pema, you may go now. We'll talk later.' Pema, in tattered jeans and strong boots, nodded and marched across the room.

So there were just four of us in the war-room: the pock-faced general, Gyapon, kurta-clad Phuntsok and me. Phuntsok spoke up first. 'I need help. I won't be able to enlist Indian politicians to speak at our demonstration alone.'

'I too need help,' I said. 'Writing releases, petitions and contacting the press, it's too much work for just one man.'

Gyaltsen had the ruler resting upright on the table, supporting his hands and chin. He released the ruler and it fell with a clutter. 'In that case, you two team up,' Gyaltsen said. Dhondup, you help Phuntsok to find Indian politicians willing to speak at the demonstration. And Phuntsok you help Dhondup with contacting the press and writing the releases. But first start drafting the petition to the Chinese foreign minister. And do it now.'

'And what do we say in the petition?' I asked.

'Two important issues. First, make it absolutely clear that the Tibetans will fight for independence right to the bitter end,' Gyaltsen said. 'To the bitter end. No compromise will be accepted. No delegation diplomacy will prevent Tibetans from re-claiming our birthright and dignity. This must be made absolutely clear to the Chinese.' Gyaltsen strode toward the corner table with the Remington. He shuffled the loose sheets, placing them in a neat pile on the table. 'As for the second point, make it clear that China has no right to initiate any discussion on the border. The border is between Tibet and India, and not between India and China. Only the Tibetan people have the right to make any decisions on the Indo-Tibetan border. And write about the McMahon Line. This should be a message to the Indian government. The validity of the McMahon Line is based on Tibet's treaty-making powers. You can't make treaties without being sovereign. The Government of India can't have it both ways, recognise old Tibet's treaty-making powers to give legitimacy to the McMahon Line and in the same breath deny Tibetan independence.' Gyaltsen handed me the sheets. 'There are more points in these. Use the arguments in here,' Gyaltsen said, jabbing at the sheets with his finger.

Phuntsok and I found a table at the far corner. Phuntsok said he would draft the fight-to-the-bitter-end part. 'I like this kind of stuff. You draft that lawyer's angle, McMahon Line and stuff.' Phuntsok raised his voice and shouted across the room, 'How long do you want this to be?'

'Two typed pages. Anything longer is tossed into the wastepaper basket. Nobody reads it,' Gyaltsen shouted back, as if he knew.

'I bet his was,' Phuntsok said, giggling wickedly. 'He's talking from experience.' Phuntsok rolled his kurta sleeves up to his elbow and his fountain pen flew across the page.

I read the typed sheets Gyaltsen had handed me. It was a well-researched pamphlet. I liked the sarcasm of the title: Sino-Indian negotiations on Indo-Tibetan border. The arguments were cogent and the writing was fluid. It was a fine example of Tibetan exile pamphleteering. 'Where did you get this?' I shouted, holding up loose sheets. 'It's very good. I can't add anything to this.'

'Dharamsala, Centrex,' Gyaltsen shouted back. 'Then tick the points you think should go into the petition.'

I ticked the parts I liked and wrote a connecting paragraph to link Phuntsok's piece to the points raised in the leaflet on the reasons why India had to recognise the independence of Tibet for it to legally lay claim on Arunachal Pradesh. Then I walked out for a smoke. By the time I returned, Phuntsok was done with his piece. We turned over our pieces to Gyaltsen. He said he would get the schoolteacher to type it on TYC letterhead.

'So which politicians do you have in mind?' Phuntsok asked Gyaltsen.

'Any, the bigger the name the better,' Gyaltsen said. He and Gyapon were going over the expenses of the demonstration. These included the fee for the hired buses, the cost of printing the pamphlets, the fee for hiring lawyers to bail Tibetans out of prison in case they were rounded up by the police and food and accommodation expenses for a group of youth activists coming from Dharamsala.

Phuntsok suggested we see Raj Narain.

Gyaltsen thought it was a good idea. 'Yes, go and see him. He is sympathethic to Tibet and will speak at our protest demonstration.'

As soon as Phuntsok and I were seated in a three-wheeler, I raised the issue that had been bothering me. 'Why did Tashi and Samdup do that thing, walking out like that? They were actually trying to sabotage the demonstration.'

'I think it's a political stunt,' Phuntsok said, wiping his face with his kurta sleeve. 'To get support. To recruit members for their party. To let Tibetan refugees know that the communist party is working hard for the cause. I can find no other reason.'

'But you can't play politics with our national cause,' I added, finding it difficult to believe that someone like Tashi could stoop to such a cheap trick. 'Putting their party over and above Tibet. What do they hope to accomplish? A rally of just two commies?'

'Tell that to them,' Phuntsok said dryly. 'But I thought Dolma acted with courage,' Phuntsok commented. 'Don't you think?'

'Acted with courage? She sounded so glib with her "my friend and not my comrade in arms" talk. Tell you something; don't trust anyone who talks like that. I won't be surprised if she passes details of our demonstration to Samdup.'

'No, I don't think so. Dolma means well. Even if she has plans to do that, I think Gyaltsen took care of it when he sent her packing with Nyima on the money-raising errand.'

We reached Ashoka Road and Raj Narain's residence. Before we got off the three-wheeler, a thought struck me. 'We can't walk in like this. With nothing to show for ourselves,' I said. 'We need a letter on the TYC letterhead requesting his presence at the demonstration. And we need khatas to present to him, to show our respect. We need to make this look formal and serious so that Raj Narain will take our request seriously.'

'You're right,' Phuntsok said. He directed the driver of the three-wheeler to take us to Majnu Ka Tilla. In Majnu Ka Tilla we found Gyaltsen and his foot soldiers hard at work. Banners and posters filled the war-room. One poster just said, 'Chinaman, go home!'

I drafted a short letter addressed to Shri Raj Narain, the honourable Member of Parliament, invoking more than 2,000 years of relations between Tibet and India to persuade the honourable Member of Parliament to address the planned demonstration. I hammered on the repeated theme that India was the master and Tibet the disciple. In times of crisis it was the master's moral responsibility to come to the aid of his disciple. I had the draft approved by Gyaltsen. He toned down the rhetoric and asked the schoolteacher to type the letter on the TYC letterhead. Meanwhile Phuntsok and I proceeded to the Gyapon's shack to get hold of khatas. He gave us two silk khatas.

Armed with the missive and the traditional Tibetan gift, Phuntsok and I, fortified and heartened, jumped into a three-wheeler and prayed that the honourable Member of Parliament, Shri Raj Narain, would be at his residence and accept our invitation.

On Ashoka Road in front of a colonnaded one-storey building, the three-wheeler stopped and we jumped out. Phuntsok paid the driver and didn't bother to haggle over the fare.

The place was full of people, petitioners and seekers of favours. We knew instinctively that the great man was home. Suddenly I was swept by a fit of nervousness. 'Phuntsok, we haven't prepared what we should say to him.'

'What?' he said, glancing at me sideways, twitching his moustache and then flapping his kurta to cool himself. 'What's there to prepare? We only need ask him if he'll speak at our demonstration. That's all.'

But my fit of nervousness was eased by the sudden realisation that unlike the usual Indian politicians, who surrounded themselves with a bunch of praetorian guards to either announce their exalted status or to distinguish themselves from the puny masses, Raj Narain kept a simple house. No sign of grandeur, no intimidating bodyguards, no public image cultivated to impress, no trappings of power so that a big, insecure ego could find some reassurance that the rest of the world was at its beck and call.

'Wait here,' the young man, behind the low desk, said when we entered the house. Phuntsok took over the whole venture and whispered something to the young man in rapid Hindi. I was a bit surprised when Phuntsok mentioned the Dalai Lama, several times. The next minute the young man was back. To our delight and surprise he told us to walk in. Just like that.

Phuntsok and I walked into the large, airy audience room. Raj Narain, bare-chested and without the green bandanna he always wrapped around his head in public, was massively lolling on a deerskin spread on a cement floor. A man was massaging his feet.

'Namaste,' quick-witted Phuntsok rushed forward. We presented the khatas and Phuntsok handed over the invitation letter with both his hands. Raj Narain, thinking the khatas were scarves, immediately wrapped them around his neck. Phuntsok got to work without wasting time. In chaste Hindi he thanked Raj Narain for seeing us at such short notice and was at the point of touching the great man's feet in total subservience when Raj Narain tucked in his feet and turned to us with a huge smile. 'How's Lamaji?' the ponderous man asked. He was on one side, his right hand supporting his face, his elbow resting on a large green divan. He looked approvingly at Phuntsok.

Raj Narain's inquiry about the health of the Dalai Lama made the atmosphere electric. It also changed our equation. It made us feel equal. We were no longer the nervous, unsure supplicants, requesting a huge favour from an erratic, unpredictable but important person. But there were more surprises in store. Raj Narain agreed to address the demonstration even before Phuntsok had finished. He asked Phuntsok to give a date and time.

'April 21,' Phuntsok said. He said it would probably be in the morning but would depend on when the President received the Chinese foreign minister.

'You don't know the time?' Raj Narain asked, draining the last dregs of tea from the steel tumbler and tossing the empty tumbler over his shoulders. It clattered on the bare wooden floor. Someone immediately picked it up.

We shook our heads, mournfully.

'Not to worry, I'll find out the time for you,' Raj Narain said. 'Call later. My secretary will pass the information to you.'

Raj Narain snapped his fingers and asked his secretary what his schedule for 21 April was.

His secretary flipped through several sheets of paper on the clipboard and said, 'You are very busy that day, sir, very busy. You are up here,' the secretary said, bringing his free hand to his neck, 'in programmes, functions, seminars, an all-party meeting and parliamentary debates.'

'Keep the parliamentary debates and the all-party meeting. Cancel the others,' Raj Narain commanded, snapping his fingers. He rolled over on his back, crossed his legs, and propped up his head on the divan, gazing at the whirring ceiling fan.

'But sir, you promised to address the World Wrestling Conference and the seminar on good governance and clean elections and later the samellan on the Khalistan imbroglio,' the secretary protested.

'The World Wrestling Conference, oh, that's very important,' Raj Narain said, sitting upright and flexing his arms. 'I must attend that one. I am giving the keynote address. My point is that the World Wrestling Federation must convince the International Olympic Committee to introduce kabaddi as an international sport in the next Olympic Games.'

Raj Narain continued to flex his arms. Turning to Phuntsok, he suddenly asked, 'You play kabaddi in Tibet?'

'Yes, sir,' Phuntsok said, with lightning speed before I could vigorously deny it. My limited bazaar Hindi prevented me from understanding the nuances of Phuntsok's conversation with the minister, but Phuntsok affirmed that kabaddi was Tibet's national sport, a favourite of the monks. In fact he said the Tibetan monks were crazy about kabaddi. According to him there was one whole monastery devoted to the practice of kabaddi. It had the name—Sera. The practitioners of kabaddi in the Sera monastery were called dob-dobs, monks with blackened, menacing faces and huge keys as weapons. 'Kabaddi came to Tibet with Buddhism,' Phuntsok said. 'It used to be an important tool for meditation. Now it is banned,' Phuntsok said with sad, downcast eyes, 'by the Chinese communists.'

'Arrey bhai, suno! Did you hear this? They play kabaddi in Tibet! I told you kabaddi is an international sport! Spreading from India to the rest!' a delighted Raj Narain told his hugely impressed courtiers. 'I must mention this in my speech. Monk kabaddi-wallahs, a tool for meditation! wah, wah!' Raj Narain said, stroking his beard. 'What time does the World Wrestling Conference start?' a beaming Raj Narain, asked of his secretary.

'Eleven in the morning.'

'Keep that one and cancel my appearance at the other two, the one on good governance and clean elections and the Khalistan imbroglio. My appearance at both the good governance and Khalistan seminars won't make the slightest difference. The first one will never come to India, the second will never go away.' His courtiers laughed and, on cue, Phuntsok and I joined in, heartily.

'Well, the two of you can go. I'll be there. And please convey my respects to Lamaji.'

We namaste-ed and walked out. Phuntsok literally crawled to Raj Narain's secretary and pleaded for his direct number. It was given to him. 'Sahib, please remind Barra Sahib about finding out the time of the Chinese foreign minister's visit to the President,' Phuntsok pleaded again. Secretary sahib nodded his head vigorously.

We performed our namastes again in deep gratitude and bowed ourselves out of Raj Narain's audience room.

'How did you do that?' I, asked my friend in wonder after we emerged from Raj Narain's spartan residence.

'What do you think I did?' Phuntsok said, his eyes seriously questioning my intelligence. 'I introduced myself to the young man behind the desk as the Representative of His Holiness the Dalai Lama in New Delhi. The head of the Bureau, in case you don't remember. Don't look at me as if I committed a crime. That's how you operate in Delhi.'

'But how could you? How could you pretend to be the Dalai Lama's representative and then go on to speak on behalf of the TYC. We'll be in deep trouble,' I protested, but then thought the better of it and shut my mouth. In any case, the excitement had caught on and I was bubbling with it, ready to kiss the ground beneath Phuntsok's chappals, every footprint, wherever the mustachioed Phuntsok walked the earth.

But this other side of Phuntsok's personality, the smooth operator, was new to me. 'Phuntsok knows the Indian mentality,' Gyaltsen said, tapping his forehead with his chopsticks when he, as thrilled as I was, took us for dinner at Gyapon's chang shack. 'Put that in the press release, that Raj Narain will speak at our demonstration. That will attract the media. Don't say a word to the communists,' Gyaltsen said. We made a promise and kept our secret.

'The two of you can go now,' Gyaltsen said. 'Gyapon-la and I need to tend to a lot of other work. We have only three days left before the big day,' Gyaltsen said, digging his chopsticks into the chow-mein. 'I want to make it the most successful demonstration. And guess what? The president of the central executive committee of the TYC will be here to address the crowd.'

'We are happy to stay and help you. We have nothing pressing today,' Phuntsok said.

'Much of the work is done,' Gyaltsen said. 'Gyapon-la and I need to seek police permission to hold the rally and hire some good lawyers. The rest is taken care of.'

'You keep saying we need to hire lawyers. Whatever for?' Phuntsok asked, twirling his moustache.

'In case the demonstrators turn unruly and assault the police. People get emotional, you know. We need lawyers to bail them out of prison or get out of police custody. It requires a lot of paper work and legal knowledge.' Gyaltsen wiped his face with his handkerchief.

'Anyway, we'll be hanging out at Ama Penpa's chang shop if you need us,' I said.

'Remember, nothing of the Raj Narain appearance goes to the two communists,' Gyaltsen sternly reminded us. 'And remember to ring Raj Narain's office to get the exact timing of the Chinese foreign minister's call on the President.'

'What do you think the two communists are up to?' Phuntsok asked.

'Search me,' Gyaltsen said. 'It's all drama, man, drama. Trying to get publicity for their stupid revolution. They think that by organising a demonstration Tibetans will come rushing to enrol themselves. Fat chance!'

Phuntsok and I decided to walk back with Gyaltsen to the war-room. The foot soldiers had completed their work. 'Free Tibet' posters were stacked against the wall, ceiling high. There were cardboard boxes full of 'Free Tibet' headbands. I was curious about the one-slogan battle that we were about to fight. 'Earlier we used to have a variety of slogans, like UNO we want justice, China quit Tibet, etc. Why just free Tibet this time,' I asked Gyaltsen.

'Because different slogans confuse people. It also indicates we don't know what we want. Keep one core slogan and stick to it throughout. The core slogan identifies the core demand of our struggle. It tells people what our struggle is about. It will remain in people's mind along after the demonstration,' said Gyaltsen, an old war-horse of protest demonstration battles.

On the day of the demonstration Phuntsok and I were at Majnu Ka Tilla at five in the morning. Six buses were lined up, ready to roll. Through battery-operated megaphones Gyapon and his lieutenants were urging the demonstrators to get into the buses. The early risers, monks, nuns, schoolchildren and scattered men and women clambered into the buses. We marched into the war-room where Gyaltsen was barking orders. On spotting us he ordered us to grab copies of the Sino-Indian negotiations on the Indo-Tibetan border and to go ahead and wait at the intersection of Mathura Road and Raj Path where the procession would start its march to the venue. Phuntsok woke up a rumpled man asleep in his three-wheeler and directed him to take us to Pragati Maidan. Traffic was sparse and we were there before we could recite om mani padme hum a thousand times. We got off on Mathura Road between Pragati Maidan and Purana Qila. And waited.

Phuntsok unloaded the pamphlets from his shoulder bag and ventured onto the street. He stopped passing motorists and others and handed them the learned discourse on Sino-Indian negotiations on the Indo-Tibetan border. Some motorists angrily threw the discourse back at him. Unperturbed his kurta-pyjamas flapping in the pre-monsoon early morning breeze, Phuntsok picked them up and shoved them through the windows of other passing cars. I sat on the sidewalk and smoked, contemplating the jagged outlines of the ramparts of the Purana Qila, a mute witness to the past, the wizened elder brother of the Red Fort. A group of khaki uniformed policemen joined my contemplation of their heritage to act as escorts and minders in case the protest rally erupted in anger.

Around seven, the six buses lumbered by and coughed up the Tibetans who tumbled onto the street and sidewalk like so many illegal immigrants caught crossing the border. Gyapon and his stern lieutenants got to work. Through blaring megaphones they ordered the contingent of monks and nuns to head the procession and to form two single columns. The school children in their uniforms were ordered to march behind the exotic clergy. The other adults were to follow. The Tibetan flag emblazoned with two snow lions in front of a snow mountain lit by a blazing rising sun was distributed. Free Tibet banners and posters were unfurled and everyone wore a Free Tibet headband. A monk at the head of the procession carried aloft a framed photograph of the Dalai Lama. He was followed by two monks who between them shared a long banner held by poles that said 'Tibet's freedom is India's security'. This was followed by a sea of fluttering Tibetan flags and Free Tibet posters and banners. One flag, one slogan. A complex struggle reduced to an extravagant symbol and a defiant slogan.

Gyapon and his lieutenants shepherded the procession under the watchful eyes of the cane-swinging men in khaki. The march started with a chant that almost sounded like a fervent prayer. 'Dalai Lama zindabad,' the megaphones intoned. There was an immediate roar of an echo. And the procession started its slow shuffle on Raj Path, the avenue that ends at the doorsteps of the President's residence.

Phuntsok was still busy distributing the pamphlets. I stopped him. 'You don't need to do this. There are many others who are doing this. We need to go ahead and contact reporters who are at the venue.'

'It's too early,' Phuntsok protested. However, he stopped distributing the pamphlets and we strode ahead of the procession. The venue for the rally had been changed. It was not at the Boat Club, but on the grassy patch in front of the National Museum. Scattered khaki-clad policemen were at the site, looking on indifferently. They were reinforced by plainclothes men of the Intelligence Bureau who kept watch from a distance. Police ropes cordoned off the rally site. Within the cordon a wooden platform was being constructed. On it was Gyaltsen who was supervising the men who were hammering nails into the wooden planks to make the platform. With Gyaltsen were some well-dressed Tibetans and two Indians.

Phuntsok and I, hopefully, looked for reporters. There were none in sight. 'I told you. It's too early,' Phuntsok said.

Gyaltsen jumped off the platform and joined us. 'Where are the reporters?' he demanded.

'It's too early,' Phuntsok countered. 'We told them the demonstration starts at ten. Told them to be here by nine-thirty. It's only eight. And what are we doing at this spot?' Phuntsok asked with dismay. 'It's so far from the motorcade path.'

'Doesn't make a difference. The important thing is that the Chinese foreign minister will hear and see us. He will see the spirit of the Tibetan people.' Gyaltsen started to punch the air and stopped midway. 'No reporters, but here's more of the other ones,' he groaned. We looked in his direction and saw three vans speeding towards our spot. The vans stopped and disgorged more khaki policemen in full riot gear. One van was empty. A jeep had pulled over earlier. The commanding officer and the riot police made their way to our spot. The junior officers were barking into their walkie-talkies.

'Who is Gyaltsen?' superintendent of police K.L. Jha asked, walking briskly towards us. His name tag was clipped on his shirt.

'I am, sir,' Gyaltsen said, almost saluting the man.

'I hope there won't be any more nonsense here,' the police superintendent demanded.

'What nonsense? No, no, sir, ours is a peaceful protest. There won't be any trouble, if you mean that. Here is the police permission slip for the rally.'

'But what about the report we received from Chanakyapuri. Someone pelted homemade petrol bombs at the Chinese embassy! Crude homemade petrol bombs! Explain this,' the officer demanded.

'No, sir, we've got nothing to do with that. The person must have acted on his own.'

'Then how do you explain this?' K.L. Jha whipped out a copy of our memorandum to the Chinese foreign minister. 'This was pasted on the Chinese embassy gate. Look here, this has your name on it. You said you had nothing to do with this. How did the arsonist get hold of this and what is your name doing here?' K.L. Jha asked, slapping the petition.

'No, sir, he was acting on his own. He volunteered to paste our memorandum. But we had no idea he would do this dastardly thing. No, sir, we had no knowledge.'

'You're sure about this?'

'Yes, sir, very sure. And where is the culprit, sir?'

'He's under our custody at the Chanakyapuri police station.'

Gyaltsen shouted in the general direction of the platform which had been done by now. 'Mr Sharma, please come here.' We could hear the distant chants of Free Tibet. Gyaltsen turned to superintendent of police, folded his hands and requested the officer to release the culprit. 'Please, sir,' Gyaltsen pleaded.

'Release him? No, we are charging him with arson.'

'Please don't do this, sir. He didn't mean it. He's a good person at heart and he's all alone in the world, no father, no mother, and no country as you can very well see...to give him good guidance. He's all alone. This might have had an effect on him. Nobody to steer him on the right path. We'll stand surety for his good behaviour in the future.'

'No!' K.L. Jha barked. 'This is not the done thing. We will hand him over to the court. The court will decide.' K.L. Jha walked away, directing his men, deploying them at strategic points.

'We must put this in the press release,' I said.

'You're mad! And claim responsibility. We'll all be locked up in Tihar jail,' Gyaltsen said.

'We don't have to claim responsibility. This is news! Big news! And who's the one who did this thing?' I asked.

'Pema, the one who was with us the day the two communists decided to stage their own separate demonstration.'

Before we could obtain any more official clarification of the petrol-bomb assault, Mr Sharma, the lawyer, walked over. Gyaltsen took Mr Sharma by the arm and guided him towards Jha and his men.

'They'll try to bail him out,' Phuntsok said. 'And that pock-face kept this to himself all the time. Didn't even trust us,' Phuntsok said, beating his chest. But before we could explore the issue further and reason why Gyaltsen kept the assault on the Chinese embassy to himself, we were distracted. The procession was streaming into the venue and the policemen were fanning out. Gyapon climbed on to the wooden stage and speaking through the megaphone, told everyone to sit down.

Once everyone was seated, Dolma took the megaphone from Gyapon. She was the master of ceremony. She blew into the megaphone and told everyone to stand up.

'What's this,' someone muttered. 'Sit down, stand up. Make up your mind,' the critic shouted.

Dolma blew into the megaphone and said, 'Stand up for the Tibetan national anthem.'

A forest of Tibetan flags went up and the anthem was sung. After the anthem, Dolma listed the speakers of the day. She said that Shri Raj Narain would grace the demonstrators with his presence. Meanwhile she requested Gyaltsen to come up on the stage and address the crowd. Gyaltsen made a moving case for Tibet. To his credit, he decided to make his speech short. The president of the central executive committee of the TYC was asked to speak next. He was followed by a loquacious Indian who said that Tibetan independence was around the corner and told the Tibetans never to lose hope. He rattled off a long list of eminent freedom fighters, men and women and their impossible struggles to prove his point.

There were loud whisperings and restlessness. The human sea parted and the bearded Shri Raj Narain, his head wrapped in the green bandanna, accompanied by his smart secretary, climbed on to the stage amidst cheers and loud applause. Dolma gave a short introduction and requested the great man to speak.

'Where are the reporters?' Phuntsok asked, exasperated. 'They should be here by now.'

'Must be in the crowd. It's a big crowd.'

I whipped out my notebook and Bic from my shoulder bag, ready to scribble every word the great man spoke. Raj Narain stood up and waddled past the monk holding aloft the large framed photograph of the Dalai Lama. He grabbed the megaphone from Dolma and bellowed, 'My fellow wrestlers.'

There was stunned silence. Raj Narain's secretary quickly whispered something in the great man's ear. Probably he whispered that this speech was for a later programme, the World Wrestling Conference.

The giant-killer wasn't to be bothered by such petty distinction. 'My fellow wrestlers,' he repeated. 'There comes a time in everyone's life when we need to wrestle. Some of us need to wrestle with our fellow men and women. Some of us need to wrestle with our fears and neurosis. But you,' he pointed at the faces in front of him, 'you are wrestling with a country, a big country, which started the 1962 war with India and still occupies parts of our sacred territory. It is the worthiest wrestling match. But let me tell you, you are not alone in this wrestling match. The Janata Dal is with you.' Raj Narain paused and the expected thunderous applause that followed whipped him into fuming rage. 'The Congress sold Tibet down the river but the Janata Dal when it comes to power again will recover Tibet for you. Yes, the Congress sold you down the Brahamaputra River. That is why you are in India. But we, the Janata Dal, will send you back up the river...to Tibet,' Raj Narain declared. The applause that greeted this piece of promise never seemed to end. 'Yes, my fellow wrestlers, Tibet will never die. This is what our leader, Jaiprakash Narayan said. He said, "Tibet will never die because there is no death to the human spirit." Yes, we will win this wrestling match and when we win, we will install the Dalai Lama on his rightful throne in the Potala Palace. This is not an election promise. This is our party manifesto.' The air was ripped apart with shouts of 'Raj Narain zindabad'. Raj Narain handed the megaphone back to Dolma and stepped down from the stage. He was escorted to his waiting car.

As my eyes followed him and his secretary, I spotted the two communists. Tashi and Samdup were out in the distance. The lama was with them. So was Metok. The lama and Metok held Tibetan flags and were flanked by Tashi and Samdup who hoisted a banner above their heads. Their backs were turned toward us. A photographer was taking their pictures. I nudged Phuntsok. 'The two communists have joined our demonstration,' I said. Phuntsok looked in the direction I pointed and laughed. 'It seems a family affair, almost a family affair,' he commented. 'And they threatened to organise their own separate demonstration. What a joke!'

It was then that I spotted the welcoming committee for the Chinese foreign minister. Out in the distance on Raj Path was a group of people with welcome banners and bouquets of flowers. The group was lined up on either side of the avenue. Several policemen looked and watched the group from a distance. I could hear their chants, Chini-Hindi bhai bhai.

'Are they Chinese?' I asked Phuntsok, pointing to the group.

'Must be,' Phuntsok said. 'No Indian would grovel like that before any Chinaman.' But before Phuntsok could finish venting his contempt for the welcoming committee, he was distracted by the one event we had all been waiting for. 'He's coming!' Phuntsok screamed. 'The Chinese foreign minister is coming!' Beyond India Gate a long motorcade was making its way on Raj Path. 'He's coming! He's coming!' Phuntsok shouted at Gyaltsen who was sitting on the stage.

As if on cue, the crowd surged forward and was confronted by a phalanx of policemen with lathis in hand. The megaphones went ahead of the crowd and police walkie-talkies crackled. Tibetan flags bloomed like flowers and banners and posters were raised a little higher. The megaphones spewed angry slogans that filled the air: 'China quit Tibet' and 'Human rights for Tibetans'. The crowd echoed these slogans in a fervent uproar.

'Phuntsok, I think we should go,' I said. 'We have a lot of work ahead of us, writing the release and distributing it to the news agencies.'

'And miss the action?'

'The action took place at the Chinese embassy when it was lobbed by petrol bombs. This is real and we need to mention this in the release. Let's go, man.'

I noticed that the motorcade had stopped at the spot where the welcoming committee waited. 'Look, I think the Chinese foreign minister will be getting out of the car to receive flowers,' I said.

'No, I think there's some kind of trouble there,' Phuntsok said. 'Look! Look! Some people are lying on the path of the motorcade. Policemen are hauling them up and dragging them away.'

The crowd too had noticed this and an expectant silence fell. The silence was shattered by distant chants of 'Free Tibet' that came from the welcoming committee. 'They are Tibetans!' Phuntsok shouted. 'They are one of us!'

Police walkie-talkies crackled and about ten policemen from our spot dashed to the area where the Chinese motorcade stood still.

Several Tibetans broke the police cordon and rushed forward. They were immediately stopped by lathis. Seeing this, a Tibetan woman assaulted a policeman. Two policemen brought her down and bundled her into the police van.

'Phuntsok, we must go. We have enough material for the release.' I grabbed Phuntsok by the hand and dragged him away from the crowd. We stepped into the first three-wheeler that passed by.

We reached Majnu Ka Tilla. The place was silent. The school hall was empty except for the schoolteacher who sat behind the Remington, reading a novel.

'That Gyaltsen,' I said, 'didn't even bother to tell us that some Tibetans pretended to be a part of the welcoming committee. How are we expected to write releases when all important information is withheld from us?'

'Just shut up and get to work,' Phuntsok said.

'I think the lead should be the petrol-bombing of the Chinese embassy,' I said.

'No! It should be what Raj Narain said. He said his party supports the independence of Tibet. No other party has expressed such unequivocal support for Tibet. That should be the lead,' Phuntsok said.

'In that case you draft it. Here are my notes of what Raj Narain said.' I walked out of the school hall and made my way to Ama Penpa's chang shack. She set a glass of chang on the table, which I gulped. She refilled the glass and I lit a cigarette. Ama Penpa asked how the demonstration went. I explained every detail. She seemed happy when I told her that Raj Narain promised to install the Dalai Lama on the lion throne in the Potala Palace. When I exhausted the details of the demonstration, I asked for a jug of chang and two glasses and took these with me to the school hall. Phuntsok frowned when I placed the two glasses on the desk and poured chang.

'Here, have a look,' Phuntsok said, pushing forward several pages on the desk. He took a sip from the glass. In the draft Phuntsok had Raj Narain's declaration of his party's support for Tibetan independence as the lead. He followed it up by mentioning the petrol-bomb incident at the Chinese embassy and how the Chinese foreign minister's motorcade was stopped by a group of Tibetans who lay down on the motorcade's path.

'Great,' I said and went to the schoolteacher and asked her to type and make about fifteen carbon copies. While she typed, Phuntsok and I took the jug and glasses and went back to Ama Penpa's and ordered momos, which we dipped in chilli sauce and washed down with chang.

'I wonder how Gyaltsen managed to sneak Tibetans into the group that welcomed the Chinese foreign minister?' I asked.

'He must have told them to pose as Chinese, Chinese students who were there to welcome their great leader,' Phuntsok said, indifferently.

'But why didn't he tell us? About the petrol-bomb and this. It helps us in drafting a more detailed release.'

We went back to the school hall. The schoolteacher had typed the release and made fifteen carbon copies, all neat and legible and stamped with the TYC seal. Armed with this clear evidence of the strength of the Tibetan struggle, we, the delivery boys of news of an earth-shattering nature, did the rounds of New Delhi's media circuit.

When we returned to Majnu Ka Tilla, the demonstrators were back. The place was bustling again. Gyaltsen wasn't there and on inquiring we learned that he was with his lawyers at the police station trying to obtain the release of the petrol-bomber and the five Tibetans who laid down on the path of the Chinese foreign minister's motorcade.

Phuntsok and I avoided Ama Penpa' chang shack. We did not want to confront Tashi and Samdup. Instead we went to Ama Bhuti's place and bought several jugs and went back to the school hall. We drank to rangzen, to our demonstration, to the five Tibetans and to Pema of the tattered jeans and strong boots, whom we came to learn, was the one who assaulted the Chinese embassy with the petrol bombs. Late in the evening we heard loud cheers and went out of the hall to see what was happening. A huge crowd had gathered and in the middle of the crowd were the five young Tibetans and Pema. They were being carried on excited, patriotic shoulders and looked as though they were surfing on waves. The crowds were welcoming the day's heroes.

Outside in the school compound the president of the central executive committee of the TYC addressed the crowd and thanked the people of Majnu Ka Tilla for their dedication, and Pema, and the five Tibetans from Dharamsala for their patriotism. We met Gyaltsen later. He said he had managed to bail them out, but every now and then they would have to make court appearances. 'It's a long-drawn process,' Gyaltsen said. 'Will take years for their case to be settled.'

The next day when we opened our newspapers, the two communists, grinning triumphantly, stared at us from the front pages of most dailies.

There was no mention of our demonstration. No mention of the petrol-bomb assault on the Chinese embassy. No mention of the five Tibetans flinging themselves on the path of the Chinese foreign minister's motorcade. No mention of Raj Narain, the honourable Member of Parliament, promising the crowd to install the Dalai Lama in his rightful place in the Potala palace. Just a photograph of Tashi and Samdup, flanking the lama and Metok, holding a banner which declared that the newly formed Tibetan communist party demanded independence for Tibet. The extended captions focused on the Tibetan communist party and carried a few quotes from Tashi saying that communism would be the salvation of the Tibetan people. All the papers carried the same photograph, which was credited to Sygma.

Media savvy Tashi and Samdup had put an interesting spin to the lama's presence at their demonstration. They made it seem that the lama was a member of the Tibetan communist party, a riveting and fascinating news peg.

Phuntsok and I faced the firing squad. 'What happened?' a furious Gyaltsen demanded, the pockmarks on his face jumping up and down, as if on a warpath. 'How come the two communists are in the news and we are not?'

'Why are you blaming us?' Phuntsok said. 'You are the one who withheld important information from us.'

The president of central executive committee of the TYC intervened and said the important thing was that we were able to send a strong message to the Chinese foreign minister. 'This is nothing,' he said.

'Media doesn't make or break our struggle. We have been able to tell the Chinese that we will never give up. That is what matters.'

We called for a truce. Phuntsok and I went to Ama Penpa's chang shack to shake off the demonstration fatigue. There we found Tashi and Samdup smirking over their chang glasses. Phuntsok confronted them. 'I hope you know that a struggle is not made by cheap publicity tricks.'

'We know that,' Samdup said smugly. 'But it helps. Tibetan masses will know that the TCP has their best interests at heart.'

'And revolutions are not made through cheap tricks. Tricking the lama into joining you. That's a cheap trick,' Phuntsok retorted.

'We are not saints. What did Mao say? A revolution is not a garden party. We believe the end justifies the means,' Samdup said, still smirking.

I turned to the lama and asked him whether he realised that Tashi and Samdup had used him in getting publicity for themselves and their party.

'What does it matter? They are doing something for Tibet. Why does it matter whether I join them or the rest of you?'

'I just wanted to be sure. At least you know that you were used.'

'Used? I volunteered. I have never done this before. I went on my own accord. Now it is time I catch my bus to Manali,' the lama said.

The two of us walked out of Ama Penpa's chang shack, cursing devious communists, pliable lamas and youth leaders with political ambitions. We spent the night at the office of the *Tibetan Review* and managed to convince Nyima not to mention a word of the Tibetan communists when he wrote his piece on our demonstration in the coming issue of *Review*. 'The Tibetans need to know only the truth,' he said. He, mustachioed and kurta-clad, was a loyal soldier of the Tibetan exiles' protest rally generation.

Tashi and Metok

☯

I was back in college to collect my stuff. It bore a deserted look. All my neighbours had left, most for their summer holidays and, others who had graduated, to the wider world. Doors left wide open revealed silent, empty rooms strewn with cardboard boxes and paper wrappers. In my room the whir of the ceiling fan and the listless chirping of birds outside broke the stifling silence of the place that once burst at the seams with the effervescent energy and mischief of the young.

When I had done my packing, Samdup, in his usual safari suit but this time appearing as if a starving yak had grazed on it, barged into my room. He was breathless, dripping in sweat, his glasses filmed in a moist haze. He slumped on the chair, panting. Wordlessly, he took off his glasses and polished them. He looked like a monk who had just been defrocked before the entire monastic assembly and banned from reincarnating. Just as Samdup made an effort to open his mouth, Dolma stepped into the room. She looked from Samdup to me and back to Samdup, perhaps wondering what had transpired between the two of us. The blank look on my face must have told her that I hadn't received the breaking news of the day because she demanded, 'Where is Tashi?'

'Yes, where is Tashi? You know where Tashi is?' Samdup asked, coming out of his shock and perhaps remembering the reason why he had suddenly found himself slumped on my chair.

'No!' I shouted. 'You are comrades in arms, aren't you? You should know. You mean to say that you don't know where the other half of the revolution is or what it is doing!'

'If you know where Tashi is, please tell us. It's urgent,' Samdup said. He was pleading. I had never known Samdup, self-confident and brash, in a situation where he had had to abase himself thus. He was doing it now. His communist revolution must have suffered humiliating reverses. 'Metok's pregnant!' Samdup said, as if this explained the plaintive tone in his voice. 'Ama Penpa is raving mad. She wants to play Golok on Tashi...she wants to kill him!'

'Good for her,' I said. 'Means one less communist. Can't blame her. I'd do the same. And doesn't he know that there are such things as condoms? Anyway, how does Ama Penpa know it is Tashi's?' I asked.

'Because Metok said so,' Dolma said.

'Why would Metok do such a silly thing?' I asked.

'Because she wants to live with Tashi, she loves him, you fool,' Dolma shot back.

'Well, in that case, congratulations! You have a brand new member of the Tibetan communist party, a brand new legitimate member,' I said. Dolma stared at me with cold angry eyes. Samdup ignored my comments and went back to cleaning his glasses. We stared at one another in silence. I finally suggested that we step out and we wound our way to the cafe.

'This morning,' Samdup recounted, slurping his coffee, spilling some on his wrinkled safari suit, 'Ama Penpa made her way to Tashi's college.' Tashi wasn't there but Gyaltsen was, Samdup said. Ama Penpa told him to tell Tashi that she was after his blood. She told Gyaltsen that Tashi had ruined Metok's chances of going to Switzerland to be married. 'Gyaltsen was the one who broke the news to us,' Samdup said. 'There was smirk on his face and a wicked gleam in his eyes when he told us this. He's laughing at us. That pock-faced one! This will spread like wildfire in the Tibetan community,' Samdup said, his anxious eyes darting from Dolma to me. 'How are we to get mass support with this kind of story floating around?'

'You should purge him. You form a party and the first thing you get is a scandal?'

'You're missing the point. He is the party. Without him there's no Tibetan Communist Party,' Samdup said seriously.

'Apart from the party and all that, aren't you concerned about what Tashi feels? What Metok feels?'

'Yes, yes, also that,' Samdup said, giving me a look which said I hadn't still got it.

'That's why we need your help,' Dolma said. 'It would be best if Tashi and Metok could live together. Ama Penpa would allow this if only the lama approves of Tashi. So go with Samdup to Manali to give the lama the full story and get his approval for Tashi's marriage to Metok.'

'Why me? Why can't the two of you do it? The two of you need a holiday. I've got to go to Dharamsala, you know that.'

'Dharamsala is next door. Manali first and then you could make your way to Dharamsala. The lama knows you better than us.'

'But I can't deal with these matters. You know these are delicate, personal matters,' I protested. 'You need somebody more mature.'

'That's why Samdup will accompany you,' Dolma said. 'He knows how to talk. That's how he got me,' she said, flashing a smile and coolly sipping her coffee.

But I had a problem of my own. 'What will people think if they saw Samdup and me together in Manali? They will think I'm also a part of the Tibetan communist outfit.'

Dolma flew into a rage. 'Your friend is in trouble and here you are thinking of yourself and your image. You don't have an image. What do you care what people think of you, as long as you can squeeze out a few free drinks?'

I must admit that was true. I did not have an image. The more I thought about the Manali trip, the more I liked it. I would get the chance to hear some more lama stories. I might disagree with Tashi's politics or snigger at his exalted post as the chairman of the Tibetan Communist Party, but at least if this plan succeeded, I would help Tashi acquire a wife who, according to the public opinion of Majnu Ka Tilla, deserved someone far better. Tibetans in Majnu Ka Tilla took a dim view of Tashi's ability to provide for Metok. Instead of happiness and prosperity, they said, Tashi would give her a lot of verbiage and expect her to survive on it. She might get smart in his company, but she would starve. Besides, I would also see a new place. I had never been to Manali and here was the chance of a free trip. But I had to make sure it was a free trip. I asked, 'So who's the jindak?'

'You are like the rest of them,' Samdup erupted. 'A parasite, living off the jindak system. A sponsor for your kids' education, a sponsor for your aged parents living at the old people's home, a sponsor for your monastery, a sponsor for everything. I'll pay, of course,' Samdup volunteered. 'I'll be your jindak.' Samdup said, disgust clouding his face and somehow finding its way down to his safari suit, which seemed to wear the same resentful look.

'Hope it's not coming from party funds? Don't want to be pulled up later in front of the entire politburo for misappropriating precious fund meant for the second liberation of Tibet.'

Dolma burst out laughing. I noticed then why Samdup was attracted to Dolma. It was her laughter, open and robust. When Dolma laughed she had a habit of flinging her head back and at the same time running both her hands at the back of her neck to raise her long, luxuriant black hair and let it tumble down to rest in an overflowing heap on her narrow shoulders. That was how she preened. But Dolma's laughter was the laughter of a woman who knew that in the survival game, a pretty face came in handy but there were other attractions, other skills, which if used with effect could devastate any man. She knew she possessed these skills. When she laughed she hinted at these skills. Her uninhibited laughter arose from the vast, invigorating open spaces of the Tibetan highlands dotted with black nomadic encampments in which, around the fading warmth and ebbing smoulders of the fireplace, beyond the next yak-skin bed, lay promises of shared happiness.

I took a three-wheeler to deposit my stuff at the *Tibetan Review* office and late in the evening took a bus to the Inter-state Bus Terminus where I found Samdup waiting for me. When we reached Manali the next day we walked to the lama's monastery, which turned out to be a two-room apartment in a run-down, two-storey wooden building, mostly occupied by Lahaulis, people from beyond the Rohtang Pass. The lama occupied the ground floor. The door to his apartment opened onto a long, low verandah, which he shared with his next-door neighbours.

There was a short, expectant queue of Tibetans and other devotees, with khatas in hands, khatas as white as the snow of the Tibetean mountains. A couple of tall Tibetans, swaddled in yak skin, manned the nervous queue. The two Tibetans were probably new arrivals because they gave off the stench of Tibet: of butter-tea and unwashed bodies.

Samdup presented Tashi's case in a long-winded sort of way, which put off the lama. He praised Tashi's great qualities, and tried to explain the tragic loss his indiscretion could lead to, especially the damage it would cause to his career. But the more Samdup tried explaining Tashi's predicament to the lama in his high-flown Lhasa Tibetan, the more the lama narrowed his eyes, an indication that he didn't like Samdup or didn't understand what the hell he was talking about. People from eastern Tibet, rough-hewn, straight-talking, had a traditional suspicion of the tactful, polite ways of the people of Lhasa. They knew through experience that no good news lay behind such exaggerated politeness.

Since Samdup did most of the talking, I gazed at the walls of the lama's room. Nineteen thangkas, portraits of all the nineteen Drubtop Rinpoches, hung carelessly from the walls. I examined the nineteenth Drubtop Rinpoche. He was a young man, probably in his mid-twenties with his left eye shut. Permanently. Covered by skin.

At last when Samdup had finished, the lama said he would come with us to Delhi and sort out what he called 'a fuss over nothing'.

'When?' Samdup asked.

'Tomorrow,' the lama said.

The next day we walked to the lama's place to pick him up. He didn't have much baggage, except for his steel box which contained the thangkas of the nineteen Drubtop Rinpoches, a maroon cotton shoulder bag and a larger brown canvas bag which could be zipped and locked. A huge Tibetan in the yakskin, who called himself Rabga, hauled the steel box and the large brown bag, which seemed heavy and probably contained the lama's scriptures. Rabga clambered up the roof of the bus and deposited the lama's box and bag in a secure spot. He clambered down and said goodbye to the lama with a dignified bow. Once in the bus and ready to face the long drive back to Delhi, we discovered that except for narrating Drubtop Rinpoche stories the lama wasn't much of a talker. I slept while Samdup gazed out of the bus window mesmerised. You couldn't blame him because some of the passing scenery was so stunning that you wished you could have them in your dreams. Except for the intermittent jolts and sudden and unexplained halts, I slept all the way to the ISBT.

Samdup said he would accompany the lama to Majnu Ka Tilla. I was headed for New Delhi to the office of the *Tibetan Review*. I saw the two of them off. The lama's bulk filled the taxi and Samdup perched himself on the front seat with the driver. Above the roar of traffic, I shouted that I would come to see them in Majnu Ka Tilla the next day to learn the fate of Tashi. 'He'll be all right. He'll be all right,' the lama shouted back.

Nyima was holding fort at the office, since Editor was away in Mussoorie to escape the heat. Nyima said that most of my friends had left Delhi. Phuntsok had left for Dharamsala, leaving a note with Nyima which simply said 'See you in Dharamsala'.

'Only you and your two communist friends are left in Delhi,' Nyima said. 'By the way, are you with them?' Nyima asked, looking me in the eye.

'No way!' I screamed. 'Tashi is in trouble and I went to Manali to seek help,' I said, alarmed that Nyima could even entertain such thoughts. 'I'm not a part of that communist package.'

'Oh, I see,' Nyima coolly responded, 'But there are mere rumours.'

'Ignore the rumours,' I said and spread out a mattress on the floor and lay down with a thump, switching on the cream-coloured small portable fan to its full whirring strength. I slept off my exhaustion and Nyima's rumours.

Late afternoon the next day, Nyima and I took the Ring Road bus and headed for Majnu Ka Tilla. With the Editor away, it was a slow month for Nyima. He didn't have anything which couldn't wait for the next day.

We got off at the ISBT and took a rickshaw to Majnu Ka Tilla. With some dread I crept into Ama Penpa's shack, still unaware of the fate which awaited Tashi.

There were six of them in the inner room which was filled with the pungent smell of chang and cigarette smoke. They were celebrating something! The lama, Tashi, with Metok beside him, Samdup and Dolma and Ama Penpa were all laughing, drinking and swapping jokes. But Ama Penpa was the happiest of the lot, pouring chang from her favourite plastic jug, the one she reserved for her privileged guests. The lama had worked a miracle. But I couldn't make myself believe that Ama Penpa had accepted Tashi so quickly and with such little fuss into her home. A few days before she had vowed to wring Tashi's neck.

I stood there, mouth hanging open, in stunned bafflement, like some stupid muleteer working himself into a trance after witnessing for the first time the spectacle of an oracle.

'Metok's going to be a mother,' Ama Penpa said in an effort to explain the sudden merriment. She put her paws on my shoulder and dumped me on the empty steel chair. Nyima pushed aside Tashi and sat next to him.

I didn't say anything but stretched my hand for the nearest chang glass and gulped the iced cold drink in the hope that I would find some explanation at the bottom of the glass.

'I have forgiven Tashi,' Ama Penpa explained sweetly, a sweetness quite out of sync with her usual blunt and no-nonsense personality. 'When two young people are in love, this kind of thing sometimes happens. Anyway, the Tibetan man in Switzerland is worse than Tashi,' Ama Penpa whispered, looking sideways at the lama. 'I hear he keeps several women at the same time. And he's old!' she said, with an exaggerated grimace.

'Well then, when's the marriage?'

'We'll have a simple ceremony,' the lama said, grinning. The lama consulted his astrological chart and decided that the following Sunday was auspicious enough for Tashi and Metok to be married.

'Since you are marrying into their family, who will give you away?' I asked, turning to Tashi. 'Someone needs to give you away at the ceremony. Someone has to act as your parent. You are going to be a magpa, marrying into their house.'

Ama Penpa and Metok too were curious. They turned to Tashi and waited for his answer. Tashi took his time responding. He picked up the chang glass and drained it. He set it on the table and nodded to Metok to refill it.

'I've asked Tsering Migmar-la to give me away,' Tashi said. 'And he agreed,' Tashi announced grandly.

'Tsering Migmar!' Ama Penpa screamed. She turned to the lama who had pricked up his ears and stared at Tashi questioningly. Samdup, Dolma and Nyima were alarmed by the fright in Ama Penpa's voice.

'Yes, Tsering Migmar-la,' Tashi said, nodding his head. Tashi looked at the lama in answer to his questioning stare. 'Tsering Migmar-la, the Golok, of the Tangshawa family,' Tashi continued, 'He agreed to act as my parent and grandfather to that one,' he unabashedly pointed at Metok's stomach. 'As grandfather he will guard that one and those related to it with his life. Goloks, Tsering-la said, when he agreed to my request, needed to stick together these days.'

The lama's eyes had a new sparkle in them, in dawning realisation of the deft way Tashi had defused a sticky situation. The lama had rescued Tashi from a 'fuss over nothing'. Tashi had returned the favour. With one masterstroke, Tashi had delicately put an end to a protracted feud that had lasted a century or two. 'That's good,' the lama said. 'It means that he will prevent the past from spoiling our present,' the lama said, telling his prayer beads. 'He is a brave man who is able to overcome inherited hatred.'

I was happy. Tashi was safely married. The lama was at peace with himself once more. Tsering Migmar, the China expert who was reluctantly threatening to reincarnate into an avenging Golok, too seemed to have made his peace with his past and with the lama's grandfather. After the marriage, for a week or so I camped at the office of the *Tibetan Review*, helping Nyima proof-read the articles for the new issue of the *Review*. I also had time to work on the guide on Ladakh, a request from Rigzin, my Ladakhi college friend, who was keen to start a travel agency in Ladakh and had done stints as a guide to trekkers.

I was soon reading everything on Ladakh from the books Rigzin loaned me and from the *Review*'s well-stocked library. I divided the guide into six segments: a brief history of Ladakh, description of the four schools of Tibetan Buddhism, the major monasteries in the area, the three geographical regions of Ladakh, the best time to travel, and hotels to stay and places to eat, though there wasn't too much to choose from in the last. Rigzin too was against the idea of naming all the hotels and restaurants. For him there was only one hotel in Leh worthy of both the rich tourists and the backpackers. Rigzin insisted that I mention Hotel Dreamland, owned by his brother as the best in town. In case, the tourists missed the point, Rigzin made me write a one-page ad on Hotel Dreamland. The selling point for Hotel Dreamland was that it had such luxuries as running water and flush toilets. That itself was of enormous tourist interest. And there were two whole pages on Leh, the capital, where Rigzin preferred the tourists to confine their activities and interest to the enrichment of his brother's hotel.

I dropped in at the Ladakh Dharamsala where Rigzin was camping.

Rigzen was in his shorts and greeted me with a hearty laugh. I took out the brown envelope from my Free Tibet shoulder bag and handing it to him said, 'I hope you'll make lots of money from this.'

'No cash from this, man. We will distribute this free. These tourists, they keep asking questions. I hope this will shut them up for good,' Rigzin said, in an attempt at humour, leafing through the pages. 'This looks great. Thanks. I'll print about a thousand copies. The printer said it would take about three days. By the way, what are your plans for the summer?'

'Going to Dharamsala. I have a job in Dharamsala but that's one month away.'

'One month! Come to Ladakh. Take a break,' Rigzin gushed.

'Can't,' I said.

'It's on the house. It's my way of saying thank you for this,' Rigzin said, waving the envelope.

'If that is the case, yes,' I said, jumping at the idea. It was like going to Tibet.

Rigzin told me to come to the Dharamsala after three days when the first proofs for the guidebook were off the press. 'We'll discuss our travel plans then.'

4

On the Silk Road to Shambala

In Search of a Cave in Srinagar

☯

Two days after the marriage, when the searing heat of the evening was about to be swallowed by the hot, greedy night, I went to Majnu Ka Tilla to see the lama, knowing that perhaps I would never see him again. Ama Penpa had gone shopping and Metok was serving chang to the rickshaw-wallahs who sat silently at high wooden tables, their chang glasses and plastic jugs staring back at them with the same gloom. They were the underdogs, underdogs of even the working class, a people who had nothing to look forward to but another day of grinding work. Metok indicated the lama was in the inner room. Tashi was sitting on a steel, folding chair, his legs stretched out, reading *The Wretched of the Earth*. 'Gathering material for laying the ideological foundations of your party? By the way, your toiling masses are having a silent party in the other room,' I quipped. Tashi looked up, frowned and continued reading. The lama sat cross-legged on the bed, his face impassive, his fingers telling his prayer beads. I mentioned to the lama that I was going on a trip to Ladakh, through Kashmir.

The lama became animated. 'Kashmir?' he said, checking whether he had heard right.

'Yes, through Kashmir, to Ladakh.'

'But that's where the first Drubtop Rinpoche received his teachings,' the lama said. 'In Kashmir!'

'So what about it?'

'Find the exact spot where the first Drubtop Rinpoche met Birupa. Bring photographs!'

I thought the lama was teasing me at first, but I later realised that he really meant what he was saying, almost as if he had spotted the twentieth Drubtop Rinpoche. I asked the lama whether he had discovered the twentieth Drubtop Rinpoche and was on the verge of announcing his identity. The lama nodded. 'In which case,' I said, 'why don't you let him lead you to the exact spot in Kashmir? Will save a lot of trouble. It will also be a method of testing whether your little boy is the authentic reincarnation. There is a saying in the English language, killing two birds with one stone. If he is not able to lead you to the place where the first Drubtop Rinpoche met Birupa, he is not the reincarnation you're looking for. I think it is a great idea. You must try it out,' I said excitedly.

'Find the place,' the lama said, quietly. 'And stop being smart,' he said, his cold eyes staring into mine. 'This is not a game or a time to show off how smart you are. You can always refuse my request but stop playing games with my faith and the faith of many other people.' The lama uttered these words so quietly and with such force of conviction that I inadvertently accepted his request by first protesting the absurdity of carrying it out.

'Find the place? But that's like looking for enlightenment. I'll never find it. And where in Kashmir did the two meet? Did the first Drubtop Rinpoche leave hints, descriptions of the place?'

'The place is called Pallahari.'

'I'm looking for a real place, a place where people still live and can be found on maps. But Pallahari! Is there still a place called Pallahari in Kashmir now? It's like Shambala, everyone longs for it but no one finds it. Pallahari is just a place in a story.'

'A story!' the lama growled. 'It's my faith. And Pallahari is the origin of Tibetan culture.'

'I need descriptions of the place and where it might be located.'

The lama held up his hand. He stood up and lowered the steel box from the wooden shelf. He called it his inheritance and took his time, rummaging through it. He finally found what he was looking for and lowered it on the table. It was a bundled manuscript. He gingerly opened it, mumbling a prayer. 'The biography of the first Drubtop Rinpoche,' the lama said, as he picked up the ancient text and touched it to his forehead. He quickly flipped through the loose sheets. 'Here it is,' the lama said, a broad hint of a smile softening his hard face. He read aloud, 'In the region of Kache, above the wondrous and heavenly valley of Pallahari, abundant with apricots and apples, on the little hill, a day's journey from the shores of the great expanses of water that look like a giant lotus in bloom, on the exact location where the immediate and direct descendants of Emperor Ashoka built a temple dedicated to the Great One, there, on that blessed day, our master, the bringer of the light of the wisdom of India which dispelled the darkness of ignorance of the Land of Snow met his teacher and master, Birupa, the naked one, as naked as a newborn baby, except the beard he wore on his chin.'

'It's here, all in here,' the lama said, his face suffused with a glow of excitement.

I was making furious notes but missed some points and asked the lama to read the passage again. He read the passage, slowly for my benefit.

'Any more information on the place?' I asked, after a while. One question was answered. It was definitely Kashmir. Kache is the Tibetan name for Kashmir and the generic term Tibetans use for Muslims.

'That's all. No other description of the place,' the lama said, bundling the book back in the maroon cloth.

'Wait a minute,' Metok said. She re-filled the lama's chang glass. 'I think it may be Srinagar. There are lakes in Srinagar. And there are lots of small hills which overlook the place,' she said, straightening her pangthen, a symbol of happy matrimony.

'But how do you know that,' I asked.

'Because I've been to Srinagar several times, to sell sweaters in winter. If the great expanses of water is any hint, then it is Srinagar.'

'But small hills, there must be plenty of small hills in the place. I can't go clambering up all of them,' I said, getting exasperated as the impossibility of the task dawned on me. 'But the text says Pallahari, not

Srinagar,' I said, doing a semantic nit-picking in order to shake off the assignment. 'And all this took place centuries back. No one will be able to trace it. You need a team of archaeologists, not a college student.'

'It's a small hill with a cave and a flat rock before the mouth of the cave,' the lama said, with a scowl on his face that brooked no attempt at shirking.

'What if all the hills have a cave and a piece of rock on it? How would I know the real hill?'

'Trust your instinct,' the lama said in an attempt to be helpful.

'Anyway, if I did locate the exact place, what are you doing to do about it?'

'Built a chorten,' the lama said, astonished that such an obvious thing didn't occur to me. 'Built a chorten in his honour, in their honour. That cave, that rock was his home for seventeen years. Despite little comfort, what he learned and mastered on that hill transformed the whole of Tibet. All Tibetans need to know the exact location where their present heritage began. Don't you see?'

'Okay, but I can't promise you anything. I'll try but can't make a promise. But if I happen to stumble on to the place, I'll bring photographs of the place, the cave and the rock included. Remember I will be in Srinagar for a week only, or maybe less.'

'Good. If you are going to do any serious work, I suppose you would need some of this,' the lama said, pushing forward five crumpled hundred rupee notes.

I took the cash. I had one last question for the lama. 'If the cave and rock are so precious to you, why didn't you think about finding them before?'

The lama remained silent. The vacant stare on his face, as if he was looking into the distant future or the past, made it seem that he hadn't heard my question, so I asked again, 'Why didn't you or someone else look for the cave and rock before?'

'Dhondup, I heard your question the first time. I was only pondering on how best to answer it. Don't flatter yourself, but we have the karmic link. You were in my dreams last night.'

'What was I doing in your dreams?'

The lama just stared blankly ahead of him and started murmuring his prayers, his fingers counting his prayers beads. With his other hand he dismissed me. I nodded to Tashi and Metok and stood up to leave. This was news to me and I couldn't help but savour the feeling. Or was this a form of lamaist flattery to ensure that I got the cave-and-rock job done? Just as abruptly the lama motioned me to sit down again. 'You are right. You can't do this thing alone. You need help. Tashi will help you.'

Tashi shook his head in disbelief. 'But I just got married!'

'That's right,' the lama said calmly. 'Because of me. You needn't say thank you. Just do this thing for me,' the lama said in a sharp tone that I had not heard the lama use before. Metok nudged Tashi and he threw his hands up in the air. His seeing right eye looking straight at me. Any object before that cold, angry stare could be laser-beamed into a heap of dust. And I knew I had a problem. 'Tashi won't be of help if he refuses to cooperate.'

'Don't worry, he'll help. You just buy the train tickets whenever you like,' the lama said.

I stared back at Tashi for some reassurance, but all I got was a hard and angry stare. The anger in his eye was quickly reduced to a wink of mischief and a hint of a smile. Tashi nudged Metok who stood up and offered the chang glass to the lama. Her face now lit into a dazzling smile, Metok said, 'Rinpoche, I think I can help Tashi and Dhondup. I know Srinagar. Can I go with them?'

The lama gravely nodded his head and I bowed myself out of Ama Penpa's chang shop.

I wasn't going to rely on my instincts as the lama had suggested and thought of doing some research before leaving. The lama had assigned to me what I assumed was detective work with a touch of spirituality. The broad clues were that the place contained water, perhaps lakes, maybe even a big river, that a son or daughter of Emperor Ashoka had built a temple on the hill overlooking the place and that the place was in a beautiful valley. My immediate task was to find out whether

Drubtop Rinpoche's Pallahari was our modern-day Srinagar. If I was able to establish any connection between Srinagar and Pallahari, my task would be made much easier. When I got back to the *Tibetan Review* office, I looked for books on Buddhism and Kashmir on its well-stocked shelves. The books were silent on any connection between Pallahari and Srinagar. I picked up a battered copy of Gendun Choephel's famous guide to the Buddhist pilgrim spots in India. In it Gendun Choephel had mentioned a hill named Pulahari, but this was located between Rajgir and Patna in Bihar! The Mahabodhi Society of Calcutta published Gendun Choephel's slim volume, *A Guidebook for Travel to the Holy Places of India*, in 1939. Since its publication, countless Tibetan pilgrims were provided guidance by Gendun Choephel's slim volume. How could one of Tibet's towering scholars be wrong?

I mentioned this to the lama who simply said that place was called Pallahari and it was located in Kashmir and not Pulahari. More to the point, the lama said, 'That madman, he did not know anything. His guidebook is full of errors.'

Gendun Choephel had scampered all over India but it seemed he never set foot in Kashmir. There was no mention of Kashmir in his guidebook. Although Gendun Choephel was silent on the Buddhist spots in Kashmir, a poem he had composed in English in 1941, which I had accidentally come across in one of the biographies of the renegade monk came as a gift from the past, and echoed the longings of my own battered, confused soul, and have served as an inspiration since.

> My feet are wandering 'neath alien stars,
> My native land, the road is far and long.
> Yet the same light of Venus and Mars
> Falls on the small green valley of Repkong.
> Repkong, I left thee and my heart behind,
> My boyhood's dusty plays, in far Tibet.
> Karma, that restless stallion made of wind,
> In tossing me; where will it land me yet?
> ... I've drunk of holy Ganga's glistening wave,
> I've sat beneath the sacred Bodhi tree,

Whose leaves the wanderer's weary spirit lave.
Thou sacred land of Ind, I honour thee,
But, oh, that little valley of Repkong,
The sylvan brook which flows that vale along.

I met a fellow Tibetan, a fellow exile, and a fellow wanderer, one who had been there before us and sang about it, lyrically.

However, after several days of trying to play the detective and burying my nose in clueless books, I gave up the search. I just couldn't figure out where the lama's Pallahari was. I took a bus to Ladakh Dharamsala to meet Rigzin to have a look at the tourist brochure on Ladakh and to hand over the leather bag of books on Ladakh I had borrowed from him.

Rigzin, shirtless as usual, was in his bare room on the second floor, with the ceiling fan whirring full blast. I dropped the leather bag of books on the cement floor. Rigzin grinned and handed me the ten-page brochure: *A Guide to Places and Pilgrim Spots in Ladakh*. The brochure loudly and boldly announced that it was printed at Modern Press and published by Ladakh Travels and Tours.

I went through the brochure and was pleasantly surprised to spot some good quality black and white photographs of famous monasteries, Hemis, Lamayuru and Thiktse, the palace in Leh, and of other sites to illustrate my text. There were several photographs of Hotel Dreamland taken from various vantage angles. 'Looks great. I want several copies.'

'Take as many as you like,' Rigzin said, pointing at two bulky, tightly packed cardboard boxes lying accusingly on the floor as if to say that better research could have chiselled them into a finer shape. 'These are going to Ladakh with us,' Rigzin said. 'The first printed guide book on Ladakh. By the way, we leave tomorrow. I bought the train tickets, second class A/C. Here's yours. These two are for your friends. I want these two to be reimbursed.'

'Tomorrow is fine,' I said. I had nothing in Delhi to detain me.

Rigzin suggested lunch. We walked around the temple to the Gyuto monastery's restaurant, perched precariously on the edge of the Yamuna.

While we waited for our food, I explained to Rigzin what the lama expected of me and Tashi while we were in Kashmir. 'Do you know anyone in Srinagar who could help me?' I asked.

Rigzin said he knew the owner of the Lhasa Restaurant in Srinagar, a Tibetan Muslim, who had the history of the town stored up in his head. 'He's the person. He'll know,' Rigzin said, digging his chopsticks into the pile of vegetarian chow-mein on his plate and slurping his soup. 'We'll spend about a week in Srinagar. I have some business to do and I think a week will be ample time for you to get to the bottom of the cave and rock story,' he said, amused.

The next evening, Tashi and Metok reached the crowded, milling, suffocating railway platform of the Jammu Mail before us. Tashi was staring at the masses, his arms folded, his legs astride. Metok wore jeans and was chatting with Rigzin who squatted on one of the cardboard boxes containing copies of the Ladakh guide. 'Ha-ha,' he grunted when I introduced Nyima. He immediately handed Nyima a copy of *A Guide to Places and Pilgrims in Ladakh*. 'I have given him a copy,' I said. 'Doesn't matter, take another,' Rigzin said. He encouraged Nyima to get it reviewed in the *Tibetan Review* or even to print excerpts from the brochure. Nyima said he would mention it to Editor.

That was when the Jammu Mail pulled into the station. I said a hurried goodbye to Nyima. The four of us had the cabin next to the carriage door. A large Bengali family, of husbands and wives and their broods and the patriarch and his wife were already camping in our carriage and some members of the tribe spilled into our cabin. We shooed them away.

As we settled into our seats, a stocky man, in a half-sleeve shirt and jeans, drenched in sweat, entered our carriage and ordered the coolie to push his luggage under the seat across the passageway. He had a bristling military moustache. Sometime later, his wife, plump and panting, followed him. The man gave a sigh of relief as he faced us and started wiping his perspiring face, bald head and hands with a clean handkerchief. He pointed to the fan switch and said, 'Fan, fan.' Rigzin switched the fan on. 'Thank you,' the stocky man said. 'My vehicle took us to platform sixteen, the last one. And the traffic, it's bad! I thought I would miss the train. That was my main anxiety,' he sighed, as he made way for his plump wife. He then pulled out a long steel chain from his bag and started to tie his luggage under his seat. 'Gentlemen use chains, but thieves cut through them like thread,' he said and gave a loud laugh. 'But still, it is better to take precautions.'

Tashi pointed to the man's black brief case and the name tag, 'Wadhwa, is that a Gujrati name?'

'No, no!' he shouted. 'I myself, originally from Pakistan. Lahore. You know the Partition? It made many Hindus to come to India and many Muslims to go to Pakistan. That was in 1947. I was only fifteen years old. Worked as a typist. Thirty-five years of service. Moreover, I retire with pension and other benefits in two and half years' time. I have a son, married and and he has a son.'

'You're a grandfather,' Tashi said pleasantly. 'And I will be a father!'

'Yes, yes, I have been through the father stage. Now I like my grandfather role better,' Shri M.C. Wadhwa beamed, extending his hand to Tashi.

As the Jammu Mail coughed and spluttered out of the station, we dozed off.

The next morning the train stopped at the sleepy one-platform railway station of Pathankot. It was an open air station with a fin-like corrugated blue tin awning, protecting passengers and hawkers from the sun and rain. As the train slowed, the station burst into activity with shouts of hawkers advertising their wares: 'chai garam, coffee, puri, pokora!' On the right side of the Jammu Mail, away from the platform, in the green patches between the tracks several cows and scattered goats nibbled on the grass without bothering to give us a second look. Under the train and between the tracks, scavenging dogs scurried like rats sniffing for leftovers.

About two hours later we arrived at the dismal town of Jammu. We waved goodbye to Shri Wadhwa and his plump wife, and lodged at a spare hotel near the Tourist Reception Centre, next to which was located the deluxe bus stand. Rigzin bought four tickets for Srinagar.

We got up early the next day. Our deluxe bus had all the colour and vibrance of a peacock in full plume. The driver was a strapping man in his early thirties, who spat crisp commands to a young, eager deck hand who doubled up as the ticket collector.

Our fellow-travellers comprised of a sprinkling of excited Western tourists, a group of polite Japanese, several Ladakhi men and women and honeymooners from South India and the large Bengali family who we had first encountered on the Jammu Mail. Their incessant chatter filled the bus and succeeding even in drowning out the loud filmi music the deck hand had switched on. We were delighted to find the garrulous Shri Wadhwa and his plump wife as fellow passengers once again.

Here out in the bracing air of the hills of northwest India Shri Wadhwa's pet topic of conversation was his health. 'Yes, yes,' Shri Wadhwa said, in a manner of someone divulging confidences, 'I retire. Retirement at age sixty. But I'm in good health. Moreover, I can still read without glasses. Look, I really can read without glasses. Yes, that one. Otherwise, I'm fine,' Shri Wadhwa said, patting his stomach. He rubbed his hands together. 'And by the way, you're from Ladakh?' Shri Wadhwa asked, with genuine curiosity.

'No, Tibetans,' Tashi said. 'You know those wandering refugees who peddle sweaters.'

'I see, Tibetans,' Shri Wadhwa said. 'The Dalai Lama's people. A good man. Once I attended a talk of his. Very good, everyone liked him, including myself. It's good that India gave him asylum and that he is our honoured guest. We nearly refused at one point.'

'Refused? To give asylum?' Tashi asked.

'Yes,' Shri Wadhwa nodded his head gravely. He leaned forward on the table and whispered, 'You want to know the real reason why India decided to give him asylum?' He slumped again on the backrest of the steel chair. He chuckled, gently at first, and then his whole body was convulsed, the beginning of a vast mischief shaking his body, playing on his face and dancing in his eyes.

'The real reason?' Tashi repeated, confused. I too wondered why was Shri Wadhwa rolling in laughter.

'Yes, the real reason.' The year was 1959, Shri Wadhwa recounted, recovering from his laughing fit. All the Indian dailies carried the news of the fighting in Lhasa. The Dalai Lama was reported missing. Some papers speculated that he was making his way to India. A representation was made to Pandit Nehru, a strong representation at his Teen Murti residence. Nehru spotted the crowd that had filled the manicured lawn and shouted, 'Mathia, why are these people here?'

'To request the Government of India to grant asylum to the Dalai Lama. You agreed to meet them, Sir.'

Nehru stood up, pushed the chair back and strode across his study room and flung the door of the main entrance of Teen Murti wide open. He confronted the crowd, surveying it from the verandah, lined with flower pots. Now and then Nehru sniffed the red rose stuck on the lapel of his Nehru jacket. 'This Dalai Lama business,' Nehru began, impatient. 'It is an extremely delicate matter. We can't make any hasty decision. There are important factors to take into consideration. One of them is our judgement of Chinese sensitivities. That is of utmost importance. The other factor is the Dalai Lama has yet to make a request for asylum. We will wait for further development. The parliament will be informed of whatever decision the Government of India arrives at. Now off you go,' Nehru said, a little ill-tempered and as always impatient.

'But Sir,' said an old man, clad in dhoti and carrying a walking stick that was more of a hindrance than help. He waddled up, barely able to carry his walking stick. 'But Sir, how can the Dalai Lama request for asylum when he's busy escaping? Please announce immediately that the Dalai Lama is welcome to India. The whole world is watching how India will react. I hope the government's decision will be made according to our traditional hospitality and in keeping with India's dignity.'

'What do we have here? A schoolteacher, teaching me about India's dignity,' Nehru said, his thin lips, quivering with impatience. 'India's dignity will best be served if we are circumspect about these matters. We—India and China—are together in this great partnership of leading Asia on the road to peace and prosperity, after years of western colonial domination. Our partnership is based on the Panchsheel. China's cooperation is vital for the success of carrying forward the five principles of peaceful coexistence so that the whole of Asia, not just India and China, but the whole of Asia, can stand proud in the community of nations. Without Chinese cooperation our vision of a prosperous and peaceful Asia will come to naught. These are the key factors to consider when making a decision on the Dalai Lama issue. Now off you go. I have a parliamentary debate to attend.' Nehru swerved around and was about to march back into his study when a new voice, shouting, 'But Sir,' stopped him. Nehru turned on his heel and faced the crowd. 'What is it now?' he demanded.

A sadhu, clad in saffron, carrying a trident, staggered forward and said, 'But Sir, one of ours up there is residing in Tibet and ...'

'What nonsense is this, one of ours is residing in Tibet? You mean the staff of the Indian consulate in Lhasa? They are safe.'

'No, Sir. I didn't mean that. I didn't know that there was an Indian consulate in Lhasa.' The sadhu pointed his trident up in the sky and continued, 'I meant one of ours residing up there is residing in Tibet. So...'

'Stop this gibberish. You are testing my patience. Gentlemen, I gave you a fair hearing. Now leave!'

'But Sir, I mean Shiva. He is residing in Tibet, on Kailash. If one of our gods can live in Tibet, why can't one of their gods live in India. It's only fair, I say.'

Nehru was about to erupt into a Kailash-sized temper himself. Instead he flew down the steps of the Teen Murti verandah and confronted the sadhu with the trident. The Prime Minister of India, arms akimbo, legs astride, stood before the sadhu and sniffed. 'What's this I smell? Ganja? Hashish? Charas?'

'All three, Sir,' the sadhu replied, sheepishly. 'Only to praise Shiva. Yes, Shiva, the destroyer of all our illusions.'

Thus spoke the child of the original culture. With these words, which made headline news in the scattered hashish joints around the world, the sadhu inadvertently unleashed a new invasion on India.

Having missed out on the earlier assault, these new invaders rushed in, the sadhu's words to Nehru, coming out in whiffs of exhalation, making eminent good sense.

Nehru screamed, 'Mathia!' Throw this bunch out!'

'Also Sir, Parvati is with Shiva. They've been there for ages and not one word of complaint from the Tibetans,' the sadhu said, earnestly. 'No visa-shisa problem from the Tibetans for centuries.'

Shri Wadhwa collapsed on his chair, convulsing uncontrollably. He had been standing to act out how Nehru had confronted the sadhu, arms akimbo, legs astride and his sharp, aquiline nose sniffing the sadhu's mouth. 'And that's the real reason?' Tashi asked, breaking into a hearty laughter. 'Yes, yes,' Shri Wadhwa nodded, tears streaming down his cheeks.

At Metok's pestering Tashi translated Shri Wadhwa's story. Rigzin immediately dozed off, so did I, dreaming of Shiva, sacred Kailash, the stoned sadhu, a furious Jawaharlal Nehru and a cave and a rock on a hill in Srinagar. I awoke just as the bus entered the Jawahar Tunnel, an engineering marvel dug through an entire hill. As soon as we passed through the long spine-chilling tunnel and emerged out in the open on the other end, the soft, translucent valley of Kashmir magically appeared down below the snaking road, lit and gently revealed in the simmering sunlight which bounced off trees and villages and streams. A hidden valley, a Shangri-La!

Early in the evening the bus dropped us off at Srinagar's crowded Lal Chowk, enveloped in a Silk-Road ambience which transformed a journey and made it into a pilgrimage, to some fabled, faraway Shambala with promises of ladened caravans and unknown adventures and loads of merits to last a lifetime.

But the gentle picture of the valley clung hopelessly with the brazenness of the autorickshaw-wallahs. Rigzin bargained hard and furiously with several autorickshaw-wallahs on Lal Chowk. Finally he found someone who seemed less inclined to rip us off our savings. That their haggling took longer than the journey to our destination, Rigzin's sister's apartment, is another matter altogether. Disket, bluff, oval-faced, ruddy-cheeked and clad in a light salwar-kameez, ju-led us.

Disket and Norbu, her husband, worked at the Ladakhi service of the local All India Radio station and the apartment where they lived on Maulana Azad Road was spacious, comfortable and subsidised by the Government of Jammu and Kashmir. Metok said she and Tashi would drive on, some distance away and stay at the same place she used to stay during her sweater-selling days. 'They are very nice people,' Metok said. Tashi added that the two of them would be back in the morning to plan our expedition in search of the lama's hill with a rock and a cave.

Rigzin was eager to catch up on family gossip with his sister and her husband and I spoke no Ladakhi. So after dinner, I went to bed, flipping the pages of my notebooks and wondering whether we would be able to identify the lama's hill on which that historic encounter between India and Tibet took place. The thought weighed on me like a nagging marathon college exams but unlike the exams we did not have any textbooks or extensive lecture notes to rely on for guidance.

The next morning I was up early. Telling Disket, who was busy in the kitchen, that I was going out for a walk, I took a stroll on the Boulevard, squeezed between the lake and a line of restaurants and fancy shops. It was the tourist season and the Dal Lake was swarming with houseboats with small, agile shikaras ferrying well-heeled tourists from their houseboats to the shore or carrying supplies of fresh vegetables to the numerous floating hotels on the lake. The other side of the Boulevard was flanked by restaurants and hotels and expensive shops. They were shrouded in the shadows of a low hill. Was this the hill where the first Drubtop Rinpoche met Birupa? But there were other hills in the valley. It could be any one of these. Anyway, how was I to know that Srinagar was Pallahari except for Metok's suggestion that the great expanses of water in the first Drubtop Rinpoche's biography meant the lakes of Srinagar.

I strode back to Disket's Maulana Azad Road apartment. Rigzin sat crossed-legged on the floor, having breakfast. So was Norbu. There was another man, whom Rigzin introduced as Chhewang, the one who would drive us to Leh in his Tata truck. Chhewang said ju-le and I ju-led back. After breakfast I told Rigzin about the urgency of the task assigned to Tashi and me by the lama and how important it was for us to start our detective work soon. 'I don't want to disappoint the lama. He trusted us to do this for him. The matter is dear to his heart,' I said.

Rigzin was cavalier. 'Relax, man, relax. Why bother about such a thing so early in the trip? You have plenty of time. I told you the owner of the Lhasa restaurant knows everything. We'll pay him a visit this morning. Before that I have some business to attend.'

'What happens if he doesn't have the information?'

'He knows, the man knows everything.'

Just then there were several loud, rapid knocks on the door. The doorknob turned vigorously and Tashi, his face clouded in a severe frown, and Metok, looking radiant, walked in. Rigzin, Disket and Chhewang greeted them. When Tashi had decided sufficient time had been spent on social niceties, he turned towards me and said, 'Let's get started.'

'Start what?' I asked in total bafflement.

'To find the lama's hill, his rock and cave.'

'But we haven't done any serious research. We don't have a clue.'

'There's a certain Mr Namgyal. Metok says he will point us to scholars who could help us,' Tashi said.

Rigzin ha-ha-ed. That was his way of saying I told you. 'Let's go,' Tashi said. 'Metok knows where Mr Namgyal is. Let's be off,' Tashi said again with growing impatience.

'Not so fast,' I said. 'I went through the notes I made of the brief reading the lama did from the biography of the first Drubtop Rinpoche. Maybe we should start with the temple built during the time of Ashoka. This might be a starting-point, rather than taking a cave and a rock on a hill as clues. Still I am not sure whether Srinagar is really the place where Drubtop Rinpoche met Birupa. We need to ascertain that.'

'Then let's start with the hill with the Buddhist temple,' Tashi said. 'But first let's go to Mr Namgyal's place.'

Rigzin volunteered to accompany us. He said he had some business with Mr Namgyal. He asked Chhewang, his business partner, to drive all of us to the Lhasa Restaurant in his sturdy Mahindra jeep. 'Hello, Mr Namgyal,' Rigzin said, when we arrived at his restaurant, taking the large man's hand in both his hands and giving it a firm, respectful shake. 'We have lots of business to discuss but first I want you to meet my Tibetan friends, Tashi and Dhondup, who are here in Srinagar on a mission. To find a hill,' Rigzin laughed.

'Tibetans,' Mr Namgyal said, his second chin drooping over the knot of his striped blue tie. 'Tibetans, I see. Anyway, welcome to Lhasa,' he said lightly. 'Tibetans wanting to find a hill in Srinagar?' Mr Namgyal said, with a sly laugh. 'That's easy. Plenty of hills in Srinagar.'

Tashi explained, firmly, clearly. To our dismay Mr Namgyal slowly started shaking his head, and drumming the table with his fingers as if in deep thought. 'That's a tough one. It's very old history,' Mr Namgyal said gravely. 'But sure, Kashmir was once a Buddhist kingdom, but to identify the place where the two met, that's going to be extremely difficult.'

But he asked us not to worry and gave Tashi the names of two people who might have the information we were looking for. One was a Professor A.P. Bamzai who had migrated from Jammu to Srinagar and had taught at the Kashmir University, was retired now and lived behind Lal Chowk. Mr Namgyal scribbled his address on a paper napkin. The other was an American, a Collin Zimmermann who was doing his PhD. on ancient travellers to Kashmir. Unfortunately Collin Zimmermann was not in Srinagar, Mr Namgyal said. 'He used to eat here, every day. He's in Leh at the moment, doing research.'

'See, I told you, Mr Namgyal knows everything and everyone,' Rigzin said.

'Yes,' Tashi conceded and thanking Mr Namgyal for his information suggested that we go to visit Professor Bamzai after we were done with the Lhasa Restaurant. Rigzin wanted to stay back to discuss business with Mr Namgyal and asked Chhewang to drive us to Professor A.P. Bamzai's place.

'Drive to Lal Chowk and ask anyone where Professor A.P. Bamzai's place is,' Mr Namgyal said. 'Everyone knows Professor Bamzai. 'He's the town scholar. He has written many books on Kashmir.'

On our way to Professor Bamzai's place, I turned to Tashi and asked him the reasons for his sudden enthusiasm. 'It's only a rock and cave story,' I said.

After a long time Tashi turned to me and said, 'Dhondup, you are wrong. The enthusiasm isn't sudden. It has always been there. Now it has been sparked off. You think you are the only one doing research on what the lama requested us to find. You wrong. I have been carrying on my own research, at the library of the Delhi University. I have also met with scholars. All of them think there is a distinct possibility of the cave and rock still existing. Srinagar was once a Buddhist stronghold and the centre of learning for many centuries. Don't you think it would have been easier for Tibetan scholars to trek to Srinagar than to far-off, sweltering hot Nalanda? You don't just have to take notes. Stop and think and use your brain. This is a real study of history. It's called research. Just taking down notes is parroting someone else's biases. We need to get to the bottom of this.' Tashi said.

Chhewang, not understanding, turned his head and good-humouredly asked what was happening. Metok in her sweater-selling Hindi explained. Chhewang for a split second let go of the steering wheel in a gesture as if to say that he couldn't see the purpose behind our wild-goose chase. 'Make money, get rich. Don't disturb the past. Or it will trouble you. It will come to haunt you,' he said.

Tashi wore a scowl. He had his arms crossed in guarded alertness, his eyes, or rather his seeing right eye hidden under dark gleaming glasses, looked right ahead. In broken Hindi I told Chhewang that Tashi was a communist. Chhewang turned around and looked at Tashi with mock concern and pleaded, 'Please don't come to Ladakh. We have been poor, equally poor and now we want to be rich, very rich, all of us, equally rich.' Metok giggled and Tashi burst out in a hearty laugh and assured Chhewang that Ladakh won't be touched by communist egalitarian poverty, not under his watch. Chhewang, the businessman, expressed huge relief and looked confidently at the road ahead of him.

We arrived at Lal Chowk. As promised by Mr Namgyal, it was easy to spot Mr Bamzai's house. Chhewang parked his jeep and we took a by-lane that opened to wide paddy fields. A two-storey building, standing all alone at the edge of the fields, was Professor Bamzai's residence. A tall, slim woman was washing clothes under a water pump. When Chhewang asked her whether Professor Bamzai lived here she drew the fold of her sari across her face and shouted, 'Papa, Papa' and fled up the wooden stairs. A tall man, in his sixties, dressed in a kurta and pyjamas, stared down at us from the wooden banister that framed his small upstairs verandah. Seeing who it was, a foursome belonging to an indeterminate race, he said, 'Yes? I'm A.P. Bamzai.'

'We're from Delhi University. Doing research on the Buddhist period in Kashmir,' Tashi said, trying to elevate our status before the scholar of Srinagar. 'Mr Namgyal of the Lhasa Restaurant said you could help in our research, or at least answer our questions,' Tashi said.

Professor A.P. Bamzai hesitantly beckoned us upstairs. We climbed the stairs and on the way Chhewang said he wouldn't be staying long. He needed to get back to work. That was okay with us. Metok wanted to go back with Chhewang.

We namasted our way into Professor Bamzai's study room, which had an unimpeded view of the hills and mountains. We had to slip off our shoes since the floor of his room was thickly carpeted. Shelves were stacked with books on Kashmir. In the far corner, next to the main window stood a bare wooden table and a low, easy chair where Professor Bamzai enthroned himself, legs stretched out, his hands gripping the armrest. This was the only part, which was not carpeted and revealed a mud floor.

Tashi explained the details of our research while Professor Bamzai sat back on his chair, silent, observing. The professor had alert eyes, sunk in deep sockets festooned with bushy, bristling eyebrows which branched over his glasses, like a hairy eye-shade. He wore a threatening scowl that started from his eyes, settled on his grim jaws and drooled down his grey beard like the first drops of a sudden burst of monsoon. Now and then his eyes softened into a brief spell of compassion or curiosity, or of some deep sadness. His shoulders, like his room, drooped with the weight of centuries of scholarship. After a while Professor Bamzai leant forward from his chair, his legs apart, his hand resting on his walking stick, and demanded, 'Which period are you researching on?' Professor Bamzai asked, unexpectedly, a faint hint of interest brightening the severity of his face.

'Sixth century,' Tashi said quickly. 'We are particularly interested in the Indian master Birupa who taught a Tibetan called Drubtop. They spent seventeen years together here in Srinagar.'

I'd had enough! I couldn't take Tashi's long-winded explanations anymore. I brushed aside Tashi's explanations which could easily misfire and told Professor Bamzai the truth, the whole story: our chance encounter at a chang shop in Majnu Ka Tilla with the lama who was in search of the twentieth reincarnation of the Drubtop Rinpoche and the stories he told of the first and the last Drubtop Rinpoches. Professor Bamzai, listened, his head cocked to one side, sometimes lifting his glasses to focus on my facial expression or the movement of my eyes, trying to assess whether this was another concocted story. I pleaded strongly on behalf of the lama and his unshakable belief that the place where the first Drubtop Rinpoche met his teacher could still be found in Srinagar. When I had finished, Professor Bamzai vigourously tapped the mud floor with his walking stick. In answer, the tall, slim woman appeared hovering at the doorstep, uncertain of what was expected of her.

'Beti, chai,' Professor Bamzai barked.

'I see, interesting,' he mused, turning his attention back to me after he had ordered his daughter to make tea for us. I interpreted this to mean that Professor Bamzai might help.

'And why is this lama interested in making this search, the search for the hill in Kashmir?'

The lama, Tashi explained, was the abbot of the Drubchen Monastery situated in Kyitsel which lies in the Amdo province, in northeastern Tibet. Drubtop Rinpoche was the monastery's highest incarnate lama. The last Drubtop Rinpoche, the nineteenth incarnation, and the lama were half-brothers. The last Drubtop Rinpoche was struggled to death by the Chinese communists and the lama fled his homeland to India, like thousands of other Tibetans. 'The lama thinks that it is here in Kashmir that the first Drubtop Rinpoche mastered the various branches of Buddhist learning at the lotus feet of his Indian teacher. The lama wants to identify the spot where this historic encounter took place between India and Tibet and he wants to celebrate the event by constructing a Buddhist stupa,' Tashi said. 'But we don't have any clues. Or means of tracing this encounter.'

'Yes, you're right. You can't prove anything if no traces of such an encounter are left,' Professor Bamzai said calmly, sipping tea and gesturing to us to do the same.

'Traces of the encounter after nearly thirteen hundred years?' I said, astonished. 'Even if the two had built an entire city, it would be hard to trace it now.'

Professor Bamzai ignored this and said, 'Now we need to establish that Srinagar was the place where the two met. What did the lama say was the name of the place where Birupa and the first Drubtop Rinpoche met?'

'Pallahari. There was a hill overlooking the place. A temple, a Buddhist temple, was built on it by one of the descendants of Ashoka,' Tashi said.

Professor Bamzai stood up and walked to a shelf from where he picked up a thick book and waddled back to his chair. 'Kalhana's *Rajatarangini*, the chronicle of Kashmir, written in the twelfth century, annotated by Max Mueller himself,' Professor Bamzai intoned, as a way of explanation, adjusting himself in the chair. I thought Professor Bamzai was making excuses for the sheer size of the book because he kept repeating Pallahari like a new mantra, as he flipped through the pages of the tome. I made a silent prayer that the book would reveal the site of that famous partnership. After a while, Professor Bamzai looked up from the book and said, 'No Pallahari here. During Ashoka's time Srinagar was known as Puranadishtana and later in the seventh century as Pravarapura, the old official name of Srinagar, but no Pallahari.'

'Wait! Say those names again,' Tashi said.

'Puranadishtana and Pravarapura.'

'Perhaps Pallahari could be a Tibetan corruption of Puranadishtana or Pravarapura. Pronunciations change when rendered into another language,' Tashi said.

'Possible, possible,' Professor Bamzai said, nodding at Tashi, a tiny trace of a smile appeared on his lips. 'But here we are on a scholarly research and need to prove our thesis with solid empirical evidence,' Professor Bamzai said. 'Deductions, logical conclusions are fine. These form, if you like, the circumstantial evidence, but we are looking for solid, incontrovertible evidence. Scholarly research is like detective work. You go through a process of elimination. Anyway tell me what the lama said about the place. There may be clues there.'

Tashi gave me a prod in the ribs and told me to read from my notes of the lama's reading of the biography of the first Drubtop Rinpoche. I took out the notebook from my bag and read the passage. 'This is from the biography of the first Drubtop Rinpoche,' I explained to Professor Bamzai who was cradling his chin in his hand. I read the passage, slowly, 'In the region of Kache, above the wondrous and heavenly valley of Pallahari, abundant with apricots and cherry trees, on the little hill that overlooks the great expanses of water that look like a giant lotus in bloom, on the exact location where the immediate and direct descendants of Emperor Ashoka built a temple dedicated to the Great One, there, on that blessed day, our master, the bringer of the light of the wisdom of India which dispelled the darkness of ignorance in the Land of Snow met his teacher and master, Birupa, the naked one, as naked as a newborn baby, except the beard he wore on his chin.'

'Naked, except the beard he wore on his chin,' Professor Bamzai repeated. His face did not break into a smile at this piece of ancient humour. 'Come, hand that dirty notebook to me,' Mr Bamzai, demanded. He took his time reading the passage consulting his volume of *Rajatarangini* every now and then.

'I think we can say that Drubtop Lama's Pallahari is our modern Srinagar,' Professor Bamzai gravely announced. Before we could make any excited interjection, he continued, 'Look here, here in your passage it says "the great expanses of water which look like a giant lotus in bloom". That's a revealing metaphor, don't you think? I think it refers to Wular Lake, the big brother of Dal Lake. Wular is the biggest expanse of water in Kashmir. In ancient times Wular Lake was called

In Search of a Cave in Srinagar 177

the Mahapadma or the Great Lotus Lake. Doesn't the giant lotus in bloom of Drubtop Lama's passage capture the meaning and imagery of the Great Lotus Lake? Wular Lake is about thirty kilometres up north,' Professor Bamzai said.

A surge of excitement swept over me. I could sense the same excitement suffused Professor Bamzai. There was a glint of scholarly thrill in his eyes, his nostrils were quivering, sniffing for ancient scent. I looked at Tashi. His face mirrored my emotions. Tashi took off his glasses and ran his hands over his face. He questioned Professor Bamzai's connection between the reference to the giant lotus in bloom and Wular Lake. 'But that's just an inference. What about the solid empirical evidence you were talking about? How could we prove this conclusively, with facts, evidence? If only we could locate an Ashokan temple on any of these hills, then we would have solid, archaeological evidence in our hands,' Tashi said.

'That's right,' Professor Bamzai said. 'We need empirical evidence. However, we have two inferences. The first is the one which yourself pointed out: that Pallahari could be a Tibetan corruption of either Puranadishtana or Pravarapura. The second is the lotus lake connection I made. In research that's a lot to go by. But you're right, we need factual evidence and most importantly, we need to locate and identify the hill where a Buddhist temple was built during the Ashokan era. That will clinch the matter.'

As he said this, Professor Bamzai stood up, gazing at the view of hills and mountains from his window. He stood there for a long time, his back turned against us, his gaunt, tall figure silhouetted in the soft evening light, silent, brooding. Suddenly, he turned around and faced us with the full force of his scholarly passion and thumped his walking stick on the mud floor in the manner of the Buddha calling upon the Earth to bear witness to his enlightenment. 'But I have found the hill, some ten years back!' he proclaimed.

'You have?' I managed to bleat, a wave of relief and faith surging up and lashing against the rock of scepticism, producing a whisper of a collision.

'Yes, I have!' Professor Bamzai announced. The professor was actually doing a scholar's equivalent of a strut, dexterously twirling his walking stick and throwing it up in the air and catching it in mid-fall. 'Some ten years back.' He strode to the nearest bookshelf and picked up a book and dropped it on Tashi's lap. 'It's all there,' he said. In Tashi's hands was a copy of *Buddhist Kashmir* by A.P. Bamzai.

'It made news, here in Srinagar and across India,' Professor Bamzai said.

'And which hill is it?' I asked.

Professor Bamzai peered over his glasses, ignoring my question. Very much the professor in the comfortable world of his lecture-room crowded with admiring students, he launched into a discourse on the main points of his discovery. 'Emperor Ashoka introduced Buddhism to Kashmir,' Professor Bamzai said. 'His was the first historical name we come across in *Rajatarangini*. According to the Tibetan historian Taranatha, Emperor Ashoka gifted the valley of Kashmir to 5,000 Buddhist monks and built viharas for them. From Kashmir he sent missionaries to the whole of the northwest, including the kingdoms of Taxila, Gandhara and Bod, a reference either to Ladakh or Tibet, and onward to the Central Asian kingdoms of Transoxania. Because of Ashoka's efforts the string of Silk-Road kingdoms from the principalities in Chinese Turkestan through the numerous kingdoms in Central Asia to Ladakh and Kashmir vibrated with a common Buddhist culture. A son was born to Ashoka, one Jalauka, and when he became of age, his father gave him independent charge of Kashmir. Jalauka was the one who constructed the temple in his capital city of Puranadhistana, dedicated to the Buddha Sakyamuni.

'Well, this is my thesis,' Professor Bamzai said, taking out a handkerchief from his kurta pocket and wiping his mouth. 'I needed archaeological evidence. What did I do? I consulted the writings of all those who had visited Kashmir, particularly that of Huen Tsang, the famous Chinese traveller who did so much for Buddhism in China. The passage you brought from the Drubtop Lama's biography wasn't available then. Even without it I managed to locate the hill,' Professor Bamzai said.

The conclusive clue, Professor Bamzai said, which converted his tentative scholarly conjectures into full-blown conviction was in Huen Tsang's writings, who wrote that in Pravarapura, where he spent about four years, he constantly prayed on Vihara Hill before a temple which stirred faith because of its elegant simplicity. The Chinese traveller said the low hill ornamented by the temple was located east of the beautiful lake of Pravarapura and this scene constantly brought to him memories of his own native Chang'an. According to Huen Tsang the temple on Vihara Hill was considered particularly sacred because it was built and consecrated by the son of emperor Ashoka.

My legs were aching from sitting cross-legged for so long and to ease the ache I stood and did a little walk-about. 'And which hill is it?' I asked, wanting to get to the bottom of things. I was a little bored of Professor Bamzai's historical details.

Without paying heed to my query, the professor continued, 'So what did I do? I organised an archaeological team, naturally, from the local office of the Archaeological Survey of India.'

'So which hill did you go digging?' I demanded. I wanted Professor Bamzai to name the hill and skip the details.

This time Professor Bamzai glowered at me, raising his glasses, disapproving of what he considered to be youthful impertinence. 'Be patient,' he growled. 'I know you want the name of the hill so that you can tell your lama that you have discovered the Drubtop Lama's hill. I deliberately avoided telling you the name because I want you to go through the pain and dismay of historical research. Didn't Marpa do this to Milarepa, didn't Tilopa do this to Naropa? And you want it just like this,' he said, flicking his fingers in the air.

I sat cross-legged on the floor in humble supplication before the scholar of Srinagar.

Equipped with the clues Huen Tsang had left, Professor Bamzai said, he went to see Mr Gupta, the director of the Archaeological Survey of India, Srinagar branch. Mr Gupta was sceptical at first and refused to give Professor Bamzai access to the resources and skills of his department. 'So I asked the man, what he stood to lose. Nothing. Whereas if my research was correct, he would have the credit of finding one of the riches of ancient Indian history,' Professor Bamzai said. 'Someone who had added to our knowledge of ancient India.'

That, Professor Bamzai said, proved to be the carrot before the donkey. Led by Professor Bamzai and Mr Gupta, the archaeological team drove to the foot of Shankaracharya Hill. 'That's the hill you are looking for,' Professor Bamzai said. 'It is Shankaracharya Hill. We can't see it from here. But it's the little one in the east overlooking the Boulevard and the Dal Lake. And the rest, as they say, is history,' he said, sipping his tea. 'The ruins of the temple were found, along with coin offerings, little Buddha statues and terracotta figures of tutelary deities. Archaeological examination supporting my own research, proved that the temple ruins, the style and quality of the coins and the statues belonged to the Ashokan era. The news made headlines, here and nationally, and Mr Gupta was promoted as the director-general of the Archaeological Survey of India, Dehra Dun and I wrote that book, the first of its kinds.'

'And did you find a cave and a rock?' I asked.

'No, I wasn't looking for a cave and a rock. I was looking for ruins of a Buddhist temple built during the reign of Ashoka and I found them,' said Professor Bamzai, an exasperated tone creeping into his steady voice.

But this left us with nothing, practically nothing. The lama instructed us to look specifically for a cave and a rock. 'In which case, this doesn't prove that Shankaracharya Hill is the hill where the first Drubtop Rinpoche met Birupa,' I said.

'You fool! You have found the damn hill!' Professor Bamzai burst out. 'And what did you say your name was?' Professor Bamzai demanded, suddenly.

'Dhondup, friends call me Don,' I said, breezily.

'Don! Well, Don, it seems your mission matches your name. It's quixotic! Quixotic! You fool, use your imagination. Put two and two together. What do you think we have been doing all this time? Putting two and two together. We have two inferences and one solid fact, all derived from the Drubtop lama's biography. That Pallahari is a Tibetan corruption of Pravarapur or Puranadishtana, that the giant lotus in bloom refers to the Great Lotus Lake or the present Wular Lake and the passage from the Drubtop lama clearly states the hill had a Buddhist temple, built by the direct descendant of Ashoka. And there are the ruins of a Buddhist temple on that hill. What more do you want as way of proof?' Professor Bamzai demanded, nostrils flaring.

'A cave and a rock on a hill,' I said again.

Tashi was having a quiet laugh at my discomfort and I realised what Professor Bamzai said made perfect sense. We had for all practical purposes found the Drubtop Rinpoche's hill. The thrill induced by the rapid advances we made in our research was shattered by his daughter who shouted, 'Papa, papa'. The shouts came from below but as soon as they died away the daughter was at the door telling Professor Bamzai that Rigzin and Chhewang had come to pick us up. 'Go away,' Professor Bamzai said.

'May we see you again? Tomorrow?' I ventured.

'What for? You've found what you have been looking for. Haven't you?' Professor Bamzai demanded.

'Yes,' I conceded and folded my hands together in sincere namaste and thanking him profusely for all his time and hospitality, made a quick exit.

'What a peevish man,' I complained when we were out of earshot.

'Peevish?' Tashi said. 'He's brilliant, man! Wish we had professors like him in college, instead of all those sermonisers. Professor Bamzai,' Tashi said, walking ahead and swinging around to face me, his forefinger wagging in my face, 'has found the hill for us. He's done all our work for us. You are the one who's peevish, peevish and silly. Nagging on about the cave and rock. And you still don't seem to get into your head the stunning significance of the work Professor Bamzai has done for us. You are just a note-taker, and you don't even understand the significance of the notes you take down. We have a lot to thank Professor Bamzai for. He has changed, no, he has discovered our true past,' Tashi said.

Rigzin interjected and asked, 'You didn't find your hill?'

'Yes and no,' I said, testily. 'I think we have found our hill. We have yet to find our cave and rock. The hill is there,' I said, pointing to Shankaracharya Hill. 'But we are looking for a hill with a cave and a rock. And Professor Bamzai said there's neither a cave nor a rock up there.'

Tashi turned to me and said, 'Tomorrow we'll make an assault on Shankaracharya Hill. We'll call on Drubtop Rinpoche and his teacher.'

'Sure,' I said.

Professor Bamzai's Tibetan Theories

☯

Tashi strode importantly into Disket's apartment early the next morning. He was buoyant but alone. Walking with a bounce in his step, he rubbed his hands in nervous excitement. 'Let's go!' he almost shouted, pushing us forward with his hand as though coaxing us to confront past mysteries, to battle history's demons. 'Let's make this assault on our hill.'

Ignoring his commander-in-chief attitude, I asked, 'Where's Metok?'

'I told her to stay back. She has friends visiting her.'

'But we need her help. Wasn't she the one who volunteered to help?'

'What help do we need? The hill is there,' Tashi said impatiently, pointing his finger toward the rising sun casting long shadows from behind Shankaracharya Hill. 'We have to simply climb it and find the cave and rock and we don't need a guide to do this.'

'As you wish,' I said, not wishing to turn Metok's absence into the subject of a prolonged argument.

That was how we launched our two-man expedition to Shankaracharya Hill. Just like that. Just with a few words that substituted a detailed discussion and careful planning.

The good thing about Srinagar was that it was a manageable town, any part of the town could be reached by walking. The walk was pleasant enough but when we reached the foot of the hill our explorers' enthusiasm turned into moans of disappointment. The local TV tower taunted us. The trace of antiquity and our hopes of stumbling across a major historical relic dissipated in the drab, familiar presence of the Information Age. Regardless of this, spurred on by Tashi's stubborn instincts, we soldiered on and trekked past the Hindu temple. On top of the spur we discovered that Shankaracharya Hill constituted three hilltops. We clambered all over the three spurs but found no cave or rock. On top of the eastern-most spur were the ruins of the Ashokan temple, discovered by Professor Bamzai. A half-hearted attempt had been made to cordon off the place. A rusting tin plaque, its coat of paint peeling off, nailed on a wooden pole stuck to the ground simply said that this was once a Buddhist temple built during the reign of emperor Ashoka, a grudging confirmation of the spot's historicity.

From here we could see the city of Srinagar lying below, the buildings and streets with scurrying ant-like figures of people and cars and beyond that the numerous lakes and the Jhelum River which snaked its way through the luminous valley. Did the view from this spur remind Huen Tsang of the glories of his native Chang'an? The summit had a gentle incline on the western side where we stood. In the east it dropped sharply about ten feet down into a wide plateau covered by an overgrowth of shrubs, undersized firs, starved birches and an enormous mass of tanglewood. Tashi stood at the edge of the precipice, looking down at the plateau covered by the overgrowth. He stood there for a long time, silently. The buoyant glow still visible on his face. I joined him and stared down the precipice and asked, more to myself, 'I wonder what's down there?'

'Seems to be a tableland, taken over by the jungle,' Tashi said in response, not taking his eyes off the overgrowth. 'Yes, I too wonder what's under the jungle. No sign of a cave and a rock, though. But this is the hill,' he said with conviction.

'We need proof and not a statement of assertion. The lama told us to look for a cave and rock,' I said.

'The cave and rock don't matter,' Tashi said. 'We could tell the lama that we found his hill minus the cave and rock. We have the words of Professor Bamzai and he is an exacting scholar. The ruins of the Ashokan temple are another piece of irrefutable historical evidence. The lama could build his memorial to Drubtop Rinpoche on Shankaracharya

Hill. If only we could hire extra hands to clear the overgrowth down below,' Tashi said.

'And after clearing the place, what if we find no cave and rock?' I said. 'It will be a lot of money wasted.'

'I know,' Tashi said and we reluctantly made our descend. On the way down Tashi asked whether I had a copy of the lama's stories with me. 'Yes,' I said. 'It's at Disket's apartment.'

'Let's go through that. Perhaps there are some clues there.'

At Disket's apartment, I handed Tashi my notes and said, 'Good luck. You seem to reek of desperation. The first Drubtop Rinpoche's stint in India is here,' I said, opening my notes.

'I'm testing the accuracy of your notes,' Tashi said heatedly and immediately started reading, loudly. '"In the valley of Pallahari, Drubtop came across this pretty girl. The Tibetan translation of her name is given as Dolma. Drubtop didn't speak her tongue and Dolma was ignorant of Tibetan. But this hardly mattered. As the months passed, Drubtop became competent and even fluent in her language. The early Tibetan translators were that sort of people..."' Tashi stopped abruptly, slamming down the book and demanded, 'What sort of notes are these? No useful information in them!' He frowned and went back to the notes and read aloud. '"Some magic made him follow the path which led him to the top of the hill and to the mouth of a cave lit by the flood of morning sunlight rushing in. In the cave was seated Birupa, the best of all teachers. Drubtop had found his lama."' Tashi paused and thought. 'That I think is a clue,' Tashi said, excited. Hear this, 'a cave lit by the flood of the morning sunlight rushing in'. This is the clue. The cave faced east to receive the morning sun. Let's go to Shankaracharya Hill again,' Tashi said, pushing me forward. 'The eastern-most spur. That's the spot.'

We rushed back to the eastern-most spur of the hill beside the ruins of the Ashokan temple. Tashi stood at the edge of the gentle incline that sharply dropped off in a precipice and he peered at the overgrowth at the bottom. 'So much for your clue,' I said to Tashi who picked a stone and flung it down the precipice. Ignoring my comment he said, 'I'm researching, Tibetan style.' I gave Tashi a puzzled look.

'See here,' Tashi said in response, 'stone hitting stone produces a sound, if there is a rock down there. Unless we engage a whole army to clear the overgrowth, there is no better way to find out.' Tashi picked up another stone and flung it down the precipice, but we couldn't hear a sound. That was when I thought Tashi's stock of wind-horse started falling.

I don't know how it is with other people, but for Tibetans a good portion of our existence is geared towards increasing one's wind-horse, a combination of good karma and good luck, with lots of spiritual grace thrown in. The wind-horse rituals are our own private lines of communication to the gods of Tibet. We perform the rituals by stringing woodblock-printed prayer flags from treetop to treetop. Or from the summit of a hill we hurl prayer flags that carry the image of a flying horse with a wish-fulfilling jewel hunkered on its back in the hope that the wind would carry the horse and our prayers to the demanding, tempestuous gods.

One rule of thumb of the wind-horse ritual is to never throw down stones from a summit, any stone from any elevated ground. Instead you build a cairn and each traveller would add his share of stones to this landmark claimed for the gods of Tibet. Throwing stones down a summit will cripple your wind-horse and send it stumbling down the precipice. In crippling your wind-horse, you shorten your life and reduce your stock of good fortune.

Tashi continued pelting stones, quite oblivious to the peril he was putting his wind-horse into. But that day on the summit with a stiff breeze whipping our faces, I think Tashi, the communist, was less concerned about Tibetan beliefs and more focused on research, Tibetan style. The overgrowth was too thick for the stones to cut through and reach the ground below. No luck. He looked around for more stones and spotting a big one, he picked it up with both hands and to my surprise mumbled a prayer. He spat on it as a form of communist benediction. Then lifting the stone and aiming it at the eastern edge of the jungle below, he flung the stone with all the force he could muster. It ripped through the overgrowth and landed with a loud 'thwack!', the welcome sound of stone greeting rock.

Call it premonition. When Tashi stood with that pose at the edge of the summit, his legs apart, his hands above his head holding the stone aloft, I was gripped by dark foreboding and overcome by a sense of disasters to come. I shouted, 'Tashi, be careful!' The force he used to hurl the stone made him lose his balance. I dashed to grab him. But I was too late. Tashi plunged down. The speed with which I made the dash swept me over the precipice and with hands and legs kicking and flaying in the air, I followed Tashi down the precipice. This was the end. I was going down to meet our cave and rock. As long as I had my consciousness about me, I remember screaming my guts out, spreading out my hands in the hope that they would spout wings. The sky and the clouds rushed backwards and disappeared into a receding whirlpool of nothingness.

I regained consciousness, I don't know how long we lay there, a few minutes, perhaps a few centuries, and was instantly aware of the pain in my back. I opened my eyes. Just scratches, no major damage. My wind-horse had saved me. Streaks of sunlight streaming through the canopy of undergrowth above me lit the floor of the tableland with a soft, subdued glow. A giant freak ivy had gathered together all the overhanging foliage and formed an interlocking roof over the place. Luckily for me, I fell on a mass of undergrowth of thick shrubs of saffron and rhubarb, cushioned by grass and leaves.

'Dhondup, we found them! The cave and the rock are here!' I heard Tashi's excited shout.

'Are you all right?'

'Of course, I'm all right. So are you, by the sound of it,' Tashi said.

Lying as I fell, flat on my back, I glanced sideways and spotted a large rock, covered in moss. I slowly turned on my stomach and looked ahead and believe it or not, the mouth of a cave that wore the unmistakable yawn of centuries stared me in the face! Yes, we had found Drubtop Rinpoche's cave and rock! Our wind-horse had never flown higher, nor with such accuracy.

Tashi was some yards away, trying to recover his glasses that had been caught in the tanglewood above him. Finally he succeeded in retrieving them.

'Let's enter the cave,' I said, excited, frightened and shaken.

'No, let's call extra hands to clear this mess,' Tashi said, dusting his shirt. 'We can't do this alone. We must have help. Let's inform Professor Bamzai. I think, he'll get official help for us.'

We fought our way through the foliage to the edge of the plateau, jumped down the steep ravine and crawled on all fours to the footpath on the other side that led to the summit of the spur. As we walked down the footpath, I tried to sum up the significance of what we had discovered. I turned to Tashi and said, 'We have found the place where the Tibetan Word was minted, the Word that articulated our culture.'

'Yes,' Tashi said with good humour and then continued, 'Yes, your word, not mine, your culture, not mine,' and strode ahead down the footpath. I didn't want another ideological argument to spoil the joy of our discovery and as I straggled down the footpath, eager to give news about our discovery to to the simmering valley below.

'Professor Bamzai! Professor Bamzai!' I shouted when we reached his place. The professor, clearly disturbed by our unwelcome sight, glared at us from the upstairs verandah, his hands gripping the banister in an attempt to control his flaring temper.

'We have found the cave and rock! They're on the third spur,' I blurted out excitedly.

'What happened to the two of you?' Professor asked, instead, eyeing our torn shirts.

'We fell, but we found the cave and rock. It means we have found the spot where Drubtop Rinpoche spent seventeen years of his life.'

'But I have already proved it, you fool,' he shot back.

'But this is physical evidence.'

'Fine, so you have your proof. Now what do you want from me?'

'Your help, Sir,' Tashi intervened. 'Your friends at the Archaeological Survey of India could get the place cleared. The cave and rock are buried under a whole jungle,' Tashi said.

'Well, why don't you clean up first,' Professor Bamzai said, pointing to the water pump. He looked at us with the slightest hint of amusement and said that he would speak to Mr Dogra, the new director of the local Archaeological Survey of India. 'He's a good friend and I think I will be able to persuade him to clear up the hill. You look exhausted, after your... fall from grace.'

On the way back, Tashi said he wanted to go to the nearest post office to place a call to the lama. He wanted the lama to visit Srinagar as soon as possible.

Professor Bamzai was right. I was exhausted, mentally and physically. Reaching Disket's place, I immediately took to bed, happy to be alone, trying to weigh the import of the discovery. I dreamed of flying, riding on the back of my wind-horse and landing on top of the rock. While I explored the cave and surveyed the rock, my wind-horse nibbled the grass at the mouth of the cave. When I emerged from the cave, my wind-horse was nibbling the English alphabets. Half-eaten letters fell at its forelegs, only to be scooped up again.

My dream of the wind-horse munching vowels and consonants at the mouth of the cave gave way to a brilliant morning. But clearing the tableland took more than two days. On the morning of the third day Tashi, Metok and I, as suggested by Professor Bamzai, made our way to his place behind Lal Chowk. Mr Dogra, the director of ASI and his assistant, Mr Bhatt, were already in Professor Bamzai's study.

'Well, we should make a move,' Mr Dogra said. 'Let's go and see how far my men have done their job. I think they must have cleared the place by now,' he added, beaming. We drove to the foot of the Shankaracharya Hill in ASI's open jeeps and made the ascent to the summit. A whole army of workers was on the plateau, hacking away. They had already cleared a large patch. We could spot the rock; it had a flat surface and was situated at the edge of the plateau. We stood on the summit in silent wonder. A stiff, cool breeze fanned us as we watched the workers toss the debris of deadwood and hacked foliage down the edge of the plateau. Once this was done, their boss told us that we could come down to have a look.

'The throne of Solomon!' Professor Bamzai whispered, with breathless awe as we stood at last gazing at the find. It was a throne. The plateau formed the seat of the throne and the cone-shaped precipice the backrest. The mouth of the cave, lit in the streaking sunlight, was still giving the yawn of centuries. Mr Bhatt, equipped with a powerful torch led us into the cave but the torch was not necessary. Sunlight lit the whole cave, all the way to the innermost corner. It was bare except for three stone slabs. One was aligned on one side of the cave wall and the other on the opposite wall, separating the two was a rectangular slab. 'Must have been used as beds and table,' Mr Dogra commented. Mr Bhatt, the young, budding archeologist, shone his torch in every unlit corner, on every darkened cave wall, sniffing, looking, searching, scanning for history's leftovers. Professor Bamzai on the other hand said he was feeling claustrophobic and lowered himself out of the cave. Tashi, Metok and I stayed on with the two officials from ASI. Looking at the two stone slabs, I wondered who used which bed. After a while, Professor Bamzai shouted from outside the cave, 'Mahesh, have a look here. There's some sort of writing engraved here on the rock.'

Professor Bamzai was standing on the rock, facing us, his back to the sun. There were stone-steps leading to the rock. We mounted them and reached the rock to look at the script engraved on it. 'Here, here, here,' Professor Bamzai said, pointing to distinct letters with his walking stick. 'They look like the Sarada script to me, of Brahmi origin,' Professor Bamzai said.

Suddenly Tashi screamed, 'It's the Tibetan alphabet!' making us all jump. I went over to his side and stared down. The letters did look like the ancient Tibetan script. 'It's true after all, Drubtop Rinpoche invented the script. It's huge, it's a huge discovery!' I screamed.

'They look like the Sarada alphabet to me,' Mr Dogra frowned, ignoring our excitement and walking to our side to look down at the engraved script.

'Sarada or whatever, I can read this!' Tashi said and rattled off the entire Tibetan alphabet.

'Yes, very much a Sarada derivative of the Brahmi,' Professor Bamzai said, looking at the script from our angle.

'But this is Tibetan, Tibetan,' I shouted.

'Yes, yes, we can see that,' said Professor Bamzai, nostrils flaring again. 'We're not about to take your script away from you. This is

Tibetan. We agree. But we are saying that this script is derived from the Sarada alphabet, which is directly descended from the Brahmi script. The Sarada script once flourished throughout the northwest, Gandhara, Pakistan, Ladakh, Jammu, Himachal, the Punjab, Delhi and here in Kashmir. It's used here even today though it is confined to the Hindu priestly class. Your Drubtop Lama must have learned it from Birupa.'

Professor Bamzai then launched into a specious theory of Kashmir's evangelisation of Tibet. He said the evangelisation of Tibet had a political motive, to subdue the hordes of Tibetans who were harassing Buddhist Kashmir. 'Not to subdue them by force of arms, but to convert them to Buddhism, to stop them from harassing Buddhist Kashmir.' Professor Bamzai said the idea came to Durlabhavardana (627-663), the founder of the Karkota dynasty of Kashmir. His kingdom was penetrated from the north, through the corridors of Baltistan and Gilgit, by these marauding hordes. They had already occupied the outposts of Hunza and Ladakh. There were rumours that they would descend to the Valley through the impregnable Dzoji-la. Before that catastrophe occurred, Durlabhavardana sent emissaries to the Tibetan king who he heard was amenable and even well disposed to Buddhism and had taken a Tang Buddhist princess as his queen. He chose Shyambhadra, an astute administrator and a scholar of vast knowledge, to head the delegation. Laden with gifts the royal caravan wended its way through Ladakh where it picked some Ladakhis who spoke the Kashmiri dialect and across the bleak barren land and beyond to the Tibetan capital. In Tibet, Shyambhadra because of his Buddhist erudition and vast knowledge of distant lands rose to be a minister of the Tibetan king Songtsen Gampo (620-649). And Tibetan harassment of Buddhist Kashmir stopped.'

'Professor Bamzai is a miracle!' Tashi said afterwards. 'And I thought the lama was talking crap when he related the first Drubtop Rinpoche's story. This will make news.' Tashi, the iconoclast, dying to overcome Tibet's past, to correct our perspective, was going full blast when I turned to him and asked, 'You believe in all that nonsense? What proof did he produce, except a scholar's ranting? No proof, except theories! A theory is nothing but an opinion and everyone has one.'

'The cave and rock, that is evidence enough, man!' Tashi said. 'That is good enough for me.'

That night I pored over the notes I made of the story the lama had told me of the first Drubtop Rinpoche and I came across this passage which in the light of Professor Bamzai's Tibetan theory made interesting reading. It echoed his conspiracy theory and made it more plausible. It was an excerpt of a speech given by Gar Tongtsen, an able and important minister of Songtsen Gampo, to the first group of students Tibet ever sent abroad, as chronicled in the biography of the first Drubtop Rinpoche. According to the biography, Gar Tongtsen made this speech to the first Drubtop Rinpoche and his group,

> You are being sent to India to master the art of
> reading and writing, and the ideas and philosophy
> of the country. Tibet is a powerful military state.
> But military force is fickle. It is here today and
> gone tomorrow. Far more than military might, ideas
> will hold our empire together. It will make our people one.
> Arrows rust, bows no longer bend and swords
> lose their sharp edge, but ideas, no matter how
> defunct, tend to retain their power.
> Well, go and get those ideas
> and bring them back to Tibet in writing,
> whatever that means!

Tibet defeated by an idea? I mulled. Did the conversion of Tibet really happen this way? Was there a plot to convert Tibet to Buddhism, to tame the country and avert military harassment? Or were they mere theories. I didn't think there could be an answer. Any one of the theories could be dressed up in the shining garb of truth.

Anyway, I was grateful to Professor Bamzai for coming up with this theory. It opened up many historical possibilities, possibilities trapped in the past but waiting to be released. Past possibilities imbued the future with similar promises. They made you look forward to the future, rather than seek for things in the wreckage of the past. Or was it the other way round? The future merely an excuse for the past? An excuse because it always, sooner or later, turned up as the past. I didn't really know. But above all, Professor Bamzai's theory was an affirmation of our historicity: a people with a past, bad or good, but still a people with a past. Because we had a past we were a people with a future. This thought made me happy because refugees were dismissed as people without a future. That was why we were called refugees, seeking refuge and shelter in someone else's future. We were the gatecrashers, fleeing our present and gatecrashing into a future defined and shaped by somebody else. Tashi's and my fall from the eastern-most spur of Shankaracharya Hill landed us in our past. Yes, we had found our past, at least some of it, and this was an omen that numerous possibilities lay in the future.

The next day all Srinagar newspapers carried the story. *Greater Kashmir*, Srinagar's English paper, announced the discovery thus: 'New discovery confirms Kashmir's evangelisation of Tibet'. Kashmir's better known paper, *Kashmir Times*, had a witty headline: 'Tibetan Refugees Stumble on Their Past'.

That day also brought the lama to Srinagar. He took the first available flight from Delhi. It was Tashi who came to Disket's place to say the lama had arrived. We hurried to the Tibetan Guest House and I gushed, 'We have found our past for you!'

The lama squinted at me and said, 'Dhondup, the only thing you've found is your faith.' He said he wanted to visit Shankaracharya Hill, the home of the first Drubtop Rinpoche as soon as possible.

The place was guarded by three khaki-clad policemen, courtesy the Government of Jammu and Kashmir. I ran to the rock and shouted, 'Here's the rock with the Tibetan alphabet.' But the lama paid no attention. He was prostrating before the entrance to the cave and encouraged Tashi and Metok to do likewise. Before he lowered his massive frame into the cave, the lama slipped off his brown Bata shoes, folded his hands in reverence, and entered the cave. I pointed to the three stone slabs. On each slab the lama offered a khata while murmuring a prayer. He stood in there for a while and when he came out, I pointed to the rock and the script engraved on it. I started to climb the rock when the lama shouted, 'Come down immediately.'

'But the script is up there, engraved, on top of the rock,' I said, surprised.

'That ground is sacred,' the lama said, as a way of explanation. He prostrated three times before the silent rock before placing another khata of the finest Benares silk on it. Touching his forehead to the big stone, he launched into another round of prayers. He then lumbered to the western edge of the plateau, facing the cave and rock, his back against the evening sun, and sat down, cross-legged. Pulling out a pile of scriptures, he started reciting from the text, now and then twirling his damaru and ringing his vajra bell. The rituals lasted a good half hour. Tashi and Metok sat beside him. I was a little bored and started to light a cigarette when the lama motioned to me, with all the ferocity of a marauding bandit, to desist. I quickly snuffed the matchstick. At last he was done. He folded his text and wrapped it neatly in the maroon cloth. Finally, we made our way down Shankaracharya Hill.

Tashi urged the lama to visit Professor Bamzai to thank him for his help. The lama agreed. He referred to Professor Bamzai as a terton-pa, a discoverer of buried treasures. The lama and Professor Bamzai hit it off right from the word go. These were two people who were destined to meet. The lama offered Professor Bamzai a long silk khata and a small statue of the Buddha and through Tashi thanked the professor for using his knowledge for the discovery of the place Drubtop Rinpoche stayed for seventeen years. He said of all the pilgrimages he had made in Tibet and India, there was nothing to compare with the depth of faith his pilgrimage to Shankaracharya Hill stirred in him. That hill, the lama said, would become an important monument of the efforts made by Kashmiri and Tibetan scholars to introduce the light of Buddha's teachings in the dark land of Tibet. The lama said that Professor Bamzai was a true Buddhist master.

For the lama's benefit Professor Bamzai briefly dwelled on the history of Shankaracharya Hill. It was also called The Takht-i-Suliman, or the Throne of Solomon. Professor Bamzai said the hill was called Shankaracharya either in deference to the two Hindu kings who ruled Kashmir in the ninth century, Shankara and Charya or named after Shankaracharya, the famous Indian scholar who did much to revive

Hinduism in the four corners of India. He went through the list of the Kashmiri scholars who had visited Tibet and helped in the translation of the Buddhists texts, but made no mention of his Tibetan theory. He also assured the lama that he would see to it that he was able to complete his stupa. 'After all,' Professor Bamzai said, 'this spot marks the meeting point between Tibet and Kashmir.'

The lama had found the source of his faith and Professor Bamzai a piece of Kashmiri history. This made them share a common past.

That evening the lama hosted a dinner for us at the Tibetan Guest House. After dinner, the lama handed me a thousand rupees for my pains. It was a fortune! I stared at the lama in disbelief. He also put a fine silk khata around my neck. 'With Tashi you've discovered our past,' the lama said with a wink and grin. 'Now go and discover your own future. I am confident that as you have so spectacularly stumbled onto our past, you will also stumble onto your karma and your future. You seem to have the knack,' he said, patting me on the shoulder.

But I had a question for him. I wanted to know whether he was any closer to revealing the identity of the twentieth Drubtop Rinpoche, now that we had found his cave and rock.

The lama simply put his finger on his lips. It was his way of saying that the constellation of the stars and the karma of the day didn't allow him to make the important announcement. The lama shook his matted head with immense finality. I wondered who the lama would identify as the twentieth Drubtop Rinpoche. It certainly seemed that he had someone in mind. The question was, who?

The next day the lama, Tashi and Metok returned to Delhi. The lama said that he was determined to build a stupa on what he called Drubtop Rinpoche's hill with Professor Bamzai's help.

I headed for Ladakh.

Shambala Dreams

☯

We set off for Leh in Chhewang's Tata truck. The truck, a cross between a grunting yak and an unyielding camel, was packed a metre high with provisions for Hotel Dreamland: rolls of tissue paper, cups, saucers, glasses, plates, spoons and forks, chopsticks, vegetables, noodles, sacks of wheat and rice and tins of vegetable soup. 'We're ready for the kill,' Rigzin said, his face brightening at the prospect of a busy tourist season ahead.

When the truck negotiated the Dzoji-la, we knew we were on the Roof of the World. A biting wind churned in the valley, picked up pace and lashed our stone-cold faces. We sniffed the air and looked at peak after peak of rolling desolation canopied under an azure sky lit by a brilliant, cold sun.

There are places that trigger your imagination. Landscapes to which you immediately relate. Just seeing them, breathing that air, walking those paths, you surrender to them. You say to yourself, I'm made of this earth, of these mountains. The dust and stones of this place are in my bones. The woolly clouds pinned to the sky like a picture postcard are my hopes. This recognition became immediate in Kargil, where we spent the night.

'That road,' Rigzin explained, pointing north, 'leads to Zanskar.'

I thought I heard Rigzin say that the road led to Shambala, a homeland once vividly imagined and still meditated upon. As the imams called for the evening prayer through the loudspeakers, and cries of 'Allah ho Akbar' filled the one-street town, you knew that you were enveloped in the magic of the Khyber Pass, the gateway that saw the march of armies and ideas that shaped India and beyond. You could almost hear the tramp of soldiers' feet trapped in the mountain air, the roar of their victorious trumpets. You realised that locked in these mountains, were the spells and mantras that created Shambala. And the Silk Road that took in Srinagar and Leh in its ambit enabled the cross-fertilisation of ideas that moulded Tibet. We were in the birthplace of spiritual Tibet. You felt it in the mountain air and in the haunting magic of the stark landscape. You knew that these mountains were once the playground of the Gods of Tibet and you knew that you had entered holy ground.

Shambala is a promised land. The Silk Road a grand highway that led you to a prayer that ringed a spiritual homeland, a sanctuary so closely guarded that it is allowed to exist only in enlightened minds. Shambala and the Silk Road! They conjure up visions of weary travellers, stout in heart, leading their caravans across the deserts of Central Asia, determined to make their way to Shambala. And how you wanted to be a part of one of the caravans, set against the background of fantastical sandscapes, the elastic shadows of camels and travellers stretched across the dunes by the setting sun! This is the yearning of every schoolboy whose wanderlust is sparked off by books of explorers. And you ask, did the Silk Road finally lead to Shambala, once upon a time? Islam and the expanding Taklamakan desert buried both the Silk Road and the towns that thrived on the traffic and commerce that flowed on it. With the loss of the road, did we lose the way to Shambala forever? In Tibetan mythological memory Shambala is located northwest of Tibet. Were the oasis towns, that once served the Silk Road civilisation and which for a long time in history were thriving centres of Buddhist learning, the source of Shambala rumours?

With these thoughts swimming in my head, I slept the night in Kargil and dreamed of Leh, awashed in a Silk Road cosmopolitanism. I dreamt of caravanserais. Of merchants, monks and pilgrims. They came from neighbouring Yarkand and Kashgar, Ngari in Tibet, Gilgit and Hunza, Kashmir, Lahaul and Spiti and as far away as China. Amongst them were tall, fur-hatted tribesmen from beyond the Hindu Kush, with red hair and red beards and eyes as blue as Tibet's Turquoise

Lake. In the bustling crowd were high Tartars from High Tartary and low Tartars from Low Tartary. Just as I was marvelling at the diverse ethnic composition of the bazaars of Leh, the lama of Hemis monastery passed by with his retinue on a sedan chair in a colourful, trumpet-blaring procession. The Buddhist crowd lined the street, clucked their tongues and stuck them out to prove their innocence, of not reciting any black, un-Buddhist mantras, which made tongues black and hearts blacker. The high lama parted the tasselled curtain of his sedan chair and inspected the rows of tongues stuck out in respectful greeting. Seeing no black tongue, he nodded, beamed benignly and raised his hand in benediction.

I turned right and came across a large door that led to an enormous courtyard. I entered the courtyard and stepped into an assembly hall. Sitting on a high throne was Huen Tsang. Kow-towing before him were the great Central Asian explorers. None other than Marco Polo headed the distinguished delegation. He was followed by Sven Hedin and Aurel Stein, the manuscripts they plundered weighing heavily on their hunched backs. They recited the mantra of world exploration. 'We will go where no man has gone before and find what has not been found. But you, O, the first of all travellers were there before us and found and brought back what was not found and brought back before. Your journey to the west is our sutra, our tantra and our daily mantra.'

Huen Tsang raised his hand in benediction and said, 'Now go and find Shambala. And don't steal anything. Ask permission first if you must bring back anything.'

Perhaps Huen Tsang Rinpoche needed some updates on the latest developments. As I was about to raise a point of objection, Huen Tsang, looked at me and said, 'By the way, take that one with you. Yes, that one who has just crept in without invitation,' Huen Tsang said, pointing his famous forefinger in my direction. 'He looks familiar, probably one of the characters I encountered on my journey to the west, perhaps one of those barbarians who attempted to loot my Indian wisdom scriptures. Take him with you to Shambala.'

That was exactly what I wanted to hear. I shouted my joy in the assembly hall, 'I found the Word. Now I will find the Place!'

Aurel Stein stepped forward, the manuscripts still pressing him down. He kow-towed before his patron saint and said, 'Huen Tsang Rinpoche, he'll become my ward. I'll unload my textual loads on him. He'll be my beast of burden, my ship of the desert, the carrier of the ancient Word.'

'Very good, make him your ward,' Huen Tsang said, still sitting cross-legged on the throne, his hand held up in benediction. 'As I said before, no stealing this time.' Huen Tsang was now wagging his finger at Aurel Stein, like a teacher admonishing an awfully bright but naughty student who was pickled in kleptomania.

'I'll make sure he doesn't steal this time,' I volunteered. 'I, his beast of burden, his ship of the desert, his carrier of the ancient Word, will refuse to carry any stolen goods.'

Huen Tsang eyed me suspiciously. 'I'm not sure. I think I remember you. You are one of the barbarians who tried to loot my Indian wisdom books. I'm sure of this. No, it will not do. It will be like the thief being confronted by a bandit. No, you carry what you have been told to carry.'

The delegation of noble travellers turned to me and looked at me in utter disgust. The noblest of all travellers then beamed forth rays of courage and wisdom on the awed, assembled crowd. That was how Huen Tsang sent us off to Shambala, a caravan of the mind, the place of dreams, that already emerged from the horizon, its golden roofs glittering, gleaming and drawing us forward. And I shouted a form of farewell and expression of gratitude to Huen Tsang, 'I have found the Word and the source of the Word. Now I will find the Place and the geography of the Place. We are going to Shambala! And I thank you Huen Tsang Rinpoche for this great honour.' Up in the sky was Huen Tsang, riding on a cloud, driven by a breeze. He continued to beam rays of courage and fortitude on men and beasts alike.

'No, not to Shambala, we are going to Nimmu!' The next thing I knew was that I was being vigorously shaken by Rigzin, 'Wake up, man. Wake up! Time to go. We'll be in Nimmu this evening. And stop this, I'm going to Shambala nonesense.'

That early morning as we headed for Nimmu in the dangerously lurching truck winding its way between overhanging cliffs and deep canyons, I wondered what the lama would make of this dream.

The Ladakh Interlude

☯

On arriving in Nimmu I discovered that the lama was right. I did discover my karma. I found myself a Ladakhi wife. Thinking back on it, I suppose the landscape of Ladakh had something to do with it. It was as barren and scarred as the moon with the same haunting glow which could catapult people to flights of fantasy. Or, perhaps it was just the fact that a wandering man like me had finally reached the place where I belonged. In that old and familiar environment I felt I belonged to something. Or something belonged to me.

Whatever the reason that triggered my impulse, as soon as my dazzled eyes spotted a pair of ruddy cheeks, I decided that the one thing that to me was Skelsang. I found her in Nimmu's oasis of a village where we spent the night before reaching Leh. I ju-led her. She ju-led me back with downcast eyes. The downcast eyes did it. I strode to Skelsang's parents' house and greeted them in respectful ju-les and more to the point demanded their daughter's hand, or rather her cheeks, in marriage. They didn't return my ju-le. On the contrary, Skelsang's parents viewed me with grim suspicion. They thought me mad. Then they burst out laughing and their laughter was echoed by the bare hills, which reverberated down the mocking green valley washed by the Indus River. The Indus River! That reminded me of something. The Senge Khabab, From the Lion's Mouth, Tachog Khabab, From the Horse's Mouth. I must say I got the inspiration from the horse's mouth. Skelsang and her parents were drinking Tibetan water. They were made of Tibetan stuff. As I said, I got this from the horse's mouth. With this sudden burst of an inspiration for an argument, I left them laughing and marched to Rigzin's house to solicit his aid as an interpreter, matchmaker, and go-between. Rigzin too burst out laughing.

'You don't strike me as the type interested in girls,' Rigzin said.

'I am the type and I'm interested now. Very interested.' The look on my face must have convinced him of my earnestness or desperation. He grabbed a copy of *A Guide to Places and Pilgrim Spots in Ladakh* and marched off. I followed hot on his heels to Skelsang's parents' house. The pair hadn't got over their laughing fit, which congealed into icy Himalayan seriousness when they spotted Rigzin. He spoke in rapid-fire Ladakhi, now and then showing the tourist brochure, as if to say there was enough money in those pages to turn their amusement into a profitable business proposition. After Rigzin had concluded his argument for a potentially great business partnership, the mother and father, a practical pair not easily fooled by new-fangled ideas of the young, made a gesture of putting food in their mouth. Rigzin swung around and asked, 'They want to know how you're going to support her?' Rigzin then slipped into literal translation. 'They want to know how you will tsampa and butter-tea her?' Rigzin asked, pointing to Skelsang, who stood demurely with downcast eyes.

I mentioned my job at the Library of Tibetan Works and Archives in Dharamsala. 'That's how I will tsampa and butter-tea her.' I also pulled out the thousand rupees the lama had given me and I said I could also start a business. 'Sweater-selling,' I announced. 'Whatever Skelsang prefers. Here's the capital,' I said, with the naivety of one who had suddenly risen from rags to riches.

The parents ignored this and instead asked me what my salary would be at the Library of Tibetan Works and Archives. I mentioned the princely sum of three hundred and seventy-five rupees per month. They were dismayed. They showed it by sticking out their tongues, as if feeling sorry for their daughter or me.

'Sweater-selling' the father made me promise, pointing his index finger high up in the thin Ladakhi air.

'Yes,' I said, putting up my hand in the air in the manner of the US President promising to deliver the desired goods. 'From Nagpur to Kanpur, I will sell sweaters and make sure that no single Indian is left cold and shivering in the winter, every single Indian, from Nagpur to Kanpur. Or if you prefer, from Lhasa to Leh, if you think there's more profit on this route.'

Rigzin translated this and a smile of suspicion or satisfaction, I didn't know which, scurried across their dry, parched faces. In Skelsang's father's case, the hint of a smile started from the lower part of his left jaw and rolled rapidly upwards and disappeared in between his right ear and his furrowed brows. That settled the matter, I thought. But no, I was wrong. The parents still had dark suspicions deeply furrowed in their faces. Meanwhile I noticed Rigzin speaking to the pair in his usual rapid-fire Ladakhi and I heard the words 'the Dalai Lama' mentioned several times. It was then that their chapped faces broke into broad smiles of consent and they stuck out their tongues and bowed in total appreciation of an unknown favour I was about to bestow on them.

'What happened?' I asked.

'I said, suppose if you live in Dharamsala,' Rigzin, explained, jabbing his finger at me, 'the two of them would have the chance of receiving public audiences with the Dalai Lama every time they visited you and Skelsang. That, I told them, couldn't be measured in money or by your job. I think they like the idea.'

That was how I acquired a wife. That was also how I got into the sweater-selling business. Scratch any Tibetan refugee and not far below the surface, you will find a committed sweater-seller. Sweater-selling is the mainstay of the community. Come winter, the peripatetic Tibetans flock to Ludhiana, haul bales of ready-made woollen sweaters onto trains and scatter in all directions, scouring the subcontinent for cold weather and shivering Indians.

I say, scratch any Tibetan and not far below the surface you will find a committed sweater-seller. This is largely true. In my case, consider me a reluctant recruit. I talked about this with Skelsang. She ridiculed my predicament, clearly indicating that beggars could not be choosers. She wanted me by her side when she peddled sweaters in the streets of Delhi. But not before I made a few corrections to ensure that I was not only sweater-selling. I applied for a teaching job at the Tibetan Children's Village at Choglamsar. I was accepted. I became an English language teacher. It didn't matter that I was' teaching 'Twinkle, twinkle, little star' to the children from Jangthang.

'This is where we sell sweaters and make money,' Skelsang announced when we reached Delhi and settled into rooms in the Ladakh Buddh Vihara, or Ladakh Dharamsala as it is sometimes called, in Delhi.

Important for our tsampa and butter-tea issue, she proved to be a practical businesswoman. She had a flair for languages and spoke Hindi with the purring suppleness of Hindi film actresses. She was also a sharp saleswoman. If a man hesitated over a sweater, Skelsang immediately helped him make up by his mind by saying, 'That's exactly the type of sweater Amitabh Bachchan bought from me last year. And you have his height!' A buyer, touched by the magic of sharing something in common with the the superstar, did not even haggle over the price, and walked away as if he had won a major lottery.

On lean days I would walk off to Majnu Ka Tilla to see Tashi. I found that Tashi had put on weight and Ama Penpa's chang shack had gained in size. The two-room shack had been converted into a regular chang bar. The wooden partition that separated the inner room and the original chang bar had been torn down. The chang bar doubled up as a restaurant and it was brimming with clients, eating noodles and drinking chang. A small thatched passageway led to a three-room hut constructed on the vacant plot behind the chang bar. This was where the family lived.

Tashi was grappling with his teaching job at the school in Majnu Ka Tilla. But he was vague about the progress of his revolution. In his reticence the message I received was, ask about anything except questions about the coming revolution. Either he didn't really know how the future would treat his revolution or he was not willing to reveal details. Instead he counter-attacked. 'So what are you doing in Ladakh?'

'I teach at the Tibetan Children's Village in Leh,' I said with an expression of bored casualness.

'Great,' Tashi said, his attitude now softening. 'And the students, are they Ladakhi or Tibetan?'

'There are Ladakhi children but most are Tibetans, children of the nomads of Jangthang. Very sweet, very obedient. The children in Choglamsar are the dream students of every teacher. Where're Metok and Ugen?' I asked.

'Up in Manali, with the lama. She'll be there for a couple of weeks. She's helping the lama refurbish his apartment,' he said. 'Dhondup, I don't think it matters whether you teach here or up in Ladakh. Perhaps the children in Ladakh are more deserving, but I prefer if you teach here.' Tashi stopped abruptly. He scratched his chin. Just as abruptly he added, 'And next time bring your wife with you.'

'I'll discuss this with my wife,' I said. 'But I'll see you before we leave for Ladakh.'

On the day when the last sweater was sold, Skelsang declared that the sweater-selling season was over and that the season for social calls had started.

Skelsang was a practised social caller. She always armed herself with a package of the choicest dried apricots, prized by Tibetans. If the person we were visiting happened to be a fellow sweater-seller, Skelsang's package of dried apricots was enlarged to twice its normal size. And she took over the conversation, forcing the host to impart vital sweater-selling information in broken Hindi.

We learned that Metok had returned from Manali with her son. Skelsang, equipped with several packages of dried apricots, and I, equipped with nothing but the good cheer of having endured a season of selling sweaters, got off the lumbering rickshaw and took the maze of alleyways that criss-crossed Majnu Ka Tilla. I could not help notice that many of the old familiar faces of our college days were gone. Majnu Ka Tilla from a dismal refugee camp was rapidly transforming itself into a hub of refugee commerce with spokes radiating all over India, Nepal and Bhutan. There were a lot of new, younger faces. New restaurants and new chang shops, roomier, better furnished, had sprung up. The old Majnu Ka Tilla in which everyone knew everyone else was giving way to a bustling settlement where one could easily lose oneself in the sea of new faces.

Skelsang and I made our way to Ama Penpa's chang shop. Metok was bustling about, serving chang and chow-mein to clients. She looked up and beamed at Skelsang and told us to go right through the thatched passageway that led to their new three-room hut. ' Tashi-la's in,' Metok said above the clutter and noise of the busy chang bar. Ama Penpa was hovering before the altar emptying the seven copper bowls of the day's water offering. A line of butter lamps spluttered on the altar before the familiar Buddha statue and black and white photographs of the Dalai Lama and other lesser lamas. Ama Penpa swung around beamed her benevolence and went back to cleaning the copper bowls with a spotless strip of cotton. She seemed eager to finish this as soon as possible and her murmurs of *om mani padme hum* picked up pace. Tashi sat on a low armchair below a large open window and was going over the class work of his students. He set the exercise books aside on the low table and said, 'At last we get to see your wife.' Just as Tashi greeted us, there was a loud wail from the inner room. 'At last I get to hear your son,' I said. Tashi nodded happily. Ama Penpa quickly stacked the seven copper bowls on the altar in a row, face down. She rushed into the inner room and rushed out with a little boy buried in her arms and strode out of the room. Skelsang gave a little bow to Tashi and followed Ama Penpa.

Tashi nodded and said, 'That's Ugen.' He, the angry, frustrated communist whose revolution hadn't really taken off, seemed quite content to have settled down to domestic bliss. Here was a man who was at peace with himself and who intended to wage a war against the world. And this naturally led me to ask what I thought was the obvious question: 'So, how's the revolution?'

At this goading, the angry young man took over. The mocking world had intruded into Tashi's world of domestic happiness. He, the angry young man who wanted to change the world, didn't want the world to remind him of the lack of progress in this particular area. Tashi's face now wore a deep scowl that threatened to burst into revolutionary wrath. 'What do you care?' he demanded. Just as suddenly his mood changed. He seemed meditative, lost in his thoughts. He looked out of the window for a long time, gazing into the distance or perhaps into his mind. His face looked concerned and at this point he mentioned that Tsering Migmar, the China expert who in the nick of time had avoided transforming into an avenging Golok, was in Tibet. 'Visiting his relatives,' Tashi said brusquely.

'How long has he been gone? You sent him to Tibet?'

'No! Said he wanted to visit his relatives. It's been a year now,' Tashi said, slipping off his glasses and running his hands over his face.

'That's a long time. I hope nothing has happened to him.'

'I hope so too,' Tashi said.

Just then Metok entered the room. The way she radiated her happiness, it seemed as though she thought herself to be in paradise. And her paradise trailed behind her everywhere she went. Ugen was endowed with his father's grim, determined jaws and his mother's charm. Skelsang followed the pair.

I turned to Metok and asked, 'So how's Rinpoche in Manali?'

'Rinpoche's fine and very busy. These days he spends more time alone, reciting prayers, meditating and writing,' Metok said, putting down two chang glasses and serving Skelsang a cup of tea. Metok said that hordes from Golok, wrapped in yak skin, had camped outside the lama's residence, now demanding, now imploring, and now cajoling the lama to search, discover and recognise the twentieth Drubtop Rinpoche. Metok said these men never tired of telling the lama that they had waited all these years for their master and refuge and that they wouldn't leave Manali until the lama had found and installed their true master. Apparently the lama told them that they had waited for more than thirty years so another year or two wouldn't make a difference. The lama promised these men that they would see their ancient master in his new incarnation very soon. And the men, Metok giggled, would fall down on their knees and make full body-length prostrations at the feet of the lama who dismissed them from his presence with a wave of his hand. 'And they,' Metok said, pinching her aquiline nose with her two fingers, 'they smell, of butter and butter-tea. But they are so devoted to my uncle. They are building a new residence for him so as to encourage him to speed up the process of recognising their highest lama.' Metok was amused and laughed softly at the idea of the men wrapped in yak skin using a subtle form of bribery to quicken the pace of the descent of Kyitsel's highest lama in their midst.

'And do you know who the next Drubtop Rinpoche is or when he will be recognised by the lama?' I asked.

Metok made a face that said search me. I turned to Tashi and asked him, 'And you Tashi, do you know anything about this?' Tashi shrugged off the question making it plain that he had far weightier matters, like leading a revolution, to be bothered by such feudal beliefs. 'Reincarnation!' Tashi snorted and gulped his chang down and gestured to Metok to refill his glass. 'And certainly these men from Golok smell. To me they smell of superstition. I'm surprised that not even one communist idea penetrated through their yakskin.' Tashi's dismay was understandable. The enthusiasm of the people of Golok for the return of their lama was an annoying evidence that the Tibetan Communist Party's vision of zealous Tibetan communists working day and night for Tibet's second socialist liberation was going down the sewage of grimy Majnu Ka Tilla.

'Tashi-la!' Metok said. She raised her voice and her face wore a look of severe disapproval. Little Ugen joined in the protest. He freed himself from his mother's arms and ran towards his father who collected him in his arms and installed him on his laps.

Metok turned to me and asked, 'Have you met Samdup-la and Dolma-la?'

'No,' I said. 'What are they doing?'

'Samdup-la is a reporter for the *Indian Express* and Dolma-la works at Tibet House,' Metok said. 'They live in a rented apartment near Tibet House.'

'Yes, we'll go to meet them,' I promised. Remembering that Skelsang and I had other social calls to make, I asked, 'Do you think Dechen, Tsering Migmar's wife, is at home? Or, has she gone sweater-selling?'

'She's at home,' Metok said. 'I've heard she has stopped selling sweaters.'

'But with Tsering Migmar in Tibet, how does she manage to support herself, if not by selling sweaters? By her pangthen business?' I asked, curious and concerned.

'Don't know,' Metok said.

Well, there was only one way to find out. A couple of days later on a Sunday, Skelsang and I paid another one of our social calls, this time on Dechen. Grave and sullen Dechen greeted us at the door.

'Is Tsering-la back from Tibet?' I asked, cheerfully introducing apricot-armed Skelsang.

'No,' Dechen said, opening the door wider to let us in. 'Said he wanted to visit his relatives. That was a year ago.' Dechen was bitter and fearful. She fretted that Tsering Migmar might be imprisoned. She worried about him, their children and their future. 'It's those communists. I curse the day Tsering-la came across the pair. The two of them just talk big and my husband suffers. I really don't know whether he's alive,' Dechen said, mournfully.

'But what's he doing in Tibet for so long? Do you know?'

'No!' Dechen said. 'But I have a feeling that the two communists must have asked him to go. To build support for their party. To increase the party's ranks. If you happen to see the pair of them, tell them I will cut them into small pieces.' Dechen who did not have time for idle chatter now seemed to have all the time in the world to bare her soul, to vent her anger. I guessed she was glad that Skelsang and I were there to listen to her. She stood up to refill our cups of tea from the large Chinese thermos flask and then slumped back on the chair and said more to herself, 'I think I will never know that husband of mine.' Dechen wiped her moist eyes with the sleeve of her pink cotton blouse. 'You see, I keep receiving these cheques, every month. The envelopes always bear a Kathmandu postmark. The cheques are for large amounts, unbelievably large amounts and each of them is accompanied by a note that says "From Tsering Migmar." No "hello, how are you." No "how are the children". As if money makes up for his callous absence,' Dechen said with an angry grunt.

'That means he's alive! And more importantly, it means he's rich! Why keep worrying and crying for nothing,' I said, surprised by these mysterious cheques that kept coming to Dechen to taunt her, to mock her.

'Crying for nothing?' Dechen said, shooting me an accusing look. 'Why shouldn't I worry? I have a feeling sometimes,' Dechen said, hesitating, 'that he is keeping another woman! Otherwise, what's keeping him from coming to his family? Those cheques are the price he's trying to pay for his guilt. That's what I think.'

'Tsering-la, with another woman!' I laughed. 'Stop this. That's the last thing he'll do. You know it in your heart. He'll come back when he wants to come back. Tsering-la is a political man. He's a man who will not allow carelessness to come in the way of his political beliefs. He learned that through hard experience. Anyway, if that is what you suspect, make a trip to Nepal and clear it up. Trace the source of those mysterious cheques. That's one way to find out.'

'I did, I did, for two long months!' Dechen said, with vehemence. 'All over Kathmandu, all over Nepal and there's no Tsering Migmar in Kathmandu or in the whole of Nepal. That makes me think he's in jail in Tibet,' Dechen said and her face creased into furrows of anxiety.

'If he's in prison, who keeps sending you these cheques and how?'

'That's what I want to know myself and why I think he's keeping another woman,' Dechen said, jealousy reddening her sullen face, hope and suspicion tugging at her thoughts.

'You're too suspicious to think right. The important thing is that Tsering-la is alive. Thank the gods for that,' I said.

'Maybe you're right,' Dechen said. 'But why would he want to do a disappearing act on me and our children?'

'He's alive and that is the only thing that matters. Sooner or later, he'll show up,' I said.

I tried my best to console Dechen and give her some hope. Seeing she was feeling better we decided to leave. Skelsang presented Dechen with a packet of dried apricots. As Skelsang and I headed for the bus stop, I turned to her and said, 'That should be a lesson for you. Whenever you decide to do the Tsering Migmar on me, keep sending those cheques.'

Skelsang glared at me. 'What you mean do the Tsering Migmar on you? You mean run away with someone else?'

'Oh, forget it. But that Dechen, she's so suspicious and so confused because she's so suspicious,' I said.

'I don't blame her,' Skelsang said, looking at me sideways as we walked to the bus-stop. 'If a husband disappears for one long year, the wife will certainly have lots to think and worry about.' Skelsang stopped walking and gave my shoulder a gentle push and wagged her forefinger in my face and said, 'And you, you don't do a Tsering Migmar on me. Is that clear?'

'Sure, whatever you say,' I said. 'I feel Tsering-la is not in prison. The cheques are proof of that. Besides, he's too smart and he knows the Chinese system inside out. He'll show up one day. He'll show up one day,' I said. Perhaps I was trying to console myself. ' I wonder how he is able to make all that money? And not leaving a trace of where he is?'

Back in Majnu Ka Tilla, Skelsang and I stepped into a new restaurant that was the talk of town. The restaurant was dimly lit and it was playing Beautiful Rigzin Wangmo, the Tibetan pop song that had taken the world of the Tibetan exile community by storm. As my eyes adjusted to the dimness, I could take in the people eating and drinking. In the far corner, I spotted Samdup and Dolma. They seemed to be still on their honeymoon, speaking in intimate whispers. I walked up to them and said by way of a greeting, 'How's the revolution?'

'It's going fine. Thank you. And I see that you've joined the toiling masses,' Samdup said. It was a counter rebuke. I interpreted that to mean that sweater-selling was the last desperate act of a Tibetan refugee who just hadn't been able to make it. It was a job for losers. 'What's the point of a college education, if you land up hawking sweaters all over India?' Samdup asked.

In answer, I patted my fat wallet, smugly, as if to say I didn't care as long as the cash was coming in. 'By the way, I have a message for you from the toiling masses. The message is that a revolution is a luxury they can't afford. Got that?'

'Yeah, yeah, yeah,' Samdup said. 'We know all about it. I also know that you can't sell sweaters if your face is always buried in the pages of my newspaper. See, word gets around,' Samdup said. Dolma moved to the next chair to make space for Skelsang and me at the table.

'At least I sit beside my wife selling sweaters, making a decent living. And yes, I read the *Indian Express* and guess what? I haven't come across your byline. Not even once. The all-knowing editor of *March*, sabotaging every issue with communist mumbo-jumbo, is yet to make his name in the world of real journalism. I hope you are not using the paper to tell Tibetan refugees to rise up in revolution.' I blurt out, hitting the point home and then remembering Tsering-la asked him in the same breath, 'Why have you sent Tsering Migmar-la to Tibet? To enlist members for the communist party?'

Samdup immediately became defensive. 'Tsering Migmar-la went on his own. We tried to dissuade him. He refused to listen.'

'What's he doing in Tibet?' I demanded.

'What's he doing in Tibet? That's a party secret! And since when did the Tibetan Communist Party become accountable for its actions to a Tibetan sweater-seller?' he demanded.

'I'm just asking. I'm talking about a friend's life. He could be in prison, you know. Possibly tortured and killed by the Chinese. Did you think about that? Why didn't you or Tashi volunteer to go instead? You're putting a friend's life in peril just to enlist a few more members in your party.'

'Drop that self-righteous air,' Samdup said. 'What do you think a freedom struggle is? Being nice to each other? People die for it. And I refuse to continue this conversation. You have no right to demand an explanation.'

'Well, Tsering Migmar's wife demands an answer. *She* wants an explanation. I met her today and she asked me to tell the two of you that she will cut you into tiny pieces.'

Samdup glared. 'When you meet her again, tell her that it was his decision. We had nothing to do with it.'

'You Tibetans!' Skelsang blurted out in anger later on. 'Do you always talk like this when you meet your old friends?' she continued. 'No inquiries about health, wealth, family, job and mutual friends. It's the loss of your country. That's it!' Skelsang shouted. 'You're all frustrated and angry. You need to constantly remind one another that you are a people without a home. You need to squabble because you are trying to help one another come to terms with your humiliation. Otherwise, there is no reason for you not to behave like normal people. You like talking such stuff because you are trying to make up for your loss. Don't you think? And the same goes for your finding this cave, finding that rock. You need to talk big and prove something to yourselves because you have already proved that you are totally incapable of doing what everyone else does naturally, which is being able to defend and keep one's country.'

'Skelsang, you keep to your sweater-selling business. I think you'll make a lousy observer of the Tibetan refugee scene.'

'But don't you think I'm right?' she persisted. 'You're making up for your loss by arguing all the time. Hurting and being spiteful to one another. If it weren't for the Dalai Lama, you Tibetans would be doing what Dechen promised Tashi and Samdup: tearing one another into tiny pieces.'

I was surprised by Skelsang's sudden outburst. She wasn't the kind who usually paid attention to such things. For her, everything else was idle chatter and irrelevant to the business of earning a living. Partly to retain her interest, I asked her, 'Why this sudden interest in the Tibetan refugees' state of mind?'

'No, not on the Tibetan refugees' state of mind. I'm interested in your state of mind because your state of mind affects me directly.'

'My state of mind? What's wrong with my state of mind?'

'What's wrong? Something is wrong because you Tibetans don't behave like normal people. Normal people are nice to each other and they talk about practical things. About tsampa and butter-tea issues. They talk about business, their jobs, their livelihood, their career, of their children's education, of inflation. But you guys! Any two of you meet and you are literally at each other's throat, quarrelling, arguing,' Skelsang said, coming up with another theory. 'It's because your body is owned by China and your mind colonised by India. Contradiction, contradiction, having the misfortune of being caught between two cultures. You,' she said, pointing her accusing finger at me, 'you people are the victim of two big suspicions. Because of this you are a split people, psychologically. Yes, yes, I have it,' she continued warming to her subject and going on relentlessly. 'I know your problem. You've been a good student of India but a bad student of China. Why can't you become a good student of China? Your problems will melt away.'

'What nonsense! A good student of China!' I growled, offended.

'Just a suggestion,' Skelsang said, mischief dancing in her eyes. 'You don't need to work yourself into an oracular rage. It's just an opinion.'

'And where did you get all this stuff?' I asked, not sure whether to take her seriously or go along with the teasing.

'I've been thinking. Don't need to read fat books. Don't need to go to a big school to think about these things, especially when it affects me directly. You know what your problem is?'

'My problem?'

'No, not you personally, the problem of you Tibetans as a whole. You are caught between two cultures that make our modern world go round. China invented gunpowder, paper, paper money, the compass, rocket, printing and a lot of other things. And you Tibetans just refuse to admire and assimilate these. On the other hand India invents the mathematical zero and produces its spiritual equivalent and you Tibetans go crazy. You don't have to look as if you have seen a ghost,' she said noticing my dumbfounded face. 'I've got your lama stories translated. It was the translator who added that India invented the mathematical zero and the other zero our lamas teach. And coming to my point, there is something called cultural jealousy, you know. That's why the Chinese are so hard on you. You refuse to be like them. You refuse to pay your rent to your landlord. Instead you go about making your offerings to your spiritual landlord. That's why your real landlord is so hard on you and that's why you're split. There lies your problem and the irascibility of you young Tibetans. You don't seem to get the point and be reconciled. On the other hand, look at the older Tibetans, those who are buttered in the butter-tea culture of Tibet. They are so calm, so collected and so secure.'

'China is not our landlord!' I shouted, nit-picking and, perhaps as Skelsang said, missing the point. 'Tibetans are the landlord and receive no rent.'

'It's just an expression. Don't get worked up.'

'An expression,' I screamed. 'A gross injustice is whitewashed by that expression of yours.'

'That's the point,' Skelsang said, popping a dried apricot in her mouth. 'It could have been otherwise. You could have saved yourself the gross injustice. You took from one and not from the other. If you had also taken from China what you had taken so diligently from India, Tibet's fate could have been quite different and you would not have grown up so skewed.'

'And you?' I demanded. 'Aren't you a bit imbalanced yourself?'

'We got what you gave us. And we are happy about it. And you just proved my point. You like to quibble, trying to hide your insecurity under a veneer of modern education. Yes, China is hard on you because you are doing free promotional work for your neighbour in the south.'

'Free promotional work for our neighbour?' I repeated, trying to guess where this would lead.

'Yes, free promotional work for the zero culture, the culture of emptiness. And you are doing it quite well. Surely, the culture, which invented the gunpowder, paper rocket, all those tools would not take this free advertisement kindly. Stop it and they will be nice to you.'

At that moment, on behalf of all the yabs of Tibet, I invoked the spirit of the yums. Yums are the embodiment of the mother of all the Buddhas, those who in turn nursed and mothered all the lamas of Tibet. The lamas did and still do free promotional work for the wisdom of ancient India: that in our common nothingness we are bound to the Earth that we have inherited, not to hold dominion but to share, and to see something of our own nothingness in the birds that fly, the fish that swim, the herds that roam the pastures and the wildlife. The lamas still teach us to hold all these sacred. In this positive nothingness, the lamas have given each of us a lamp to show the way, to search, look and to light the path that leads to enlightenment.

Most of our social calls became a platform to re-state old arguments, a clinic to nurse and lick old wounds. More than the tedium of sitting out in the hot sun, my face buried in the loquacious pages of the

Indian Express, these social calls to old friends frayed my nerves. So it came as a relief when Skelsang declared the season of social calls was over. She ended the season by saying, 'Wasting time on listening to silly, angry and empty words is time taken away from the pleasure of making money.' For once I agreed with un-becoming enthusiasm.

We took the train to Ludhiana and paid our dues and that of Yudon's to Badal Singh who beamed with pleasure and said he prayed that the next winter be a severe one. We, the sweater-selling lot, had the same wintry hope in our over-heated hearts and minds.

That spring I taught at the Tibetan Children's Village at Choglamsar. Skelsang and her parents tended to their barley fields. Two years went by. Skelsang had a miscarriage which nearly snatched her life away. After this, we both gave up hoping for children. Meanwhile I became fluent in Ladakhi with a strong Nimmu accent.

My learning to speak fluent Ladakhi was the only exciting thing that happened in Leh. Otherwise, from the perspective of the living on the moonscape of Ladakh, news of the Tibetan community in the rest of India mutated into rumours and travellers' tales reaching us from distant planet Earth. They reached us after months, after they had become history for the rest of the country. In Ladakh since one was deprived of the sense of immediacy and urgency, one could look upon events with a calm objectivity provided by distance and time. Sometimes, however, in being so deprived, one was reduced to a curious spectator or a hungry reader. Occasionally I read about Tashi and the Tibetan Communist Party in the *Tibetan Review*. In fact one whole issue was devoted to the Tibetan Communist Party and the running debate it engaged with the Tibetan democrats, scholars and members of the TYC. The issue carried the TCP's manifesto. Under a blazing red emblem of the hammer, sickle and an original Tibetan contribution of a pen, the manifesto said, 'The TCP, as the revolutionary vanguard of the exploited and oppressed people, will struggle for a socialist Tibet...In this relentless struggle for self-determination, the TCP will unite with all patriotic and progressive Tibetan forces according to time, situation and place.'

The democrats countered by saying that communism was like pimples that 'latch on to most young people at that awkward age when they are most confused and most misunderstood'.

The *Review* in its editorial, 'Seeing Red', thundered, 'It is also not certain how many people would agree with the TCP assumption that the majority of the present generation in Tibet have willy-nilly become communists. It may be true that there are many Tibetans who carry red scarves, attend gloomy meetings and raise blood-curdling slogans. But whether they are doing so as true believers in the communist ideology or whether they are prompted by reasons of personal safety and comfort is a debatable point. If the accounts of refugees and visitors are anything to go by, evidence is strongly in favour of the latter assumption.'

The editorial raised the question, uppermost in most people's mind that the TCP did not seem to be making any significant contribution for the liberation of Tibet, except for generating a lot of verbiage.

The controversy raged full steam. The *Review* even carried a news item that the TCP was trying to contact the Soviet Union for solidarity, fraternal advice and aid.

No sooner had the debate spilled from the pages of the *Review* to the streets of Leh and into the small chang shops that some of us frequented, than the obsessive fuss over the TCP died down. The Soviet Union might have been deeply sceptical of the three-member TCP demanding full-fledged membership of the socialist bloc. Or the debate might have exhausted the revolutionary fervour of the politburo. Or the bemused, quizzical look on the faces of the Tibetan masses might have prompted the TCP to think this mass of benighted faces was just not ready to receive the blessings of liberation. No matter what the reason, the TCP was silent on the *Review* front. No publicity meant no existence.

That was the time when Phuntsok, still clad in a kurta, showed up in Choglamsar. Several weeks ago I had heard of Phunstok's impending transfer to Choglamsar. The Choglamsar TCV was upgraded to a high school. Along with a group of other experienced teachers from the parent school in Dharamsala, Phuntsok was dispatched to Leh to teach English literature.

I immediately went to Phuntsok's place with two plastic jugs of home-made chang. Phuntsok sat on the bed and I took the chair and faced the open glass window, which framed the bare hills of Leh. I poured chang into two rumpled aluminium mugs and handed one to Phuntsok, who before sipping, dipped his middle finger in the brew and flicked drops in the air, an offering of nectar to the gods. I could tell by the way he leaned forward and cupped his chin in his hands that he expected me to fill him in, to give him a report of my life. I obliged and told him about Skelsang and narrated Tashi's and my adventures in Srinagar, about the lama's obsession with the cave and rock on Shankaracharya Hill, about Professor Bamzai and how Tashi and I literally fell upon the two objects of our search. All Phuntsok could do was repeat 'a cave and rock, eh?' I could tell he was amused and wanted to burst out laughing but feared that I might stop my narration if he did.

At the end of my story, I expected Phuntsok to fill me in on what had happened to him. He did not oblige. Instead he was brimming with ideas about how to introduce the wealth and range of Western literary attainments to the nomadic children of Jangthang's northern plains. After he had exhausted his literary plans for the Choglamsar TCV children, I asked him whether he had heard anything from Tashi.

'Tashi? Oh, yes, they closed shop. They purged themselves. The Tibetan Communist Party has been dissolved.'

'Why?'

'Because they were not able to mobilise the toiling masses who are too busy toiling and have no time for a revolution. I told you that, remember? That they won't last. It was a game. To attract attention.'

'But Tsering Migmar-la. I think he was sent to Tibet on a mission. His wife is furious and worried.'

'Yes, I know,' Phuntsok said. 'I hear he's imprisoned. Accused of being a splittist. No one has heard of him since.'

'It's like betraying him. He has given his life for the communist party. He will feel betrayed. It's not right.'

'Who's to say,' Phuntsok sighed. He helped himself to more chang and took a long gulp. 'I met Tashi sometime in April in Dharamsala. He was there for a teachers' conference organised by the Education Department. He told me as much. He was despondent, nay devastated.'

'I think they were having serious internal differences.'

'That's not the reason,' Phuntsok said. 'They had no mass support. There were no takers for their revolution.' Phuntsok took another swig from his aluminium mug and let out a long sigh as if he had a daunting task ahead. 'At least they tried. They did something. Whereas we, what about us? We are doing nothing and we did nothing! Nothing!' Phuntsok looked at the bare hills framed by his window. He turned around and said, 'I don't believe in any of these fancy isms. But it's bad the communists dissolved themselves. It means we have no stamina. How can we show our face to the world? It shows that we don't take things seriously. How will the world take us seriously? A slight trouble and we duck for cover.' Phuntsok picked up his rumpled, dented aluminium mug and gulped down the last drops of chang and waved both his hands in front of him like a referee at a football match, as if to say that the game was over. But he wasn't finished as yet. 'And we, you and I, we, we sit on the fence watching the show, not applauding, not approving, not disapproving.'

The news of the folding up of the Tibetan Communist Party hung like a huge embarrassment between Phuntsok and me. We were not a part of it, but our generation had dreamt of it and because of that we felt we were a part of it. Unfortunately, we awoke before the dream could reach its rightful end. After all the effort, what did we have to show for ourselves, show others of ourselves, except a failed dream?

Tashi was the cause of our despondency and the object of our eventual contempt. But where was he? We learnt that he had hid himself, as if in shame and guilt. No one knew where Tashi, the chairman of the recently deceased communist party, was. He was in hiding because he wanted to be spared the insults and slanders of busy, mocking refugee tongues. Or had he run away fearing arrest and imprisonment for attempting to point to a new subversive future for himself and his fellow refugees. Or had he vanished to conceal himself like a wild beast in some mountain fastness to lick his wounds and recover his self-esteem. Rumours reaching us in Ladakh whispered that he had become a secretary to the lama in Manali. Others said with sniggering glee that Tashi too had taken to the livelihood of the proletariats of the Tibetan refugees. He had gone sweater-selling at an unknown city of India. Still others whispered that he had become a recluse, a hermit living on nettles and meditating in caves in some part of the Himalayas. He had abandoned the world because the world had abandoned him and his revolution. Some even claimed to have spotted him out in the distance, staggering like a yeti on icy mountain slopes. Man or a beast, they wondered aloud. Man, they agreed when they saw the glint of his dark glasses giving off the morning sun. Or, was it a yeti that was sporting the glasses of its latest human victim, they wondered. Like the yeti, Tashi left no concrete evidence of his real whereabouts, only legends of footprints, rumours of sightings. The first and only chairman of the Tibetan communist party in exile had reincarnated into a shaggy yeti-like legend. Would the legend reveal its mysteries?

There was only one way to find out. Before winter came, shrieking and howling through the valleys of Ladakh and burying the region in ice and snow, Skelsang and I hurriedly made our way to Delhi to sell sweaters. When the train pulled into old Delhi's railway station, I rushed to Majnu Ka Tilla to Ama Penpa's chang shack to obtain confirmation of Tashi's actual whereabouts.

'He's in Manali,' Metok said with an uncharacteristically grim face. Where had Metok's vivacity gone, I wondered. Her radiance had dimmed and the glow had disappeared.

'Hope nothing is wrong with him,' I said. I did not know what else to say. I certainly did not want to tell Metok that we had heard rumours that her husband had turned into a yeti and was roaming the mountain slopes, his trademark dark glasses glinting in the sharp sun.

'He's a little ill, but nothing to worry about. Recuperating from tuberculosis. That's all,' Metok said. Yes, clearly Metok's radiance had dimmed. Her vivacity was stifled by worry that was out of character. But the glow in Metok must have returned like the warmth of spring when back in Ladakh I heard that Tashi had just as unexpectedly re-appeared in Majnu Ka Tilla and was teaching at the school with greater enthusiasm. Strange, I thought. Did this mean Tashi had recovered? Or was he really stricken by tuberculosis? Or was it a case of diplomatic ill health, political indisposition? Or maybe Tashi's sense of shame and failure really dealt a blow to his usually robust health? But why the sudden disappearance? Why the unexpected appearance? For an intensely political man there must be a political reason for doing so.

The Enthronement of the Twentieth Drubtop Rinpoche

☯

Surprises come in small packages. So people say. Mine came in a Manali postmarked envelope, torn, dog-eared and re-directed. The envelope was addressed to Dhondup Kunga, C/O TCV, Choglamsar, Leh, Ladakh, Jammu and Kashmir. A thoughtful staff of the Tibetan Children's Village had crossed out the TCV address and added Nimmu in a distinct, confident handwriting. I was in Nimmu with my wife's family, celebrating Losar when the dirty dog-eared envelope caught up with me. It was an invitation from the lama to attend the enthronement ceremony of the twentieth Drubtop Rinpoche in Manali. To say that I was delighted would be an understatement. I was hopping mad with joy that the lama had returned from Tibet, that he was safe and that he had at last decided to announce the discovery of his master. I jumped all over Nimmu village. Older people stared, shook their heads mournfully and gave up on me. Children pointed at me, giggled and pointed again. But I continued dancing the dance of discovery, singing the hymn of recognition and howling the latest Hindi hit in celebration of the end of a long wait.

I asked Skelsang to accompany me. She took time to consider the suggestion and concluded that there was no profit to be made out of this trip. 'No!' she said tersely. 'I have better things to do.'

I hitched the first available ride to Srinagar and spent a night at Kargil and another in Srinagar. I made a detour to Dharamsala and met Phuntsok, who was recalled from Leh to Dharamsala to teach the increasing number of students arriving from Tibet. He said he was very busy. He handed me a khata and an envelope with cash to offer to the new Drubtop Rinpoche. He parted with the information that the secretary of the department of religion and culture of the Tibetan administration was taking a jeep to Manali. I met the secretary, who wore a red chuba, signifying his important status in the Tibetan Buddhist hierarchy and requested a ride. 'Sure,' the secretary said. 'There's enough room in the jeep.'

We started the journey around eight the next morning. At the insistence of the secretary, we spent the night at Tso Pema in Mandi district, where the secretary murmured prayers on its shore, prayers dedicated to Guru Rinpoche, the apostle of the Buddhist Himalayas and the one responsible for introducing tantric exuberance into Buddhist quietism. It was at this spot that an outraged local king had ordered that Guru Rinpoche be burnt to death. Rumours reaching King Arshadhara's royal ears had it that his daughter, Princess Mandarava, was having an affair with the spiritual teacher. She, as innocent as a newborn babe, was only thirsting for the milk of the Guru's teachings. Guru Rinpoche was condemned to the stake. The flames and smoke lapped around Guru Rinpoche and engulfed him. The flames died but the smoke remained and covered the whole country of Zahor like a thick blanket of monsoon mist. The awed onlookers felt water swirling around their feet and rapidly rising to their waists. They fled to the hills and looked down in fright. Suddenly the obscuring smoke was sucked clean into the blue sky, revealing a large lake. Then the onlookers saw the real miracle. Borne on a stunning giant lotus was Guru Rinpoche, reciting his mantras of magic. Guru Rinpoche had transformed himself into an eight-year-old boy. When later, as a remorse-stricken King Arshadhara of Zahor offered his kingdom and princess, the teacher from Uddiyana changed back to his old self, the slayer of Tibetan demons, subduer of Himalayan spirits. Since then Tso Pema became the most important pilgrim site of Buddhism's magical realism. Local myth which soon turned into a fervent Himalayan belief dictated that after you had prayed on the lake's shore, if a lotus flower came skimming and shimmering your way, your prayers had been answered. Briefly, I joined the secretary in prayer. It felt good to be sitting beside the secretary. I caught some of his equanimity of mind. I prayed with him because I believed that the Tibetan struggle was also a prayer, for ourselves and others, a prayer that the fire of rumours spread by the reigning satrap would be extinguished by the calm waters of our beliefs, to produce a harvest of a lake of floating, prayer-answering flowers. For a split second I thought I saw all the lotuses of the lake converge, dance and float towards us. The image was just as quickly washed away by the lashing white waves whipped up by a sudden fierce wind.

We started our journey early the next morning while it was still dark. On the way I asked the secretary who happened to be a Nyingma lama about the importance of the Drubtop lineage. 'The oldest lineage,' the secretary said, as he closed his eyes and clasped his hands. And I wondered whom the lama had recognised as the inheritor of this lineage. Was it Ugen, Tashi's and Metok's son? The lama had a habit of recognising members of his own household as the reincarnation of the highest lama of the Drubchen monastery. I would soon find out.

When we drove into Manali, the whole town was crawling with Tibetans in chuba, carrying khatas and incense sticks in their trembling hands. And the stretch of field, which the lama's residence overlooked, seemed a scene from nomadic Tibet. Groups of Goloks, tall and swaggering, were camped in tents. We drove directly to the enthronement ceremony, which we were told, would take place behind the lama's residence.

The enthronement space was canopied under a giant shamiana. A large wooden platform was erected on which was installed a high throne, covered in brocade, silk and satin. Hanging from the roof of the shamiana directly above the throne was a square parasol fashioned out of brocade, wavy with folds of satin. There was another throne, smaller and lower, beside the central throne. Flanking the two thrones was a crowd of shaven heads and maroon robes, all seated on rows of bodens. Low detachable Tibetan tables were set before these rows of guests and important lamas. The secretary was shown his seat on the platform and I sat behind him. The general public was already seated below the platform. The crowd sat cross-legged on the carpeted ground, murmuring prayers, whispering. At times the crowd turned its collective head and craned its neck to find out whether the sudden upsurge of movement at the entrance of the shamiana heralded the procession of the new Drubtop Rinpoche.

After a long wait and a lot of murmuring, trumpets blared and longhorns moaned. The crowd below and on the platform stood on its feet and a sea of khatas rippled in waves toward the procession that made its way to the throne. The crowd prostrated.

The procession mounted the steps of the platform. I was looking for a small boy who would soon inherit the legacy of the Drubchen monastery, but there was no small boy. The focus of all this spiritual fuss, of people carrying burning incense sticks and juniper twigs, of hushed voices and the prostrating crowd, was a young man in his early twenties, all wrapped up in his ngaba robes! He resembled Tashi, the communist. There was no mistake. It was Tashi! Who could mistake his confident strides, the exaggerated, military swinging of the arms, his large, dark glasses that covered half his face? The lama had recognised Tashi, the communist, as the reincarnation of the twentieth Drubtop Rinpoche! The lama had done it again. He had recognised one of his own as the exalted Drubtop Rinpoche. Yes, it was the chairman of the now defunct Tibetan Communist Party, the one who at one time was prepared to tear down the Buddhist religion at the first opportunity, blaming Tibetan Buddhism and what he called 'its mumbo-jumbo' for the Tibetans' present political misfortune. 'I know him! He's a communist!' I whispered to the secretary of the department of religion and culture, who gave me a look of biting disapproval. This was a spiritual charade, a mockery of our beliefs, this elevation of a political animal to high religious status. I didn't know who to be angrier with, the lama for recognising Tashi or Tashi for accepting the recognition.

The lama helped Tashi mount the steep steps to the throne. When Tashi sat down, there was another round of formal prostrations, heads bobbing, arms outstretched and lips whispering prayers. When this was done, the assembly, led by the clergy on the platform, burst into a long chant.

I looked up at Tashi to stare into his atheist eyes, to pierce the heart of his hypocrisy, to prick the bubble of his soaring egotism, to puncture his confused and conflicting aspirations. But Tashi sat on the throne, cross-legged like a meditating, bespectacled Buddha. He sat there, looking ahead, impassive, composed, swaying slightly from side to side to the rhythm of chants. Below him on the smaller throne sat the lama, the Drubchen Rinpoche, a figure as familiar as a mother churning the morning butter-tea. Indeed after a few chants, the whole assembly was served the ritual sweetened boiled rice sprinkled with drolma, and cups of butter-tea. First Tashi was served sweetened rice brought on an elegant tray by a monk who had his mouth covered in the fold of his robe. Then lama was served and the guests and the members of the clergy on the platform. Groups of fast-moving novices, carrying large kettles of butter-tea and basins of sweetened rice, fanned out amongst the crowd, pouring butter-tea and dolling the ritual rice in paper plates.

After a while, long-horns were blown, cymbals clashed and the dull drums of the lamaist band were beaten and the assembled monks burst into a short, triumphant prayer. After this the lama rose and stepped down from his throne and stood below Tashi and recited several short verses, which staked Drubchen monastery's claim on Tashi. In Tibet this claim was directed to the parents, but Tashi had no parents but the lama nevertheless read the verses.

Do not look
But in reverence
Parental ties
Severed forever
Born of your flesh
Fed by your milk
Today's laughter
Tomorrow's tears
Born of the Sangha
Fed by the Teachings
Today's joy
Lasting forever.

When all this was over, the lama enacted the scene, which he first performed five decades ago in a different era. He read the proclamation recognising Tashi as the twentieth reincarnation of Drubtop Rinpoche, the highest lama of Drubchen monastery of Kyitsel.

Homage to You, Our Precious Protector
Plunged in sorrow
By Your departure,
We roamed in the darkness of night.
Until Your blessed reappearance
Lit our lives with joy.
For guiding us away from slothful slumber,
And from the darkness of ignorance
For this glorious awakening,
For this blessed dawn,
We bow in humble homage.
May you never depart,
May you never forsake us,
But forever be our guide,
Be our lamp,
To that goal,
To that joy
Called Enlightenment.

After this incantation, the lama made three prostrations, and then placed before Tashi a scroll of parchment paper, the Drubchen Monastery's letter of recognition, two seals and a red upturned hat, which made its owner the true and ultimate spiritual authority of the oldest monastery in Tibet. The presentation of these sacred and priceless articles was the Drubchen Monastery's way of declaring to all Tibet, to the Tibetan people, to the world, to the gods, to the spirits, good and evil, to the nagas of lakes and rivers, to the deities of the mountain and deserts, to the guardians of the high mountain passes, to the human world, to the spirit world that their user was Drubtop Rinpoche whose name meant, the Accomplished, the Victorious Mystic Wanderer, the Good and Compassionate who was both the guide and path to enlightenment.

This was followed by a long-life prayers, which in essence said that the mind, speech and body of the whole assembly was offered for the long life and merit of the new Drubtop Rinpoche. Led by the lama, offerings were made by a long queue of selected followers, bearing ritual objects of mandalas, statues of the Buddha and gifts of bags of tea, tsampa, wheat and butter. After this, headed by the secretary, the whole assembly prostrated again and made a single file to offer khatas and envelopes stuffed with money and in return to receive blessings from the new Drubtop Rinpoche.

By this act my communist friend became the Drubtop Rinpoche, heir to Tibet's oldest lineage. I could not help but be moved by the incredible beauty of these prayers and the unquestioning fervour of the assembled crowd as it drank in these ageless words with sniffling, and fervent tears streaming down their cheeks. These were the same prayers of invocation uttered when the first Drubtop Rinpoche was recognised. The ceremony had the weight of centuries of tradition of absolute belief, but this did not make me blind to what I considered the rank opportunism of my friend, who made a mockery of the Tibetans' belief, their faith and their culture. Why did not Tashi say, 'I'm a communist, I don't believe in this stuff? I'm not what you think? Recognise someone else and spare me your beliefs.' Why didn't he come clean?

For money? For power and prestige?

I was torn. Decorum and face dictated that I join the crowd and queue to offer respects to the throne and receive blessings. But my conscience just didn't allow this. I couldn't imagine myself kow-towing and humbling myself before this one-eyed reincarnation of opportunism. I sought anonymity in the rush of crowd and sneaked away. I thought I had a perfect biological excuse, with a touch of a personal weakness. After sitting cross-legged for three solid hours, my legs were aching and needed stretching and I was dying for a smoke. I also desperately needed to use the toilet. In an exaggerated and loud voice I asked direction to the toilet and without bothering for an answer stepped down from the platform and squeezed through the crowd and slipped outside the shamiana. I stretched my legs and lit a cigarette and wondered the route I should take on my return trip to Ladakh. Just then someone shouted my name. I looked around. 'Dhondup Kunga!' a familiar voice shouted again. The pathway that led to the entrance of the enthronement space was full of people going in both directions and from amongst this crowd emerged dapper Samdup and Dolma, both with a broad smile and leading a group of Tibetans who carried trays covered in cloth.

'Good to see you, man,' Samdup said.

'Tashi delek, Dhondup,' Dolma greeted.

'Good seeing you. How are you?' I said. But at the same time I couldn't help but slide into sarcasm. 'You just missed a historic event. Your chairman has just been formally enthroned as the new Drubtop Rinpoche. Go in, go in, to receive his blessings. There's a big rush. Hurry, or you will miss his blessings.'

For Samdup it was an awkward moment and I could sense his discomfort. He grabbed my hand and shook it. Samdup didn't say anything in response but continued to grin. Perhaps he was also in the same dilemma as I was. Perhaps he too was trying to make sense of Tashi's sudden elevation to an exalted spiritual status. I empathised with him. Samdup had lost his comrade to Buddhism and I lost a friend to rank opportunism. At last Samdup said, 'Still tense, still irritable. Cheer up, man. Relax!'

'If there's any cheering you want to do, do it. You lost your comrade to Buddhism.'

'Dhondup, we'll talk later. At the moment our hands are full. These are the lunch trays for the lamas and rinpoches.' Samdup waved and pushed beaming Dolma forward and told the men with trays to hurry up. He turned around and said, 'Dhondup, go, have your lunch. It's being served. It's behind this tent.'

A good idea, I thought. I strolled behind the shamiana where there was an enclosed space. I entered the enclosure, which was milling with people and food was splashed on a long table. I stuffed my plate with food and found a quiet corner and dragged a chair to the spot and ate with an appetite. I was halfway through lunch when Samdup joined me. 'Ah, there you,' he said, carrying a plate stacked with food.

'So, what do you think of all this? Do you really believe he is the Drubtop Rinpoche?' I asked.

'Still at it,' Samdup said. 'Leave it alone, man. Who cares what I think? Aren't you happy that a friend has been recognised as an important lama?'

'What about you, are you happy?' I countered, surprised by Samdup's pragmatic attitude.

'Can't you tell? Sure, I'm absolutely thrilled.'

'Wow! Very convenient. What about your commitment, commitment to an ideology, to a cause?'

'That's history. It was a mistake. We were young and naive. Still in the inquisition mood. Leave it alone, man. It's not your headache.'

Just then Metok came rushing towards us. Ugen trailed her. Happiness was written all over her excited face.

'The Sang-yum,' said Samdup, teasingly, and Metok giggled. Metok said, 'Rinpoche wants to see you.'

'Which Rinpoche?' I asked.

'You know which Rinpoche,' Metok said, giving me an irritated stare.

'Oh, I see. You mean the real Rinpoche. Sure, I too look forward to meeting him.'

Metok's irritated stare turned into a glare. Samdup chuckled and his safari suit chuckled with him. I accompanied Metok to the lama's place. He gave a broad, exultant smile and said, 'I have completed the biography of the nineteenth Drubtop Rinpoche and will start on the new Rinpoche's life story soon,' he said, pointing to a pile of paper. The lama exuded good health. He was animated and was crackling with energy and bursting with new enthusiasm. Perhaps his recent visit to Tibet and the day's enthronement contributed to the lama's renewed dynamism. He wasn't praying but sat cross-legged on the bed, shooting off orders to individuals who entered his room for instructions.

'So how was your visit to Tibet?' I inquired politely of the lama.

'I have repaired Drubchen monastery,' the lama said. There was genuine pride in his voice, a sense of accomplishment. The lama leaned towards me and in a whisper said, 'The faith is strong, very strong in

Tibet. No one,' the lama said, wagging his finger, 'no one can take that from the people.'

'No trouble from the Chinese authorities?'

'No trouble whatsoever. They let me repair my monastery and permitted me to recruit some limited number of monks. I appreciate this.'

I thought sufficient time had elapsed for me to ask the one question I had been dying to ask without seeming to question his motives. Normally one doesn't ask such questions. One is just told to accept things, and explained later. But no one questions a lama on his decision. It is a breach of protocol. It is blasphemy. Delicately, in a sort of disinterested way, I asked, 'So about the new Drubtop Rinpoche, what were the signs which convinced you that Tashi was the one?'

'Isn't it obvious to you? Rinpoche managed to stumble on to the first Drubtop Rinpoche's cave and rock. Who can find a needle in a haystack, except the person who put it there? Who can find a footpath up the mountains, except the traveller who made the path? And then the physical characteristics,' the lama said, his face dipped in devotion. 'His eye, his blind left eye! It is exactly like that of my half-brother, the late Drubtop Rinpoche. Look at that,' the lama said, pointing to the thangka portrait of the nineteenth Drubtop Rinpoche, hanging from his wall. 'Look at the blind left eye. We are looking at the same eye! We are looking at the same person!' the lama whispered.

The lama was right. The flesh that covered the left eye was of the same texture, colour and shape. 'Yes, I noticed that when I was last here. But that's only one indication. And Tashi, you know, he's a communist! Or at least he was till they closed shop.'

'Understandable. It's the lingering effect of his two years' stay in Beijing. Remember, the last Drubtop Rinpoche had two years of communist education. That's natural,' the lama rationalised. 'I know in my heart, in my dreams that he's my half-brother, my rinpoche,' the lama said. 'When I first saw him I knew that he had come back! Back to his family, back to claim his sacred inheritance.'

'But Tashi doesn't know anything about Buddhism. He can't even distinguish a monk from a nun.'

The lama laughed. 'That's why I brought with me the finest Buddhist scholars from Amdo. Or at least those who survived. We will revive Buddhism in Tibet. We will make Tibet what it used to be. Why do you think Rinpoche and Metok were so attracted to each other? It's karma,' the lama said, as if that explained everything.

'But these are circumstantial evidence, so to speak. What concrete evidence do you have that Tashi is your man?'

The lama ignored the sting in my voice. 'I told you long ago that I am an interpreter of dreams. Tashi came into my dreams again and again. Always in auspicious circumstances. There was one dream that I will tell you about. I dreamt that I was visiting my monastery in Golok. From a distance, I caught the sparkle and glitter of the golden roofs of my monastery. It was surrounded by tents. The whole area was covered with tents and people sat, cross-legged, listening to someone giving a sermon. There were no loudspeakers, but the lama's voice as if descending from the skies, was rolling over the monastery, over the tents and throngs of followers. I thought I recognised the voice. I knew that voice. It was the voice of the nineteenth Drubtop Rinpoche. I entered the monastery courtyard, and the main assembly hall. There sitting on the throne of the Drubtop Rinpoche was Tashi. He beckoned to me. As I passed the line of assembled lamas, they all whispered, "Rinpoche has been waiting for you." When I was below his throne, Drubtop Rinpoche bent his head over and whispered, "I have brought Buddhism back to Tibet again." Those were the only words he spoke. But those were enough for me. If happiness could be compared with enlightenment, I was enlightened in my dream. No one, no one can take away the joy I felt in that particular dream. When I woke I knew that this was an important spiritual guidance for the search and recognition of the twentieth Drubtop Rinpoche.'

Moved by the power of his own dream, the lama had tears rolling down his cheeks. He wiped them and said, 'Didn't Drubtop Rinpoche discover the place where he had first studied in Kashmir? You were there with him. You should know. It was no accident. It was intuition. It was karma. He fell down on his cave and rock and not a bone broken, not even a scratch. Don't you think this is evidence enough, if one ever needed evidence? Tashi is the authentic reincarnation of the inventor of the Word. At this point the lama joined the palms of his hands in prayer and closed his eyes and recited the prayer invoking the Word.

The Word!
The one that makes us speak,
The one that makes us remember
And to store what we remember
For those in the future to learn
Again and again and remember
And pass on to others
Through the endless cycle of birth
And death and rebirth.
It's the Word,
The one which opens to us
The wisdom of the Sakyamuni
Who frees us from
The cycle of karma.
The Word
Which leads to us freedom
And saves us
From going around and around
In small, meaningless circles
Drawn by our ego
Forever going,
Forever reaching nowhere.

The lama's faith was unshakable, his motivation true and his belief that Tashi was the original Drubtop Rinpoche absolute. In face of such faith, my cynicism seemed silly and irrelevant. I had first planned to confront Tashi, to expose his blatant hypocrisy. Now I wasn't so sure. Resorting to reason to expose the other person's faith did not seem right.

At this point the lama said he had to see some people in the other room and lumbered out. Just then Tashi, in his ngaba robes, walked in. I did not acknowledge him. I sat there, glum and silent. On the spur of the moment, my feelings brushed aside my caution and I barked, 'I refuse to recognise you.'

'Blame the lama,' Tashi said calmly. 'I didn't volunteer to become Drubtop Rinpoche. At the same time how can I deny his and other people's faith by saying I am not the reincarnation of Drubtop Rinpoche?'

'How can you live with this pretence your entire life?'

'Pretence or not, this is what people believe. How can I, one single Tibetan, deny the belief of the whole bunch?'

'Because it suits you. Because it benefits you. That's why,' I choked. With that I walked out of the room.

Later as I was having a bowl of noodle soup at a restaurant when Samdup and Dolma walked in. 'What's wrong with you?' Samdup asked. 'You are jealous. Why aren't you happy that a friend of yours has been recognised as a rinpoche?'

'Jealous, me? What about you? You of all people, why aren't you mad that your friend has dumped you and your revolution and abdicated to Buddhism? He has betrayed you!'

'Let's talk this over,' he said. 'Anyway, I don't understand you,' Samdup said, his face breaking into a puzzled frown. 'When we formed the communist party, you, like the rest of the bunch, were dead set against it. Now it seems that you want us to start the communist party all over again. Why?' Samdup waited for an answer. I had no answers, only feelings, conflicting, contrary and pulling in opposite directions.

'About Tashi. About Drubtop Rinpoche,' Samdup said. 'He has no choice. How can he deny that he's not Drubtop Rinpoche? It would break the lama's heart. He's been searching for Drubtop Rinpoche's reincarnation since the last one died way back in the 1950s. The lama is convinced beyond any doubt that he has found the authentic reincarnation. How can you deny that? How can you say that he is not the one. Go to Tashi. Say you understand, if not approve.'

Next morning in the broad sunlight of reason, to the music of singing birds, I viewed things differently. What would Skelsang make of this? I supposed she would blurt out, 'You Tibetans!' and continue with her close study of the state of the Tibetan refugee mind. Well, Samdup was right. I would need to go to Tashi, to apologise. Armed with the khata that I refused to offer during his enthronement, I strode to the lama's place and was met by a beaming Metok, followed by Ugen.

'Is Rinpoche in?' I asked.

'Which Rinpoche?' Metok asked with a mischievous smile.

'The other one, the new one, the one with the one eye,' I said.

'Oh, he's inside. Go in,' Metok said, picking Ugen in her arms and bustling away.

Tashi was alone. He sat cross-legged on the bed and was flipping through the pages of some Buddhist text.

'Good morning,' I said, awkwardly. 'May I come in.'

'Hope it isn't to deliver another lecture,' Tashi said, looking up, a hint of a smile lighting his face.

'No, no. I'm here to say sorry,' I replied. I placed the khata on his table and carefully spread it out lengthwise before him. 'I was supposed to have given you this yesterday. Sorry. And these are from Phuntsok.'

'Oh, that's all right, man,' Tashi said, adjusting his jaws with his hand. 'You made your point. At least, you are honest. You may be right. This communist experience...my heart wasn't into it,' Tashi said, as if Buddhist wisdom were now fully open before him. He started bundling the loose pages.

'I see,' I said.

'It didn't feel right. It was as if I had reincarnated in somebody else's old dream. I didn't feel comfortable.' Tashi paused, perhaps for effect, or to allow his words to sink in, maybe he was just gathering his thoughts. 'I don't know whether you would believe me or that I should tell you this,' Tashi said, wrapping the text in its maroon cloth cover and tying the sacred bundle with the long, sturdy cotton cord attached to it. He gave himself a benediction with the wisdom book by tapping it lightly on his forehead. 'On the other hand, remember the day in Srinagar when we fell on the cave and the rock? That day I had this strange feeling that I had been at the place before. A sort of deja vu. The feeling was so strong that I wanted to act on it. I thought I even knew the exact shape of the mouth of the cave and the contours of the rock on which was carved the entire Tibetan alphabet. It's difficult to explain. It's strange,' he said, awkwardly, pulling off his glasses and running his hands over his face.

Back in Ladakh, Skelsang asked me who the new Drubtop Rinpoche was. I told her.

'That one!' Skelsang said, giggling. 'You Tibetans!' she blurted out.

Mutton Leg in Bodh Gaya

☯

That summer Leh and its neighbouring villages were awash in Kalachakra rumours. I was spending the weekend in Nimmu with Skelsang, her parents and their whole tribe. We had finished lunch, which was usually an austere affair of tsampa, butter-tea and curd, and had climbed on to the terrace to sun ourselves. The terrace commanded a stunning view of Nimmu with its green barley fields and poplar groves and the stark hills lapped by the waters of the Indus. Skelsang's mother brought out wooden bowls, their inside inlaid with fine silver. She poured her best chang and handed Skelsang's father, her three brothers and me a bowl each. She went back to Skelsang's spot to spin wool. Then as if on cue, up the rickety wooden staircase clambered Rigzin. 'Ha, ha!' Rigzin greeted us, grinning from ear to ear. He picked up a bowl and helped himself to chang. 'As usual, the best chang in Nimmu! You know, you can make money out of this,' he said, 'Bottled chang! Tourists would love this,' he said between gulps. 'By the way I came to tell you that the Dalai Lama will be giving Kalachakra teachings in Bodh Gaya this winter. I thought you may want to attend.'

'The Kalachakra empowerment teachings?' Skelsang's father asked, excited. Spiritual greed rolled rapidly up and down, like the Rajdhani Express, on his face.

'Yes, the Kalachakra empowerment teachings,' Rigzin said, gulping more chang.

'Are you sure?'

'Sure, the Representative of the Dalai Lama in Choglamsar confirmed this. There is great excitement in Leh.'

'We must go,' Skelsang's father said. 'We believe anyone who receives these teachings will go directly to Shambala in his next life,' he said. 'We didn't have the money to attend the last Kalachakra teachings he gave in Bodh Gaya. Now thanks to my daughter the whole family will be able to go to Bodh Gaya and later to Shambala. Do you have exact dates for the teachings?'

'The last week of December to the first week of January, I think,' Rigzin said. 'And you are not the only one. As far as I know whole of Ladakh wants to go. Start booking your train tickets now if you wish to make it,' Rigzin said, grinning mischievously. Rigzin took one last gulp from his chang bowl, wiped his mouth with the back of his hand and climbed down the rickety stairs. 'See you in Shambala!' he shouted from below.

A family meeting was not necessary. Skelsang's father had already made the decision. As for making plans for the trip, Skelsang eased her father out and took command of the whole operation. In fact, her father, her three brothers and I were reduced to errand boys, made to do her bidding. I knew something was brewing in that shrewd business mind of hers. She created a web of informants who were assigned to gather every detail of the Kalachakra arrangement, who was organising it, who was sponsoring it, who was arranging the accommodation to house the pilgrims, who was responsible for supplying water and electricity, et cetera. Skelsang was especially interested in numbers, the number of families going from Nimmu, from Leh and beyond, both Ladakhis and Tibetan refugees. According to the estimate Skelsang managed to obtain, the total number of pilgrims attending the teaching crossed well beyond the hundred thousand mark. 'Imagine that!' Skelsang said in disbelief. 'More than a lakh people gathering in Bodh Gaya, more than a lakh! And all of them need to eat, and all of them need a place to sleep. We are going to operate a restaurant!' she announced. 'And a big tent to accommodate as many people as possible! And not a word of this to anyone,' she warned, 'Not a word.'

Throughout that year, Skelsang was hugely solicitous to Rigzin. He was the one to whom she served chang first. We were made to surrender the best seat on the terrace to him when he made his social calls. She inquired about his health obsessively and about the fortunes of Hotel Dreamland. One day Skelsang made her move. She borrowed Hotel Dreamland's three best cooks for the winter. 'No hotel business in Ladakh in winter,' she explained. Rigzin saw the point and let her hire his three cooks. 'Only for this winter,' he said.

'Only for this winter,' Skelsang promised. 'I won't make this into a habit.'

That winter Skelsang, her parents, her three brothers and the three cooks of Hotel Dreamland set off to Bodh Gaya a month ahead. I could spot the gleam of keen anticipation in her eyes as she recited the hundred thousand number almost like a new mantra that would grant her great riches. Skelsang's father asked his young brother and his family to look after his house, fields, cattle and poultry. I had one more month of teaching to do at the TCV.

'Leave my train ticket at Tsultrim's restaurant in Pathankot,' I told Skelsang the day she and her team left Nimmu. 'And by the way,' I paused, 'how will I find you amongst more than a hundred thousand people? Do you know where you'll be staying?'

'No, we don't, but keep looking. Ask people,' Skelsang said, exasperated. 'It won't be that difficult. Besides,' Skelsang said, 'there will be an information centre run by the TYC people. Ask them.'

'Ask them and they will know where you'll be staying?'

'No, they won't, but they will announce it through the loudspeakers. Once we hear your name, one of us will come to fetch you. Is that clear?' Skelsang demanded, the exasperation in her voice rising to the pitch of the deep growl From the Lion's Mouth that drowned the whispers of the valley.

Well, if you ask me, I too was keen to go to Bodh Gaya. To meet old friends, to catch up with new gossip. And to ponder under the Bodhi tree that sheltered the world's first exile in the hope that some of the spiritual grace that lingered on the tree would fall on me. Bodh Gaya was the place where Tashi, the former communist, and now the twentieth Drubtop Rinpoche, had his mutton-leg vision, a vision of freedom from hunger. I too needed to pray at the place, which inspired people with such practical vision. And, well, as Skelsang's father promised, to pick up the one-way ticket to Shambala and to measure the distance we had covered.

But when I eventually got there, Gaya was desolation itself. It was the place from where the Buddha had gone away and perhaps the reason why he decided to renounce the world in the first place. Bandits abounded, dacoits plundered in full daylight, thiefs and thugs fooled one another and helpless pilgrims, and marauding gangs roamed at will. It reminded me of stories from Tibet's Wild East and the best place for pilgrims. Buddhist pilgrims believe that the more dangerous the pilgrimage one undertakes, the greater the spiritual merit.

But after a half-an-hour tonga ride with other pilgrims, I was transported to the magic of the Silk Road. I glimpsed at the top of the Mahabodhi Temple that commemorated the spot where the Buddha had attained enlightenment. With that one glimpse the whole place was transformed into a huge caravanserai. There they were, all figures from the past, monks, merchants, pilgrims. There were Ladakhis in their maroon woollen gowns, Monpas in their tartan-like skirts, Bhutanese in their striped bakus, Tibetan refugees, freshly-arrived Tibetans in dark woollen chubas, bringing with them the smell of Tibet, of yak dung, of butter-tea and unwashed bodies. And then there were the spruced-up white crowds from the West, their yellow-coloured counterparts from the East and the copper-skinned ones from the North, from the grasslands of Golok, swaddled and swaggering in yak-skin, ridden with lice. It was a Himalayan show time. The spectators? The whole wide world. In its homeland it might be fanatically desecrated, but it was good to see that outside the Land of Snow, Tibetan culture had spread its wings and was soaring to distances, reaching places and touching people beyong imagination.

If a religious gathering could reincarnate as a political statement, this was it. Enlightenment came to me! I was thrilled. If a culture could attract such a mass of international audience, that culture did not need to think of working on a speedy reincarnation. It would live and never die.

After having assured my culture a safe and happy future, I jumped down from the tonga, paid my share of the fare and became a part of the Silk Road romance, shuffling my way to the TYC information booth.

Skelsang, ruddy cheeked and flushed, was buoyant in a silent, suppressed way. 'We are making money!' she whispered excitedly. We waded through the crowds that were gathering thick and fast on the streets, the by-lanes and the open spaces. We walked past an elegant Tibetan building, which opened onto an enormous open ground fenced with bamboo poles. 'The Kalachakra teaching ground,' Skelsang said curtly. Behind the Kalachakra Temple on a mound was a forest of tents and wooden huts of shops and restaurants. We turned a corner and there was Skelsang's business creation: Hotel Ladakh. Although it was a tarpaulin tent, Hotel Ladakh boasted of ten tables. Skelsang was right, she was literally cooking money! The hotel was crowded. Skelsang's three brothers spotted me, grinned in my direction and with a brisk shrug went back to take orders, serve and clear up the debris on the tables. I noticed Skelsang had hired several local hands. I turned to her and asked, 'Where are your parents?' She made a circular motion with her finger and said, 'Around the Temple.' That was where I dashed off. And that was where I came across the mutton leg Tashi had written about in his Memory article.

Rather than seeing it, I heard it first. Later I had a public audience. I was doing the rounds of the outer circle of the Mahabodhi Temple when at the main gate from behind me someone boomed, 'Who wants to buy a mutton leg from Tibet?' I swung around and there right behind me was a scruffy Tibetan in a black woollen chuba. He took out a dried mutton leg from the enormous folds of his chuba and raised it high above the heads of the mantra-murmuring pilgrims and shouted, 'Mutton leg from Tibet. Two hundred rupees.' The man trying to sell the mutton leg within the precincts of Buddhism's most sacred spot seemed to hail from Rachu in Toh because this particular travelling salesman had that distinct Topa accent. I bowed deeply before this vision of freedom from hunger. But then as always, the price was too steep. I comforted myself with the thought that I was fortunate to see every refugee's vision of enough food on the table in flesh. Conditions in Tibet must be pretty good, I mused, if mutton legs were re-appearing in the pasturelands of the plateau.

After this spiritual feast on the mutton leg from Tibet what remained was only the bare bone of the story of the journey made to Shambala.

One day while I was circumambulating the Mahabodhi Temple, I spotted a religious delegation ahead of me. A man in ngaba robes, walking briskly, arms swinging, led the delegation. A couple of monks walked ahead to make way in the milling crowd. When those in the crowd realised that there was an important lama in their midst, they stepped aside and folding their hands bowed and stuck out their tongues for spiritual inspection. The ngaba nodded and reassured them of the spiritual health of their tongues and strode ahead with some importance. Two women and a little boy followed the ngaba. They were shepherded by several nomads, swaddled in yak skin. I walked past and someone jabbed me in the back and said, 'Dhondup!' I turned around and there was Tashi, the former communist in his new avatar as the twentieth Drubtop Rinpoche. He had become quite like the lama I had first met in Ama Penpa's chang shack in Majnu Ka Tilla. His ngaba robes matched his long hair which was tied by a red sash into a knotty bun that sat on his head like an imposing crown. He was reserved, perhaps wanting to preserve some measure of dignity before his fawning courtiers. Yes, Tashi, this reluctant mystic, this committed householder, was the very picture of the lama, joyfully flouting all the monastic rules of Buddhism and yet still commanding the spiritual allegiance of a whole region.

Metok was there, with Ugen in tow. Ama Penpa however seemed to have stooped a bit.

'Drubchen Rinpoche?' I asked.

'He's a little indisposed but recovering…in Manali,' Tashi said.

'I hope nothing is seriously wrong with him?'

'Don't worry. Nothing is wrong with him. The real reason he stayed back was because he wanted to complete my biography,' Tashi said with no trace of self-importance.

'Oh, the second one-eyed one,' I said.

'Yes, the other one-eyed one,' Tashi said, curtly. 'That's me.'

One of the monks walking ahead of us turned his head round and stared at me with the ferocity of an avenging Golok. Need to be more respectful to their rinpoche, I thought.

I invited him for a meal at Hotel Ladakh. He refused, saying he was busy. Instead he sent Ama Penpa, Metok and Ugen. Whenever I walked around the Temple, I spotted him at the foot of the Bodhi Tree in deep meditation. It was Tashi's way of trying to find true liberation, his inner liberation which he thought might also be needed by those around him. I left him to his meditation but from then on, whenever I thought of Tashi, that image of him sitting under the Bodhi Tree always came to my mind. Tashi, the Bodhi Tree and a mutton leg.

Skelsang's hiring of local extra hands relieved me of my dishwashing chore and I tagged along with Skelsang's parents and sat in the hot sun when the teachings began.

During the teachings we were not only issued a one-way ticket but also given a guided tour of Shambala, the kingdom of our minds, forged by our imaginations and ruled by time and space. No tyrant less than time and space could take that away from us. Yes, I could say I had been there. For about ten magical days thousands of people created it, a castle floating in the air, both Shangri-La—the outsider's stereotype of us—and Shambala—our hopes for ourselves. Ten days later, the Dalai Lama left Bodh Gaya, everyone vanished, revealing empty dirty streets lined with maimed beggars, scampering dogs and rubbish. The Silk Road magic that shimmered in the air also vanished. As though some nomads had stolen it away under cover of night.

Skelsang finally noticed that the chairs of Hotel Ladakh were empty. She folded her tent and we headed for Ladakh.

The Kalachakra teachings made me want to go to Dharamsala. To work. To keep alive the spirit of Bodh Gaya and to retain the vision of that leg of mutton from Tibet.

To Skelsang's parents, I used Rigzin's argument that they would receive a public audience with the Dalai Lama every time they came to visit us. The parents agreed. I wrote to the Library of Tibetan Works and Archives if there was a post available for me. The post for which I had applied three years ago was still vacant. So one fine May morning Skelsang and I took a bus from Leh and headed for Dharamsala.

In Srinagar as was my habit, I called upon Professor Bamzai, who reproached me in his stentorian voice, 'Delhi University student, eh? Doing your PhD thesis on the lotsawas of Tibet, eh? The first skirt or dress you see and you go chasing after it. Don, my friend, I've told you many times, your name matches your attitude. It's quixotic! Quixotic! Now get out of my sight. Anyway, where you're off this time?'

I mentioned Dharamsala and the Library of Tibetan Works and Archives.

'That's better. You've lost three precious years. Now don't fritter away the rest of your life,' Professor Bamzai said, waving me away.

So with Professor Bamzai's reproach ringing in my ears, Skelsang and I took another bus to Jammu and after a night's stop took the first available bus to Dharamsala.

The bus stopped at Tilokpur for a while. Skelsang wanted to make a pilgrimage to the Kagyu nunnery perched on the steep hillock that overlooked the Baral River and the small cluster of dhabas. 'The bus won't stop for that long,' I said.

'Well, then we will take the next available bus,' she said coolly.

'But we've paid right up to Dharamsala. We'll go there once we are settled in Dharamsala.'

'It's not the nunnery, only. It's the spot where Tilopa stayed. It's a pilgrim spot. Moreover, there will be less merit if you happen to pass an important pilgrim spot and not visit the place the first time. Dharamsala can wait. We will take the next available bus.'

I told Skelsang she could go on her own. I would look after our luggage. So Skelsang equipped with several fine silk khatas, some cash offerings and a large dirty cotton bag of apricots laboured up the hill strewn with Tibetan prayer flags.

I stayed back, guarding our worldly possessions, sipping tea and smoking and wondering why Skelsang wanted to pay a visit to the nunnery in the first place. It did not figure in our travel plan. But from the dhaba-wallah I learned that the place was also known as Do Nadir Sangam, the meeting point of two rivers, the Baral and Dehra, the confluence of which was marked by a small spiralled Hindu temple.

After what seemed like an age, Skelsang made her descent. She seemed serene, as serene as the catchment of the small gurgling waterfall below the bridge. 'I think my parents will be happy,' Skelsang explained. 'I've made a pilgrimage to the spot where Tilopa, the master of Naropa, who was the master of Marpa, who was the teacher of Milarepa, the founder of our order, stayed for many years.'

'So what was Tilopa doing here, running a roadside dhaba?'

'No, fishing.'

'So, he was a fisherman.'

'No, not a fisherman. Fishing to live, not to earn. Fishing so that he could eat and live so that he could meditate and pass on the insights of his meditation to those who wished to learn and become wise like him.'

We had to cut short our conversation on the history of the Kagyu lineage and the profession of Tilopa because a bus rumbled past, panted and stopped ahead of us. We struggled with our luggage and scrambled in.

5

Dharamsala

Homecoming

❂

To an outsider, the passer-by, the first-time visitor or to Tibetans from older and more established communities like Kalimpong of the wool trade ferried on the mule train, Dharamsala gave off an air of temporariness. You could tell from the refugee architecture, tentative, in-substantial, makeshift, which bespoke of a vulnerable readiness to de-camp anytime. Diffident, insecure wooden shacks, rose from McLeod Ganj's Bhagsu Road to the road that led to the Swarg Ashram, the old residence of the Dalai Lama, layer after layer, in a hesitant, whimpering, wooden imitation of Lhasa's confident, blazing, imperial Potala. A symbol of Tibet's one-time greatness?

Yes, the Tibetans in Dharamsala seemed rootless, alienated and isolated. They were an émigré affliction. A diaspora that stirred a dangerous mixture of sympathy, jealousy and contempt. Worst of all, they were deprived of the usual and useful traffic of people and commerce from the mother country to explain and excuse their presence in Dharamsala or for them to strike roots.

But once settled, you came to a more intimate knowledge and understanding of Dharamsala.

You then realised that Dharamsala was a place built by hope.

And sustained by faith.

And perhaps a better symbol of the greatness of Tibet's gentle culture and faith. The faith that underpinned the world of the Tibetan diaspora was carved on stones all over the hill on top of which was located the residence of the Dalai Lama. Mani stones along the lingkor footpath, piled layer on layer, rising in a conical, ascending crescendo of fervent cairns, circled the hill of the Dalai Lama's abode like a protective mantra. This act of faith climaxed at Lhagyal Ri in a celebratory outburst of prayer flags, prayer wheels, prayer poles that pierced the azure blue, cloudless skies, all of which showcased an elegant white chorten dedicated to the jealous tutelary deities of Tibet with their apotropaic power.

There was another side to Dharamsala. Sometimes—this was especially true when the Dalai Lama gave religious teachings—Dharamsala evoked the ambience of the Silk Road, a place made prosperous because it was a travel destination, with bustling crowds. A place of modern caravans, of caravanserais, of merchants, travellers, monks, lamas, nuns, mendicants and pilgrims, bringing merchandise, ideas and inspirations and in turn taking back ideas and inspirations.

About two in the afternoon, the bus disgorged us in Kotwali Bazaar, the main town in Dharamsala, the Indian part of the hill station. It was early May on a sun-splashed Sunday. The towering snow-capped Dhauladhar range, glistening in the brilliant sunlight, stood behind the hills of Dharamsala like a forbidding deity. The mountains, silent and stark, stood brooding over the lush, stunning Kangra Valley. In front were the foothills covered with stunted trees. Behind the foothills stood dark green hills, and rising above and overlooking the two layers were the mountains topped with snow. Behind those mountains, about hundred miles to the north as the crow flies, is Tibet, the country of our dreams and the roof to the rest of the world.

It felt like homecoming. For Skelsang it was exile.

Skelsang and I needed to rest and stretch our aching legs. We were also famished. We lugged our load to a nearby restaurant and ordered momos. 'It's so small,' Skelsang said in Ladakhi.

'Small, the momos?' I questioned her in my Nimmu accented Ladakhi.

'No, the place. Dharamsala is like a village. People talk about Dharamsala as if it were a big city like Delhi. And I thought I was going to a better place,' Skelsang complained.

I couldn't argue with that. Skelsang was echoing the small-town girl's longing for the bright city lights.

'Really, it's not any village. It's the village where the Dalai Lama lives!' I said, trying to console her.

Skelsang brightened up at the thought. Like any practical businesswoman, she was probably calculating the profits she would make selling sweaters to foreign visitors who were pulled to this small town by the magnetism of the Dalai Lama. She presumed all foreign visitors to be rich, every single one of them. That was her experience in Ladakh. Foreign visitors to Dharamsala would be no different. Having formed a definite business opinion of Dharamsala and perhaps relishing the prospects, Skelsang went back to her momos, stuffing herself hungrily.

Skelsang's contempt for the town did have merit. Some said it was an overgrown village, a one-yak-street, and they wondered aloud why such a tiny place managed to create such a huge international fuss. Like a village, everything in Dharamsala was walking distance and everyone knew everyone else. While we were wolfing down the momos Phuntsok, with Gandhi spectacles dangling importantly on his nose jauntily walked past.

'Phuntsok!' I shouted, springing from my seat.

Phuntsok looked around him and spotted us in the restaurant. 'Dhondup!' he greeted. Phuntsok walked in and looked from me to Skelsang and then extended his hand. 'You showed up sooner than I thought,' he said. 'The Library job, I suppose.' He peered at Skelsang, over his Gandhi glasses.

'Yes, the Library job. Skelsang, my wife…from Ladakh. Remember? I told you about her.' Skelsang ju-led Phuntsok in her best Ladakhi manner.

'And you're at your same job?' I asked.

'Yes. More children are coming from Tibet. And we need more teachers. Let's go,' Phuntsok said. 'I'll help with the luggage.'

With Phuntsok's help, Skelsang and I did our own coolie work. With our luggage secured on our backs, we made the fifteen-minute trek to Gangkchen Kyishong, the headquarters of the Central Tibetan Administration and the complex where the Library of Tibetan Works and Archives was situated. When we reached the Library complex,

Phuntsok made us wait in front of the Library building while he went to fetch the man responsible for the accommodation of the Library staff. He soon returned with him, a shuffling man clutching the key to our room. We climbed up the hill and approached a run-down building, hidden under a cluster of trees. An apso scampered in the clearing. It let out a few fierce barks but yelped and slinked away at the first threatening gesture from the shuffling man.

He unlocked the empty room and said, 'Your room.' He handed the key to me and shuffled away.

'I too had better be going,' Phuntsok said, as we stepped into the empty room. 'But I'll see the two of you later when you have settled down,' he said. His eyes swept across the dismal room. He turned to Skelsang and said in a consoling way, 'I hope you'll come to like Dharamsala.'

'I hope so too,' Skelsang said. I translated. She rummaged in her bag and produced a package of dried apricots and handed this to Phuntsok who waved and took the short cut to McLeod Ganj.

We dumped our stuff on the wooden bed fitted with a thin mattress. I surveyed the room with its hollow mud walls and blackened ceiling. Holes, made by rats, dotted the walls, just above the slate floor. The earlier occupants had stuffed the rat holes with mildewing newspaper pages. The whitewash was peeling off and splotches of brown mud were surfacing beneath the fallen paint, defacing the walls. Except for the wooden bed, table and chair, there was no other piece of furniture, and this gave the room an air of uncluttered spaciousness.

While on our way up to my shack, I saw that the house, a part of which constituted my new home, was old and dilapidated. Small and rectangular, more forlorn than forbidding, with blue slate tiles for its roof, the house stood all by itself, on the hillside.

It was divided into three rooms. Ours was in the middle and had three doors. One was our own, the one which Skelsang and I would use. The other two on either side served as connecting doors, but were sealed. It was apparent that before the coming of the Tibetan refugees, in more prosperous or less crowded times, the whole house was the undisputed domain of just one family.

The only window with glass panes opened into the room and was wire-meshed. The hinges of the window were broken. As for the door, for whatever reason, the lower half was of wood and the upper half of glass. Through the glass panes, I could see the overhanging foliage and possibly people, if they stood on the steps leading to the door. The room had only one electric bulb hanging from the ceiling. The light it emitted was dim and paled in the scattered patches of sunlight peering in through the holes in the roof.

Skelsang was devastated and showed it by being unusually peevish. It was while we were contemplating our new situation typified by this graceless room that we heard a loud 'O-loi'.

For me that one word—a sound, a tone, a piece of Tibetan memory—opened up the world of old Tibet. Depending on its pitch, 'o-loi' means either 'hello' or 'is anyone at home?' In Tibet that word with much else has been obliterated from the social life of the people. Here in Dharamsala an echo from old Tibet still lingered.

Skelsang stepped forward and opened the door. Outside stood our neighbour. She, we later came to learn, was a goddess. A slight, portly figure but gaunt in the face, the goddess wore her chuba carelessly and her smile warmly. She was followed by Chodon, her daughter who was about eight years old, with her hair tied in a ponytail and a pair of bright eyes rounded off by fresh protruding cheeks.

The goddess tashi deleked us. Skelsang ju-led back. She carried a Chinese thermos flask and two glasses and quite out of breath, she said, 'Tibetan tea for you. You know, you got a very good room. It's cool in summer and warm in winter.'

'But there are holes in the roof and I think there must be a lot of rats,' I protested.

'The rats won't bother you. Leave them alone. They mean no harm.'

I sipped the tea. It was good butter-tea, properly salted.

'And the best thing about this place is that you won't have your things stolen,' the goddess consoled, seeing the expanding area of dismay on my facial landscape. I wasn't surprised. The sight of the bleak house must put off even the local thieves.

'And the water here is good.' The goddess meant that the tap outside my room and the one, which was shared by all three neighbours for washing, cooking and drinking, ran out of water less often than the others in the neighbourhood.

I found that the goddess' pet apso was between my legs, sniffing away.

'Senge, go away. He's a nuisance,' the goddess said, raising her arm threateningly.

The goddess blew her nose with the lower part of her pangthen, which she raised to her face with her free hand. Her rainbow-hued pangthen, now faded and far from ornamental, had been reduced to a mere symbol of matrimonial bliss, now used for purely utilitarian purposes like blowing her nose.

'Anyway, this place is quiet and I think you will like it. If you need anything, let us know,' she said. Before she waddled off with the glasses, Skelsang produced a package of dried apricots and presented it to her. She said thank you and disappeared around the corner of her part of the house.

Skelsang and I stayed outside for a while, surveying the house. Post the goddess' visit, I saw the place with new eyes. The place was quiet and I noticed, for the first time, birds chirping on the trees above, which gave the house and the surrounding area, a refreshing change from the suffocating congestion of Delhi. As for Skelsang, she spat out her opinion of our room by saying, 'It's worse than our cowshed in Nimmu.'

Our first morning in Gangkyi, Skelsang and I were awakened by a strange, chilling sound. Heavy, almost painful breathing followed a noise, half human, half animal, that turned into shrieks and groans and seemed to come out of the bowels of a beast that roamed the muffled light of dawn. The glow of dawn coupled with the swaying branches and the mysterious shrieks created an atmosphere of impending, unknown danger.

Where did the shrieks come from? And what were those cries, human or the howling of a beast?

'Kyee Heek! Kyee Heek! Kyee Heek!' Skelsang, startled and frightened, sat upright on the bed, wondering, fearing and dreading. Then her face broke into a smile of understanding. She cupped her mouth with both her hands to suppress her laughter. Slowly withdrawing one hand from her mouth, she pointing to the goddess' wall, she rolled her eyes, jerked her head back and made a motion of staggering, an act of someone going into a trance.

Yes, that was it. The goddess had opened her spiritual consultancy firm, and was working herself into a terrific trance to predict, advise, caution and point a way in the confusing darkness.

As we settled down in Dharamsala, we became friends with the largely bureaucratic crowd. So much so that we came to be included in their whispers and gossip. From these whispers we learnt about the goddess' strange powers, all of which pointed to her formidable reputation as a soothsayer, an unofficial oracle, a finder of lost, precious items, of important and sometimes highly confidential official documents which were mysteriously misplaced or lost. Everyone had heard about the devastating accuracy of her predictions.

Meanwhile, the Mess gong struck, summoning us for breakfast. I grabbed a towel, a cake of soap and my toothbrush and strode out of my room. After Skelsang had done washing her face and brushing her teeth, we walked down the hillside to the Mess. In the clearing before the goddess' room we spotted a Tibetan couple squatting on large slabs of stone, waiting for their turn to consult the goddess.

Soon Skelsang's attitude toward Dharamsala changed from petulance to one of tolerance and even acceptance.

As for my work at the Library, it was fun and rewarding. The fun part of the work came about mainly because of comparison with my earlier part-time sweater-selling profession and the daily grind of sweat and struggle to survive. The sweater-selling business was all about keeping body and soul together, eke out a living. The work at the Library, for want of a better phrase, was otherwise.

The director of the Library, a retiring, soft-spoken man with immense scholarly inclination, assigned me to collect Tibetan folk tales and translate these into English for a book the Library was planning to publish. I made myself busy, interviewing people, picking their brains for folk tales from different areas of Tibet. This assignment was a part of the Library's project to preserve the oral traditions of Tibet before the memory of Tibet's entire repertoire of fire-place stories was wiped out by the passing away of the old generation. I was told that the project came under a grant from the Ford Foundation. My Elephant notebooks, the Bic ballpoint and the Remington typewriter I was trying to master were kept furiously and noisily busy. I imagined I was racing against time. If in our small community, I heard some old Tibetan had died, I thought there went a story untold, unrecorded. I felt personally responsible for the death. I gave my assignment a sense of epic proportions, I and the grim reaper struggling for the memory of traditional Tibet, I retrieving, he taking it all away. I kept a score sheet. A Tibetan popping off before I had the chance to interview was a score for my adversary. A Tibetan who I had interviewed was a score for my side.

I was completely engaged in my epic battle.

Skelsang too became equally active and busy. Bustling with energy, she grew more confident by the day. She discovered that hand-knitted woollen sweaters were favoured by the growing number of foreign visitors to Dharamsala. Skelsang was not a person to let a business opportunity slip away. She had bales of wool transported from Ladakh and our single room soon became a godown for Jangthang wool. I suggested to Skelsang she should knit a logo, a trademark, an emblem, on the sweaters to indicate that these came from Dharamsala or that these sweaters were hand-woven by Tibetans. 'Tibet and Dharamsala sell, you know. The image of a yak would do the trick for you.' Skelsang liked the idea. However, as a precaution she consulted the goddess who went into a friendly trance and approved of the yak brand. So that was how Skelsang settled on the sturdy yak, the Himalayan beast of burden, whose shaggy hair conveyed the message of warmth and comfort during the winter chill. 'Yak' sweaters became a brand name. Skelsang hired extra hands. Skelsang's parents who visited us every winter became a regular conduit of this one-woman wool trade.

That year Dharamsala's monsoon was particularly savage. The rains lashed and the high wind, howling and screaming, swept through town, smashing windows and uprooting trees. This despite the best efforts of Ngapa-la, the town's weatherman. He would be present at every open-air public function under threat. During the monsoon season, his services were urgently required. Dressed in his usual white ngapa robes worn under a maroon shawl, Ngapa-la would strut about. He carried a large conch shell, his instrument for stopping or inducing rain. He had his hair tied in a bun. Ngapa-la wore thick glasses and sported a scattered, untidy salt and pepper beard. He would come armed with his big black umbrella. He would face the Kangra Valley and direct his conch at a particularly dark, threatening band of clouds and blow on the conch. As he blew, his cheeks bulged with the effort of packing such a powerful spell. The sound that issued from his conch, infused with the power and energy of many hours of recitation of potent, rain-smashing, cloud-scatttering mantras, would burst out in a series of low thunderclaps. The conch sound would rip the clouds apart with the force of cosmic energy. Well, if his conch didn't work, he always had his umbrella, which he used as a walking stick and when the heavens brought down the deluge, he would tweak it open and under it his gnome-like figure scurried forth ducking for a more dependable cover. More often than not, his conch shell did its work; the ominous clouds dissipated and the day became bright and sunny. At such times the community's regard for Dharamsala's only practising weatherman would be restored. For the community his success was a reflection of the potency of Tibetan culture. A spontaneous we-beat-the-monsoon celebration took place. The refugee children, as cheerful as the bright sun and the cheerful sky, would break into their exultant Ngapa song.

That summer Dharamsala was deprived of the rain-stopping services of Ngapa-la. He had been invited by the Tibetan refugees of Mundgod settlement in south India to bring more rain for their parched cornfields. That was one reason why the hot sullen summer of Dharamsala was washed away in one noisy downpour. As the rainwater rushed down the drains and gullies of the hill, it triggered off a riot of stench from last year's clogged sewage.

A part of the monsoon rain also leaked into our room through the cracks where the slate tiles overlapped. One night a strong gale lashed the roof and swept away a tile. We had to place a plastic bucket below the gaping hole to catch the pouring rain. Skelsang and I took turns throwing out the rainwater. The next morning I lifted the bucket and under it, also trying to escape the monsoon, was a little red scorpion. Rats, rainwater, a scorpion, all in our room. That wasn't all. Later a snake slithered down roof and dropped gracefully on our bed.

I can't make up my mind on how to describe Skelsang's reaction. Like people from cold places, Skelsang was horrified of anything that crawled. Either she spat out Dharamsala to exorcise herself of the place or she spat at it. Or, should I describe her reaction as volcanic because she erupted? Skelsang went into a screaming fit. The goddess, thinking that she had a new rival anxiously came around to ask what the matter was. She was visibly revlieved to learn that it was only the rats, snakes, scorpions and rainwater which had caused the fit.

When Skelsang came to her senses, she said that I should demand a better room.

'But you know as well as I do that there are no vacant staff quarters. All of them are occupied.'

'I demand a better room,' Skelsang said. 'If you don't have the spine do this, I will do it. I will go and see the secretary to demand a better room. I don't want to spend our nights with all these creatures.'

One day I casually mentioned our leaky-room problem to the secretary of the Library. He said he would put me in the wait-list. Sure enough, two weeks later, one of the translators of the Library migrated to America to set up his own dharma centre and I was given his apartment. It had a bedroom, a kitchen and a common toilet and bath. We said goodbye to the goddess.

The Lama Visits Dharamsala

☯

One day after we were confortably settled in our new apartment, I received a call.

'Telephone,' the Library accountant said, grunting as he came into my office, apparently annoyed at being disturbed and having to perform the errand.

I followed him to his office and picked up the receiver. It was a call from Tashi. He said that he and his family, including the lama, were at Hotel Tibet in McLeod Ganj and wanted to see me. 'Phuntsok too will be here,' Tashi said.

This was just the call I had been waiting for. I marched to the secretary's office and I told him that I was taking the afternoon off. Then I walked to my apartment to collect Skelsang. She packed two sacks with her Yak brand woollen sweaters to be sold wholesale to shop number seven in McLeod Ganj.

At McLeod Ganj, while Skelsang went off to sell her wares, I joined the crowd before Nowroji's store, which overlooked the bus stand. I spotted Phuntsok walking briskly on the TCV road. This time he wore jeans and a woollen Tibetan that buttoned next to the armpit. He had a cotton bag slung across his shoulder. I joined him on our way to Hotel Tibet.

'Why do you think the lama and the whole gang are here?'

'For an audience with His Holiness, I suppose,' Phuntsok said.

'Yes, an audience, but what for?'

'No idea.'

We stepped into Hotel Tibet. A familiar change had come over the place. Instead of the foreign faithfuls who usually came for darshan of the remnants of old Tibet, old Tibet had taken over the lobby. Gone was the cackle of many different tongues talking among themselves wondering how a piece of the old Tibet had taken roots on foreign soil and was actually flourishing. Instead, a crush of men and women, wrapped in yak skins, filled the lobby. The knot of people spoke excitedly in a dialect that we did not understand. The women spoke in whispers. In their hush, excited tones and in the burning devotion in their eyes, these people seemed to have reached the final destination of their Himalayan pilgrimage. They were new from Tibet. We could tell from the clothes they wore. They all held on to long flowing silk khatas and carried bags of tsampa, rancid butter packaged in yak skin and brick tea bundled in torn yellow paper wrappings inscribed with Chinese characters. The smell of rancid butter laced the air and heightened the intensity of the whispers.

I steered Phuntsok to the hotel restaurant and said, 'We'd better wait. With this crowd calling on Tashi or the lama, I think it will be quite a while before we get to see them.'

'Who are these people?' Phuntsok wondered, hitching his Gandhi glasses higher over the bridge of his nose.

'I think they are nomads from Golok. Perhaps they are here to pay their respects to the new Drubtop Rinpoche. Let's wait in the restaurant. It will take a while for us to see Tashi. He's the object of this crowd's excitement.'

'They all come to see him?' Phuntsok said in disbelief.

'Yes, they have all come to see Tashi, the one who failed to get the toiling masses excited about his revolution but who now commands the allegiance of a people of one far-flung corner of Tibet. Yes, it is amazing, the transformation of a failed revolutionary to a messiah.'

We stepped into the restaurant and spotted more Goloks, silently overflowing tables and chairs. They were all men. Gifts to their lama were stacked high on the tables. 'Amazing!' Phuntsok commented. 'I didn't realise Tashi had such spiritual influence. I thought he is a reincarnation of an ordinary lama. A neighbourhood lama. I didn't expect this! And they've come all the way from Tibet to receive his blessings?'

'Yes, all the way from the farthest corner of Tibet. Risking their lives and limbs.'

Phuntsok's Gandhi spectacles hung from the beak of his nose in astonishment. He hitched them higher on the nose to survey the restaurant with greater visual clarity and in open-mouthed astonishment. 'It's hard to believe,' Phuntsok said. 'A communist who failed to recruit a single new member is now a spiritual leader who commands the loyalty of these rough and tough lot.' Phuntsok stared long and hard at the silent Golok crowd. 'They look like bandits to me.'

'They are nomads,' I said dryly, irritated that what was obvious to a lot of Tibetans of our generation was new to Phuntsok. It seemed to me that being an orphan, Phuntsok had been cut off from a part of his past and a general knowledge of his country.

'Yes, yes,' Phuntsok said. 'Nomads, bandits, what's the difference?'

A hushed hubbub arose from the lobby and two Goloks stepped into the restaurant and gestured to those who were camped inside to follow. The crowd in the restaurant rose as one. Struggling with their khatas and gifts, they rushed out of the restaurant, leaving behind the smell of rancid butter and the whiff of a monastic kitchen. Suddenly there was silence and the excited whispers and fervent murmurs of prayers in the lobby echoed faintly and fadingly amid the general disarray of the restaurant's chairs and tables.

'Incredible!' Phuntsok said. 'It's hard to believe that someone you know is now a person who commands the devotion of such a warlike bunch. I wonder what Tashi really makes of this, of such devotion and faith? Or, does he even care?' Phuntsok said as Skelsang joined us and dumped a package of dried apricots. We contemplated the departed Golok crowd and ordered tea, each lost in our own thoughts. After a while, Phuntsok waved to someone behind me. I turned around and saw Metok striding towards us. 'There you are,' she said. 'Come up to Rinpoche's room. The Goloks have left and he is waiting for you.'

'Rinpoche?' Phuntsok asked. 'You mean Tashi?'

'Yes, Tashi, Rinpoche, whatever you like. Your friend is waiting for you,' Metok said sharply.

The three of us followed Metok out of the restaurant and up the balustraded stairway to Tashi's room. Ama Penpa, looking very busy and harried, with Ugen in tow, met us at the door and managed a weak welcoming smile. The equation had changed. Tashi sat on the bed, cross-legged and the lama sat on a low armchair below the bed. The lama beamed at us. When he spotted the khatas in our hands he deferentially pointed towards Tashi and we filed past the lama and offered them. Phuntsok smothered a laugh when he saw Tashi all wrapped up in tantric dignity, his long hair tied in a bun on the crown of his head. Tashi ignored Phuntsok's suppressed hilarity and accepted the khatas as if these were his due.

Tashi's room was a mess. The table overflowed with khatas and the corners of the room were stacked with gifts: packages of brick tea, large chunks of rancid butter packaged in greasy yak hide and bags of tsampa.

'So how's Dharamsala treating the two of you,' Tashi asked, once we were done with the ritual of paying him our respects.

'I'm back at my same old job of taking notes,' I said. 'So what brings you to Dharamsala?'

'To see the two of you,' Tashi said quietly. A change had come over Tashi. Gone was the young man seething in anger at the unfairness of the world. He had gained a quiet confidence and was measured in his words and actions. And he had a glow in his face.

The lama sat quietly in the chair. Seeing that his friends had shown proper respect to the twentieth Drubtop Rinpoche and perhaps to forestall any embarrassing interrogation of Tashi, the lama took over the discussion and staring at Skelsang asked, 'And who's this?'

'My wife, my karma which you said I would stumble upon,' I said quickly.

'Yes, yes,' the lama said and let out a hearty laugh. Skelsang decided that the lama's inquiry about her deserved acknowledgement and she brought out another khata from her handbag and bowed and presented it to the lama. She placed a package of dried apricots on his table.

Phuntsok turned to the lama and asked, 'These people who came visiting you...are they from your part of Tibet?'

'Not visiting me. They've come to receive Rinpoche's blessings,' the lama said, pointing to Tashi. 'And of course to receive the blessings of His Holiness the Dalai Lama. And yes, they are all from my part of Tibet. From Golok, my ancestral home.'

'Those tough-looking men sitting in the restaurant, they looked as if they were ready for a serious fight, so silent, so fierce.' Phuntsok said. He flicked dust from the sleeve of his shirt and hitched his glasses higher. 'I still can't get over the fact that these mean-looking men have come all the way from Tibet to receive his blessings!' Phuntsok blurted out, pointing at Tashi.

A look of annoyance leapt across the lama's face. 'These mean-looking men are tribal leaders. Important people.'

'They still have tribes in Tibet?' Phuntsok asked.

'Yes,' the lama said, irritably. 'We still have tribes in Tibet. Old ties are not that easy to break.'

Phuntsok turned to the lama and said, 'Rinpoche, I've heard from Dhondup here that you have been to Tibet. How did your visit go?'

'Very good, I think,' the lama said. 'I'm a happy man. I've fulfilled my life's dearest wish, to see my monastery before I die. And I have also accomplished other important tasks. I have completed writing the biography of the nineteenth Drubtop Rinpoche and I have succeeded in discovering him,' the lama said, pointing to Tashi. 'The new reincarnation. We are all returning to Tibet, to make what I said come true. We came here to seek His Holiness' permission and it has been granted,' the lama beamed. 'Well, I need to rest,' the lama said. 'It's been a long day for me. It's hard meeting people you knew as children. Suddenly meeting them as adults! It's hard explaining what happened in between. Perhaps for them and certainly for me. Yes, I need to rest. But the two of you may stay, if you like. I am sure the three of you have a lot to talk about.' The lama smiled knowingly. He stood up and gave a slight bow to Tashi and beaming his benevolence at the two of us lumbered out of Tashi's room.

We too stood up to go but Tashi stopped us. He said, 'Before I go I want the two of you to have this.' Tashi handed me a diary. 'This will answer a lot of your questions. At least it will. This is the diary I kept during my travels in Tibet. Please keep it. I hope you'll find it interesting. It is also a record of why I returned to the faith of my native land.'

'We'll return your diary after we have gone through it,' I promised..

'No, no, keep it. Remember, I am going back to Tibet,' Tashi said. 'I can't take it with me to Tibet. It will be incriminating. You keep it. I went to look for Tsering Migmar in Tibet and I found my faith and I have it here,' Tashi said, tapping his heart. 'Consider this diary my own lama stories for you. A fresh addition to your other lama stories. Well, it's getting late,' Tashi said, suddenly businesslike. 'Don't want to keep the two of you long.' He rose from his bed in a bid to say goodbye.

As soon as we got back to our rooms I opened Tashi's diary. It was written in his neat longhand. A random opening of the pages revealed this entry.

The Blue Lake
6 July 1983

I didn't know that we had a piece of Sri Lanka in Tibet. I think this is a sort of an exchange. Earlier on, Hanuman, ancient India's superman, had carried off a Tibetan mountain blessed with herbal plants to Sri Lanka to cure one of the main combatants mortally wounded in the day's war. Like that tropical island, Mahadeva Island was very much surrounded on all sides by water of the deepest blue. I discovered this when I visited the Blue Lake. My travelling companion, well, let's say, was Sherab, a former monk of Drubchen Monastery. When the lama was the abbot of the monastery Sherab was a novice. I told Sherab I knew the abbot of Drubchen Monastery. In fact, I said I was married to the lama's niece. But I needn't have made any extra effort to ingratiate myself to him because he said he knew this.

After the 1959 uprising when the monks of Drubchen Monastery were dismissed, Sherab disrobed and took a wife. Since then he had become a trusted cadre, first promoted to a commune leader. He slowly rose through the ranks. Now he is the first party secretary of Kyitsel district, a minor king and a new tribal chief within the communist system. He was the one who suggested that we take a motor-powered boat to one of the islands in the middle of Lake Kokonor. Today Sherab and I and Dorje, the captain of the feisty motor boat, drove to Mahadeva, the heart of Lake Kokonor. Sherab said it took about three whole days on horseback to make a complete circle of the lake. That was his way of saying the lake is very, very big. And I believed him because it took us about three hours on the motor boat to reach Mahadeva Island. Sherab added that according to Chinese scientists, Lake Kokonor would dry up within the next three hundred years. He looked despondent as he gave this piece of state secret.

A monk greeted us on the shores of the island. He wore the robes of a Gelug monk but his long hair would make any woman of Tsang proud. It reached his ankles and was dishevelled. I expressed surprise when Sherab said he was a monk. I pointed to his long hair. Sherab said he was alone on the island and had no barber who could shave his head. The monk was as emaciated as Milarepa. He greeted us as if he had been expecting us for a long time. He had a reason to welcome us. Our party was bearing his provisions. Sherab handed him a bag of tsampa, butter and brick tea. Karma, the monk, was twenty-four years old and hailed from Chamdo and had been in retreat on this island for six years now and hoped to complete twelve. He depended on the goodwill of the nomads scattered along the shores of Kokonor to keep supplying him with food.

Karma gave us a guided tour of the island. During the course of the tour Karma explained why a piece of Sri Lanka was located in the middle of Tibet's largest saltwater lake. As with all Tibetan beginnings, the story started during the reign of Songtsen Gampo, who had dispatched his wily and able minister, Gar Tongtsen, to China to ask for the hand of Tang China's most celebrated princess in marriage to the Tibetan king. The princess was none other than Wengchen Kongsho. The Tibetan demand for a matrimonial alliance was backed by the might of Songtsen Gampo's army. And Wengchen Kongsho was released to the barbarians. During the journey back to Tibet through the grasslands, Gar Tongtsen's son became thirsty and there was no water in sight for miles around. Gar Tongtsen told his son to pick up a large stone and water would gush out and return the stone to the same spot when his thirst was quenched. Gar Tongtsen's son picked up a stone and sure enough sparkling clear water shot up in the air like a fountain. The son drank enough water to last for many days, but in his relief he forgot to place the stone over the gushing water. The water kept gushing out and formed Lake Kokonor and threatened to engulf the roof of the world. That was the time when Gar Tongtsen prayed. His prayers happened to be answered by Guru Padmasambhava who was on a hilltop in Sri Lanka. Guru Padmasambhava grabbed the nearest hill and hurled it towards Tibet. This hill plugged the hole and prevented the inundation of Tibet. It later became Island Mahadeva, the heart of Lake Kokonor.

As a grand finale of our tour of the island and its history, the four of us walked to the top of the island. Sprawling ruins dominated the island top. The five-star Chinese flag fluttered over the ruins. According to Karma these were the ruins of a monastery. During the Cultural Revolution, the island was converted into an open prison. He pointed to the vast stretch of water on all sides and said that these served as prison walls.

Sherab suggested that we string prayer flags from one ruined wall top to the other. A strong wind arose from the shore and blew the prayer flags in a fluttering rage. We took this as a sign from the gods and threw fistfuls of tsampa into the air and shouted, 'Victory to the Gods. Lha Gyalo! Lha Gyalo!' Our cries rang throughout the treeless island and flocks of gulls rose into the sky and encircled the island as if in frantic attempts to convince us to leave them in peace and quiet.

Afterwards we sat down on the island top amidst the ruins and fluttering prayer flags for a simple meal of boiled yak meat and tsampa. We washed these down with green tea kept hot in thermos flasks.

The last image of Karma that springs to my mind is when he stood on the hilltop waving to us. This modern-day Milarepa, who stood there amidst the ruins of his heritage, was the reigning deity of this piece of Sri Lankan territory. The fluttering Chinese flag dominated both the figure and the ruins. That image stays in my mind. It still stays because I am intrigued by the different identities trying to assert and impose themselves on that stark island. That image somehow mirrored what was going on in my own mind. Anyway, I am glad to reflect that Karma's presence on the island seemed to have cleansed it of the evil days of the Cultural Revolution. I am sure that he is still at it. His story of the origins of Island Mahadeva endowed the island and the lake with mythic enchantment. More than the mad fluttering of the Chinese flag, the meditations of Karma seemed to permeate the island and its cold rippling waters.

That was how Sherab, without saying a word about it, led us into celebrating the forty-eighth birthday celebrations of the Dalai Lama and allowed me to have a peek at the inner world and secret longings of the Golok nomads.

In his diary Tashi had made some efforts to disguise the people who had helped him. But in the case of the first party secretary of Madoi, even giving him a new name wasn't enough. By mentioning his official position, Tashi had compromised him. I wondered whether Tashi had ever worried about his diary landing in the wrong hands and jeopardising the lives and careers of those mentioned therein. What made Tashi so sure that his dairy would never leave him? I read on. This was Tashi's entry on his way to Lhasa.

Communist lessons on the journey to the West
4 August 1983

Before I left for Lhasa, I told Sherab the real reason for my travels. I told him I was looking for Tsering Migmar. Sherab handed me several references and introductions. One introduction was to a fellow Golok who was doing business in Lhasa. Sherab said he could be trusted and was in the thick of the world of guanxi in Lhasa and knew almost everyone. Gyatso was the fellow's name. He's s the one who greases the wheel and keeps the circle of personal connections in full rotation, to everyone's benefit. For a change I was happy to realise that the corruption that has reared its ugly head was actually convenient for everyone. This meant that my task had been made much easier. To enable me to grease the wheel to its full effect, Sherab equipped me with loads of rancid butter wrapped in yak skin, the gift of the nomads to the inhabitants of the City of Gods. He also handed me several scriptural texts. He said I was to give them to the lama. 'He couldn't take these with him,' Sherab explained and pointing to the butter he added, 'Make offerings for me.' With these words, he flagged me off from the sullen grasslands of Golok. But Karma on Mahadeva Island had given me an idea, so before setting off, I shaved my head and put on a monk's robe. If I wanted people to believe that I was an itinerant monk, I had to look the part. Sherab laughed and commented that I would make a fine monk and pilgrim.

I headed for Gormo. From there I took a bus to Lhasa. On the way I met a Chinese student who spoke English. 'Call me Charlie,' he said cheerfully. Charlie had an open honest face and the unthinking excitable nervousness of a Red Guard about to stage a struggle session to expose a major reactionary. He talked incessantly, only now and then making inquiries about me. 'My father,' Charlie said as if confiding a secret, 'came here, to liberate Tibet.'

I said, 'Thank you and thank your father for a job well done.' Charlie beamed and asked, 'Your English, strange English?' I told him my English was Indian English. Charlie said, 'I see. My English BBC, BBC Radio English.'

Having established the superiority of the source of his linguistic wisdom, Charlie said with a flash of bitterness, 'But my father no longer alive to receive your thank you. He was killed during the Cultural Revolution. That's the thanks he got for a job well done.'

Charlie, I discovered, was a victim of the violence of the Cultural Revolution and bore the psychological scars with a loud and open grudge. I was on my guard and guardedly expressed my attraction to communism. I thought that was the best policy. Charlie quickly disabused me of my communist illusion and let out a loud and disbelieving laugh. 'Communism?' he asked, startling the other travellers crammed in the bus. 'Not even those old turtle eggs in Beijing believe in communism. It's a mistake, this communist thing. But no one will admit it and that's a bigger mistake,' Charlie said with deep bitterness. 'As for me, no one can tell me what or what not to believe in. I am a Buddhist!' he declared with grim, open defiance. 'I'm on pilgrimage to all holy places. To get rid of the bitterness in me.'

I asked him why he chose Tibet. 'There are many Buddhist pilgrimage sites in other regions of the mainland.'

'Tibet is different,' Charlie said. 'It is remote. The mountains of Tibet, in fact, all high places have spiritual significance. Because it is so remote,

a pilgrimage to Tibet becomes spiritually meaningful for me. The harder the journey, greater is the merit you gain. A journey tests you, prepares you for the blessings you receive when you reach its end. That's why The Journey to the West has a meaning for me. It's just you, the road before you, the destination and the spiritual force that drives you to the end. That is freedom. That is happiness. That,' Charlie paused and searched for a word and said, 'is liberation.'

I was intrigued by Charlie. I didn't know what to make of his openness and frank comments. Charlie bore a grudge against the system, but his personality gave no hint that he had lived through an era of suspicion and the midnight knock. This made me cautious and alert. I quickly wished him a safe journey. 'Remember, we liberated Tibet. Now I am going to Tibet to seek personal liberation. I want the courtesy to be returned. This is how much we hope.' He laughed lightly and covered himself with a blanket and dozed off. I did not know what to make of this. Was Charlie joking or was he hinting at something deeper? Or was he trying to ferret out information and opinion? Charlie started snoring, loudly, and his snoring was as carefree as his opinions. To me he became Checkpoint Charlie, the point where one suspicion merges into another.

It was my turn to be intrigued by Tashi's entry and the route he took in his travels in Tibet. The normal route for anyone travelling to Tibet when he enters through Nepal is to make the journey from west to east and if one was foolish enough to maintain a diary to at least make the entries according to this route. But Tashi had waited till he had got to Kyitsel to start the record of his journey. The natural instinct of anyone who was returning home after years of separation would be to first head to his hometown. Tashi's was Shigatse. Why did he not first visit Shigatse? And he had left out the account of half of his journey. What was more intriguing was his dismissive entry in the dairy on Lhasa. What was supposed to be the climax of the journey was reduced to a few cursory lines. Where his entry on Kyitsel and the Blue Lake was careless and rich in information, his entry on Lhasa was vague and irritatingly tight-lipped. Where earlier he had been loquacious, throwing caution to the wind, Lhasa made Tashi seem at a loss for words. It appeared as if he had eventually realised the potential damage his diary could do to him and to those he had come in contact with if it were to fall in the hands of the Chinese authorities. Except for a few subtle hints, he refused to confide about his doings in Lhasa.

The City of the Gods
7 August 1983

To the rest of the world it is the Forbidden City, the Vatican of Asia, the seat of the Grand Lama. To Tibetans, it is the City of the Gods and the repository of their cultural wisdom and faith. But for the Potala, Lhasa is just another Tibetan town, only a little larger than the others. The romance of Lhasa has been greatly exaggerated. Maybe it is the case of distance lending enchanment to the place for examining it at close quarters, one wonders whether there is much to it. I am in the City of the Gods and to me it does not mean anything.

In Lhasa, I met my own god. He is Gyatso the Golok, the one recommended by Sherab. I told him that I was looking for my Uncle Tsering Migmar. Gyatso assured me that he would find my Uncle and ensure his wellbeing. That was the only consolation I had in a city that has over the centuries drawn the attention and energy of the some of the finest travellers. I wondered why they bothered at all.

As promised, I made a hundred butter-lamp offerings in Jokhang. I suppose my reputation as a pious monk must have spread! I also gave several chunks of butter to Gyatso.

I wondered whether Tashi's dismissive remarks about Lhasa were prompted by age-old Tsangpa envy for seeing its power and prestige being wrested by Lhasa. Shigatse, the capital of Tsang, once dominated Tibet. But I was wrong. Tashi was equally dismissive of his own birthplace. In fact, his entry on Shigatse started as an attempt to write a treatise on the effects of colonialism on human nature and seemed to have been interrupted in mid-sentence by the proverbial midnight knock.

Tsangpa Sulleness
15 August 1983

Shigatse is a sullen place. The city's inhabitants are furtive and speak in whispers and look at you with suspicious eyes. I wondered what happened to the Tsang humour, Tsang's self-deprecation. Shigatse is a place that has been robbed of its pride and now lives in self-hate and double humiliation, humiliation of having been overshadowed by Lhasa and then the humiliation of having been forced to lend a reluctant hand of cooperation to the new conquerors from further afield. The pride of Shigatse and the symbol of Tsang's dominance of the whole of Tibet, the once magnificent Samdrup Tse Dzong, on which was modelled the Potala Palace, is now wiped clean from Shigatse's skyline. And the people of Shigatse had a hand in it. The ruins of Samdrup Tse Dzong serve as a daily reminder of Tsang's secret guilt. That seems to explain the furtive looks and the whispers.

At Tashilhunpo Monastery, which has kept its architectural dignity unsullied, I offered a lavish butter-lamp offering and thanked the gods for this.

Like Lhasa, Shigatse is a place not worth looking at and I did not. I did not even bother to trace my relatives, aunts and uncles. I decamped on the first available truck for Ngari but not before I bought a prayer wheel and...

Wit and wisdom on the road to Ngari Korsum

17 August 1983

For the last two days I had been trekking, hitching rides in overcrowded trucks and surviving on tsampa and black tea. I had also paid my way for great distances in crumbled reminbi notes when transportation was available and the drivers sober. In this part of Tibet, the passengers cheer on the drivers by offering mugfuls of strong chang and the drivers, their resolve to get their passengers safely through another day greatly stiffened, would cheerfully lurch forward their trucks on slippery, precipitous roads. I discovered that keeping the drivers constantly supplied with a steady flow of chang was a form of tipping. It is like giving a hundred-dollar bill to a taxi driver for a one-mile drive and saying, 'Keep the change, man.'

By the time we reached Sakya, I'd had enough of drunken drivers, let them keep their trucks, I was prepared to trek. I think I made the right decision. The weather is pleasant and the people, away from the politicised and oppressive atmosphere of Shigatse, are cheerful and hospitable. In fact, I am writing this in the tent of Dhargye with my namesake, the black *mastiff, barking loudly outside. I had wandered into Dhargye's tent one evening in the hope of him allowing me to boil some tea for myself over his fire. Out in the distance with a stream running by were a couple of tents, with smoke rising from them. I walked towards the tents and was soon greeted by the vicious snapping and barking of a huge mastiff tied to a pole. I shouted. Dishevelled Dhargye popped his head out of the tent and gave me a good look. Seeing me in my monk's robe with my prayer wheel twirling in my hand and a load of scriptural wisdom on my back, Dhargye beckoned me in and asked where I was headed for.*

'On a pilgrimage to the Precious Mountain,' I replied.

Dhargye was suitably impressed. He shouted 'Dolma!' Dolma hurried in and Dhargye asked her to lay some food before me. Dolma lost no time in setting down a cup of steaming butter tea, a large wooden bowl of tsampa and a plate of boiled mutton, with a knife, before me. 'Eat,' Dhargye said, sticking out his tongue and sucking in his breath. I dined on this nomadic feast. Dhargye said he was recuperating and that was why he was indoors. Usually he was out with his herds. Now his children were out in the upper reaches, herding his yaks.

While enjoying the generous food laid before me and feeling a great deal of gratitude for Dhargye's hospitality, I looked around. It was a large tent. By the arrangement of the mattresses and the low cushions, it was clear that the family's domesticity was centred around the hearth located in the middle of the tent. The part of the tent directly above the hearth had a small hole to let out the smoke from the kitchen fire. The altar was a profusion of statues of the Buddha, renowned teachers and deities. Photos of lamas in exile and those in Tibet were stuck on the glass frames of the altar. To my surprise there on the altar provocatively displayed with a khata over it was a small black and white photograph of the Dalai Lama when he was in his teens. Somehow this act of defiance and faith moved me deeply. Was it a political statement? I turned to Dhargye and asked him whether keeping a photo of the Dalai Lama did not land him into trouble.

Dhargye thought about it and said, 'What do we nomads know? We tend to our herds and watch the changing seasons. But, yes, we nearly got into trouble.' Dhargye recounted the episode of the Dalai Lama's photograph in his possession. It was two years ago, Dhargye said. The usual team of cadres came to collect the annual animal taxes. Dhargye said he was foolish enough to invite them into the main family tent for tea and refreshment. That was when the cadres who were all Tibetans spotted the Dalai Lama's photograph. The leading cadre of the team gave Dhargye and his family a long lecture on the benefits the Chinese Communist Party had brought to Tibet. The cadre listed the roads, schools, health care, electricity, etc. The cadre then pointed at the photo of the Dalai Lama and demanded, 'What has that man done for you?'

Dhargye in turn listed all the good things the Party had done for Tibet. He said the Tibetan people, including him and his family, remained deeply grateful for these wonderful benefits. Then pointing at the photograph of the Dalai Lama he said, 'As for him, he has done nothing for us. Yes, he has done nothing for us, nor does he want anything from us.'

There was a sly gleam of a smile playing in Dhargye's eyes. He said, 'They fell silent and silently handed me the usual list of annual taxes I owed the state. I thought the taxes would be higher, but they weren't. They were the same as the year before. The usual number of yaks, the same amount of wool, etc. Since then whenever they come, I offer them tea and meat in the other tent, which I call the tax tent. That tent has a large photo of Mao. You want to see it?' Dhargye asked.

'No!' I shouted. But I am grateful for this encounter with nomadic wit, wisdom and hospitality.

When I had finished, Dhargye asked me whether I did divination. I asked him, 'What for?' Dhargye said he wanted to know how much of his herd of yaks would survive the coming winter.

'I don't do divination,' I said sharply. Making a show of relenting, I said, 'But better still I will read the appropriate religious text for the protection of your herds.' Dhargye nodded gratefully. I unpacked my load and unwrapped the lama's scriptures. I chose a particularly slim text and read. When I had finished reading the text, I heard the bells of the yaks and the whoops and yodels of the herdsmen coming home for the night.

Dhargye thought that was a good omen. The coincidence of my finishing the prayers for the protection of the animals and the herdsmen and their herds coming to the nomadic encampment from the greener pastures of the *upper reaches pleased him. Because of this Dhargye referred to me as the Golok Lama. And I didn't mind.*

Tashi's diary became rich in detail and information when he was travelling through western Tibet. But the account which struck me and which perhaps constituted the real reason for his opting to become the twentieth Drubtop Rinpoche is this short account of his experience in the Mount Kailash region. This seems to be his road-to-Damascus experience. The account is surprisingly reticent, as if he didn't want to reveal too much or he couldn't find the words to express the emotions that overwhelmed him during his meditation in the area. But this account sparkled with some kind of spiritual energy.

Gangkar Tise and Mapham Yumtso
2 September 1983

I am on the southern shore of Tso Mapham Yumtso, having a steaming cup of butter-tea over a roaring fire kept alive by slabs of yak-dung. A couple of days earlier, I had joined other pilgrims and done a complete kora of the Precious Mountain. I felt I did something significant, something meaningful, something truly Tibetan.

I completed the kora of the Precious Mountain. It took me three days. Then I headed south…to the Eternal Lake. On the southern shore of the lake, to my astonishment I came across a group of Indian pilgrims, all from West Bengal. The men and women dipped in the lake fully clothed and chanted prayers and hymns. One particular Bengali was loud in his prayers. When he paused I asked him in English what was he chanting. He turned around in astonishment and instead of answering, he shouted to his group and said, 'Here's a monk who speaks our colonial masters' language.' The others turned around, contemplated me for a while and waved their hands and continued their chants. I asked the man once again what he was chanting. In answer he showed me two books, both in English. One was A Mountain in Tibet *and the other,* The Wonder That Was India. *'The English translations are better,' he said, as a way of explaining why he was praying to his gods in his colonial masters' language. 'This one is from the Puranas,' he said. He chanted with his face turned to Mount Kailash,*

As dew is dried up by the morning sun,
so are the sins of men dried up by the sight of the Himalaya,
where Shiva lived and where the Ganga falls from the foot of Vishnu
like slender thread of a lotus flower.
There are no mountains like the Himalaya,
for in them are Kailash and Manasarovar.

*'This one is by Kalidas,' the loud Bengali shouted. 'You know Kalidas?
Shakuntala, Meghdoot? He's like our Tagore. You know Tagore? Gitanjali?'
And the Bengali loudly and proudly ,vocalised another verse, subjecting me
to his literary pride.*

In the northern quarter is divine Himalaya,
The lord of mountains,
Reaching from Eastern to Western Oceans,
Firm as rod to measure the earth...

*He continued to chant ancient Sanskrit paeans to the mountain and the
lake. I was struck by ancient India's lyrical homage to the sacred geography
of Tibet. This was new to me. So much spiritual energy and devotion
generated by a place that I had earlier regarded as a piece of real estate,
to be bought, sold or pillaged.*

*Contemplating the clear waters of Manasaravar, I thought I too
needed to have my sins washed away. I stripped and had a quick dip in
the waters of the lake. Perhaps I soaked my sins too, wet and dripping. I
was freezing.*

*Watching Kailash out in the distance in the north from this end of
the lake, I realised this is Tibet, the very heart of our spiritual geography
and sacred space. The children I taught back in Delhi at Majnu Ka Tilla
are made of this stuff. This is their identity. The lonely eternity of that
mountain in the distance, as lonely and as eternal as the act of creation
itself, and its rugged, exposed dignity is their real character. No matter what
ism or human interpretation we put forth to explain our life on Earth,
it cannot compare to the fact we have been given birth, sustenance and
nurturing by Mother Earth. That I think explains the nomadic kora of a
mountain and lake, as a form of reverence and gratitude to the Earth for*

tolerating our petty adventures on its sacred soil. What right do I or anyone else have to say it is otherwise. Before the Eternal Lake and the Precious Mountain, I thought I had found my true vocation. Let me say that I have just demoted myself from being a communist to an animist, someone who worships Nature and our very own homegrown religion called Bon. Before the Precious Mountain and the Eternal Lake, I am convinced that man is not certainly the measure, not of anything. We are merely some uninvited guests who decided to stay on, with the delusion of staying forever. And changed things in the home that offered us so much. If there is any greater exploitation, it is the human exploitation of Mother Earth, eternal and mute and forbearing. There are no more relentless or devastating predators than human beings. Dinosaurs have come and gone but now is the age of human-saurs, bent on devouring the resources of the Earth to their bare bones. The question is not whether we will become extinct. The question is how soon we will consume ourselves into an early extinction. But the Mountain and the Lake, the yin and yang of creation, will remain, mute witnesses to humans ravishing the Earth and themselves.

The real issue is not class struggle, the battle between the exploiters and the exploited. The real struggle is species struggle. It is about how long man, the ultimate exploiter, will hold dominion over Earth. In view of this, class struggle becomes a mere side show. We need not bother too much about it.

'So this is the reason!' I shouted.

My shout startled Skelsang out of her sleep. She glared and slumped back to sleep. I slapped the diary shut and placed it on the altar.

The next morning Skelsang wanted the diary dethroned.

I refused. I said I had placed the diary on my part of the altar. It deserved its place before the flickering votive lamps and bowls of pure water offering. Tashi's diary remained on the altar, which now constituted a new prayer of hope from a refreshed soul.

The Year of Protests and Other Years

⊚

It was not in the Water-Rat Year. It was not in the Fire-Tiger Year, either. It was in the Fire-Rabbit Year (or, as some people insisted, in the Fire-Protest Year) of 2114 of our Lord and Master, Heaven-descended King Nyatri Tsenpo and the one who was the first to sit on the throne of the Land of Snows, that he mysteriously showed up in Dharamsala. Out of nowhere, really, just like Heaven-descended Nyatri Tsenpo himself. Claimed he fought in the war between the two reigning superpowers. That was Nyatri Tsenpo, not his modern avtar. Claimed lightning and thunderbolts were used as weapons. Shafts of cosmic light streaking across the sky burst upon armies like thunderclaps and tossed warriors, chariots, elephants, horses and maces high up in the air. Well, it seemed he fought on the losing side and escaped. It took him a long time to find his way to Tibet, centuries, maybe a millenium or two. At last at the foot of Mount Lhari Gyangto in the forests of Kongpo, he found himself surrounded by a group of despondent Bonpo priests who had just succeeded in losing their king. A new king was sourly needed. Not having discovered the Word and not being bilingual as yet, the despondent Bonpo priests made a spontaneous collective gesture to find out from where he came. The man pointed at Mount Lhari Gyangto that pierced the turquoise blue Tibetan sky. The Tibetan crowd looked up at the sky, knelt down and thanked the heavens over Tibet for sending down their king. They made a sedan chair, enthroned their heaven-descended lord on it and carried him off to the empty throne. The new king became known as Nyatri Tsenpo, the Neck-enthroned One. Later when he became fluent in Tibetan, he told his Tibetan subjects tall tales of the Mahabharata wars. He continued to sit there, on the throne, telling his stories, a storyteller who had come to rule our kingdom—for a song and a new story.

Well, after the Fire-Rabbit Year of 2114, another figure crossed the mountains in the opposite direction. He did not make any claims of having fought in the war between the day's two reigning superpowers. He had been on a sowing, planting and spreading mission. The year was 1990.

Several years before he showed up in Dharamsala, the TYC people were especially insistent and strident. They wanted the Year of Fire-Protest to be added to the sixty-year cycle of the Tibetan calendar. Nothing like this had happened before, the TYC said. We were witnessing Tibetan history, they said. The Fire-Protest Year must make it into the Tibetan lunar calendar, they repeated, nay demanded. The old fogies of the Tibetan Medical and Astro Institute, compilers of the Tibetan almanac, poring over dusty scriptural texts, their glasses perched on their snuff-stained noses, sadly shook their heads and said that the Fire-Protest Year was not mentioned in the Tibetans' traditional astronomical wisdom. The neighbouring Nechung Oracle went into a prolonged trance and said that the Fire-Protest Year was not predicted in the ancient predictions. Looking into the future, the oracle shook his head and pronounced, nor in future ones.

So two of the most venerable institutions of Dharamsala shot down the TYC's political demands couched in the preservation-of-culture language. But everyone else agreed that 1987 should be declared the Year of Protest, many protests, in fact. There was also an element of refugee jealousy involved. They had been bringing out protest rallies every year, on 10 March, on any occasion which offered itself as the best possible excuse for staging a demonstration, but received no mention, leave alone coverage, in the media. But look, some of the jealous refugees pointed out, one fine day a group of religious-minded Tibetans in Lhasa taking advantage of the more relaxed attitude to religion decided to take a lingkor walk around the Jokhang temple and they managed to grab headlines internationally. Not fair, the jealous ones complained. Leave aside the fairness of the issue, the demonstration the Tibetans in Lhasa staged in September 1987 triggered a decade of protest rallies in Tibet. That particular year was certainly the Year of Protest, many protests. Yes, the September 1987 protest rally triggered the cycle of protests and supporting protests between Tibetans in Tibet and those in the rest of the world. The September 1987 protest demonstration triggered an explosion of protests by refugees, to support the protest in Lhasa and condemn the subsequent Chinese crackdown in the Tibetan capital. The refugees and their countrymen in Tibet received new energy, new enthusiasm from each other. Each echoed the others' dissent. This cycle of protests and supporting protests was moving quite nicely on both sides of the Himalayas when suddenly the Chinese students in Beijing got all excited. They started a mass demonstration. Some said it was a million strong. The authorities imposed martial law. The students were furious. They demanded, 'How dare you! Beijing is not Lhasa!' For once the authorities did not discriminate.

However, the September 1987 demonstration and the demonstrations that followed in Lhasa electrified Dharamsala, like nothing else had ever done. The refugees felt that the Tibetan people had given their verdict. The efforts of the exiles, however feeble, to bring international attention to the dismal situation in Tibet was sanctioned and bravely supported in words and deeds by Tibetans in Tibet. That gave new courage to the exiles.

It was sometime in September 1989 that Phuntsok, who was spending a week with us, and I couldn't believe our ears. We were ecstatic. The uprisings in Lhasa vindicated our exiled existence. We no longer felt that we were one people divided by the Himalayas. We sat up late to discuss the news. That particular night Phuntsok and I were hunched over our bowls of noodle soup. Skelsang had left for her winter sweater-selling business. This time it was Bodh Gaya. Her parents had joined her there.

'Wow! I take my hat off to them,' Phuntsok kept repeating. 'They have proved to the world that our struggle is alive and real.'

I think that was the exact moment when he showed up at our doorsteps. Out of nowhere really. There was rapid, insistent knocking on the door.

'Wow! I didn't know that it will be that soon,' Phuntsok said. 'The bearer of good news,' Phuntsok said eagerly. He stood up and strode across the room and into the passageway to open the door. 'Here's a monk who has come to see you, Dhondup,' Phuntsok said, not letting the visitor enter the room. Then there was a long silence. 'It's Tsering Migmar-la!' Phuntsok shouted and flung the door wide open. Judging by the intensity of the shout, I thought Phuntsok might have jumped right out of his pyjamas. I rushed to the door and an emaciated figure in maroon robes limped into our room, hesitant and unsure, a knowing smile of familiarity softening his lean, harsh face. The face and eyes fell into place. In spite of his shaven head and that his swaddling robes, the face of Tsering Migmar, the China expert who briefly wanted to be an avenging Golok, was softened by the warm glow of a smile. His eyes, quick and sharp, playfully darted back and forth from Phuntsok to me.

'You're alive!' I managed to greet Tsering. 'And in monk's robes! What happened?'

'I managed to escape! That's what happened,' Tsering said choosing a chair and settling himself comfortably, as if nothing had happened.

'And Dechen-la, she knows you are in India?' Phuntsok asked.

'Sure, she does. She was the first one to know. She's my wife, my long-suffering wife.'

'But you have become a monk! Does she know about this?' Phuntsok asked.

'This?' Tsering said, feeling his robes. 'Disguise, disguise all the way from Tibet, all the way from Lhasa to Kyitsel in Golok and back here. An effective disguise. It worked for me. That's why I'm alive.'

'Unbelievable!' an astonished Phuntsok said. 'Tsering-la, you know that your comrades have disbanded? They closed down the Tibetan Communist Party. And Tashi has been recognised and enthroned as the twentieth Drubtop Rinpoche. You know that?'

'Yes. I met the Drubtop Rinpoche and the lama in Kyitsel when I managed to escape from prison. They were the ones who saved me, the ones who made it possible for me to escape to India again. I owe my life to them.'

Phuntsok scurried to the corner of the room where he had stacked his bag and retrieved a 3-X rum bottle from it. Setting three teacups on the table, he poured generous helpings. Tsering, wrapped in his monk's robes, unconsciously reached out for the nearest cup and gulped down the fiery liquor. 'I really needed this,' Tsering said, as if his act required an explanation. He set the empty teacup on the low table. Phuntsok immediately refilled.

Tsering Migmar, with great effort, slipped off his tan Bata shoes, tucked in his feet and sat cross-legged on the low chair. His face had become leaner, emaciated, half his teeth were gone. He looked old and exhausted. But his eyes retained their old, darting intelligence. He knew that we expected him to tell us about his adventures and the reasons for his prolonged absence. He launched into his adventures immediately and told them with great gusto, glad of an attentive audience. He gave the impression that he had long wished to get the story off his chest. I picked up a ballpoint pen and opened my notebook. I sensed that Tsering Migmar had a riveting story to tell.

'As you have rightly suspected, I was a member of the Tibetan Communist Party, one of the founding members,' Tsering said. 'But that was a long time ago when we were younger and quite foolish. But we had our differences. Tashi and Samdup wanted to start a revolution in the exile community while I wanted to mobilise the Tibetans in Tibet. There was an intense debate. I pointed out to them the futility of their plans. We are all refugees. A social revolution had already taken place. Our refugee status rendered us equally poor. Our trying to start a revolution in exile would make us look foolish. The two disagreed, vehemently, right to their last bitter teardrop. So I told them to do things their way. Tashi and Samdup could start their revolution in the refugee community and I would return to Tibet, for whatever it was worth, to make the masses more aware. So I went to Tibet on my own. Tashi and Samdup pleaded. They said it was not necessary for me to go to Tibet. They said, think about your family. You would be more useful outside prison walls, they said, but I went ahead and crossed the Himalayas. I suppose once you start a thing you would have to go through the whole thing, right to the bitter end.'

Phuntsok was transfixed. He hung on to Tsering's every word. He sat cross-legged on the cement floor, on three layers of bed-sized Tibetan carpets and covered in a Chinese blanket, nursing his drink and looked quite ready for the warmth and comfort emanating from the fiery cup of liquor and the story of one man's return to the place of his youth. Phuntsok was both the stern inquisitor and the fawning fan, asking sharp sceptical questions and solicitously refilling Tsering Migmar's teacup with rum and water. 'And you,' Phuntsok intervened, 'told Dechen-la about this, your decision to return to Tibet?'

'Yes, I told her, but only the half-truth, that I was visiting my relatives. She was apprehensive at first, but she let me go when she realised how much I missed my relatives. Later I learned that Tashi and Samdup had the decency to tell her the truth, but only that they were the ones who had egged me on. But she knows the truth now and she is happy, not because she learned the truth, but because I managed to return to India, to freedom, to her and our boys, in one piece.'

Except for Phuntsok's openly sceptical questions, getting fewer and far between, I could only hear the relentless narrative of Tsering Migmar's story, punctuated by the quick rustle of the pages of my notebook. These notes grew into the following story, translated from Tsering's Tibetan into my English, edited from his defiance and anguish into this inspiration.

'It was an impulse, my going to Tibet,' Tsering Migmar recounted that first night when he suddenly re-surfaced from the darkness of the great beyond. 'Yes, an impulse drove me back to my country,' he said. The gaze of his penetrating eyes fell ruefully on the large framed black and white photo of the Potala Palace Skelsang and I had hung on the wall above our altar.

He said he wanted to do what all refugees did, he simply wanted to walk across the border. He wanted to retrace his escape route to India. But silly, irritating details got in the way of his plan. In the end he said he established himself as a credible Sherpa businessman in Kathmandu. He bought a Nepalese passport and learned to speak Nepali with a Sherpa accent. It wasn't too hard. Tsering's Migmar's lavish distribution of money helped him make most of his plans fall into place. He had the persistence of a zealot and the tenacity of a yak.

He set up shop in Thamel, Kathmandu's fashionable business spot, catering exclusively to tourists. He melted his business with that of Thamel's. He decided buying and selling Tibetan antiques, stolen from Himalayan monasteries, or smuggled across the border from Tibet, was the most effective front. But first things first, Tserng Migmar said. First, he had to select a new name for himself. After considerable thought, Tsering introduced himself as Sherpa Kusho and Sherpa Kusho he came to be known as in his expanding business circle. When people talked about him, they talked about the antique operation he was running throughout the Nepal Himalayas and across the border into Tibet. That explained the man's wealth, they agreed. Rumours flew thick and fast in Kathmandu's business circles, among the Marwaris, the Newars, the Sherpas who tended to dominate the trekking business and the Tibetan refugees who dominated the carpet-weaving business, all captains of industry of the world's only Hindu kingdom. Sherpa Kusho joined the ranks of successful businessmen of the Himalayas, who, though burdened with little education were blessed with wit and took advantage of the money-making milieu created by the collapse of old restraints after the independence of India and the fall of Tibet. Tibetan refugees, scattered along the whole length of the Himalayas, added a new burst of energy to the rush for prosperity, and Sherpa Kusho determined that if it was antiques they wanted, then antiques were what he would sell. Most of the antiques that slipped across this side of the Himalayas from Tibet tended to converge in Kathmandu. They were ferried by the peripatetic Tibetan refugees operating from Ladakh in the west to Arunachal Pradesh in the east. Sherpa Kusho soon had the lion's share of the booty.

Sherpa Kusho's choice of Kathmandu as a base for his business operations was smart and proved opportune. A benign monarch ruled Nepal and tolerated anything that did not smack of political restlessness. The Nepalese, gentle and friendly by nature, were only beginning to stir from rural poverty and caste restraints. There was no anger yet in their poverty, nor humiliation in their caste oppression, only a resigned fatalism. It hadn't reached the depth of anger that would later drive the Nepalese to knock off their country from the world tourism map.

The 1980s were the years of prosperity and peace. They constituted the golden decade. Nepal was dubbed the fairyland, a Shangri-La. Peace, social cohesion, the gentleness of the inhabitants and the highest mountains in the world were Nepal's chief attractions. Tourists flocked in. Trekkers clambered all over the foothills. With oxygen cylinders strapped securely on their backs, mountaineers goggled at Everest. More determined souls scaled the height. Those years coincided with China's opening of Tibet. Border trade grew. Through Nepal tourists poured onto the Roof of the World. For the commercially ambitious, Kathmandu was an ideal business base. And unlike the big Indian cities where business interests were entrenched and impenetrable, Kathmandu was a manageable town and there were business opportunities waiting to be grabbed. Small but aspiring businesses were drawn to the place and Kathmandu became the commercial hub of the Himalayas.

'I was fascinated with Kathmandu,' Tsering Migmar said. 'Especially with the Newars. I felt at home with them. Their art, architecture and sculpture spread throughout Tibet and has enriched us. Yes, I enjoyed playing the Sherpa Kusho part. That was the only time I felt that I was no longer a refugee, but a man of substance with people at my beck and call. Yes, it was Sherpa Kusho who amassed wealth and very quickly.'

In keeping with his new wealth, Sherpa Kusho decided he needed a grand reputation. He started gambling. He frequented the casino, the only one this side of Aden, and carelessly gambled away huge sums. So in this money capital of the Himalayas, Tsering Migmar successfully buried his real self. He buried himself in the persona of the glamorous Sherpa Kusho, the famously rich Sherpa businessman who had a weakness for gambling and the good life. But before he forgot his real identity, Tsering Migmar through the Royal Bank of Nepal arranged for an instalment of money to be transferred to Dechen in New Delhi, every month. The note that accompanied each check simply said, 'From Tsering Migmar.'

One day Sherpa Kusho called a business meeting of his operatives. He told them that he was now branching into tourism. 'I want to start a travel agency. Foreign tourists are flocking into Tibet. This means that there is big money in operating a travel agency. It will also prove a nice front for our real business of antique smuggling. We must diversify and survive,' Sherpa Kusho announced.

Sherpa Kusho's business operatives were excited by the idea. They dreamt of good hotels, great cuisine, comfortable travel and generally the good life associated with rich foreign tourists. They were from the impoverished countryside, fascinated by Kathmandu's glitter and cosmopolitanism. They were from the less privileged castes, the Rais, Chhetris, and the Limbus, all young, all absolutely devoted to Sherpa Kusho. He was their ticket to Himalayan riches, their road to freedom from caste neglect and poverty.

Sherpa Kusho found that it wasn't that difficult to get a foothold in Tibet. The group of Nepalese young men working for him and his Tibetan identity buried deep in his Sherpa one became a convincing front for his travel agency operation in Tibet. Three years after he had set up shop in Nepal, Sherpa Kusho launched his travel agency: Shangri-La Tours and Travels. Nepal's tourism minister himself, Dr D.Y. Rana presided over the launch, saying Nepal's tourism industry, the kingdom's biggest income generating section, would be a big beneficiary. Sherpa Kusho paraded all the young Nepalese men, before the minister who then went on to add that Shangri-La Tours and Travels would reduce Nepal's unemployment problem.

Shangri-La Tours and Travels found office space in Thamel. It concentrated on two routes: the Kathmandu-Pokhara-Mustang route in Nepal and the Kathmandu-Lhasa-Tsetang-Gyangtse route in Tibet. Before the start of each tour, Shangri-La Tours and Travels organised a two-day seminar on the history of Nepal and Tibet at which experts on the two countries spoke and answered questions. This new feature gave it a great reputation as a travel agency that imparted tourists with in-depth historical background.

Sherpa Kusho accompanied the first batch of tourists on the Tibet route. The Tibet he returned to was different from the Tibet he had left behind. Corruption seeping from China had reached Tibet and made his work that much easier. Money bought a lot of things, even in Tibet. He discovered that money and the power of money ruled China. China's communist enthusiasm had died with Mao.

A week after Sherpa Kusho had returned to Kathmandu from one of his frequent visits to Lhasa, he happened to be in his office. He was discussing a new trekking route in western Nepal with his business associates when through the glass window he spotted a man staring at him from the street. Sherpa Kusho thought he was a shy potential client and beckoned him in. The man hesitated and kept staring at him. His brows were creased into deep wrinkles and his face was strained with the effort of picking up the right piece in the jigsaw puzzle of faraway, battered memories. After a while, he seemed to have found the right piece, which notched his confidence levels a few pegs higher and he strode right into the office of Shangri-La Tours and Travels. He flung his arms wide open in anticipation of a bear hug. His face was wreathed in a huge smile of recognition and utter relief. 'Tsering Migmar! Tsering Migmar!' the man shouted. Sherpa Kusho cowered and abruptly dismissing his men told the man stepping into the office that he had got the wrong person. 'I'm Sherpa Kusho.'

'You may be Sherpa Kusho now, but you were Tsering Migmar in Tibet,' the smiling man said. 'I'm Trutung, remember the minority institute and your constant vows to kill the Drubtop Rinpoche and his lama because many of your grandfather's tribe were massacred by their ancestors? I said I would be right there besides you because my grandparents' people too were killed by them. And remember the legend of how the Drubtop Rinpoche is supposed to have made Beijing clean and beautiful? Remember?' Of course, impassioned Tsering Migmar hiding in the glamorous Sherpa Kusho remembered. He remembered them all, to the last painful detail. The floodgates of memory released by this unexpected encounter with his past, forced Tsering Migmar to shake off his assumed identity and greet Trutung like a close relative who had returned from a hazardous pilgrimage to Tsari. 'Trutung!' Tsering Migmar burst out. 'How did you recognise me, after all these years!'

'Who can forget your lean, intense face and your darting eyes?' said Trutung.

'And what are you doing here?' Tsering Migmar asked in disbelief.

'What do you think? I escaped, like you, like everyone else.'

What followed were many nights of reminiscing into the wee hours of the morning, unburdening their memories, baring their souls. But not once, not even to Trutung, did Tsering Migmar mention his wife and their children or his work in India. Instinctively Tsering Migmar knew that some information was better not shared. Tsering Migmar explained to Trutung that he had assumed the identity and name of Sherpa Kusho, a Nepalese national, because it was good for his business. He asked that Trutung refer to him as Sherpa Kusho. In return Sherpa Kusho employed Trutung as his trusted business partner, and the two, feeding on each other's partial trust, made their business the model of success in Kathmandu's commercial circles.

It was in 1986 when Sherpa Kusho was at the height of his business success, that he was picked up by members of the Public Security Bureau at the border crossing in Dram. He said Dram was a frontier town. Everyone in Dram was there to make a fast buck and move on. In view of this he was a little surprised when the long arm of the law grabbed him in what he considered a lawless frontier town. Three Tibetans in dark glasses and green uniform took him by the arm and walked him to the police station.

'What is this for?' Sherpa Kusho demanded. 'What have I done?'

'Just some questions. That's all,' said the man who seemed to have authority over the other two.

'You can't do this to me. I'm a Nepalese national. I demand access to the Nepalese consulate.'

The three policemen laughed aloud. 'We'll see about that,' the senior policeman said.

And still laughing they shoved him into a small, windowless room. A naked bulb lit the cheerless place. A steel, folding chair was placed in the middle. They pushed him down on the chair. He was left alone for a while to ponder his fate. Sherpa Kusho wondered whether the police were after Sherpa Kusho, the smuggler, or Tsering Migmar, the political activist. Or, both. In his heart, he knew the police were after Tsering Migmar and he wondered who had tipped them off. His Nepalese business associates hadn't the faintest clue. He knew that his best strategy was to stick to his Sherpa Kusho story and not to admit being Tsering Migmar unless the police produced incontrovertible evidence. He took comfort in the fact that six million Tibetans had at the most about a hundred different names to go around. There must be perhaps thousands of Tibetans who answered to the name of Tsering Migmar. He thought it his best strategy to refuse to confess to whatever accusation was hurled at him. It was certainly not possible for the Chinese authorities to keep a record of all Tibetan refugees or their activities.

After an hour the same three men led by a Chinese officer trooped into the room and crowded around him. The Chinese officer whipped out a Panda brand packet of cigarettes. He lit one, blew the smoke and calmly surveyed the captive.

'Tsering Migmar!' the Chinese officer shouted. 'You have been involved in splittist activities,' the officer said in Chinese. He stared at Tsering Migmar's eyes for any tell-tale reaction to this piece of information. Tsering Migmar turned quickly to the three Tibetans, his eyes pleading for enlightenment, shrugging his shoulders to say that he was ignorant of Chinese.

'Tsering Migmar, don't pretend that you don't understand Chinese. We know. We have records.'

Tsering Migmar turned to the three Tibetans again to plead innocence. 'What's this man talking about?' Sherpa Kusho asked. There was no reaction from the Tibetan policemen.

'I said we have records of your splittist activities,' the Chinese officer said, flinging the cigarette butt on the floor and stamping on it. The officer opened his briefcase and pulled out a file. 'Here's the evidence,' the officer said. He held a frayed, cyclostyled copy of *March*, a January-February 1978 issue of the Delhi TYC magazine. 'And here's your article and your name. In the article you said "The Chinese people will find peace only when the mask of communism is ripped off the face of China." How dare you blaspheme the ideology that has united our country and made China great!' The Chinese officer spoke rapidly.

When he had finished, he looked into Tsering Migmar's eyes for signs of acknowledgement of guilt and contrition.

Sherpa Kusho was relieved. Far from contrite, he became indignant. Turning to the three Tibetans, Sherpa Kusho shouted, 'What's this man talking about and why is he talking to me in Chinese? And why are you not translating. I'm a Nepalese citizen and I demand consular access.'

The three Tibetans silently looked at the Chinese officer, for a cue, or instruction. The Chinese officer nodded and Sherpa Kusho knew that he had won the first round in this psychological war. The senior of the Tibetan policemen put a hand on Sherpa Kusho's shoulder and said in Tibetan, 'Comrade Liu says your real name is Tsering Migmar and that you are a Tibetan and you have written critical articles in reactionary magazines brought out by splittist elements. You must confess to all this. Confess and we will be lenient.'

'Why should I confess to things which I have, leave alone doing, never even dreamt of. I'm a businessman. I'm a Nepalese citizen. Now let me go. I have work to do.'

The Tibetan, his hand still on Tsering Migmar's shoulder, pressing him down, translated this to comrade Liu.

Comrade Liu lit another cigarette and considered what Sherpa Kusho had said. 'First things first,' he said, flicking the ash of his cigarette. 'Are you or are you not Tsering Migmar? And are you or are you not a Tibetan? Be honest and we will be lenient.'

The question and the hint of uncertainty implicit in the tone inwardly delighted Sherpa Kusho. He knew that his tormentors were clueless. But again he turned in puzzlement to the three Tibetans. Sherpa Kusho looked offended. 'What's he saying now?' The senior Tibetan policeman translated.

A thought came to him. It was more a feeling, a sense of frustration and guilt, Tsering Migmar said. All his life he had been proud to be a Tibetan. Why deny the fact at this critical time? Why deny being a Tibetan, why deny being Tsering Migmar? His patriotism swept aside his common sense. Tsering Migmar, the political animal, decided to take over Sherpa Kusho, the shrewd, cautious businessman. He sprang from his chair. 'If it makes thing easier for you, I am Tsering Migmar and

I am a Tibetan. But I needed a Nepalese citizenship for my business. So now I am a Nepalese citizen. What's wrong with that? Is there a law that prohibits people from changing their nationality? Everyone else is doing it. But they are not questioned. But I must say you have the wrong Tsering Migmar. The Tsering Migmar you're looking for is not me.'

After the translation comrade Liu stood in silence, perhaps pondering over his next question. Very quietly, as if wanting to share a secret, comrade Liu asked, 'And you are the Tsering Migmar who had studied at the minority institute in Beijing?'

'It's a privilege I did not ask for,' Tsering Migmar retorted in Chinese. 'I was forced to go.'

This time his confession was more a matter of calculated risk than impulsive disregard for the consequences. With this question he realised that the police were on the mark. He instinctively knew that the only person who was aware of his identity and who could have betrayed him was Trutung. But he would deal with that later. Right now it was more important to deal with the situation by coming clean on his past. But he took comfort in the fact that not even Trutung knew about his living and working in India or his association with the Tibetan Communist Party or his articles on China for *March* magazine. He felt that his best policy was to admit to his Tibetan origin and his period of study at the minority institute in Beijing but he would disavow of having ever set foot in India. That, Tsering Migmar said, was the best policy to ensure that he survived the ordeal.

Comrade Liu listened and said to his subordinates, 'Pack him off to Drapchi.' He turned to Tsering Migmar and said, 'This will be your privilege. You'll get the education you deserve. You will be tried by the people's court.'

Tsering Migmar fumed. 'What's my crime? Being a Tibetan? Becoming a Nepalese national? You don't have anything on me.'

'Your crime will be decided by the people's court in Lhasa,' comrade Liu said with a cold stare.

'I didn't protest too much on being arrested or being sent off to Drapchi,' Tsering Migmar said. At this point he finally seemed to break loose from his story. He seemed to have come out of his reverie and realised that there were two attentive listeners before him one of whom was taking copious notes of his adventures. After saying, 'I knew this would be another opportunity for my sowing, planting and spreading mission,' Tsering Migmar clamped up. He gave the impression that he had said too much. Garrulous Sherpa Kusho became Tsering Migmar, the man of few words and the one who wanted no record of this conversation to survive. Despite Phuntsok's best efforts to quiz him, Tsering Migmar never revealed what he actually did in Tibet. He was seized by extreme reticence. His story, now became disjointed and scattered, vague and evasive.

Now it was Tsering Migmar and not flamboyant Sherpa Kusho, who started to give monosyllabic grunts to Phuntsok's exasperating questions. Yes, when I looked up from my notes, the person who was speaking or in this case, not speaking, was Tsering Migmar. He had shed his earlier persona. Tsering Migmar was once again wrapped up in the robes of reticence. I was too busy taking down notes to ask cogent questions and we had come to an important turn now. It was Phuntsok who persisted. 'Did they hurt you?' he asked.

'I kept saying I was a Nepalese citizen and that they got the wrong Tsering Migmar,' he said. 'I demanded to see the officials at Nepal's consulate general in Lhasa. Besides, they had nothing on me. It was good that I confessed to my Tibetan identity. As I had guessed, that double-faced, double-headed Trutung had betrayed me. He had entertained the fond hope that with me safely behind prison walls, he could take over my business operations, the entire outfit. This was what I learned from the manager of the Lhasa branch of my travel agency after I had escaped from Drapchi prison. Well, I told the manager that no one must know that I was out of prison and the business operations must go on with Trutung at the helm.

'To cut a long story short, with money supplied from my office of the Shangri-La Tours and Travels in Lhasa, I bribed the Drapchi prison warden. 10,000 renminbi bought my freedom. These days, freedom comes cheap. One day after the delivery of the first instalment, the prison warden, a Tibetan, took all prisoners outside the prison wall to plant turnips on Drapchi's vegetable farm. Through a deliberate oversight, he took only a single armed guard with him. When evening came and the sun was about to set, I asked permission to relieve myself. The warden nodded his head. I took my time. That was when the warden ordered the guard to round up the prisoners and marched them into prison. They left me behind. Perhaps they forgot. Perhaps the warden gave a commission to the guard. I made a quick visit to my Lhasa office and collected enough money to finance my escape. I shaved my head and told my manager to get me a monk's robes. I also told him to hand the next instalment of the bribe to the warden of Drapchi prison as discreetly as before and to ensure that the news of my escape remained a secret, especially from Trutung. Instead of taking the route to Nepal, on which I knew the Public Security Bureau personnel would keep a close watch, I headed north, to Golok. I disguised myself as a monk who had come on a pilgrimage to Lhasa. I reached Kyitsel and the Drubchen Monastery. I found the lama and the Drubtop Rinpoche. They provided a safe haven for me in their sprawling monastic community until it was safe for me to head to Nepal again. And here I am.'

Tsering Migmar paused and thought for a while. 'Tashi, the present Drubtop Rinpoche, also put in a word on my behalf in the right ear. That's why my escape seemed so unbelievably easy. Yes, thanks to his intervention and his protection I am here today.'

'How is the lama?' Phuntsok asked lightly. 'Health-wise?'

Tsering Migmar sighed and his face crumpled into sadness. He told the story, holding nothing back, the story of the death and rebirth of the Drubchen Rinpoche, the one who had discovered the twentieth Drubtop Rinpoche. This time it was not Tsering Migmar, the ardent communist, nor Sherpa Kusho, the seller of Buddha statues, who told the story. It was a simple monk, perhaps a potential disciple, who, seeming to have lost his teacher, wanted to recount and immortalise the last days of his master. Tsering Migmar blew his nose into the one end of his robe. He said the lama died after a year he had arrived in Kyitsel. Tsering Migmar, the communist, actually used the term 'passed into the heavenly field'. His attendants spread the word that he had passed away while he was in meditation, an indication of the high level of his realisation. They cremated his body. The day after the cremation, in a memorial service, the acting abbot of Drubchen monastery read the deeds and accomplishments of the nineteenth Drubtop Rinpoche. This biography was composed by the lama, a spiritual duty of each successive abbot of the Drubchen monastery who had the privilege of looking after and being the teacher to the Drubtop Rinpoches of the Drubchen Monastery.

The acting abbot prayed for the long life of the current Drubtop Rinpoche. A senior monk recited the accomplishments of the lama himself. He expressed the gratitude of the entire monastic community of Kyitsel for the lama's many deeds, including his greatest, the discovery of the twentieth Drubtop Rinpoche. He prayed for his speedy re-birth and discovery. The Drubtop Rinpoche set up a search party for the discovery of his teacher's reincarnation and before Tsering Migmar left Kyitsel, a bright two-year old from Ngari in western Tibet was installed as the new Drubchen Rinpoche.

The authorities in Beijing acknowledged the growing spiritual prestige of the Drubchen monastery. They did it by making an inept attempt at imperial diplomacy of another era, both Manchu and the Raj. They dispatched a note of congratulations to the new Drubchen Rinpoche. The note simply said, 'We were greatly alarmed by your sudden demise but all our alarm and confusion has been removed by your speedy rebirth. The Central Committee of the Chinese Communist Party joyfully puts its stamp of approval on your holy self, O, You Precious Soul-Boy of the Obedient Buddha of the Western Paradise.'

When the note reached Kyitsel, there was an intense debate within the Drubchen monastery's hierarchy. Many senior khenpos were against reading the message to the larger sangha. They argued that this insult would make the monks furious. They feared for the direction in which the monks' fury would take.

Drubtop Rinpoche intervened. He said, 'I can control the fury of the monks, but not of Beijing. If we do not read out their congratulatory note in public, we will be seen as spurning it. No, we must read it at the enthronement ceremony.'

Drubtop Rinpoche, the originator of the Tibetan Word, had made his judgment and the senior hierarchs reluctantly nodded their shining, shaven heads. When the day of the enthronement came, nervousness gripped the shaven heads of the monastic hierarchs. First, the Kyitsel district party secretary read out the Tibetan translation of Beijing's high-sounding note. The party secretary, a tall Golok, dressed in a yak-skin chuba, rapidly droned the greeting. Stunned silence greeted it. Then the party secretary quickly read the Chinese original, in a guttural Golok accent. The Chinese sangha too greeted the message with stunned silence. Later all reports agreed that it started from the section where the Chinese monks and nuns were assembled, sitting cross-legged. A Chinese monk is supposed to have whispered to those sitting next to him, 'What turtle egg in Zhongnanhai thought of this insult! Yes, what turtle egg decided to hatch itself into this absurdity!' There was a quick snicker, which grew and spread throughout the Chinese quarter and gave way to respectful Tibetan laughter that swept and convulsed the entire assembly.

The party secretary, believing the laughter was directed at his barbarian attempt to speak the language of high civilisation, sheepishly withdrew. 'Otherwise, Drubtop Rinpoche is fine,' Tsering Migmar said in response to Phuntsok's insistent inquiry about the health of his college friend. 'The young Drubchen Rinpoche is growing up nicely. And all the others, Metok, Ugen and Ama Penpa, are fine. Ugen is turning out to be a fine young man.'

'The Drubtop Rinpoche, he is on a class of his own,' Tsering Migmar continued in a whisper, bringing his hands involuntarily together in an unsaid prayer. 'Tashi, irreverent, opinionated and argumentative, has been transformed into a luminous personality, radiating the gentleness of the Buddha's teachings. But it is in his role as a teacher and master that he excels himself. Like all great teachers, Drubtop Rinpoche has the ability to explain complex Buddhist concepts in a simple language, reinforcing his explanations with examples from every-day life. Above all he lives out his teachings. That is the reason that has made Kyitsel the magnet of all serious practitioners of Buddhism throughout Tibet and beyond.'

Having said this Tsering Migmar remained silent for a while. Phuntsok and I thought he had dozed off. But we were wrong. Tsering

Migmar picked up the teacup and drained it for the last time Braced by the rum, Tsering Migmar spoke again, rapidly. He said he spent more than two years in Kyitsel. The monastery provided him with food and lodging, and shielded him from suspicious eyes and questioning local policemen. The monastery insisted that Tsering Migmar desist from any attempt to contact his relatives in the area. The monastery's survival as the only ecumenical institution in Tibet was at stake. To make amends, Ama Penpa, Metok and Ugen would come frequently to his cell with a flask of hot thenthuk. In return he regaled them with the adventures of Sherpa Kusho. Sometimes they invited him to their quarters for a big dinner. They lived in a one-storey building outside the monastery's compound. They served Chinese dishes which reminded him of the delicious, exotic smell of Beijing in his student days. Sometimes Drubtop Rinpoche would leave his official residence and join them at meals. During such occasions Tsering Migmar itched to ask Drubtop Rinpoche the reasons why he had abdicated to Buddhism. He had so many questions and all of them started with the word 'why'. The opportunity, however, never came because Metok insisted that he tell them more of the adventures of Sherpa Kusho, and it seemed to Tsering Migmar that Drubtop Rinpoche wasn't too keen on being questioned. So he thought it wiser to oblige Metok by re-telling his adventures as the glamorous Sherpa Kusho. Ama Penpa and Metok marvelled at his business acumen and suggested he set up a travel agency in Kyitsel. They groaned at Trutung's betrayal and moaned Tsering Migmar's imprisonment and encouraged him to stay as long as he liked.

Tsering Migmar said he did not have to wait too long to get a glimpse of the impulses that drove Tashi to accept the Drubtop lineage. One day in July 1989 Drubtop Rinpoche invited him to accompany him on a journey. He was travelling to the headwaters of the Yellow River where his Chinese students would join him. He had sought permission from the concerned authorities to make the journey. Because of anti-government demonstrations both in Lhasa and Beijing months before, the two cities were still under martial law. Drubtop Rinpoche explained to the authorities that the trip was a summer retreat camp. The nervous officials after much delay thought that the trip was harmless enough and gave permission. Drubtop Rinpoche, his retainers and his bands of Chinese students set out in an unhurried yak caravan. A group of Golok tribesmen riding on horses and driving yaks laden with provision had set out earlier. They were the advance team, to pitch tents at every halt and prepare meals for Drubtop Rinpoche and his retainers. Drubtop Rinpoche led the main party, with black mastiffs barking and leaping and bounding, yaks grunting and retainers shouting and yodelling in the thin air to marshal some caravan discipline over this large unruly band of travellers. Rinpoche rode a white yak and led his band of students on a trip to the source of the river that had nurtured and nourished the Chinese civilisation. Tsering Migmar thought this could be Drubtop Rinpoche's way of reminding his students that the real life-giver of their civilisation had its origins in the heart of this barbarian territory. The large band of travellers did the rounds of two lakes of Tso Kyaring and Ngoring and journeyed to the source of Huang Ho deep in the shadows of the Kunlun Mountains. The journey took about three weeks.

Tsering Migmar said he enjoyed those night halts when the travellers pitched tents and tethered their yaks nearby and over a fire fed by yak dung swapped tales over bowls of noodle soup or balls of tsampa washed down with butter-tea. Tsering Migmar said those nights and the whole experience of the journey were magical. During those halts, he came to know his Chinese companions. One of them was an excitable young man named Charlie. Charlie said he had come across Drubtop Rinpoche many years ago when he was travelling in a bus from Golmud to Lhasa. 'He referred to himself as Tashi then,' Charlie told him. 'And you know what?' Charlie said in great disbelief. 'He tried to explain to me the virtues of communism. I quickly disabused him of the notion. Because of this he's a Buddhist now and a great teacher. I think I made some contribution in this regard.'

Tsering Migmar said he enjoyed this experience because in Kyitsel he kept to himself. He was, after all, a fugitive on the run. He had to be careful not to expose himself too much. He occupied himself by attending teachings of Drubtop Rinpoche, more out of necessity than interest, and by reading. Despite the meals brought to his cell by Ama

Penpa and Metok and the occasional invitation to Drubtop Rinpoche's residence, Tsering Migmar said he felt isolated and lonely in Kyitsel. Here on the journey, he felt free and he enjoyed the companionship of his new friends. Through Charlie he came to know the rest of his group. To Tsering Migmar's surprise, those in his group were outcasts and misfits. Many were in their sixties and seventies. They survived the Cultural Revolution or avoided the chaos by exiling themselves deep into the Tibetan Plateau, out of the reach of the turmoil in China. They did not want anything to do with communism or the madness unleashed by those in Beijing. They were rebels. They too were refugees and exiles. They did not belong to the new China that was being shaped by Mao. The China they knew, the China they belonged to was being destroyed before their very eyes and they wanted no part in this madness. They packed their bags and their savings and took to the mountains and grasslands of Tibet, living off the land like Tibetan nomads, herding yaks and sheep. Or simply by surviving on the goodwill of the nomads. These rebels took with them a part of the old China they loved: medicine, acupuncture, poetry, literature, history, astronomy, astrology, calligraphy, opera, each and every brick of the foundations of Chinese civilisation. They guarded these with their lives. No fancy ideology, no revolutionary madness could take this knowledge away from them. These would be guarded, preserved and handed down to others when China came out of this madness. Tsering Migmar discovered that those Chinese who studied at the Drubchen Monastery, more than being Buddhists, were Confucianists and Taoists who after the liberalisation that swept China flocked to the Drubchen Monastery to practise their art under the tolerant gaze of Tibetan abbots.

Tsering Migmar soon found that his Chinese companions were not just feng-shui masters but also practising shamans, rainmakers, weathermen, diviners, oracles, high priests of the occult, keepers of the mysterious and practitioners of magic. Their enthusiasm for magic and mysteries was on full display when they reached the source of the Yellow River. As for Tsering Migmar, reaching the source was a disappointment. Water from stretches of wetland converging at points beyond the two lakes of Kyaring and Ngoring constituted the source. The water made its way in two major flows and once again converged south of Madoi to become what the Tibetans call Machu. He expected something more dramatic at the source, something spiritual. But the Chinese students were ecstatic. For them the journey was a journey across centuries to behold the source of the very antiquity of their culture. That was enough for them, regardless of the rather undramatic beginning of the river. They spent most of the day and night, catching fistfuls of dust and mud and scattering them over the place, walking up and down with their compasses focused on the ground and burning joss sticks and murmuring invocations and paeans. There were solemn rituals. The seriousness with which the feng-shui masters went about conducting these gave the impression that they were determined to rid the place of some evil spirit. Tsering Migmar with his communist education did not care for these rituals. It was nothing but a lot of mumbo-jumbo to him. 'Where has communist China gone?' he wondered aloud. 'Where is the age of reason and liberation? Superstition has taken over and overthrown the revolution,' he muttered to himself. He silently bemoaned the loss of the world that may have come down hard on his people, but was a world that he was familiar with and in which his ideals were shaped. But that night his vision for an egalitarian Tibet was exorcised in a thunderous clash of magicians' cymbals.

After the journey, Drubtop Rinpoche told the travellers to rest for a day in the upper reaches of the grassland of Madoi with the distant Amnye Machen Mountains in the west and the Kyaring and Ngoring lakes in the east. While the travellers recuperated, Drubtop Rinpoche gave a talk that later became known as his water and river teaching. He made the talk informal. It was a simple presentation with no apparent spiritual significance. To Tsering Migmar the water and river teaching contained the kernel of the reasons for Tashi's rejection of communism and his transformation into the twentieth Drubtop Rinpoche. The talk was a lesson on the sacred geography of Tibet. It was a celebration of Tibet, the source of the life-blood of Asia.

Drubtop Rinpoche spoke in Tibetan. A Golok translated into Chinese. 'When I was small and in school,' Drubtop Rinpoche began, 'our geography book taught us that Tibet is the heart of Asia. This observation could be dismissed but for the examples that the author of the textbook gave. The author said that the mountain ranges that encircle Tibet are like the ribs that protect the human heart. The many rivers that originate from Tibet and flow to the rest of Asia are the blood vessels that give life and sustenance to the human body. Similarly, the rivers of Tibet and the mountains that feed these rivers sustain much of Asia. Here, I am talking about basic physical sustenance, not cultural, not spiritual. What to eat and drink. And this Tibet supplies to most of Asia. Ten or eleven of Asia's most important rivers have their source in Tibet and they feed about forty-seven per cent of the Earth's total human population. Can you believe this? And around these rivers grew great civilisations. For example, here in Madoi we are not far from the source of the Yellow River in the west and in the east is the Amnye Machen mountain range that the Yellow River skirts. And it was along the river bed of Huang Ho, the Sorrow of China, the Ungovernable, the Mother of Rivers, that the civilisation which later engulfed the whole of China grew. That is why our Machu and your Yellow River is so deeply embedded in Chinese memory. The Tang poet, Li Bai, who gave himself to wine and the Yangtse, celebrated the Yellow River. He wrote,

> *Torrents of the Yellow River flow*
> *Down from Heaven.*

And where is Heaven?' Drubtop Rinpoche asked. 'Here in minority territory, here in...' Drubtop said, answering his own question and scanning his amused Chinese audience. 'Here in what you used to call barbarian territory. Here in the shadows of Kunlun Shan, where the Son of Heaven worshipped and made sacrifices at the feet of the Lord and Lady of the Western Mountains. You must remember, your Heaven is in Tibet. Yes, China's Heaven is here in Tibet.' Drubtop Rinpoche paused and wondered aloud. 'The Western Mountains, doesn't that remind you of Mount Kailash, farther down south, where also a Lord and Lady, Shiva and Parvati hold court? Could it be that the mythological memory of two of the world's great civilisations have a common source, a source here in Tibet?' Drubtop Rinpoche mused and let the question hang in the air. He asked, 'And why were the ancient Chinese so reverential of Tibet and its geographical space?' He waited for an answer. There was no response from the audience. He answered his own question. Because China is nourished by Tibetan waters. Don't forget this. We are feeding you both ways, spiritually and physically,' he said.

'The fact that these rivers have their origins in Tibet is an accident of geography,' Drubtop Rinpoche said. 'The fact that in Tibet these rivers are unspoiled and remain pristine is a testimony to our people's innate reverence for the environment that has sustained us, and our belief in the basic sacredness of Mother Earth. It is our Bon and Buddhist heritage that provided us the spiritual means to look after our land and your water. For this you owe a great debt of gratitude to us and our culture because you owe your physical existence to Tibet. And now you are here because you need spiritual sustenance from a Tibetan lama. And this is as it should be. My point is that you should make an effort to cherish and protect these rivers and the land of their source while you have a chance.' There was smothered laughter from the audience. 'Yes, you may laugh now,' Drubtop Rinpoche said. 'But water is as elemental as the air we breathe and the earth we live on and it is getting scarce. Man can live without oil. But man cannot live without water. As I said, like oil, water too will become a scarce commodity. Do we have any fear that the air we breathe will one day be no longer available? No!' Drubtop Rinpoche said. 'But water will. People and countries will one day go to war for water. Yes, for water, which is Tibet's chief export along with our mountains and yaks. Yes, make an earnest effort to protect your water and its source. This is also a spiritual practice. This is my teaching to you today. And I will stop here,' Drubtop Rinpoche said. 'But not before I recite this prayer. This prayer comes from one of the biographies of an earlier Drubtop Rinpoche, from the thirteenth century.' Drubtop Rinpoche folded his hands together and recited a sort of hymn in praise of Tibet.

> The serpents that rippled with the river waters,
> The nagas who sulked in the deep blue lakes,

The stern protective deities of the mountains
Who sneezed hail and storm
And blew wind and blizzard,
Sky-fliers and the others joined in.
They sang: this won't last, military victories
And the fruits of victories.
They would all be reduced to dust
And blown away by the wind.

The tricks of Tiblomacy, the sword of Genghis Khan,
The pretensions of empire and the arrogance of conquest, won't last.
But what would last is this haven we praise,
This power-place of the world, this Land of Snow,
This measure of the earth and our life on it,
This playground of the gods,
This piece of eternity carved in mountains
Which give us our river waters.
This would last, this abode inhabited by men and women
Whose beliefs give us our existence
And blessed by countless lamas
Whose looms of wisdom
Have woven the pattern on the fabric of Tibet.

This centre of heaven,
This core of the earth,
This heart of the world
Fenced round by snow,
This headland of all rivers.

When the band of travellers returned to Kyitsel, Tsering Migmar approached Drubtop Rinpoche. He said that it was time he returned to India, to his wife and children. He felt he had nothing to do in Tibet, a place he no longer belonged to and where he was confined and isolated. His pretence of being a monk, was getting too much for him. He wanted to be out, to leave Tibet for good. 'This is not my life. I think I am wasting myself here. This is not to say that I did not receive every kindness and hospitality. But I can't go on living this pretence any further.'

Drubtop Rinpoche sat on the low cushion, telling his beads and pondered Tsering Migmar's predicament. 'My friend,' Drubtop Rinpoche said, 'I advise patience. You may think you have not accomplished what you came for. But who does? Do not think your time here is wasted. Let me tell you something. We don't know how it all began. Yes, Tibetans of my generation—you and I—don't know how it all began. Or how it will end. We can only hazard a guess. What we know is that we happened to pop in between and were caught in the crossfire of past mistakes and future exaggerations. Now thinking back on it, the real miracle is the fact of our survival, with our hope intact and our courage not blasted away by enemy fire from the camp of despair and cowardice. That is what I think is important. But I believe every beginning begins with hope. Every end ends in prayer, in thanksgiving, to the stars of hope and the moon of quiet courage that guided us thus far as we still trek back and forth across the world's highest mountains, in search of our very own Shangri-La. My prayer is that the thirst of our Chinese brothers and sisters, who search for their personal liberation, will continue to be quenched by the waters of Tibet. That is my prayer and fervent hope. Perhaps we should learn to live with each other. If we do, it will be a greater victory. Tolerance and compassion are like water. Nothing resists it. The strength of water is dependent on whether its source is continually replenished. If this is so, then water can make its way to enter the ocean. Whereas anger and jealousy find stiff resistance. The real mountains of oppression are our anger, jealousy and ignorance which obstruct rain-bearing clouds from fertilising our mind's farmland.'

Apart from this pep talk, Drubtop Rinpoche pointed to a more practical necessity of exercising patience. He said the demonstrations in Lhasa and Beijing had made the authorities extremely alert and very nervous. Leaving Tibet when the security forces were on heightened alert might land him in trouble. For now he was safe in the Monastery. When things settled down, he could slip out of Tibet. Tsering Migmar thought this was wise and reluctantly prepared himself to be confined to the Monastery for some more months, if not years.

It was around this time, Tsering Migmar remembered, that the ebullient Charlie rushed into his cell with a strange plan. He wanted to re-arrange the geomantic configurations of China and Tibet.

'What kind of shamanist nonsense are you talking about now?' Tsering Migmar demanded.

'Simply to re-arrange the configurations,' Charlie said.

'Re-arrange the configurations! Why don't you re-arrange your own configurations? You've gone mad. You are going through your very own Cultural Revolution. Even if you are able to accomplish this rubbish, what good will this do?'

'It will be good for peace and harmony. It will be good for you people. Less trouble, less hardship, greater tolerance.'

'What's wrong with the configurations now?'

'They are disturbed. Badly disturbed. We need to harmonise them.'

'That sounds simple and you have the expertise. Why bother me about it? Why don't you go right ahead? All your feng-shui masters will be behind you. Yes, this is an excellent idea and will be of enormous service,' Tsering Migmar said. His dismissive laugh made it plain to Charlie that only another turtle egg could think of an idea like this.

'I'm serious and this is serious business. This will be good for Tibet and China. Just listen.'

Tsering Migmar stared at his serious face. 'What's the harm?' he relented after a long pause. 'I have plenty of time to kill. Go ahead. Tell me your story. And by the way who decides whether the feng-shui elements are disturbed?'

'Master Kong Xun decides,' Charlie said at once. 'It was his idea. He is the abbot of Hunan Khamtsen and the Hoshang and master of all the five branches of feng-shui learning, the forms of energy, landform classification, building characteristics of both exterior and interior architecture and the flying stars system. He traces his ancestry to the best of all masters, Master Confucius himself. Master Kong Lun should know. He has it up here,' Charlie said, pointing to his temple. 'And down here,' Charlie said, as if trying to peel off some flesh from his arm. 'He is the perfect Hoshang for the people of Tibet.'

'And what does re-arranging the configurations mean? Picking some dust in your fist and scattering it about? Peering at a compass focused on the ground?' Tsering Migmar asked.

'No!' Charlie protested. 'It's not just that. Feng-shui is the universe and our place in it. It is about yin and yang, negative and positive energies. It is about the five elements of wood, fire, earth, metal and water and the energies we derive from them and our ability to read and re-direct these energies for good and bad. You Tibetans swear by the Tibetan calendar. You direct your daily life according to these energies that guide your calendar. It is not just a fistful of dust. It is about us. It is about our ability to live with nature. It is this,' Charlie said pointing to the low table. 'It is about this and this and this.' He pointed to the cup set on the table and the books on the shelf and the bowls of water offering on the altar. 'It is about how these are placed and arranged that creates the positive energy for doing good. We can do the same for our country.'

'Oh, well, what's the harm,' Tsering Migmar said. 'All the bright ideas come from you people. We tried one and failed, remember? But why leave it at that? Let's try another.'

Master Kong Xun sold the idea to Drubtop Rinpoche who was amused and left it at that. But Master Kong Xun persisted and Drubtop Rinpoche gave his good-humoured consent with a hearty laugh. When winter came the feng-shui masters fanned out, with their compasses, feng-shui charts and texts. They travelled all over Tibet. The senior masters boarded trains and buses to Beijing and other cities on the eastern seaboard. After several months, the feng-shui experts re-converged in Kyitsel. They met for a week to examine their findings. They found that Tibet was indeed a prone orgress as first determined by the celebrated Tang princess, Wengchen Kongsho, more than fourteen hundred years ago, and China a giant turtle. Both needed to be tamed again and the services of the two clearly identified. They recommended that temples, stupas and shrines be built in Tibet and China on the key parts of the bodies of the prone orgress and turtle in an effort to tame their restlessness. The setting up of these human structures on the power points of the geomantically conceived creatures took all of two years.

When all this was done—all of which went beyond Tsering Migmar and to which he looked on with tolerant disdain— as a grand finale to this mighty enterprise, complicated rituals and services were performed in Kyitsel. These took another long week. After another week of retreat and invocations, the spiritually charged and exultant feng-shui masters declared that their task was complete. They said that Lhasa was made the spiritual capital and Beijing the political one. 'One country, two capitals,' they said proudly. 'We have changed the geomantic destinies of Tibet and China.'

Tsering Migmar had come to the end of his story. Phuntsok, the stern interrogator, had long since slumped back and was in deep slumber.

I looked out of the window. The first streaks of dawn lit the sky above the Dhauladhar range. Beyond those mountains, just a hundred kilometres away as the crow flies, is Tibet, the country of our dreams.

Glossary

TIBETAN WORDS

apso	Tibetan terrier
baku	Bhutan's national costume
Bon	Tibet's native, pre-Buddhist religion
bu	boy
chang	fermented barley beer
cho-pa	meditation technique before cemetreies
chuba	gown for Tibetan men and women
Dekar	beggar who welcomes the Tibetan New Year
dob-dob	warrior monks of Sera monastery in Lhasa
dratsang	college of a monastic university
dro'ma	sweet red weed found in Tibet and used with sweetened boiled rice
gyapon	camp leader, literally a leader of a hundred men
jangshing	wooden slate for practicing handwriting
jindak	sponsor
ju-le	the common form of greeting in Ladakh
khamtsen	house in a college of a monastery
khata	greeting scarf
lama	teacher, one without peer
lha	gyalovictory to the gods
lingkhor	the circular path that surrounds any sacred spot
magpa	one who marries into his bride's family